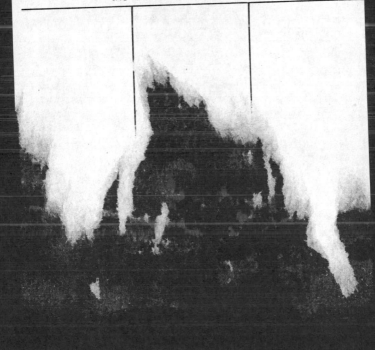

The Fall

The Fall

Simon Mawer

LITTLE, BROWN

For Gilly

A *Little, Brown* Book

First published in Great Britain in 2003 by Little, Brown

Copyright © Simon Mawer 2003

The moral right of the author has been asserted.

A CIP catalogue record for this book
is available from the British Library.

ISBN 0 316 72524 2

Typeset in Adobe Garamond by M Rules
Printed and bound in Great Britain by Clays Ltd, St Ives plc

Little, Brown
An imprint of
Time Warner Books UK
Brettenham House
Lancaster Place
London WC2E 7EN

www.TimeWarnerBooks.co.uk

Acknowledgements

For much of the more recent climbing in this book, I only had to fall back on my own memories of the highs and lows shared with my one-time climbing partner Les Littleford. Information about climbing in the 1940s came from various sources – from Jim Perrin's *Menlove* (1985) to Colin Kirkus's *Let's Go Climbing* (1941). For the Eiger, I gained much help from *Eiger: The Vertical Arena* edited by Daniel Anker (English edition 2000) and Heinrich Harrer's *The White Spider* (1959, 1965). There is also an impressive on-line account of a recent (1997) ascent of the Nordwand by Paul Harrington at www.climbing.ie/exped/eiger/eiger.html

For London during the Blitz I used a number of published eyewitness accounts, such as *Post D* (1941) by John Stachey, *Raiders Overhead* (1943, 1980) by Barbara Nixon and *Westminster in War* (1947) by William Samson. There is also Angela Raby's book *The Forgotten Service* (1999), which documents, in photograph and diary, the life of an ambulance unit during the Blitz.

The excerpt quoted by Robert Dewar on pages 29–30 is from Edward Whymper's classic of mountaineering literature, *Scrambles Amongst the Alps* (1871).

The Fall

The weather was good for the Snowdon area. The rain had held off all day and there was enough of a breeze to keep the rock dry. Damp cannot have been a contributory factor. There was even the occasional shaft of sunlight cutting down through the varied cloud to brighten up the cwm, but no direct sunlight on the fluted walls and boiler-plate slabs of the crag itself. This is a north face.

Someone shouted: 'Hey, look!' It was one of the group of walkers. Climbers would not have made a noise about it. Someone shouted and stood up and pointed towards the East Buttress: 'Hey, look at him!'

There was a lone figure climbing. He was about twenty feet off the ground. The man who shouted had been watching for a little while but at first it had not been clear that the figure was truly alone until he, the climber, had reached twenty feet up the great blank central wall of the East Buttress. The wall is a smooth, slightly curving sheet of rhyolite, a beaten metallic shield that, to inexpert eyes, appears unclimbable.

'Look at 'im. Bloody idiot or what?'

'Isn't he doing Great Wall?'

'No ropes, nothing. He's bloody *soloing*.'

The solo climber on the Great Wall moved quite smoothly up the shallow groove that gives the line of the route. He bridged easily, his feet braced outwards to make an arrowhead of his body. You could see his hands going up on the rock above him, imagine his fingers touching the rock and finding the flakes and nicks that are what pass for holds on that kind of route. Mere unevenness. What the climbers of the past would have called rugosities. They all seemed to have had the benefit of a classical education. Not the present breed. 'Thin,' the modern climber might say. Not much else.

'He seems to know what he's doing,' the walker called to his companions.

'He's not wearing a helmet,' one of the others remarked. The walkers were all watching now, some standing, others sitting on rocks – the grass was still damp – with their heads craned back to see.

The climber moved up. There was a cat-like grace about his movements, a certain slickness, a feeling that, perched as he was above nothing at all and holding nothing at all, he was yet secure in what he did. He was now fly-like, plastered across the centre of the grey blankness, laying away on a rib that he had discovered, reaching up for a further hold, bridging wide and stretching up with his right arm. He was actually feeling for a piton that had been there for the last thirty-five years, one of those bits of climbing archaeology that you find in the mountains: a peg, placed from an abseil one wet and windy day in the spring of 1962. The peg is oxidised, but smoothed by the numerous (not too numerous) hands that have grabbed it thankfully over the years. It will be there for many years yet, but not for ever. Not even the cliff is for ever.

'Look!' A gasp from the watchers, a movement up on the cliff face as the lone climber made a smooth succession of moves, reached the peg and made height above it.

'What happens if he slips?' one of the walkers, a young girl, asked.

A man's voice spoke: 'He's dead.' It brought a hush to the party. They had been watching the thing as entertainment; abruptly it had been presented to them as a matter of life and death.

'Who *is* he?' another of the party asked. There was a clear sense that this unknown, lone climber, this figure of flesh and bone and blood and brain, must *be* someone.

'A bloody idiot.'

After a pause – resting? was it possible to be resting on that vertical and hostile face? – the man had begun to move once more. The remainder of the wall soared up above him to where safety was represented by a thin diagonal terrace. There was a hint of grass up there, a faint green fringe to break the monotony of grey. It was still far above him, but it seemed to represent safety. His body swayed and moved up, his feet touching rock with something of the assurance, something of the habitual skill and poise, of a dancer. You could see that he had fair hair. Not much else about him. An anonymous performer on a Welsh crag, some time after noon on a dry and blustery day. Who *was* he?

And then he fell.

There was some argument later as to whether it was he who shouted. Someone shouted certainly. It might have been one of the walking party; it might have been one of the pair on White Slab, looking across from the first stance right out in space way over to the right on the other buttress. There were no specific words – just a cry of surprise.

He fell and there was something leaden and inevitable about the fall. After the grace and agility of the ascent, the dull fact of gravity and weight. A sudden sharp acceleration. Thirty-two feet per second faster every second. About three seconds. And then he hit the broken slope at the foot of the wall, rolled a bit, and stopped.

People got to their feet and ran, scrambled, slithered up the slopes. A pair of climbers on another part of the crag began to fix an abseil rope. One of the girls in the walking party had started to weep. Despite the hurry no one really wanted to get there. Of course they didn't. But when they did, quite absurdly they found that he was still alive, unconscious but alive. And they were surprised to discover that he wasn't some reckless youth, the kind that has no respect for the traditions of the place, the kind that doesn't care a damn about doing anything so bloody stupid as soloing a route as hard as the Great Wall – he was middle-aged. Lean, tough, weather-beaten complexion (bruised horrendously, his jaw displaced raggedly to one side), middle-aged. Bleeding from his mouth and one ear. His limbs were arranged anyhow, like those of a rag doll tossed casually out of a window to land on the grass below.

Someone crouched over him and felt for a pulse in his broken neck. One of the walkers was on his mobile phone calling the police. Others just stood by helplessly. The pulse was there for a moment beneath the middle finger of the would-be rescuer, and then it faded away. He died as they stood and watched.

1

I was driving home when I heard the news. I was somewhere on that winding nightmare of motorway, expressway and flyover that crosses and recrosses the city of Birmingham: ribbons of lights stretching away into the gathering dusk, the long necklaces of housing estates, the pendant jewels of factories and warehouses. Design without intention; a strange sort of beauty without any aesthetic to support it. Over it all the traffic moved in columns towards Liverpool and Manchester, towards London and the south-east.

The radio was on and the story was big enough to make the national news on a day when the news wasn't special, the murders a mere one or two, the rapes only half a dozen and date-rapes at that, the peace negotiations stalled, the elections indecisive, misery and poverty quotidian. 'A noted climber has been killed in a fall,' said a disembodied and indifferent voice from the radio, and I knew at once who it was even before I heard the name. Curious, that. I knew it would be him.

'Jim Matthewson, who lived in North Wales, had spent a lifetime tackling the highest and hardest climbs in the world, but died after falling from a local crag where he had first cut his teeth over thirty years ago . . .'

I decelerated and pulled into the slow lane behind an articulated lorry. *Like my driving?* a sign on the tailgate asked, and gave a phone number, just in case you didn't. The next exit was for the A5 and North Wales and I let the car slow down and drift leftwards down the slip-road. The newsman was talking about helicopters and multiple fractures and dead on arrival. I hadn't really made a decision, no conscious decision, anyway, but that was just like it had been with climbing – movement being everything, movement being a kind of thought, body and mind fused into one, the mind reduced perhaps, but the body exalted, surely. Nowadays in the ordinary round of life there was separation of mind and body, but in those days it had been different.

As I dialled home, the radio news had become a broken oil pipeline in West Africa. Villagers had sabotaged the thing in order to collect the crude oil that spilled out. The phone rang in the hallway of my house while West African villagers ranted on about the corruption of the government and the high prices they were forced to pay for what was flowing for free through the metal tube just outside their village. You had to see their point of view.

I'd hoped to get one of the girls, but of course it was Eve's voice that answered: 'Hello?'

'It's me.'

'Where on *earth* are you?' The over-emphasis in her voice.

'Have you heard the news?'

'What news?'

'On the radio. Jamie. He's dead.'

An eloquent silence. How can silence at the end of a telephone line be eloquent? But it was. 'How?'

'No idea. A fall, that's what it said. Look, I'm somewhere around Wolverhampton. I'm going.'

'*Going?*'

'To Wales.'

'*Wales?*' A note of incredulity. 'Where will you stay? For goodness' sake, Allie's got to go to choir practice this evening. She was relying on you taking her. And you haven't got anything with you.'

'That shouldn't be much of a problem. And I reckon I can get a bed at the Centre.'

Another silence. 'What's the point?'

'He was a friend. Christ alive, Eve, he was my *best* friend.' It sounded ridiculous, the kind of thing children say. Best friend. Make friends, make friends, never, never break friends. It's girls who do that kind of thing, mainly. Boys find it all a bit embarrassing, don't they?

'And now he's dead. And you haven't seen him for years. What's wrong with a letter, or a phone call or something? You don't have to go running to the rescue like a Boy Scout, for God's sake. And, anyway, there's no one to rescue.'

'There's Ruth.'

'I know there's Ruth. And how do you propose to rescue her?'

There was one of those awkward pauses, made more awkward by the fact that we were just voices, stripped of face or feature. We spoke over each other: 'Rob.'

'Eve.'

'Go on. What were you going to say?'

'No, you.'

'When . . .'

'Yes?'

'When will you be back?'

Her question hung in the balance. 'A day or two,' I said finally. 'Time to sort things out. Time to see Caroline. That kind of thing. Eve . . .'

'Yes?'

'Give the girls a kiss from me. Tell Allie I'm sorry about the choir. Next week.'

'Is that a promise?'

It was hard to read her tone. Hard to read mine too, I guess. 'Look, I'm parked on the hard shoulder. I'd better be going. I'll give you a ring later. Love to the girls. And to you.'

'Yes,' she said, but she didn't sound convinced.

Birmingham is something of a border territory. You wouldn't think it to look at the place, but the fact is that beyond Birmingham you are suddenly out of the embracing clasp of London, that disproportionate city, that selfish city that wants everything and everybody, that steals almost the whole of the south of England to itself and looks with covetous eyes on the rest. But beyond the lights of Birmingham there are the Marches, where blood was spilt, and the thin ribbon of the A5 that leads to Wales. London seems far away. I drove into the gathering dusk, past familiar names and familiar landmarks: Telford, Shrewsbury. Ahead there were black hills against the sky. Offa's Dyke was signposted for tourists. At Oswestry came the first hint of a change of language and landscape, Chirk and Newbridge giving way to Pentre and Cefn Mawr, and the road abruptly turning westward and finding a narrow gorge into the hills, and there was the sign to Llangollen, which is the furthest many outsiders get into the narrow, crabbed, secretive land that is Wales. The walls of the valley crowded in on the car.

Headlights cut into the thick Welsh evening and spotlighted Celtic names now – Cerrig-y-drudion, Pentrefoelas, Capel Garmon. With the window down I could sense the difference, that sharp scent of meltwater, the hostile chill of height, the snatch of cold mountain air at the lungs.

It all came back as I drove: an awful muddle of memory and forgetting. Eve and the children suddenly seemed very far away and in another country, a safe, literal place where nothing is left to chance and no one takes risks. But this was different: this was a haunted landscape, trampled over by the ghosts of the past. Ahead was the familiar silhouette of the mountain that was most familiar of all – Yr Wyddfa, Snowdon. Overhead were the stars, Orion setting in the wake of the sun, a planet – Jupiter, I guessed – gleaming down on the sublunary world with a baleful eye. One of our routes had been called Jupiter. I could even recall the words in the guidebook: 'Dinas Mot: start to the right of Gandalf, Extremely Severe.' I remembered Jamie floating up on invisible holds while I had sweated after him on the blunt end of the rope. I felt the sweat now in memory, even after thirty years.

I turned off the main road into a high valley. A long, narrow lake was pressed into the darkness of the mountains like an ingot of silver. At the only lighted building I pulled the car over and parked. A warm and soporific atmosphere of tradition greeted me as I pushed open the door of the bar. There was brown wooden panelling and an old hemp rope in a glass case and the signatures of history written across the ceiling, Tenzing Norgay and Edmund Hillary, Tom Bourdillon and Charles Evans, and another name scrawled somewhere there as well: Guy Matthewson.

I ordered a beer. At the bar two men were talking in low and authoritative terms about the accident. They were tweedy and pipe-smoking. This hotel and all its traditions had always been

9

a different world from ours, a parallel universe of breeches and heavy boots and pipes. We had been down at the Padarn Lake in Llanberis. We wore jeans and canvas rock boots that they used to call PAs, and ciggies. Spliffs sometimes. A world away. 'What can you expect?' they were asking each other. 'These days, people have no respect for the mountains. Of course, his father was one of the old school . . .'

There was a phone in the corner. I found the number in the directory and when my call was answered it was Jamie himself speaking. It was a shock to hear his voice: 'This is the Matthewson Mountain Centre,' he said. 'We can't answer at the moment, but if you leave your name and number after the beep we'll get back to you as soon as we can.'

I didn't leave a message. I finished my beer and left the customers to their complacency.

The road from the hotel wound uphill and over the head of the pass. The lights of a youth hostel loomed out of the blackness. There might have been a trace of snow on the hillside behind the building. On the left, the bulk of Crib Goch rose up to block out the stars. Then the descent into the pass began, and the names of the climbing crags crowded in from memory – Dinas Mot, Dinas Cromlech, Carreg Wastad, Clogwyn y Grochan. A narrow valley littered with boulders and outcrops and legends, a cradle and a crucible. Nant Peris with its little straggles of cottages.

The turn off the main road was vividly familiar, as though time had no dimension in memory and I had last taken that route only a week ago, when we had been looking for a place that was for sale. And then the headlights picked out the slab of engraved slate announcing

Bryn Derw – Matthewson Mountain Centre

10

and the low-slung grey house with the outbuildings that had been converted into sleeping-quarters, and a rough car park with no vehicles. I climbed out into the chill night air, feeling at the same time part of the place and alien, an adept and an intruder.

There were lights in a few of the downstairs windows. When I rang the bell, footsteps sounded inside and a male voice called through the door: 'You the press?'

'I'm a friend.'

'That's what they all say. You'd fucking better be.' The door opened with reluctance and a face peered out. Sallow skin and a scattering of stubble like iron filings across the chin. Long hair pulled back with a bandanna.

'Where's Ruth?' I asked, as I stepped inside. There were familiar photographs on the walls of the hall, stark monochrome ones of angular rock and scrawny climbers plastered across in balletic poses; colour shots of dark rock and enamel blue skies and untrammelled snow. One of the rock climbers was Jamie himself, poised on finger holds on some overhang; the couple of guys in down jackets and helmets and cheesy grins with an apocalyptic sunset behind them were Jamie and me together; the girl climbing a steep rock wall, with long hair streaming out below her and a skin-tight T-shirt, was Ruth a quarter of a century ago, all of them three decades ago when we were much younger and less foolish.

'She's in the kitchen. Who shall I say—'

'You shan't.' I pushed past and went down the passage. The youth followed behind, no doubt wondering whether he had failed in his duty as guard dog, no doubt wondering whether this visitor was going to pull out a notepad at the last moment and ask Ruth how she felt about Jamie's death and what it was like to be married to a man who defied death every day and crap like that.

She was in the kitchen, just as the guard dog had said. She was fiddling around with a coffee pot, occupying herself with trivial things, which is what you do in circumstances like that. She turned to look who it was who had just come in at the door, and there were whole seconds when I could watch her expression registering nothing at all, a performance that would have tried a lesser actress beyond all imagining. Her hand went up to brush a strand of hair from her forehead. She did it with the back of her wrist, a gesture that was so familiar. Her fingernails were cut short and stained with paint.

'Dewar,' she said. No surprise. A consummate piece of acting. She'd always called me by my surname, right from our first meeting. Almost always.

The minder had slipped back into the shadows. 'I heard the news on the radio,' I said.

She frowned. 'Where were you?'

I shrugged away her question and went over to her, and she stood there while I put my hands on her shoulders and leant forward to kiss her cheek. There was that awful familiarity, the sensation that somehow, even after so many years, this was where I belonged. 'I thought maybe I could be of help. I don't know how exactly.'

'Shoulder to cry on?'

'Perhaps.'

She offered me something. A beer, anything, something to eat, perhaps? I took the beer and sat at the table. While she prepared me some food she told me what there was to tell, which was mainly about hospitals – 'dead on arrival, actually' – and police statements and that kind of thing. 'There'll be a coroner's inquiry, but they say they'll release the body for the funeral.' Her mouth turned down. 'It'll be a zoo. Press, television. They've been on the phone all bloody evening.' Her Welsh intonation. People say the accent is sing-song, but that's just being romantic. It's flat-vowelled and resigned, the voice of a people who have always scratched a living on the edge of Britain ever since they were driven there by the invaders. The accent of defeat.

'What was he doing?'

'Doing?'

'Yes, *doing*. What happened? The radio report said nothing. Just a fall.'

She looked up at me. 'Great Wall,' she said. 'Solo.'

'He *what*?'

'You heard.' Her face was lean and pinched. It looked as though she was in a gale, the wind battering past, the sound of it in her ears, roaring past her ears so that it was difficult to hear what people said. You stood near and you shouted and still the wind snatched your words away.

'*Solo?* But that's the kind of thing kids do.'

She shrugged.

'I mean, it must be outside his range these days. Must have been. Even roped. What grade is it these days? E3? When I knew it, it was just ridiculous.'

'Four. It's E4.'

'E4 solo? At his age? I mean, that's suicide.' There was a silence in the kitchen. The windows were black as slate. There was that faint, infernal smell of gas from the cooking range.

'He was fit,' she said eventually, as though something had to be said. 'Always out, always climbing. You know.'

'I remember falling off Great Wall trying to second him. Had to take a tight rope. He thought it bloody funny. I remember him peering down at me from the peg belay and grinning like an idiot.'

'He would.'

'Where is he now?' For a fraction of a second it had seemed that we were talking in the present, about the living not the dead. That lithe man, the laughter in his expression, the shadows in his eyes.

'The undertakers',' she said. 'I've discovered that they take everything off your hands. Complete service. What a discovery to make. Look, you don't have to be here, you know.'

'I want to be.'

'Have you got somewhere to stay? Do you want a room?'

'If you like.'

'Okay.' She looked away and found something to do, the way you do when you want distraction. There's always something irrelevant to do.

'What are your plans?' I asked.

'Plans?'

'About this place.'

'Oh, that. Sell my share, I guess. Nic's a partner now, did you know that? Dominic Lewis. You know him?'

'I know the name. Was that the courteous reception committee?'

'He's been a big help.'

'I'm sure.'

'And I'll buy a cottage in Spain with the proceeds.' It was a joke. She smiled to show me and I smiled back, and there were echoes all round us. The past, the distant past. A whole lifetime.

She corrected herself: 'Castle more like. Castles in Spain.'

'Or in the air.'

I slept in one of the rooms in the main building beneath a low sloping ceiling and watched over by a picture of Dominic Lewis climbing Pendragon, which was one of our routes, one that Jamie and I had put up. I recognized the pitch clearly enough. Like so much else it was ingrained in memory, the feel of the rock, the precise uncompromising curve of *that* hold, *that* crack, that small nub of quartz that was the key handhold. It was like an etching, the details scored into the mind because they were experienced in every way at the time – intellectually, physically, all ways that there are to experience something. 'It's just like sex,' that's what Jamie used to say. 'The physical and the mental together. Mind and matter.' Quite the little philosopher, Jamie had been. In the photo Lewis was all flexing deltoids and purple leotards, looking up towards the camera with his fingers curled like claws over a flake hold and his mouth in a half-smile. The pink gneiss was all around him, the sea boiling in the background: very photogenic. He was soloing, of course. No doubt he'd have done Pendragon on sight, as a warm-up before tackling something hard. He was one of the new generation: bolts and chalk, abseil inspections and top roping to get the moves right.

I thought of Jamie soloing Great Wall, a climb he could never have hoped to succeed on, not any longer, not these days. And then I must have dozed, because the next thing I knew was a faint, mouse-like sound, and when I turned there was no longer the cold blackness of the wall across the room, but a faint grey trapezium of light. The door was open. A figure was standing there, a black silhouette against the grey, like a minimalist painting. Mere shapes.

'Who's that?'

Soft steps creaked on the boards. I felt her close presence in the darkness, a sensation that was midway between heat and scent. 'Do you mind? I just wanted company, you know. Feeling a bit *digalon*.'

Calon is heart; *digalon*, downhearted. It had been one of her words, one of her Welsh words that she allowed into her English. *Cariad* was another: darling, dearest, love. I said something – an apology, a warning, something – but she didn't care. She lifted the blankets and slipped in beside me. Even after a quarter of a century, she was familiar, the movements of her tough limbs, the hard angles of her body, her loose breasts, her smell.

She'd gone by the time a grey, bleary dawn opened the narrow windows of my borrowed room. The whole incident might almost have been a dream; or a memory.

2

Breakfast was a silent affair. The three of us watched each other warily, Lewis wondering exactly who I was and how I fitted into this strange little world half-way up a Welsh hillside. Ruth avoided my eye, busied herself with making tea and coffee and the kind of domestic thing that was so alien to her.

'You used to partner Jim, didn't you?' Lewis asked. He had flat Mancunian vowels that didn't go very well with a flashy name like Dominic. In the past he'd have been Don or Joe and would have driven up on a motorbike to spend the weekends in the Pass bivvying under a rock. Nowadays he was sponsored by a climbing-gear manufacturer. He had the name all across the front of his fashion shirt: Top Peak.

'For a few years.'

He smiled. 'Did quite a few routes with him, didn't you?'

'Quite a few. Pendragon was one.'

'Course. Matthewson and Dewar, alternate leads.'

'You read the guide.'

'I didn't flash it, if that's what you mean. Nearly came off at the crux. Got gripped something terrible.'

'It doesn't look like it in the photo.'

'That was for the camera.' He grinned and shovelled cereal into his mouth. 'Fine route,' he admitted, through the debris of corn flakes. Or did he say *fun* route? 'Necky. Quite something, for those days.' There was a pause while he ate. Then, 'You were on the Eiger with him, weren't you? That business on the North Face?'

'Yes,' I answered, but I didn't say any more and I didn't encourage him to ask. I wasn't going to discuss that with him. I turned to Ruth. 'Caroline. Is she—'

She smiled knowingly. 'Still alive? Oh, very much so.'

'Still at Gilead House?'

'Yes. I spoke to her on the phone yesterday. I suppose I ought to go round, but . . .'

'I'll go and see her.'

'She'll be at the funeral.'

'I'd still better go.'

You must confront your past. At some time or other you must confront your past. It doesn't flash before your eyes, I knew that; but it's always there. We are our past. There is nothing else, and none of it can be undone.

The drive took an hour and a half, back through the valley to the top of the pass, up and over and through the mountains, then down to where trees grew again and there were waterfalls and grey terraced houses picked out in white, with signs saying 'Bed and Breakfast'. A verdant valley on the edge of the mountain wilderness. Beyond the town, the road wound up into the hills. I lost the way once but picked it up again after going back on my tracks for a turn or two. Nothing had changed much, but memory is selective: it doesn't give you a route plan. A sign pointed a stern Old Testament finger to Nebo from where Moses was allowed to view, but never reach, the Promised Land; and then there was the familiar stretch of green meadow and the grey house half-way up the hillside beneath the hanging woodland. The stableyard on one side and the upper garden at the back. A drystone wall of slate. Roses and fuchsias set like jewels in a case of pewter and green velvet. Gilead the quaint name, from a chapel that had once stood there, part of whose walls were built into the house itself.

'It'll do,' Jamie's mother had said once, long ago. 'It's not home, but it'll do.'

I stopped the car and climbed out. Below, the ground fell steeply away to the river and the town. I could see the Anglican church and the Methodist chapel, and the municipal offices, which were like a hybrid between the other two. There was the silver line of the railway to balance in its directness the silver meanders of the river. There was smoke in the still air, thin plumes like old-fashioned quills stuck in ink pots. Upstream of the town was the seventeenth-century bridge that features in the postcards. They claim that Inigo Jones built it; but his surname was the only Welsh thing about the man. Jones was London born and bred.

Before opening the gate, I got Eve on the mobile. I didn't *know* when I'd be back. I'd have to stay for the funeral. Of course I would. And there would be a coroner's inquiry, apparently. And then, when everything was over . . .

'Everything was over years ago, wasn't it?' she said.

'Yes, but . . .' But what? I tried to explain, and felt the inadequacy of words at the very moment I spoke them. There was a silence on the line.

'I rescued you from them once, Rob,' she said eventually. Her voice was quiet. 'I don't think I could manage it again. Not after all this time.' And then she rang off.

I waited a moment with the phone dead in my hand. Sounds: the barking of a dog and the bleating of sheep. The sound of sheep was the constant undercurrent to the landscape, an old crone's griping or a child's whinging, a Welsh complaint. 'Bloody sheep,' Jamie's mother had said. Coming from her mouth the word 'bloody' had shocked. It was *language*. 'Bloody sheep. God, how can we live *here*?'

I had gone with them to look, a long and stuffy journey in the back of a hired car. She'd got lost and we had had to stop in a village to ask an old man the way. 'Gilead?' he repeated. 'Gilead House? That'll be up Gwytherin way. Not far, mind, not far.'

And sure enough it was not far, just up the hill above the town, on the side of the valley among the trees, a grey place picked out in blistered white, with the lawns run to rack and ruin and the field at the front full of sheep.

'Bloody sheep,' she had said, standing there holding Jamie's hand (he struggled to let go but she gripped him hard). 'However will we live here?'

But she had apparently, off and on. Forty years and more.

I drove the car through and went back to close the gate, then drove slowly up the gravel to the space in front of the house. There was no one around, but when I rang the doorbell I heard shuffling footsteps inside. Someone fiddled at the lock on the other side of the door and it was only then that I realized I hadn't really asked Ruth about Caroline's health. 'Very much alive' was what she'd said. But what did that mean when you were – what? Eighty? I tried to work it out. Seventy? Seventy-five? I wasn't certain, not because I didn't know how long ago it was but because, I understood with a sudden shock, I hadn't really known her age even then. I had nothing definite to add to the forty years that separated then from now, this hillside on the edge of summer from that same hillside so many summers ago. Listening to the scrabbling on the far side of the door, I thought about the epithets of decline and decay – arthritis? Parkinson's? Alzheimer's? – and was filled with dread at the prospect of seeing her again.

The door opened. The face that appeared in the gap was lined and toothless. It contained within its features all the closed suspicion of the Welsh hill people. '*A chi sy o'r Bwrdd Dwr?*' it said.

I felt an absurd and irrational relief at the sight. It was a woman from the village, a woman who *did*. 'I'm sorry. I've no Welsh, I'm afraid. Not really. *Bore da* is my limit.'

She looked peeved. 'Are you the man from the *Water?*' she asked, with exaggerated emphasis.

'I'm a man from England,' I said. 'An old friend.'

The woman faced this disappointment stoically. 'We're expecting a man from the Water.'

'I'm afraid I can't oblige. I just want to see Mrs Matthewson, if she's in.'

'Well, she's not receiving *people*.'

'I think she'll receive me. Tell her it's Robert. Tell her that.'

The maid considered the matter carefully, her wrinkled lips mulling over the problem as though it were a taste.

'You aren't Mary, are you?' I asked.

'I'm Alice.'

'I remember Mary.'

There was a smile there among the suspicion. 'Mary was my sister, God bless her.'

'I remember her well.'

'Do you now? Do you?' Memory was a kind of password. 'Well, you'd best come in. I'll find if Mrs Matthewson can see you. Mr Robert, you say?'

'Robert. Just Robert.'

She shuffled off. I waited in the hall, the dark brown hall with the long-case clock that paced out the silence. Stairs led upwards into shadow. There was a stained-glass window at the turn of the stairs: an Arthurian knight looking towards his lady, a piece of vapid Burne-Jonesery. I remembered that. I remembered laughing at it because she had laughed. There were pictures on the walls: watercolours of Welsh hillsides, and an oil painting of an urban street – one of the slate towns, the slate cliffs laid on with a palette knife that brought to them the very texture of the rock itself: lucid slabs, slick with rain. I knew that style well enough, even without seeing the signature at the bottom: 'Ruth Phoenix, 1979'. Then there was the jawbone of a shark, fished – I remembered the story – off Nantucket. That was what she had told me, laughing at the memory of it. 'I caught it myself, while the men jeered and told me I could never do it and all that sort of crap. But I did it. And there it is.'

How much had changed? I couldn't be sure. The illusion of memory gave me everything, all the artefacts, all the *objets d'art* (I could hear her enunciate the French phrase): a tortured glass bottle – Lalique? – that was like some intimate female organ; a porcelain shepherdess – Meissen? – that laughed at the onlooker as though flaunting her recently lost virginity; another oil painting that might have been (but she had never dared subject it to the expert's curious gaze) by Marie Laurencin. I peered at the thing with new eyes now, and knew just the man to examine it and value it. On the opposite wall there was even a photograph showing Jamie: a crouched figure in silhouette, his bandaged face looking out from under a helmet, with plunging cliffs behind him and bright alpine meadows far below. Jamie at Death Bivouac. I knew that photo well: I had taken it myself.

From upstairs there was the noise of talking, but I couldn't make out any words. Then a light footfall at the top of the stairs. 'Yes?'

I turned from the photo. Someone was coming down. She turned at the landing and paused in front of the stained glass, looking down at me. 'Yes?'

There was a shock at seeing her, of course. Something physical like a fist, a child's fist perhaps, swung playfully into the stomach when you weren't expecting it. A convulsion of heart and diaphragm. The blow had been intended as a joke so you had to smile.

'It's Robert,' I said.

'Robert, yes.' She smiled vaguely. For a moment I wondered whether she even remembered.

'I came to see how you were. I've been over at Jamie's place. With Ruth. I've come to say how sorry I am.' Paltry words. Maybe that was what made her smile. Paltriness had always amused her. She was wearing trousers (she'd have called them slacks) and a white shirt (she'd have called it a blouse), and her hands were clasped in front of her as though she had to do that to stop a tremor. As she came down the final flight of stairs she moved cautiously, with one hand on the banister and the other still clasped in front of her. 'Have you been to see him?' she asked.

For an awful moment I thought that she hadn't understood. I imagined – it was a fleeting moment of horror, like the sudden perception of a death – that her mind had gone. 'Caroline, Jamie's *dead*,' I told her gently.

She came up close to me as though it was necessary to bring my face into focus. It was like looking at someone through a screen, a Japanese screen of some kind – rice paper or whatever: the woman I had known peering out through the layers of time. 'I know what Jamie is,' she said softly. 'I know exactly what Jamie is. I have had practice in this, don't forget.' Her left hand, which had gripped the banister, which had gripped many things in its time, gripped my arm. The other remained where it was, slack and idle across the base of her belly. She leant forward and presented her cheek for me to kiss. Her skin was soft and smooth.

'You're looking very well,' I said.

She shook her head. 'Forget the compliments. The only thing about age is the surprise it brings. Death is no surprise, of course; but you never know *who* is going to die. I'll bet he put his money on me first. And I bet you did too. You probably thought that I was already dead and buried, didn't you?'

'Don't be ridiculous, Caroline.' The name seemed absurd on her aged body, a young woman's name given in error. Caro, she had been. She always said it was inaccurate. 'Caro' is masculine. It should have been 'Cara'.

'Oh, yes, you did.' Another of her traits, to brook no argument. She walked away into the drawing room where there were other photos – Jamie's father looking youthful, like a corpse preserved – other artefacts, other memories enshrined. An old, polished gramophone from the time when they still made them like pieces of furniture. And on the wall another of Ruth's paintings, a nude, this one, a woman standing beside a bed, her flesh blurred by sunlight from a window: white limbs and a smudge of pubic hair.

'What would you like? Tea?' She rang for the maid and I remembered the box of little mechanical flags on the kitchen wall, one for each room in the house, to signal which room had rung. There was even a green baize door dividing off the servants'

24

quarters. Caroline had laughed when she had shown me that. It was one of those things that accumulated, like parts of an argument, to convince her that this isolated house on an isolated hillside was a place where she might live.

'The other thing about age,' she said, 'is that it's only once you are old that you realize things are for keeps. What seemed an interesting experiment is actually the only existence that you have or are going to have. Why did you leave it so long to come back?'

'It doesn't seem long,' I replied evasively. 'It seems like yesterday.'

She laughed. 'That's another trouble with age,' she said. 'Thirty years ago seems like yesterday.'

Alice came into the drawing room with a tray. While Caroline poured the tea with her left hand, her right remained couched in her lap like a small, helpless pet. It was only then that I understood something was wrong with it, wrong with the mechanism of nerve and muscle that was meant to move it. She saw my glance. 'A stroke, my dear,' she said. 'Just a little one. My doctor assures me that I could go on for years yet.' She crossed her legs. Her ankles were still narrow, but they had a wasted look to them, as though slenderness had given way to fragility.

'So tell me,' she said. 'How is your mother?'

I shrugged. 'She's in a nursing-home. Oh, she's well enough physically, but . . . her mind wanders.'

Was there sympathy in her expression? It wasn't happening to her, that was clear enough. Her mind was there, all right. 'And tell me about you,' she said. 'Married? Of course. I remember Jamie telling me. Are you happy?'

'I'm content.'

'That's a very equivocal response. Children?'

25

'Two. Girls. Twenty-one and seventeen. University and A levels.'

'And what does Daddy do?'

'Don't you know?'

'Should I?'

'I thought Ruth might have said. I'm in the art business. Contemporary art. A gallery in London, another in Birmingham of all places. An associate gallery in New York.'

'Bisected cows in formaldehyde, that kind of thing?'

'Not often.'

She looked thoughtful. Somehow I could see the younger woman behind the mask of age. 'But happy?' she asked again. 'Is Rob *happy*?'

I shrugged. Don't you grow out of happiness? Isn't happiness what kids hope for? Wasn't adulthood the understanding that there is no real happiness, not long, sustained and unequivocal happiness? 'I told you. I'm content.'

Caro smiled, as I knew she would. Blurred by age, it was her familiar smile nevertheless. 'Equivocal,' she said. She had taught me the word, like so much else. 'Dear Robert, as equivocal as ever.'

3

There was some kind of religious service for Jamie. It was Ruth's idea, Ruth's insistence, even though Jamie had not been a churchgoer, hadn't believed in anything as far as I knew. 'What alternative is there?' she asked, when I protested. 'Just a dreadful crematorium thing?'

I rang home and suggested that Eve come, but she declined. 'They were your friends,' she said. 'Not mine. And look how they treated you . . .'

The service was held in the local church. The place was full, of course. There were names I knew, a few faces I recognized, all hard-edged and weathered, one or two bearded. The survivors. One in eight Himalayan climbers fails to return. If you are talking about going high then the statistics get worse: under half of those who go above seven and a half thousand metres survive to tell the tale. Oh, yes, there were as many ghosts at Jamie Matthewson's funeral as live mourners.

I sat in the front row between Caroline and Ruth. Caroline was in grey silk – the grey of ashes, the grey of slate, a grey that set off her still bright complexion; Ruth wore black, a sharp, black linen suit that made her look tough and vulnerable at the same time, the kind of trick she had always been capable of pulling off. She had no makeup and her hair was pulled back and gathered up to emphasize the line of her jaw. Her expression was tightly pegged down – like a tent in a storm. Beyond her was Dominic Lewis, looking uneasy in something resembling a jacket and tie.

We sang a hymn and the rector gave a little address about striving for the heights and seeing the Promised Land from the top of the mountain, and things like that. And then it was the turn of others: Carrington to say something about Jim on Everest, Jim as the selfless expedition member, the man who you could rely on for help, or a joke, or a day's hard slog at altitude to set up the top camp; Philips to talk about Jim standing in awe on the summit of K2 as they watched the sun set and steeled themselves to face the bivouac that would probably (but didn't) kill them both. There was someone else to talk about Jim the businessman, the man who helped the local economy, the Englishman who had found a home in Wales; and Dominic Lewis mumbled a poem about Icarus falling from the sky. Auden, I suppose it was. Ruth had asked me to add something. I didn't really want to but I couldn't refuse, so when all the others were done I made my way up to the lectern. Looking out over the congregation, I wondered if they knew who the hell I was.

'I first knew Jamie when I was about twelve,' I told them, just to put them in the picture. 'Later we climbed together. We shared a great deal, as one does with a climbing partner: meals, climbs, tents, bivouac bags, jokes, all that kind of thing. Occasionally we shared the lead. When he let me.'

They laughed at that. They were desperate to laugh. I stopped and looked down at them, and I wanted to say other things. I wanted to tell them about the first climb ever. I wanted to tell them about winters in Scotland and summers in the Alps. I wanted to tell about Caroline – she looked up at me with a quizzical expression, as though she couldn't quite recall my name – and my own mother who now languished in a nursing-home and wondered who I was when I visited her. I wanted to speak about Jamie's father. And I wanted to tell them about Ruth. Above all, I wanted to tell them about Ruth.

There was a great silence in the grey church, a cold and expectant silence, almost as though they were waiting for me to tell them these things. 'Probably we shared more than most,' I said. Ruth was watching with the faintest of Welsh smiles. But I didn't tell them; instead I opened a book and read to them: '"The play is over, and the curtain is about to fall. Before we part, a word upon the graver teachings of the mountains."'

I don't know if they recognized the piece – they sat there as you do at funerals, in a no man's land between misery and embarrassment, and I couldn't tell whether there was any recognition. '"Still, the last, sad memory hovers round, and sometimes drifts across like floating mist, cutting off sunshine and chilling the remembrance of happier times. There have been joys too great to be described in words, and there have been griefs upon which I have not dared to dwell; and with these in mind I say, Climb if you will, but remember that courage and strength are naught without prudence, and that a momentary negligence may destroy the happiness of a lifetime.

Do nothing in haste; look well to each step; and from the beginning think what may be the end.'"

The curious thing is how often people ignore that advice, in climbing as in life. I closed the book and resumed my seat and we all sang 'Guide Me, O Thou Great Jehovah'. It was a fine sound, no doubt.

After the funeral there was a sorry procession of cars to the crematorium. In the chapel I sat beside Ruth. She gripped my hand as we watched his coffin roll silently through a red velvet curtain to the sound of heavenly electronic choirs. Caroline sat on the other side of her. Afterwards we hung around outside, looking at the sodden bouquets, reading the labels on them before the rain dissolved the ink. 'Who are these?' I asked once or twice, but I didn't get much of an answer: 'Oh, just people he knew.' One of the cards said, 'From all of us at the City Climbing Club – keep going for the top, youth.' Ruth just looked away into the distance, across the sodden acres of grass and the miniature memorial plaques.

Caroline came over to say goodbye. There was a detached quality about her manner, as though I hadn't been to see her just two days before. 'I'm surprised you're here, Robert,' she said. 'I thought you'd quite broken with Jamie. What made you come?'

'He was my oldest friend,' I said. 'Whatever happened after.'

'And Ruth?'

'And Ruth as well.'

She smiled. It was difficult to read her expression. Perhaps I was somehow to blame, was that it? I almost said something to that effect; I almost lost my temper with the woman. 'How's Diana?' she asked.

'She's fine physically. Like I said when I saw you.'

'Did you?' The smile was wry now. 'Memory, you see. The second thing to go.'

'What's the first?'

'Robert, dear, I'm sure you can guess what the first is.' She touched my arm. 'Give Diana my love. Tell her . . .'

'Tell her what?'

'Tell her it seems that she won.'

'I don't think she'd understand. I'm not sure I do.'

She shrugged, and turned towards the big black car that waited for her. 'It doesn't matter,' she said. 'Nothing matters.'

We watched her drive away. For Ruth and me there was the journey back to the hotel where refreshments had been laid on. The beer and the wine flowed. There was talk, there was laugh ter, there was reminiscence and the relating of absurd stories and hair-raising exploits. There is so much about the climbing community that derives from the Celtic fringes of Britain, and at a wake climbers are as good as the Irish. Perhaps it's because they have a lot of practice. I stood with Ruth and smiled and nodded, and for a moment I felt as though I were part of all this.

We got back late in the afternoon. It was already dark. Someone had turned lights on in the main building, but the place was deserted. We went to the kitchen as the natural focal point of the house. Ruth put a kettle on to boil. 'He wanted his ashes scattered, did I tell you that?'

'Yes, you did.' She'd even shown me the will. 'If my body can be recovered, I wish to be cremated and the ashes scattered . . .' I liked that practical touch 'if my body can be recovered'. At least he hadn't asked to be freeze-dried and left on Kangchenjunga.

'Will you do that for me?' she asked.

'If you'll come with me.'

31

'I'll come with you.' When the tea had brewed she poured two mugs and came and sat beside me at the table. She seemed smaller, somehow shrunken, as though she had aged two decades in the last twenty-four hours. She sipped tea and stared into the shadows that had collected in the corners of the room. We began to talk.

I

4

Go back. Go back a long way. Forty years, for God's sake, so far away that the world seems a different place and the people populating it different beings altogether. My mother standing with me in the hallway of the hotel, her hand round my shoulders in a gesture that was almost protective, and the other woman coming in through the door with her own son in tow and a look of artificial surprise painted across her face. 'Diana, *darling!*' she exclaimed. 'How *won*derful to see you after all this time!'

But there had been no matching intonation of surprise from my mother: no exclamation, no excitement. Mere statements of fact: 'Meg. How long it's been.' They embraced. It was a curious embrace, designed to avoid intimacy rather than welcome it: no part of body or soul actually came into contact except two cheeks, one finely powdered, the other naked. You notice these things as a child. You stand and watch, and things lodge in the memory like splinters in the eye. The woman was coloured pink and cream and gold, and she had the air of someone from another world, an ambassador to a foreign and decidedly barbarous place. Gold jewellery at her neck (the neck showing the tendons and the first small fault lines of age), a narrow linen suit, and in the V of the jacket, the smooth curves of her breasts.

'Actually I use *Caroline* now, not Meg,' this newcomer said.

'*Caroline?* Why on earth *Caroline?*'

'I prefer it, that's all. And Caroline was always my name, after all. Margaret Caroline.'

'But you'll still be Meg to me.'

'Darling, I'd rather not. Meg sounds like a sheep dog.' The woman with two names looked round the lounge (*Guests are Requested to Respect the Presence of Others and Refrain from Turning up the Volume of the Television*) with an expression of faint distaste. I saw the expression and felt ashamed. 'So this is what you do now?'

'We survive.'

And then she paused in front of a photograph, the photograph of my father that hung there on the wall like an admonishment, like a reproach. 'Alan,' she said. 'How determined he looks.' She glanced round. 'I did write when I heard about your break-up, but to your old home address. It was the only one I had.'

My mother smiled. At the time I wasn't sure why, but now I understand. She was smiling at the lies. The woman turned her eyes on me. 'And this is your son? What's your name, young man?'

I told her I was Robert.

'Well, I'm *Caroline*. And that's what you can call me: Caroline. None of that Mrs Matthewson nonsense. And certainly' – she

36

turned down her mouth – 'not *Meg.*' We shook hands on the fact. Her grip was firm and soft at the same time, a strange sensation. 'And this is Jamie.'

He stood there beside his mother, with the sullen expression of a child who has grasped what adulthood means and resents not having yet achieved it. 'Jamie is just thirteen.' I was still a mere twelve, far below him in the precise hierarchy of child-hood, further from him then than ever again.

There was an awkward pause while the adults wondered what to do with this incongruent pair of children. 'Perhaps Robert can take you out and show you round,' Mother suggested.

Jamie hesitated.

'Go on,' said his own mother, with just a hint of impatience. 'Robert's mother and I have so many things to talk about.'

We both stood there in our uniform of the times – blue Aertex shirts, grey shorts, plimsolls, the one pair black, the other white – and waited.

'Well, go *on*, then.'

So Jamie and I walked out into the garden, side by side, but not together, walked idly down the lawn kicking at things that presented themselves for kicking, and when we looked back we could see the two women talking in the sitting room, their images latticed by the leads of the window: the one with her mouse-coloured hair, and the other a perfect blonde. I won-dered whether I could read the movement of their lips – my mother's thin and hard, his mother's perfectly carved out of coral lipstick. *Lips.* The word buzzed in my imagination.

'My father has another family,' I announced. I supposed I felt the need to explain. 'That's why he's not here.'

Jamie reckoned this piece of information for a moment, then played a winning move. 'Mine's dead,' he retorted.

'Dead?'

'Dead. He died in the mountains.'

'You can see the mountains from the hill up there.'

'Those aren't *real* mountains. They're just *Welsh* mountains. My father died in the Himalaya.' He pronounced the name Him-*ah*-lya. 'On Kangchenjunga.'

I had never heard of Kangchenjunga. 'How did he do that?'

'A storm. He died of cold.'

I thought about this. Dying of cold was the death of heroes, the death of Scott and his companions. 'What's it like to have a dead father?'

He thought about it a bit. 'It's okay,' he said.

After that first encounter the Matthewsons, mother and son, came to stay in the hotel. It was only for a couple of weeks during the summer holidays while they were doing up their house. They took three rooms on the first floor – '*Three* rooms, can you imagine?' my mother exclaimed – and for almost the first time I had a companion. Despite the difference in age, we were united in much: an alien Englishness among the Welsh, the shared lack of a father, the shared fact of being an only child, a shared curiosity in what went on around us. Powerful similarities, centripetal forces that pulled us together across the barrier set up by the years.

I worshipped Jamie, I suppose, with that dogged admiration the young can have for the immediately older – far greater than if he had been an adult. In the next few weeks I followed him like an acolyte. We kicked cans around on wasteland near by. We had a tense encounter – an uneasy blend of familiarity and suspicion – with some other kids at the recreation ground, an encounter in which Jamie's greater age and belligerence won the day. We made casual friends with a solitary girl called Bethan, who lived in the council houses. We watched contrails high in a rare blue sky and debated whether they were Russian spy planes, preparing to take the capitalist world for their own. Perhaps we could see satellites up there among the night stars, Russian Sputniks looking down on our own fragment of the Earth. Together Jamie and I went into town. I followed him along the sea front, past benches with glum holiday-makers, amid the alien accents of Liverpool and Manchester. He walked quicker than I; I seemed to spend the whole time struggling to catch up. We found an arcade with slot machines. One of them was a what-the-butler-saw machine. Jamie fed it with pennies, then stood aside for me to peer into the viewer. I could make out vague and ill-focused tits and a froth of lace. It was education of a kind.

One day we spied on people in case they might be spies, stalked random strangers round the streets, watched a Brylcreemed man going from door to door trying to sell brushes to housewives. 'Clear off, you little buggers!' he shouted, when he noticed us following. 'I'll tell your parents of you.'

I went in fear for the rest of the day in case he had that power, to know names and addresses and parentage from a mere glimpse of someone's face. But Jamie merely laughed. 'I think he fucks the ones that want it,' he said. And added thoughtfully, 'Maybe they get a free brush.'

The word 'fuck' was possessed of a strange potency, a pass-word into the unknown adult world. Jamie had got hold of a copy of *Lady Chatterley's Lover*, published by Penguin at 3/6d, phoenix-covered and newly risen from the ashes of censorship and we leafed through the pages for 'fuck' and its derivatives. They occurred twenty-six times. We counted them. The book was his mother's, he told me. My mother would surely never have read it, certainly never owned it, never in a million years uttered such words. The fact that Jamie's mother possessed it, had read it, had played those words over to herself in her mind, made her seem dangerous and subversive. I watched her with the careful eyes of a spy, saw the curve of her calves, the arabesques of chin and ear, the subtle hollow at the base of her throat and the gravitational funnel between her half-hidden breasts.

'I've seen my mother,' he told me, 'in the nude.'

'You never.'

'Bloody have. She doesn't mind. As long as you're family.'

I wondered what it might be like, the sight of his mother stark naked. My own mother was tightly prudish. I could not imagine her having exposed herself for me to feed at her breasts, never mind opened her legs to let me out in the first place. And yet Jamie's mother had allowed herself to be seen naked.

'What's she *like?*'

He shrugged. 'Like any woman. Tits. Hair.'

'Hair?'

'Down there.'

'You've *seen* it?'

'Sure.'

Hair seemed counter-intuitive. All other evidence in my possession (but there was little enough) was to the contrary – statues, paintings, anything like that, even the pictures in the slot-machine. Men were hairy. Paintings showed that, and I'd seen it in the changing rooms of the municipal swimming-pool. Men were big and dark and hairy. But not women. I discovered a book of art reproductions in the guests' lounge and showed it to Jamie as evidence. Sir Peter Paul Rubens, whoever he might be. Women who didn't seemed concerned about their figures. Flesh piled up like uncooked dough; but no hair.

'That's art,' James said dismissively.

It was Bethan who put the matter beyond doubt, round the back of her father's garden shed, hitching up her skirt for us to look. 'You can't touch,' she warned, as she pulled her knickers down. 'Touching's rude.'

There wasn't much to see: sparse brushstrokes of dark hair and a small crease like pursed and smiling lips. 'Just that?' I asked.

'There's inside, too,' she said.

'Not *hair* inside?' Hair inside seemed remarkable, like nostrils.

'Not hair, you silly. Things.' She pulled herself open for us to see, and there were indeed *things*, things coralline and glistening. Folds, membranes, a little bud. We were silent, watching. 'That's my pinkie,' she explained. 'One day it'll grow into a willy. Maybe.'

'Don't be daft,' Jamie said.

'It will, so.' Bethan hitched up her knickers. 'Now it's your turn.'

'Who said anything about *turns*?'

'It's only fair.'

We stood there between the shed and the nettles, and debated the justice of the matter. 'Not both,' I insisted. 'Both's not fair.'

'One of you, then.'

So Jamie agreed. He was the kind who would agree. It was he who had suggested trailing the brush salesman, he who had discovered the penny-in-the-slot machine with the ancient photographs of naked women, he who found the copy of *Lady C.* He unbuttoned and dropped his trousers and underpants, and stood there exposed. His penis was small and smooth, with a domed head like a mushroom. There were blond hairs round its base.

'Roundhead,' I said, anxious to break the silence. 'That's a Roundhead.' At school we divided ourselves into Roundheads and Cavaliers. Sometimes there were games of football, or tag, or even fights between the two groups. The Cavaliers seemed to

41

be courageous and carefree like their historical namesakes; the Roundheads determined and efficient with their helmeted heads.

'I've not seen one like that,' Bethan said thoughtfully. 'Can I touch?' Remarkably the thing had begun to stir, like an animal roused from sleep.

'I thought touching's rude,' I protested.

But Jamie said nothing. Everything about him was very still except the slow rise of his penis. 'OK,' he agreed finally, and she did touch, her small, grimy fingers going round it and moving the outer skin so that the head of the penis tasted, with its small mouth, the unfamiliar outside air.

'I've done this to boys till it spits sometimes,' Bethan said.

After we had left Bethan we walked home in silence, contemplating matters of sexuality. 'Does your mother miss your father?' I asked eventually.

He shook his head. 'She's got boyfriends.'

Boyfriends sounded dangerous. 'My mother still loves my father,' I assured him, although I wasn't certain. 'That's what she told me.'

We climbed the hill at the back of the hotel. From there you could look down over the estuary and the suspension bridge and the castle. The tide was out and the mud flats glistened like steel. We sat on the grass and looked at the mountains. When seen through rain-streaked clouds they seemed like stormclouds themselves; beneath blue skies, as we saw them that day, they looked like the abode of the gods, the Celtic gods who had once ruled this place of grey chapels and grey headstones and luminous green fields.

'What are you?' Jamie asked.

'What d'you mean?'

He picked up a stone and threw it at nothing in particular. 'Roundhead or Cavalier?'

'Cavalier.'

'Show me.'

'No.'

'You saw mine.'

So I unbuttoned my trousers and showed him. It was a joke, a laugh, kid's stuff. I didn't stop him when he touched me. 'You're getting a stiff,' he said. Suddenly there was a great unease in my guts, a weakness in my knees, a sensation like falling. He laughed at my discomfiture. 'You like that, don't you?'

'Did you like it with Bethan?'

'It was all right.'

I swallowed. 'Well, then.'

Later we lay in the grass and contemplated the mountains in the distance. 'They're nothing,' Jamie said. 'Kangchenjunga is over five miles high. Can you imagine five miles high? Like an aeroplane.' I was silent for a moment, trying to imagine five vertical miles, which seemed so much more than five miles horizontally. 'My father told me that it's where the gods live,' Jamie said. 'That's what the people there believe. My mother says even he believed it, sort of. No one has ever stepped on the top, out of respect for the gods.' After a while he added, 'He's up there now, you know.'

'Up where?' I thought of heaven, somewhere up above the clouds. Had Jamie's father perhaps been watching us?

'On the mountain. They never found him. They never brought him down. He's up there on Kangchenjunga somewhere. My father. One day I'm going to climb mountains like him. One day.'

'So am I,' I said, because I was going to do what Jamie did. Whatever that was.

5

'Jamie says his father was a mountaineer.'

'He was,' my mother agreed.

How do you read an adult's face? Children have little practice in the art. The thirteen-year-old that was me read her
expression as sour and disapproving. 'Was he a hero, like Jamie
says?'

'He was to some people. To others he was just a man. A
friend, perhaps. A special friend.'

'Was he a friend of yours?'

Was she smiling? A curious expression, that I didn't understand; as close to a smile as pain is to pleasure. 'He was a
wonderful man. Very brave, and a little foolish.'

'Is that why he died?'

'I'm not sure why anyone dies,' she said.

'And were you sad?'

'*I* was. But Meg really didn't seem to be. As soon as it happened she went off with some American fellow. And now she's back here calling herself Mrs Matthewson again, and wanting to move into Gilead House – which she never liked, never was happy with, never really *lived* in.'

Gilead House. The name held strange echoes, of gilded lilies, of guilt and loyalty. Jamie described the place in terms that gave it the status of a mansion or a castle. 'You can come and see it if you want.'

'I'd like that.'

He shrugged. 'No problem.' I liked the way he said that: *no problem.* I practised the phrase in front of the mirror, with my thumbs hooked into my pockets and my chest puffed out.

To my surprise my mother didn't want to come. She had too much to do. She was too busy. She turned to a pile of papers on her desk just to prove it. 'Go if you want,' she said. 'Go.' So the next afternoon it was just the three of us who drove there. The inside of the car was heavy with Mrs Matthewson's perfume and the journey was long and stuffy, so that I felt sick and they had to stop to let me get out. We were on a hillside somewhere near our destination. The air had a breathless, exhilarating texture to it; and the smell of animals. I stood there looking at the view across the valley, over the market town of Llanbedr and towards the mountains in the distance, while the bitter vomit sank back down. Jamie's mother came and put her arm round my shoulders. 'Not far to go now,' she assured me, as we climbed back in.

A mile or two later she brought the car to a halt. There was a wooden gate and a sign, the paint blistered and faded, saying 'Gilead House'. The building was set back from the road, couched in a small cwm with trees behind it. It still preserved the faint air of a chapel: a steeply pitched roof of grey slate, a turret on one corner that might have been a bell-tower, an imposing front entrance that might have led into the nave. There was a builder's van parked in the drive and men in overalls were coming and going. The lawn was unmown and the field at the front was full of sheep. They bleated a thin, petulant protest.

'Bloody sheep,' Jamie's mother said. 'However will we live here?'

But we two boys looked out, across the valley, beyond the woods on the far side, over the nearer hills to where the mountains stood darkly against the horizon. It seemed a splendid place to be.

The Matthewsons moved out of the hotel a week later. They loaded their suitcases into the boot of their car, and then they were gone, with a promise to have me to stay, with a promise to keep in touch, with a distant smile from Mrs Matthewson and an approximate wave from Jamie out of the rear window of the diminishing car; and, quite suddenly and unexpectedly, I felt alone.

'You'll soon be at the new school,' my mother told me. 'You'll soon be making lots of new friends.' But friends were a random and unpredictable entity. Jamie was a friend and a mentor and a stepping-stone into the adult world; yet Jamie had vanished.

When was the train journey? How does it fit into those distant, fragmentary days? A single-track line ran up the valley, from the estuary at one end up into the hills and on to one of the slate towns. It was the kind of line that would soon be threatened with closure, would soon have a local pressure group to preserve it from cold economic winds. At passing places where the track was double, one train would stop and wait for the other and there would be the ceremonial handing over of a kind of engraved mace, a key, a sceptre that allowed the one train to go forward on to the single track newly liberated by the other. This method was, so local lore had it, fail-safe: as long as there was only one key and as long as the driver obeyed the immemorial rule that, bereft of the key, he should not trespass on the section of the track governed by that key, there was no chance of collision. The ritual seemed occult and faintly mystical, quintessentially Welsh, hedged about with the trappings of monarchy. The baton might have been Arthur's magical sword Excalibur.

I travelled in a compartment of which I was the only occupant, in a carriage in which I appeared to be the only traveller. There was no corridor. I sat there feeling grand and important, and looking, I suppose, small: still dressed in shorts, and dull, functional plimsolls, and wearing a close, clumsy haircut that owed much to the army. The train trundled along the valley floor, past a town that had been destroyed in a landslide (you could see the boulders, fenced off as a memorial alongside the new, resurrected settlement), through another town where there was a woollen mill and a quarry, as far as the station of Llanbedr, Peterschurch; where Jamie was waiting. Memory gives all this, but not the preparation, no telephone call to make the arrangement, no discussion with Mother, nothing that surrounds the event or gives it context – just this journey on the train through the Welsh countryside, and Jamie waiting on the platform at Llanbedr station, dressed too in the uniform of the boarding-school child of the period. He still wore shorts, I remember.

I opened the door of my compartment and he climbed in, and we were together again. His mother waved from the platform, a vague blonde figure shifting away from memory just as she shifted away from our view as the train moved off.

'How's the house?' I asked, thinking that you must ask questions of that kind, the sort of questions that adults ask: How's the weather? How's the house? How's the job?

'It's okay. There's some kind of old room called the games room and then there's the stable block with rooms upstairs but the floors are weak and I'm not meant to go there in case they collapse . . .'

'But you do, of course?'

'Of course I do.'

The train trundled on – woods, cliffs, the glimpse of a mountain torrent. Green and grey were the dominant colours. It always rained, but not today. I remember waterfalls of sunlight among the trees and strange names in that strange, wild language that neither of us knew: Pont-y-pant, Dolwyddelan, Pentre-bont. Names that hovered on the edge of absurdity, that someone might have made up in a comedy film. 'Pont-y-pant,' Jamie said, as we pulled out of that station. He smiled. There was a reserved, adult quality to his smile. I looked out of the grimy window as the train passed beneath the bare slopes of a mountain, past sterile farms where sheep picked over the land like soldiers picking over a battlefield after the guns had fallen silent, past the ruins of a castle, grey beneath the open sky. Then the train vanished into a tunnel and careered on in the dark, while our twin reflections looked back at us from the black window, distant images speeding through the bowels of the earth to vanish abruptly as the train emerged into the open light and the small, squalid slate town. There were signal gantries and a deserted platform and a grimy station building. We climbed down from our compartment and watched the guard blow his whistle and wave his green flag. The train drew out and left us alone.

Why were we there? Blaenau was the name of the town.

Bline-eye, that's how it was pronounced. It sounds like a physical condition, something you might correct with pebble-lens spectacles or perhaps delicate surgery. The myopia of memory. We were there because we had taken the train and it was the end of the line.

'Let's go,' said Jamie. He spoke with his faint American intonation, as though we were cowboys or something, as though there were anywhere actually to go. But the town was no more than a ragged line of buildings along the contours of the hillside, half deserted, silent. Slate was the whole world, slate the landscape, slate the sky, slate the rows of terraced houses, slate the road. But the slate mines had been closed down now that there was no demand, now that they no longer roofed buildings like that. What did they use instead? Tar-paper? Tiles? Not Welsh slate, anyway. The mines had closed and the young men were missing and Blaenau might have been a town in wartime, populated only by the women and the children and the old.

We wandered the empty streets, went into a sweet shop and bought tubes of sherbet with a liquorice straw, went into a newsagent and bought a magazine called *Weekend* that showed girls in swimming costumes. At the edge of the town we pushed open the rusted gate in a high fence and found ourselves one step beyond 'Perygl, Cadwch Allan – Danger, Keep Out'.

A quarry. Without saying anything, without agreeing or disagreeing, we walked up the road through a narrow black valley whose sides were slopes of shattered slate. 'What if someone sees us?' I asked, as we advanced.

'What if?' Jamie was careless, brave, capable of dealing with the adult world. I marched along beside him – behind him, just half a pace behind him. The road opened out into a great arena carved out of the hillside, with steep walls and a level floor. The floor was littered with shards of slate like pieces of shrapnel from a long-finished battle. Our feet crunched in the fragments. Rusting machinery – a conveyor-belt, a hopper, some kind of chute – drew large alphabet letters over us: an N, an A, a Y; semaphore from a dead industrial age. The quarry walls were steel grey, as grey and steep and sheer as the side of any battleship, stepped and polished deliberately into edges and planes. How high were they? Two hundred feet, three hundred? I had no means of judging. Above, you could see traces of what had been before man had come here with dynamite and pickaxe: the curve of a rising hill, a slope of bracken, the ghost of a hillside. But all this had been cut away, as though torn by giant claws, as though some ancient dragon, the *draig goch*, the red dragon of Wales, had woken up and clawed away a whole mountainside.

'Cor,' Jamie whispered.

The wind buffeted us. 'Perygl Marwolaeth – Danger of Death,' it said. We crunched nearer, the walls drawing us under their shadow until we stood directly beneath them, looking up the clear vertical sweep. Hundreds of feet. The rock glistened, not wet but whetted: sharpened, honed, dangerous.

'Bet you couldn't,' I said thoughtfully. I knew exactly what I was saying.

Jamie was sucking the sherbet. He looked up, squinting against the light. He could see things, ripples in the rock, a slanting fracture line, a ledge from which a tuft of grass grew. He could see things. 'Bet I could.'

'How much?'

He finished the sherbet and wiped powder from his lips. 'My X-15 to your FD2.' These were plastic model aircraft: precious.

'Done.' We shook sticky hands on the wager. Then he reached up, found some kind of flake, and pulled himself up until his chin was at the level of his hand. For a while his feet pedalled on the slate, walking up the rock at exactly the same speed as they were sliding down. He reached overhead again, his feet skipped up, found a foothold, and he stood upright. I couldn't see what he was standing on. A mere wrinkle. Another reach and a series of darting moves up left, his fingers in a crack, his black-soled pumps slithering on the boiler-plate rock to find friction, the space beneath his feet now more than a mere jump down if he couldn't make it.

Suddenly nervous, I edged away from the wall to see better. 'Jamie, be careful,' I called.

He had reached the moustache of grass. His hands were on it. He made another move, pulling down, pedalling his feet upwards until his weight was over his hands and he was leaning down on them straight-armed. Then he brought his right foot up to just beside his right hand and stepped straight on to the ledge. What he would later know as a mantelshelf, executed (the word 'execute', with its sensation of sharp cutting, seems exactly right) with speed and grace.

He glanced over his shoulder down to where I stood directly below. 'Come on, then.'

'I can't.'

'*I* can.'

'What you going to do now?'

'You come up.'

'I just said. I can't.'

'I won the bet.'

'Yes, but you're up there now.'

'And you owe me your Fairey Delta 2.'

'But you've got to get down.' I walked further backwards to get the whole thing in perspective, to see Jamie standing in the middle of the wall, on a narrow ledge that wandered away from him on either side and vanished into the smooth slate. How high? How high was a house? Sixty feet? He was as high as a house. Not as high as Kangchenjunga, but high enough to make a dent in the ground if he fell. Not this ground, though. I kicked my toe speculatively into the brittle litter of slate and felt a tiny flutter of unease somewhere about the level of my diaphragm. I knew that was my diaphragm. I'd seen it in the plastic model of the visible man that I'd got for my last birthday. I knew a lot about the body and the innards and all that. If Jamie fell, his innards would be spread all over.

'I'll go on up, then,' he called.

'What if you fall?'

'I won't.'

'I'll get someone.'

'Don't be a silly bugger.'

That was the moment when the man appeared. I suppose he'd come from one of the buildings. Maybe he'd been having a kip, I don't know. He wore some kind of uniform. At least, he wore dark blue overalls that looked as though they might be uniform, and he was striding across the quarry floor towards us with the importance of someone who sees his whole world about to come crashing down with the fall of one stupid unknown youth. 'You come down from there, you little bugger!' he shouted. He had a narrow face, and a moustache and an adult frown. Seeing a uniform brought mixed emotions, an uneasy mixture of fear and hope. 'What the devil you boys doin', goin' where you've no right to be goin'? Eh? Can't you read the signs? You come down here this instant!'

I could see the problem with that. If Jamie were to come down this instant he would be dead. I looked up and wondered what he would do.

'This instant!' the man yelled.

And then, high up on the wall, the figure moved. A couple of shuffled steps along the ledge and upwards again – two, three, four moves, like an animal, not a human, a monkey, perhaps, or a cat, darting quietly up the wall, pausing to look, then climbing up and traversing leftwards towards a sharp corner.

'You come down here at once!' the man shouted, but he fell silent as the true import of what he saw came through to him, this boy moving up across the face of slate as though he was attached to it, as though it was his element. For a second Jamie looked down. You could see his face like a white piece of rag against the grey of the quarry wall; then he slipped round the corner and out of sight.

The guard turned on me. His face was red and shiny, sweat standing out in beads across his forehead. 'You come along with me, young man,' he said, and reached out to grab me.

I ducked away, and apologized for the fact. 'I'm sorry, sir.'

'Don't you *sir* me!' he shouted. He made another lunge and I ran. I had never run so fast in my life, not when I played rugby at school, not when I ran the hundred yards on sports day. With the guard sweating along behind me, I ran along the quarry wall and skidded round the bottom of the same corner round which Jamie, sixty, seventy feet up, had vanished. Slate clattered under my feet like fragments of brittle pottery. Round the corner, ahead of me now, there was a slope of rubble leaning against the back wall of the quarry, a tip where fragments of the rock had been cast down from the upper levels. Running up the slope was a beaten pathway. I went upwards, slipping and slithering, the fragments rattling beneath my feet. The slope reached a gangway that split the face in two, where the shot holes were bored, where the slabs of steel-grey slate had been blown out of the belly of the earth, where Jamie waited high up, beckoning. 'Come on, Rob,' he yelled. 'Come *on*. We can get out up here!'

The guard scrambled up the slope after me. I slid on the slate debris, three steps upward, two steps back, as in a nightmare – the thing you dared not look at but was there at your heels; the running that got you nowhere.

'Come *on*, Rob.'

'Stop, you little bugger!'

Perhaps because he had larger feet, perhaps because he was able to compact the slate fragments better beneath his weight, the guard was gaining on me. I slipped and fell on to my hands. Before I could get up I felt the grab of his hand on my shoulder. He pulled me to his feet and turned me round, so that I was looking straight up at him, at the angles of his face and the half-opened mouth and the glaring eyes. 'You little bugger,' he said. He was breathing hard and his breath had the smell of gas, the gas that came from the gas cooker and the gas fires in the bedrooms at home.

'Rob!' Jamie called.

The man looked upwards, over my shoulder. 'I got 'im,' he called up. 'You'd best come down too.'

'Stay there, Jamie!' I yelled. I yelled it at no one, at the grey overalls of the man who held me. 'Stay there!'

But Jamie was coming down, clambering down the narrow gangway he had found, down over some steep steps that had once been for quarrymen to reach the upper tiers. I twisted to see. He was coming down and his face was set and he was watching me and the guard there on the slope below him. 'You let him go,' he called. 'He's not done anything. You let him go.' I thought of the adventures of the times, of the *Boy's Own Paper*, and brave kids who did things right, fought for their friends, didn't abandon them in times of distress. I loved him. I recall the emotion exactly. Love.

There was a rattle of slate and Jamie joined us, standing there defiantly as the guard grabbed him too. 'You come along with me, young fellows,' the man said. I thought that maybe he wasn't so bad after all. 'Fellows' seemed a term of reconciliation. But still he held us as we slithered and stumbled down the slope of slate and on to the brittle floor of the quarry.

'What are you going to do?' Jamie asked.

'We'll see about that.'

'I want to ring my mother.'

'We'll see about that too.'

He led us towards a shed that sheltered in the shadows of the rusting machinery. It had a sign on the door that talked of the Mining Company and the need to Keep Out. And the man came up against his problem. 'Open it,' he said, holding us.

'You're hurting me.'

'Open it.'

Jamie and I glanced at each other. There was a smile of complicity.

'Open it.'

'You open it,' said Jamie.

The man's grip tightened on my shoulder. He'd identified me as the weaker of his captives. He pushed me forward. 'Open the door, you little bugger.'

I reached out, took the handle and turned it. The door was locked. 'I can't.'

The man swore. Jamie grinned at me. The man slackened his grip on my arm. 'You just stay there, you hear me?' he said.

I nodded.

'Don't you bloody move.'

I shook my head. Cautiously, as though I might overbalance if he did not set me quite right, he released me. I stood still. He reached into his pocket and I stayed there, waiting for the hand to go into the pocket, right in, and grope for the key.

'Go, Rob!' Jamie shouted.

I ran, skittering across the floor of the quarry, with the man's curses following me and freedom all around me in the grey-blue bruised colours of the slate. 'Run, Rob!' Jamie called, and I ran, panic chasing me. Only when I reached the narrow defile between slopes of slate and the road that led down towards the gate where the sign had told us to Keep Out did I pause.

I looked back. The man and Jamie were nowhere to be seen. They must have gone into the hut. He had opened it and shoved Jamie in and now maybe he would come out and start looking for me. I wondered what I should do. The problem was an acute one, compounded of fear and guilt. The man was an official and we had been trespassing. We were in the wrong. But what of Jamie, now held hostage?

I waited and there was no sign of the man, no sound from the hut, no sound at all in the whole desolate amphitheatre of the quarry. I waited, how long I don't know; but finally, cautiously, I retraced my steps. The slate sounded like glass fragments beneath my feet. I tiptoed towards the alphabet of rusting machinery and the crouching hut. There was no sound. I crept round the side of the building. There was a window, bleary with grime, and beneath it some rusting steel stanchions. Carefully I climbed up on them, raised myself to the sill and I peered in.

Events in the stained shadows: a wooden-floored hut, a single room, maybe twenty feet by fifteen. Things round the walls – a pickaxe, a spade, a coil of rope, slabs of slate. There was a bunk bed made with slats of wood against one wall. Light came in from the window that I was at and from another in the opposite wall, light from both sides creating a chiaroscuro that was as mysterious as a religious painting, was like a religious painting, in fact, with Jamie on his knees before the man as though at worship.

I was strung between childhood adventure and adult horror. I didn't understand what I saw. I sensed something, a charge, like the tension in the skin that you feel before lightning strikes, and the same dull sultriness; but I didn't really understand. Now, of course, yes. I can interpret the memory, the image that lies there somehow among the wiring of my brain. But at the time I had no real idea, nothing against which I might judge, no yardstick, no place or point of reference.

For a moment I watched the hurried, urgent movements. Then, as carefully as I had risen, I crept down from my perch and made my way round to the door. Softly, I tried the handle. There were sounds from within that I couldn't identify, sounds that drowned the turning of the handle, that drowned all innocence. The door flung open.

'What?'

Daylight came in on the man, ridiculous with his overalls round his ankles, his flesh exposed, his face a white mess of shock.

'What?' He grabbed at his clothes. 'You little bugger,' he cried, in something like relief. Jamie had slipped away from him and stood in the background watching. The man was tucking himself away and talking at me. There was a breathless quality to his speech, as though he had been running. 'Came back to see, did you? Dirty little bugger wanted me to do it. Little bugger asked for it. You're a dirty little boy as well, I'll bet. Is that right? Did you want to see what we were doing?'

'We're going home,' I said.

The man laughed. It was a sound without humour, but it was a laugh all the same. 'I've got some pictures,' he said. 'D'you want to see? Girls. Their tits and all that. You want to have a look?'

'We're going,' I repeated. I was on the doorstep, ready to run, and the man was talking and buttoning up his overalls and shuffling towards me. From behind him Jamie was looking at me with an expression of something like fear. Was it fear? I didn't really know. I'd not seen fear, except in the cinema. But it was something like that.

The man came forward. 'You want to look, don't you? Tits.'

I moved back into the full daylight. 'Come on, Jamie.'

And as though he had suddenly woken from sleep, Jamie moved. He pushed past the man and ran out into the open.

'He wanted to do it, the dirty little bugger,' the man called after him. And then, as we ran away towards the track: 'You won't say nothing, will you? It's our secret, isn't it?'

We made our way back down towards the town in silence. The railway station was deserted. We found a bench, sat down and waited. I don't know how long it was before the train appeared. Say, three-quarters of an hour. Something like that. Jamie said nothing for a long while. When he did finally speak it was matter-of-fact, as though this was just an everyday kind of thing: 'He made me do it. That's what happened. He said he'd let me go if I did it.'

'Are you going to tell?'

'Tell?'

'Your mum or something.'

'What is there to tell? He's just a queer.'

The train came. A few passengers got out. We were the only ones to climb on board. A guard in uniform waved a flag and blew his whistle, and the train pulled out of the station. Jamie seemed indifferent, staring out of the window. The train went into the tunnel. There was blackness beyond the window and

58

Jamie's face floating in the darkness. I felt immensely distant from him, as though he had gone far, far away and this was only some kind of image of him, a television image sent from a long way away. 'It doesn't matter,' he said. He was speaking thoughtfully, as though he was trying to work out whether it really did matter or not. 'It doesn't matter,' he repeated.

When we emerged from the tunnel he glanced at me, then back out of the window. 'It wasn't that bad. Just a thing. Like your own.'

His mother was on the platform when we reached Llanbedr, scanning the carriages for some sign of us and smiling, holding out her arms, when Jamie stepped down from the train. I saw her wry expression when he twisted away from her as she bent to kiss him. Then she looked up and caught sight of me through the window, and waved. *Did you have a good time?* her mouth said. Doors slammed and the guard's whistle blew and the small train drew out of the station. *Did you have a good time?* Strange how I could read the words on her lips. Lips. That buzz.

6

I didn't hear from Jamie after that. The event had affected our relationship. Friendships were like that – fragile things that might withstand a storm yet could come to pieces in your hands for no very clear reason. Brittle, like slate. Was it something to do with the man in the quarry? Maybe, maybe not. My mother had once been a friend of his mother – best friends, she said. And now? That friendship, too, had vanished. Occasionally she might say something about Mrs Matthewson, but it was always in dismissive terms: 'Oh, yes, we were close once, long before you were born. Before the war, during the war. But you know how people drift apart.'

I nodded. I knew.

So Jamie Matthewson became nothing more than a memory, one of those passing acquaintances that punctuate a childhood, whom you pick up and then let go, possibly to encounter again at some unimaginable time in the future on a street corner, or in a bar or at a party, when the differential of age no longer counts.

But then I received a postcard at school. There was no sender address and the card had only reached its destination by a fluke, for the address was a hazard of vague recollection on his part, the name of the school imperfectly recalled from a casual conversation we must have had: 'Robert Dewar, Rhodes School, Surrey', was what it said. When was this? Memory plays its trick of distorting time, bending the irreducible dimension. Years later; perhaps three. The dimensions of time are strange and plastic, like Dali's watches, which I admired in those days, like Henry Moore's sculptures with their deceptive curves, their mysterious orifices, their smooth and endless surfaces. The message was signed 'James' and I wasn't even sure who James was until I deciphered the scrawled question 'See you in Wales?' at the end. The picture on the card showed mountains quite different from those low-slung Welsh ones that we had admired as kids: they were the towering, snow-crusted peaks of the Bernese Oberland: Jungfrau, Mönch, Eiger. The Young Woman, the Monk and the Ogre, a trio of curious eroticism. 'We climbed the Jungfrau,' Jamie had written; but who *we* signified was never explained.

I felt a small tug of envy. Whoever Jamie was now, wherever he was, whoever that collective *we* signified, he had achieved something of that ambition we had casually discussed years earlier: to climb mountains. I had only slogged up Snowdon in mist and rain, and spent a miserable weekend camped in the Lake District with a school group. But Jamie had done the real thing: the Jungfrau.

When I went home for the holidays, I searched in vain through my mother's address book for the Matthewsons' telephone number. 'I don't think I ever wrote it down,' she said. 'Anyway, why do you want to go chasing around to find him?'

'He was good fun. And he wrote to me. I mean, Christ, Mum, he was a *mate*.'

But the name Matthewson did not even appear in the telephone directory. Matthews, yes, many of them. But no Matthewson. 'Ex-directory, I suppose,' Mother said, her tone suggesting that being listed in the telephone directory went with moral purity while deliberately keeping oneself out was a sure sign of turpitude. 'Typical of Meg.'

So I went to find him. I took the train to Llanbedr once again and at the station I had to wait half an hour for a bus, and even then I wasn't sure that it was the right one. Gwytherin, I remembered. The bus crawled through the town, past a church and a cinema and the cattle-market, and soon the road was climbing up, winding past drystone walls, past fields of luminous green where sheep grazed, past woods of a green so dark that it was almost black. A fox sloped across a hillside. And there, suddenly and surprisingly, was the place that I more or less remembered, but with a new sign now, the name engraved on a slab of slate:

Gilead House

In the drive, incongruous on the Welsh hillside, was a large white Mercedes.

As I pushed open the gate and walked up to the house, it began to rain, a mere drizzle out of the slate-grey sky. I rang the doorbell. There was a long pause before I heard noises on the far side. The door opened and a face peered out at me, a suspicious female Welsh face, with dark eyes and dark hair. 'Yes?'

'Is James in?'

'James?' A lilt of surprise. 'No.' The vowel drawn out, exaggerated, given a short life of meaning: disappointment, amusement, faint ridicule. I almost apologized and went away; I almost turned tail.

'Mrs Matthewson, then?'

'Who shall I say it is wants her?'

A voice came from behind, from out of sight in the shadows of the hallway. 'Who is it, Mary?'

Mary looked over her shoulder. 'It's a young man wants Master James, ma'am.' Master James. A good, servile touch, that.

'Well, what's his name?' said the voice from behind. She came forward, stepping out of memory just as Mary stepped aside. She was smaller than I recalled. The relativity of age: of course she was exactly the same height, but I had grown taller; taller than her by a head now, looking down at her standing there in the doorway in her tight white cotton trousers and pink denim shirt. But it was she who seemed to have grown smaller, and somehow – but I was uncertain of such things – younger. She had done her hair differently, the spirit of the times catching even the adults now. It no longer had that shiny nylon look, but appeared darker and more natural. Wheat-coloured: the same streaks, the same darks and lights as a field of wheat. I blushed. 'I was looking for James.'

'Oh?' She hadn't recognized me. She smiled vaguely as though trying to assemble an appearance of hospitality and wondering whether the effort was worthwhile.

'I'm Robert.'

'Robert?' And the expression changed, shifted, lightened into a true smile; a slow and remarkable metamorphosis. 'Robert, of course. Diana's son. How' – a breath's pause as she looked at me with something like recognition – 'remarkable. My goodness, how you've grown!'

'I thought—'

'You thought you might find Jamie? What a shame. He was here last Easter. I told him to try to contact you, but you know what he's like. Come in anyway. Let me get you something. Why didn't you telephone?'

I noticed things as I followed her inside: paintings, objects, particular pieces of furniture, the kind of things you collect to make a place yours. The jawbone of something, perhaps a shark, hanging there on the wall: it had the shape of an hour-glass, rimmed with ivory daggers. Since I had looked round it on that previous visit, Gilead House had become something that ours never really was: a home.

'Mary, can you get us some coffee, or tea – which would you prefer?' Mrs Matthewson's question slid easily from the maid to me, as I stood there looking up at the curious object. 'Oh, that? Yes, that's my trophy. I fished it off Nantucket. Yes, I caught it myself, while the men jeered and told me I could never do it and all that sort of crap.' The word *crap*. My mother would have been appalled. 'But I did, and there it is.' She laughed, and I had a brief, fugitive glimpse of gold. I followed her up the stairs past the stained-glass window of a medieval knight and his lady, into what she called the morning room, which was actually a sitting room looking out over the top garden and the woods at the back of the house. There was an oil painting on the wall, the portrait of a girl with a blank face and eyes like black pebbles.

'Is that you?' I asked.

She laughed delightedly. No, it was something she had picked up in a flea market. The phrase *flea market* struck me. It may have been the first time I'd heard it. I imagined a kind of jumble sale, like they had in the local church: stalls selling old clothes that hummed with insect life. 'I think it may be an original. Do you know Laurencin?'

I didn't. Together we peered at the painting, at the heavy layers of paint, at the signature scrawled along the bottom: 'Marie Laurencin'. And as we looked Mrs Matthewson's scent came to me, an insidious blend of things I couldn't put names to: musk and orange and sandalwood and jasmine, perhaps those; something far more subtle and convincing than any painting by Marie Laurencin, whether original or copy. 'The trouble is,' she said (and the scent was on her breath as well), 'I don't dare have an expert look at it. In case it isn't.'

She left the painting and settled into an armchair, and watched me with interest, curiosity almost, as though she was trying to work something out and would come up with the answer in a moment. Her feet were bare, the toes pinched by wearing pointed shoes. They were the only thing that betrayed her age. 'So, Robert, what a pleasant surprise this is. And how you've grown! I would say quite a man, but that would be patronizing, wouldn't it? So I won't.' She smiled. Even white teeth. 'Capped,' I could hear my mother saying. 'And how's Diana? I really should get over to see her, but it's finding the time. And I'm not here very often, with the house in London.'

It wasn't finding the time, I knew that. This woman was a different being altogether from my mother, almost a different gender. I couldn't imagine them doing anything together, couldn't imagine them having exchanged clothes or confidences or boyfriends, or any of the usual currency of girlhood. But whatever might have happened in the past, nowadays they certainly had no point in common. 'I'm sure she'd love to see you again, Mrs Matthewson.'

'Oh, for goodness' sake, *Caroline*.' She smiled. 'But not, repeat not, *Meg*. I don't think your mother is quite as fond of me now as she used to be.'

I protested eternal affection on the part of my mother. Caroline smiled knowingly, and changed the subject with the lack of guile that adults believe children will fall for. 'So, you came all this way to find Jamie? What a shame.'

'He sent me a postcard from the Alps.'

'He was there with friends of his father.'

'But he posted it from America.'

'Dear Jamie, so typical of him. To write a card in one place and post it in another. He's in the Bahamas now, I think. Sailing. He doesn't really like sailing. I don't imagine he's enjoying himself very much. It'll be a big change when he gets to Scotland.'

'Scotland?'

'He's going to university there. St Andrews. For me he's barely out of shorts and already he's off to university. He's eighteen. And you must be, what, sixteen?' She looked at me thoughtfully, as though trying to work out how to rid herself of this uninteresting child. I shifted in my seat.

'Nearly,' I said. 'Nearly sixteen.' I was conscious of her disconcerting eyes on me.

'So tell me. Tell me all about you. What are you doing now?'

I told her anyway, although I knew she couldn't possibly be interested – about school mainly, about lessons and exams and sport. And I watched her, seeing shadows of Jamie there – the same colouring, of course, and something about the shape of her face, the curve of her jaw – but seeing other things that she had lent no one: the strange mobility of her mouth, whose lips I had last seen mouthing the words, *Did you have a good time?* on the station platform, a mouth that seemed small when composed, but large when she smiled, a sudden, surprising change of expression that almost ambushed you.

'And at school?'

'I said. I've just done my exams.'

66

'Of course. You said.' She was looking round the room in the way people do when they are searching for something further to say. She'd lost interest. I felt myself redden and I cursed the sensation. I half rose from my chair. 'Perhaps I'd better . . .'

She lifted a hand. 'Surely you'll stay for lunch? It's a long way to come just for a cup of coffee.'

'I—'

'Of course you will. I tell you what . . .' And now there was an uncertain quality to her smile, as though she wasn't sure of what she would tell me, or exactly how. 'You wouldn't like to earn some pocket money, would you? I need someone, and it's difficult to get people out here. Someone to do some clearing out for me. We're doing some alterations, you see. This was Guy's house,' she said, 'his great love—'

'Guy?'

'Jamie's father. He wanted to live here, but of course I preferred London. He used to make me feel quite disloyal. Dear Guy . . .'

'He was a mountaineer, wasn't he? Jamie told me.'

'Oh, yes, he was a great mountaineer. A regular British hero.' Irony, or a plain statement of truth? I couldn't tell. She seemed to speak of the man she had married as though he was still there, as though he was a fool, as though she was still in love with him, as though she rather despised him. All these things in the few occasions she referred to him. 'And now we want to make the place liveable, so I need some help. You don't have to say yes straight away. Of course not. Let me show you, and then we'll have some lunch and you can tell me what you think. I'm sure a boy like you would like to earn a little extra, and I'm sure your mother would be delighted. I know what it's like shelling out pocket money all the time. Let me show you round.'

So we did a tour of the house, peering into rooms, edging through doors, tripping over steps. Unlike its owner, the place seemed awkward, a body that had been assembled out of different ill-fitting parts, with corridors from one part to another that warranted extra steps to make the join, with right-angle corners, and alcoves and crannies and doors that only half opened because of a wall in the way. Round the abrupt turn of one particular corner we came to what she called the games room. It was long and wide, occupying the whole width of that wing of the house. We looked at the rubbish left by previous occupants: a broken sofa, an old table, empty trunks, an ancient mattress, that kind of thing. There was an open fireplace with a mantelpiece of cast iron. The only evidence of games was a full-size snooker table – she referred to it as 'pool' – with its baize torn and rotten. 'We've not touched anything here, as you can see, but now the plan is to convert it into guest rooms. I just need someone to do the clearing out. And then there might be other things you could do. You know what it's like without a man about the house. There's always the garden.'

Afterwards we ate lunch together in the cold dining room – and, of course, when she asked me about the work, I said yes, I'd do it. A few quid would come in handy. And she smiled quickly, as though that was good but not so important, really; doubtless she could always have found a lad from the village.

Mother was suspicious when I told her. 'Why?' she asked. 'Why?'

'Why not? It'll give me something to do, never mind the money.'

Perhaps the money was what swayed her from outright proscription. 'Do what you like,' she said. 'Don't take any notice of me.'

'But why shouldn't I?'

'I haven't said you shouldn't.'

'Then what have you got against her?'

'Nothing, my dear. I've nothing against Meg. I'm just disappointed in her, that's all. Her horrid flashiness, the way she seems to think herself so much *better*. The way she . . .' Her disapproval died away into a vague and impatient gesture, a kind of childish petulance. It was one of those moments when I understood something for the first time, or thought I did: that adults could operate on the same level as children, have dislikes that were based on nothing more than irrational prejudice.

'Well, I'm going to take the job,' I said.

'Do what you please,' she repeated; and I realized that in some ill-defined way I was being disloyal.

So the next day I boarded the train to Llanbedr again, and took the same bus up to Gilead House and there was Caroline already at work in the games room with music from a portable record-player – a stack of forty-fives – thumping out into the dust-laden air.

'Diana didn't mind?' she asked.

Mendaciously I shook my head.

'That's fine, then.'

We worked in silence, more or less, with Caroline giving instructions every now and again. I humped broken chairs and an ancient mattress and other rubbish down awkward back stairs and out into the garden; I helped strip wallpaper. The music set the emptying room reverberating. I watched her, this strange other presence, and hoped she didn't notice my glance. I saw the outline of her breasts inside her shirt. I saw grime on her face where she had wiped sweat from her forehead with the back of her hand, and dark stains of sweat growing beneath her arms. That was disturbing, the discovery that she could sweat just as I did. She wasn't as she had seemed when she had come to stay in our hotel all that time ago. She wasn't brass and brittle; she was sandy and blurred, softened by time and fashion, paradoxically younger and more accessible – more or less the same age as my mother, yet younger by far.

At the end of the day she drove me to the station in the Mercedes. I'd never been in a car like that before: tan leather upholstery and walnut veneer. The interior smelt of her perfume, that blend of things that I couldn't decipher. She glanced at me from time to time and smiled. As I opened the door of the car to step out into the station forecourt she leant across and handed me two envelopes. 'This one's for you; the other's a letter for your mother.'

I opened my envelope on the train. Inside was one pound ten shillings in two notes. Absurdly I felt demeaned, as though my work should have been given free.

'Five shillings an hour,' my mother observed tartly. 'That's generous.' She opened the envelope with her name on it and scanned the letter inside, then tucked it away. 'Meg,' she said. That was all. The single syllable carried with it a strange tone of impatience, and suspicion, and faint regret.

'What did she say?'

'She said what a good worker you are. How like your father. Quite a dutiful Scot, were her words.'

'Did she know Father?' I knew almost nothing of him: a few photographs, a few anecdotes, a letter at Christmas and another on my birthday, nothing more. 'Dear boy,' he used to write, almost as though he had forgotten my name. I think my mother feared that as I grew up I would decide to go in search of him, and would thus unravel the intricate knot of their separation. I think she feared she might lose me to him.

'Of course she did. Meg was one of the bridesmaids at our wedding.'

That fact quite startled me. I didn't know what to do with it, how it signified. My mother's wedding seemed impossibly long ago, an event that had happened to other people in another age. But when asked she unearthed a photograph album, and sure enough there they were, those ghosts from the past: my father, blunt and prematurely balding (looking about fifty, I thought), wearing the kilt and a black velvet jacket, my mother unexpectedly pretty in a long white dress with a train thrown carelessly around her feet; and that other figure, brown hair permed in the fashion of the time, the shoulders of her dress cut wide, her smile faintly knowing: Meg.

I thought of her. I thought of the sweat beneath her armpits and the loose shifting of her breasts inside her shirt. In my room I examined my face in the mirror, looking for signs that I was something other than a mere child, something that might be attractive to Caroline Matthewson. The metamorphosis of adolescence was a slow and painful process. Enough hair grew on my upper lip to warrant shaving once or twice a week. There was a faint beard down the side of my jaw. There was a small constellation of acne spots across my forehead and a gathering of them beside my mouth. Shag spots. It was said that masturbation encouraged them: chocolate, fried food and masturbation. No wonder there was a national epidemic.

How many times did I visit the Matthewson house that summer? A dozen, maybe – a precise number with vague borders. Once she was not even there, the absence of the white Mercedes conspicuous in the driveway. Once there were friends visiting, a couple from the United States with loud clothes and a carefully wrapped and decorated daughter who avoided my eye when we were introduced, as though she had been warned about the behaviour of the natives and knew them to be dangerous. Sometimes Caroline smiled distantly at me when I arrived and left me alone – to dig out the border in the walled garden, to shift rubbish from an outhouse, to light a bonfire of all the combustible trash I had gathered together. Sometimes she seemed to have time for me, or time for the work I was doing. 'Why, in God's name, didn't we do this earlier?' she exclaimed more than once.

One morning, when I was working on my own in the games room, Caroline called up the stairs to me. 'It's Jamie. Robert, are you there? It's Jamie.' Expecting to see him, I ran downstairs. But it was only his disembodied voice in the telephone that she held out to me, not Jamie himself, coming in at the front door, eighteen years old now and so changed from when we had last been together. On the phone he sounded oddly indifferent. 'Hi, how're you doing?' And lower-pitched, adult, really.

'How are you?'

'Bored. Hey, you get my card?'

'Yes.'

'You didn't reply.'

'I didn't have your address.'

'You could have got it from my mum.'

She stood there, just beside me, close enough for me to get a breath of that perfume. 'Why didn't you get in touch last Easter?' I countered.

He ignored the question. 'I climbed the Jungfrau, and the Eiger, you know that? The Mittelegi Ridge. And you know what? The first British ascent of the Nordwand was only last autumn, can you imagine that? Maybe I'll do that one day.'

There was an awkward pause while I searched for something to say. The word Nordwand meant nothing to me, but I didn't want to ask. The line crackled ominously, like the lightning of a distant storm.

'Look, get my new address from my mum, okay? I'm going to university in the autumn. We'll be in touch.'

Would we? I felt privileged that he had even mentioned the possibility. I handed the phone back to Caroline. 'I'll get back to work,' I said. She smiled distractedly, still talking on the phone to her son three thousand miles away, saying, 'Look after yourself, don't get sunburned,' things like that. I suppose I felt privileged to be admitted to the Matthewson family, at least in some lesser, surrogate role.

One day she was going through an old trunk and she called me over. 'Look what I've found. Guy's old notebook. Jamie will love this.' It had a stout black cover and marbled endpapers. I looked over her shoulder, breathed in her scent while she turned the pages. The entries were in blue-black ink, painstakingly inscribed in an even, perfect script:

Helyg. March 1941:
Clogwyn y Grochan – Brant (Very Severe), with John B 2nd;
Carreg Wastad – Crackstone Rib (Severe);
Dinas Mot – the Nose (Very S), with JME;
Milestone B. Soap Gut & Chimney (Severe);
Tryfan – Grooved Arête/Belle Vue Bastion (V Severe);
Munich climb (without the piton!) (Very S).

Words, terms, jargon. They meant nothing to me. And what, in God's name, was Soap Gut? It sounded fatty and slimy and rather revolting.

'Those are the rock climbs he did.' She looked up at me. 'What do you think?'

I didn't know what I thought. I thought he was a hero. I thought Jamie was lucky to have a hero for a father. I thought that my own father – stout, Scottish and distant – was a poor substitute, even for a dead one. Caroline put aside the book. Among the papers and files in the trunk there was another book, a published one with a battered dust jacket. *Kangchenjunga, the Sacred Peak*, it was called. She flicked through the pages, stopped at one of the plates and showed it to me. 'Guy Matthewson, the last photograph', was the caption. A roughly bearded face grinned cheerfully at the camera. He was sunburnt on his cheeks and his lips were chapped. His goggles were pushed up on to his balaclava and the rings of pale skin around his eyes gave him a faintly clownish appearance. I found it strange that you could grin like that with your death only a day or two away, as though you should have some kind of premonition.

'There,' she said, looking at me. What was I to make of her expression? Did she want sympathy? Did she want admiration? Did she still want consolation after more than a decade? It was hard to relate her to a man who had climbed mountains, who had had a battered, weather-scorched face and who had died in the cold on some distant Himalayan peak. 'He was a wonderful man,' she said softly.

I felt a mixture of embarrassment and jealousy, jealousy of a man long dead who could still evoke this emotion. There almost seemed to be tears in her eyes. 'What's the matter?' I asked.

She blinked and wiped at her eyes with the back of her wrist. 'Nothing,' she said. 'Dust.' And maybe I was wrong and it had been dust.

On another occasion she cried, 'Hey, listen to this,' and put a record on the player. It was Chubby Checker, twisting once again. Amid laughter I watched her dancing there in the middle of the half-empty games room, absurdly, awkwardly, her hips revolving, her legs writhing like snakes. Fascinated, laughing, sweating with embarrassment and desire, I watched her.

'Come on. Join me.'

There was a moment when I might have danced with her. There was a moment when the possibility beckoned. But the disc came to an end (a mere two minutes thirty seconds) and she took the record off the turntable and smoothed her slacks down over her narrow hips and laughed either at me or at herself, or maybe at both of us together as we stood awkwardly in the middle of the half-empty room. I was aware of her eyes on me, her expression (I glanced up and saw the look) thoughtful. I felt vividly that barrier that exists between human beings, the gulf of a few feet of empty air that is so difficult to bridge. I wanted to say things to her but dared not. And I guessed, but couldn't tell, that the same ideas moved through her mind, eating away at her composure.

Caroline. The name reverberated in my mind. It had a sound to it, a colour, a scent, a mood. The colours were pale and pastel, yellow and blue, but not the intense enamel blue of the sky seen at altitude: the smudged blue of the Welsh sky when it wasn't raining. The sound was brass, but not brassy – the chiming of a bell. The scent was a musky citrus. The mood was smiling, but with an undertow of sorrow.

These were my thoughts that summer. The sixties were burgeoning with illusions of peace and love and liberation. I, too, had a dream, but I proclaimed it to no one. It was a dream of concupiscence, a scented dream, a veiled dream rehearsed to the gyration of hips and the thoughtful manipulation of hand and body in the quiet of my room with the Rolling Stones on the record-player asserting that time was on my side: a solitary, adolescent dream.

That must have been the last occasion that I went to Gilead House that summer. 'Here,' she said to me, that afternoon as I said goodbye. 'Let me give you the number of the London house. Then if you ever need somewhere to stay . . .'

I watched her scribble on a piece of embossed writing paper. Her writing had assurance and panache. 'Caroline in London,' she wrote, and the number and address. I folded the page and put it into my pocket.

She looked at me closely, her eyebrows drawn together in a slight frown as though she was trying to make sense of what she saw. 'I *mean* it. Come and see me.' And then she did something quite remarkable: she lifted herself up on her toes, with her hands on my shoulders, and put her cheek against mine. 'I'll miss you,' she said.

'And I'll miss you,' I whispered. It was a statement of great daring, hovering on the edge of confession. Then she kissed me softly on the very corner of my mouth. There was the dampness of her saliva, like a secret promise.

7

Autumn, the anti-climax of the year, the season of my birthday and the coming of the age of consent. I received a card from my mother and a shirt with a tab collar that she had bought at some boutique in Liverpool – Lord John or King Cool or something. There were some records and a few other cards, from grandparents, from an aunt and uncle, from godparents. And a postcard, days late.

Dearest Robert,
I know it's your birthday because you made a point of telling me the exact date, and even so I'm late! So, happy late birthday. I have also bought you a present. If you would like to take up my invitation to come up to town, I'll give it to you. Next weekend? Let me know. Jamie will be there.
*   Love, Caroline*

From the other side of the card a woman's face looked up at me: a woman in tears, her face broken up into jagged planes like shards of broken glass. She held a tattered handkerchief to her cheeks. The printed rubric said: *Woman Weeping, portrait of Dora Maar*, Pablo Picasso. It was, I guessed, her idea of a joke.

I phoned her number, just to check. Her voice was distracted, as though she wasn't sure who she was speaking to. Yes, it was okay that weekend. Fine. Even though . . .

'Even though what?' She seemed remote and uninterested. I felt the intricacies of mixed emotions, worse at sixteen than at fifty, worse at sixteen than at any other age probably.

'Nothing. It's okay, if you want to come.'

'How do I get there?'

"You've got the address, haven't you? Find the place in the *A to Z*. I can't possibly *explain*.' Disappointment as a counter-point to excitement, reality as a counter-balance to fantasy: a dizzying seesaw. Why should she be interested in me, for God's sake? Anyway, I was going to see Jamie, wasn't I? Jamie, who had been a friend long ago and in a different lifetime. What would he be like, having put on as many years as I had, but having in the meantime crossed the threshold of adulthood? He was now at university. He had, so he had written, been climbing on Ben Nevis with the university mountaineering club. 'Not like Snowdon,' he had written. 'More like the Alps. See you in London some time.' A man. A university student, grown up and self-assured, with the experience of sailing in the West Indies and climbing in the Alps behind him. I was going to see him, and what did it matter that his mother sounded indifferent on the phone? Shit, she was an *adult* and I was just a kid.

I went up by train on the Friday evening. I was, I thought, looking pretty good: that shirt my mother had sent for my birthday, my hair as long as they would allow it at school and

78

brushed forward something like the Beatles were doing it, my trousers narrow, my boots elastic-sided. Chelsea boots was what they were called. Sitting there among the rush-hour crowd on the Circle Line I felt part of the city. There were kids in narrow jackets, there was a greaser or two (you tried not to make eye-contact), there were dolly birds in short skirts and long eyelashes, there was scandal and outrage and the caustic laughter of the young and the silent shock of the adults. I got off the tube at Sloane Square and walked along the King's Road where the shops looked good, the crowds looked good, where life itself looked pretty good on that Friday evening, with the weekend stretching ahead.

I pulled out the map and checked the street. A couple of turns and there it was, a small backwater of quiet with a narrow house shouldered between others in one of those mews, all bright white paint and bay windows and geraniums or something on the window-ledges. Backwater Mews, Chelsea. A van was delivering a chest of drawers a few doors down. Cats sat and watched. I checked Caroline's letter just to make sure of the number, and found the name beside the bell push: *Matthewson*. I pressed the button and listened.

While I waited a car drove into the mews and a couple got out, talking in brassy voices and laughing at something. Were they laughing at me? It was a cold evening, but I felt hot, all the heat of adolescence. Then a voice spoke, a small electronic imitation of Caroline's trapped behind the aluminium grille of the intercom: 'Is that you, Robert? Come on in.'

The door clicked open on to shadows. Caroline was standing in a doorway leading off the narrow hall. She was the same as when I had last seen her that summer. Why had I expected her to be different? She was the same: same hairstyle, the same kind of denim shirt. She was wearing a skirt now. Denim, like the shirt, just above the knee. Grey stockings. Looking younger than I thought she should be. But that was the same as well.

'Robert,' she said. Almost an exclamation of surprise. 'You must be tired. Did you have a good journey? You found the house all right? Rather different from Gilead, isn't it? You know, I can't make up my mind which I prefer. When I'm there I prefer here, and when I'm here I prefer there.'

The place had fitted carpets, a luxury we didn't have at home. There was a poster framed on the wall – an abstract painting, a thing of swathes and swirls of colour and the name Kandinsky and the date of an exhibition. The Museum of Modern Art in New York. I'd never seen anything like that before, an advertisement framed.

I looked for Jamie.

'Just put your things down anywhere. We can deal with them later. You'll have a drink? A glass of sherry? I've got beer if you want it. Sherry all right? It's dry.'

I hadn't said a word. I'd just followed her through the door and into the kitchen and stood there watching her open the bottle.

'It's a *fino*,' she told me. 'I can't bear sweet sherry, can you? Now where are the glasses?'

They were already to hand, two narrow-stemmed ellipsoid glasses, not the thimbles my mother used when she drank sherry. Only two of them. I could count. The sherry was pale yellow, not brown: the colour of piss.

'I'm awfully sorry about the mess-up,' she said, as she held out a glass for me.

I could count. I could count the glasses, I could sense the atmosphere. I wasn't a fool. 'Mess-up?'

'Jamie's not being here.'

'Not here?'

'Yes. Or rather, *no*. I told you when you rang, didn't I? I'm really cross. He rang up to say he couldn't come. Something about a group going to the Lake District for the weekend. I wish . . .' She looked at me with a tired smile. What did she wish? 'This climbing. Maybe it's in the blood, his father and everything. But that doesn't make it any easier, does it? Didn't he go climbing with you once? In a quarry somewhere?'

What had he told her? I felt a moment of panic, the sudden, ridiculous thought that my past was about to catch up with me, that she would ask me about what had happened, and that I would be constrained to tell her what we had never told anybody, about the guard and all that. That moment was, perhaps, the last glimmer of childhood guilt; before adult guilt took over. 'It was just playing around,' I said.

'That's what he says, and what his father used to say too. A game. A bloody silly game where people get killed.' There was a silence. She made a wry face, a pout of disappointment, a small twist of resignation 'Anyway, Jamie couldn't come so here we are on our own. You don't mind?'

I didn't mind.

'You can put your things in his room and then I'll show you round.'

The tour of the house didn't last long. It was not like Gilead House. On the ground floor, along with Jamie's bedroom, were the kitchen, dining room and bathroom. Upstairs was the sitting room and her own bedroom. I caught a glimpse through the half-open door: the colours blue and white; a red dress hanging like a bloody skin on a wardrobe door.

'That's it,' she said. 'Hardly a palace, but at least there's no boxroom to clear out. It's going to be a bit of a strange weekend. Just us two, I mean. I hope you don't mind. Perhaps we can go to a film or something. There's this one called *Billy Liar*.'

She had prepared dinner. I had imagined going out with Jamie to a hamburger place or something. Bright lights, bright colours. But I got *boeuf bourguignon* and candlelight. She even changed for dinner – the red dress that I'd glimpsed hanging on the wardrobe in her bedroom, red satin gleaming in the candlelight like fresh blood. And there was my birthday present. It was beside my plate, a small packet wrapped in black paper and tied with a gold ribbon. 'Did you think I'd forgotten?' she asked.

'I didn't even think.'

'Well, open it.'

I fumbled with the wrapping and pulled out a box. I knew from the shape, half knew anyway, guessed. 'Tissot', it said, in elegant script. Tissot was the name of a painter. Why that should have occurred to me at that moment, I have no idea. 'Tissot is a painter,' I said.

'Well, it's not a painting, I'm afraid. It's not really big enough.' She laughed, giggled almost, as though the amusement inside her was threatening to run out of control. Was she laughing at me? 'Go on, open it,' and I went on and opened it and found there, lying prostrate on a bed of dark blue velvet, a wristwatch. It had one of those gold bracelets, not a leather strap like my old one. A piece of jewellery. She raised her glass. By now it was a Californian red, a Cabernet Sauvignon with a full bouquet and a decisive aftertaste of blackcurrants, so the label told me. 'Happy birthday, Robert.'

How would I explain it? To my mother, to my friends, how would I *explain* it, for God's sake? 'I can't,' I managed to say.

Her voice was gently mocking. 'Can't you? It's not difficult. You wind it up and it just sort of goes.'

I blushed again, fumbling awkwardly with the thing. 'I can't accept it, I mean.'

'Why ever not?'

'Because it's too much.'

'How much is my affair. It's just a watch. To help you tell the time. I noticed that yours was a little battered and I thought you'd like another.'

Mine was an H. Samuel Everite, as advertised on Radio Luxembourg, which was the only station where you ever heard decent music. Mine had been given to me by my mother for my thirteenth birthday. This was Tissot. Swiss. Twenty-one jewels, so it claimed, and who was I to doubt it? I wound the watch and it began to go with a smooth, slick movement that I could only just hear when I held it to my ear – like the hurrying away of time itself. I slipped it on to my wrist and looked at it quite casually, as though it had always been there. It had gold hands. 'Hands' was the wrong word. These were altogether sharper than hands, more piercing, more acute. Daggers, arrows. Time's arrows. I felt an uncomfortable mixture of gratitude and resentment, and underneath it all the faintly erotic sensation of having been exploited. 'I don't know what to say.'

'Try, thank you.'

Should I offer to kiss her? Should I lean across the table and kiss her chastely on the cheek? Was that what she was expecting? I glanced at my new watch and watched my dining companion watching me, and wondered if my armpits smelt and if my acne showed. Beads of sweat gathered in a swarm on my forehead and crawled like insects down into my incipient sideburns. 'Thank you.'

'I hope you'll be very happy together,' she said, with a smile. To my relief she got up to clear away the plates. I mopped my brow and sipped my wine, with its aftertaste of blackcurrant, and glanced at the cool face of my watch, which smiled at me smugly and told me that the time was nine fifteen, at which point the telephone rang. It was my mother. I could hear Caroline speaking to her out in the hall. 'Robert's right here,' she was saying. 'I'll pass you over. Lovely to hear you, Di.'

Is there, I wondered, anything quite so humiliating as mothers? I'd told her where I'd be for the weekend. It was my bloody fault.

'Robbie?' said the voice on the far end of the line. 'Is that you?'

'Of course it's me.'

'How are you?'

'I'm fine.'

'How's Jamie?'

I sweated the guilt of connivance. 'Oh, he's fine too. I guess.'

'It's been a long time.'

'Yes.'

'And Meg?'

'Meg?'

Meg smiled conspiratorially at me. We both knew she was *Caroline*. Meg was dull and old-fashioned. Caroline was sparkling new.

'Jamie's *mother*,' the voice said in my ear. 'Who do you think I meant?'

'Oh. Oh, yes. She's fine. She gave me a birthday present.'

'How nice.'

'A watch.'

There was a pause. 'A *watch*?'

'Yes.'

'Isn't that rather extravagant?'

'Is it?' I could picture her behind the reception desk in the hall, smiling distractedly at guests as they went out to find something, anything to eat in Llandudno on a Friday evening. Nothing like *boeuf bourguignon*.

'But you've already *got* a watch.'

'Not like this one.'

'What's it like? Is it expensive?'

'It's a watch. Swiss. It's all right. Fabulous, actually.'

There was a silence. 'What are you doing?'

'Doing? Having supper. Dinner.'

'That's nice.' Another pause. Then, 'Can you talk?'

'Of course I can.'

'I mean, *she's* not there near you?'

She. My mind caught its foot in the word and stumbled. 'Well, yes, of course. But it makes no difference.' It made the hell of a difference. She was standing right beside me, almost close enough to hear my mother's tinny voice in the earpiece, certainly close enough to impart her perfume to the conversation. It made a difference all right.

'He's not there, is he?' my mother's voice insisted in my ear.

'Who's not?'

'Jamie. Jamie's not there.'

'What do you mean?'

She whispered the words. Perhaps she thought she might be overheard: 'I'm not a fool.'

'Of course you're not—'

'Well?'

'Well, what?'

'He's not *there*. Is he?'

'Couldn't be, apparently.'

'So you're on your own, just the two of you?'

'I suppose so.' There was another silence. 'Mum? Are you there?'

'Yes, I'm here,' she said. 'I don't like you there on your own.'

'What do you mean?'

Another pause. 'With Meg.'

'What do you *mean*, Mum?'

'I mean *just you be careful.*'

'Of course I will, Mum. Of course I will.' Then the line went dead. I replaced the receiver with care, and looked round at my hostess.

She raised her eyebrows. 'Well? How is Diana?'

I shrugged. 'She'll recover.' Quite what I meant I don't know; but that's what I said. There was a silence. It was the silence before an avalanche, a silence punctuated with whisperings – of snow, of fracture and fragmentation, of the awful imminence of disaster. Then Caroline laughed. Laughter is the most dangerous thing. People have died laughing. I guess avalanches have been caused by laughter. Apart from sex (and that's often doubtful) the only thing two human beings can be certain of sharing is laughter. Caroline laughed and I followed her. Caroline Matthewson, forty-something years old, and Robert Dewar, barely sixteen, an incongruous couple no doubt, laughed together. And, of course, within a few seconds of this shared laughter she had put out her hand to touch my arm and I'd held her arm in return, and then both her arms, and then quite suddenly, but not unexpectedly, we were holding each other's arms and stepping inside the circle of intimacy that is drawn round every human being, and the laughter had stopped.

'She'll recover,' I repeated. And she lifted herself up on her toes and touched her lips against mine as though to stop me prolonging the joke.

This was not the first time I had ever kissed a woman. There had been a few others: a sallow, shallow girl who, on the fringes of a school dance, had condescended to have my tongue stuck into her mouth; a cousin I had once pretended to like; the sister of a schoolfriend who had come to a summer camp; that kind of temporary, expedient arrangement. But there had never been anything of this nature, never this faint brush of what seemed like silk, never the pressure of this sleek pulp, and the small bud of a tongue that grew at the opening and pushed its way between my lips and touched my own tongue, then drew back as though to invite me in. Never this intimate connection, eyes closed, head twisted as I had seen it done in the films, my head turned one way, hers the other, making what seemed a perfect fit. There was the savour of *boeuf bourguignon*, of garlic and wine, mushrooms and shallots (she had explained the recipe to me) – a bitter, complex, for-eign taste.

After what seemed an age, she released me and laid her cheek against mine. 'Oh, dear,' she whispered. 'Perhaps we shouldn't have done that. What do you think?'

'I think it's all right.'

She pulled back and looked up at me. 'Do you?'

'Yes, I do.' I did. I felt ill with the certainty that everything, but everything was all right.

'Robert, I didn't mean this to happen. I really don't know. Whatever would Diana say? Or Jamie. Perhaps . . .'

'Perhaps what?'

'I've no idea what perhaps.'

'Neither have I.'

We laughed again. Laughter seemed the easiest thing. 'I was going to suggest a film. That we go to a film, or something. *Lawrence of Arabia*, perhaps. If you haven't seen it.'

'You mentioned *Billy Liar*.'

'Or that. But perhaps we should stay in. What do you think?'

She picked up the bottle of wine and our two glasses from the table. The bottle was almost empty, but my cup was brimming over.

'Perhaps we should,' I said. 'Stay in, I mean.' *Perhaps* seemed to dominate our small and claustrophobic world. A whole world of perhaps, a whole universe of possibilities. On the stairs going up to the sitting room she stumbled for a moment. Suddenly and surprisingly she seemed rather vulnerable, a fragile figure, no longer quite in control of matters. 'Do you want some music? I went round to the record shop and bought what's just come out.' She knelt beside the record-player, her dress taut across her thighs, and scrabbled through a pile of discs, tossing them this way and that. 'What do you think?'

Of what? I thought a dozen things, but few that I could put into precise words. The music hammered out, the Rolling Stones wanting to be her lover, baby, wanting to be her man. She got to her feet. What did I think of what? What did I think of her standing there in the middle of the room reaching round to the back of that dress? Was that the question? Did she need help? That's what I thought. What does a single woman do when she needs help zipping or unzipping her dress? Had Helen Gurley Brown said anything about it? I'd read her book. Someone had brought it to school, and we'd flicked through it to find the bits about sex. Hair is sexy, lots of it, but not around your nipples. Things like that.

I heard a zip go. Apparently you didn't need help. Apparently you could do it by yourself even when you were slightly unsteady on your feet, as Caroline was, even when you are skipping on one foot, in order to kick off the shoe that's on the other. You can do both these things at the same time. I watched her shoes go rolling across the carpet. Her dress was suddenly loose at the front. 'Do you want this?' she asked. 'Please, Robert, say if you don't.'

I tried to appear relaxed about it all, as though this had happened so often that it was rather tiresome. 'I'm fine. Don't worry about me.'

And then there was a soft rush of sound, and the dress lay like a haemorrhage round her feet and she was standing there in her underwear. Golden satin. You don't forget these things. 'Do you like me like this?' she asked.

Caroline. Jamie's *mother*, for Christ's sake. My own mother's once-upon-a-time best friend. It was extraordinary how many different things I could think at the same time. The wife of the famous mountaineering hero, Guy Matthewson. The sight of her was branded into my mind, an image I'd never forget. I knew that. This moment would be always there in memory – Jamie's mother there in the middle of the sitting-room carpet undoing her golden satin bra and stepping out of her golden satin knickers, and asking, 'Do you like me like this?' and surely not expecting 'No' for an answer. I swallowed something sticky and obstructive, and said, 'Yes,' which was only the truth. I remember, with all the obsessive interest of a sixteen-year-old, that although she was blonde, her pubic hair was dark, almost black. And, for the glimmer of a moment, I thought that she had a great deal more of it than Bethan.

After a while we went through to her bedroom. She left the doors open so that the music would come through from the sitting room, but pretty soon there was just the staccato noise of the pick-up going round and round on the inside track – flip-flip, flip-flip, flip-flip, on and on. The Beatles hadn't yet had the idea of putting something, anything, even gibberish, on that inside, eternal track, and neither of us was planning to go and change the record. In the bedroom she helped me off with my clothes as though I was still young enough to need assistance with the buttons, and perhaps I was. I was shivering, I remember that, shivering as though I was dying of cold. 'This is your first time, isn't it?' she whispered.

I didn't deny it.

'It's like riding a bike,' she said.

'A *bike*?'

She giggled. As though she were sixteen as well. 'Once you've learnt you never forget.'

We laughed. Her breasts were soft and pink, and there for me to touch.

'And . . .'

'And?'

'You must keep pedalling. Or else you'll fall off.'

Laughter blended with extreme tenderness. Laughter and sex is not a bad combination. We lay down on the bed and she did everything necessary, opening for me and pulled me on to her and showing me how it went inside; and after the storm – my storm, not hers – she stroked my head as though to comfort me, as though she had just done me a great hurt. 'I'm sorry,' she whispered. 'I'm sorry, Robert, I'm sorry.'

I told her there was nothing to apologize for. Nothing whatever. I made that quite clear to her.

Morning was different. Morning is always different. Morning is for remorse. I woke to find the room bathed in an anaemic London daylight.

Caroline was still asleep. She lay amid the knotted sheets, her legs splayed shamelessly: white buttocks and loose flesh, pink-grey creases and folds, a crest of dark hair. Her face was crumpled against the pillow. Her smudged mouth was half open and there were flakes of lipstick peeling from her lips. I could hear the rasp of air as she breathed. She looked her age, like a fairy-tale character suddenly revealed for what she was, a young girl transformed into a middle-aged woman.

Jamie's mother, I thought. *Christ alive!*

Clothes were strewn all over the floor and across a chair: woman's clothes, things of silk and nylon, lace and satin, all the unknown territory of woman spread out here for me to look at; and my own clothes, dull and sordid things that you might see in a launderette. Slipping off the bed, I tiptoed to the bathroom. As I stood there peeing, I realized that I reeked of her just as she, presumably, reeked of me. Even our scents were shared. What occurred to me vividly was this sharing, this physical sharing of scent and saliva and semen. I looked at the crumpled thing that was my penis and, as I finished urinating it began to stir again, so that when I came back into the room I had an erection once more.

Caroline was awake and sitting up in bed. She had a handful of sheet grabbed up to cover her breasts. Her face was fragmented and rough-edged like the postcard she had sent, the weeping, fractured face of Dora Maar. 'Robert dear,' she said, 'I think you'd better give me some time to myself.'

I was naked and erect in front of her and she just sat there with the sheet clutched against her front, telling me to leave the room. 'Please, Robert,' she said. Then she got up from the bed, pulling the sheet with her as a kind of shroud, and went past me into the bathroom. I heard the key turn in the lock.

I was confused, of course, aware that barriers had been hastily erected, like the Berlin Wall that they'd hurriedly slammed together out of planks and barbed wire just a couple of years earlier. I just didn't want the subsequent consolidation with cement and breeze blocks and arc lamps. I took my things and went downstairs. I could hear her moving about overhead, the shower running, the lavatory flushing. I washed and dressed and went into the kitchen to find some breakfast.

When she finally came down she barely gave me a glance. She turned to the coffee machine and began spooning grounds into the filter. She was wearing jeans and a brassière. From behind she looked young, years younger than she had looked lying in bed, years younger than she was. Twenty-five, say. 'I hope you don't mind all this.' She said it almost casually, while facing away from me.

'No.'

She plugged in the coffee machine. Her movements were clumsy and she missed the connection the first time. 'Damn it,' she said, as though the problem resided in the plug or the socket, in the design of things. 'I'm sorry, if you do.'

'I said I don't.'

'Because if you want to go . . .'

'I don't.'

She glanced round. 'That's fine, then.' Her smile was hard and sharp, like a knife. 'Jamie must never know.'

'Of course not.'

'I knew he wasn't coming,' she continued, in that matter-of-fact tone. 'Before you phoned, I knew. Next weekend, he's coming next weekend; I hoped you wouldn't contact him . . .'

I shrugged. I felt a whole mess of things, the sensation that I had somehow betrayed him, for one: a feeling of adolescent guilt that would soon enough drain away through the holes in what moral principles I had. And something else: the acute sensation of focused desire that was, I realized later, sexual love. I wanted her now, again.

'I thought it might be fun, just the two of us together. Like this. You don't mind?'

'I don't mind at all,' I assured her.

She smiled. We saw connivance in each other's eyes. 'What would Diana say? What would Diana say if she knew?'

'She's never going to know, is she?'

'No, she's not.'

That morning we went to the Tate Gallery. It was like establishing an alibi after a crime, hoping that the prosecution wouldn't see that the times didn't quite fit, that there was a whole night that had not been accounted for. We took the 88 bus and sat there up on the top deck, pretending to be mother and son and hoping that somehow this deception would erase the other. In the gallery she wanted to find the Laurencins. 'You remember the portrait in Gilead House?'

I did, vaguely. A portrait of a girl, painted with soft colours, mauve and purple and pink, her eyes like two black coals. She wanted to see the ones in the Tate collection and eventually we found one, and stood in front of it with critical expressions. 'What do you think? Is mine an original?'

'What does it matter what I think? You need an expert.'

'Be my expert.'

I shrugged. 'Assume the worst.'

She nodded agreement. 'Assume the worst. I think that's what I always do.' We moved on, the question of authenticity unresolved but the worst definitely assumed. That evening we went to the cinema – *Billy Liar* as promised – and when we came back to the house we went to separate beds in separate rooms. But in the dark, when I was nowhere near asleep, when I was wondering about Jamie and about Caroline, about what had happened and what might happen, and was assuming the worst, the door to the room opened. I could see her standing there in the narrow rectangle of light from the hallway upstairs.

Just her silhouette. Rather small. Narrow naked legs. Narrow naked hips and flanks. Naked.

'Robert,' she whispered.

'Yes.'

'Can I come in?'

'Of course you can.'

And this time it was quite different, for this time what we did was quiet and soft and thoughtful. 'I love you, Caro,' I whispered to her at one point, and in the darkness I felt the small, sorrowful birdcall of her laughter in my ear as she denied it.

'You'll fall in love with a beautiful girl of your own age. You're not in love with me.'

But, with all the mournful insistence of a forsaken lover, the word 'loveliness' comes to my mind when I think of her. Not a word we have much time for these days, 'loveliness'. She *was* lovely. In my memory she remains lovely. Her face was lovely. Her body was lovely. All was loveliness, a litany of loveliness. The soft, remorseful presence of her in my narrow bed that second night, loveliness. That weekend the word itself seemed delimited by her. Nothing that was not her was lovely. It was she who defined the limits and the boundaries of my adolescent aesthetic. I was, quite simply, in love with her.

'No, you're not,' she said.

As Caroline had told me, Jamie was due in London the next weekend. Over the phone he told me there was a party at the house of a friend of his on the Saturday. I could go along with him if I liked.

'Have they invited me?'

He laughed at that. 'It's not that kind of party.'

So I travelled up to the city again, and made my way through now familiar streets to the mews where the Matthewsons lived, and when I rang Jamie opened the door. It was the first time I had seen him since the day of the slate quarry. He was changed, of course. He was taller and stronger, with the hard edge of physical maturity. His chin was rough like a man's and his grip, as we shook hands, was tough.

'It's been a long time,' he said.

'Yes, it has.' We were awkward together, wary of each other, childhood friends who hadn't yet been proved to have anything in common. He was quietly, sarcastically older than me, smiling at my naïvety and condescending to my ignorance. Not the kid who had swarmed up the vertical cliff face, not the fourteen-year-old who had knelt down in front of the quarry guard in the shadows of the hut, the victim whom I had, in some sense, rescued. This was an adult, with an adult's armour of confidence. We talked about the party. 'Maybe we'll fix you up with a bird,' he suggested. 'Is that what you'd like?'

'I'm okay,' I assured him.

'You mean you've got a girl? Or you prefer boys?'

'Oh, piss off. I've got a girl. Sort of.'

'Sort of? What the hell's sort of?'

'There's a girl at home . . .'

'Who? Bethan?' He laughed at the memory.

'Not Bethan,' I assured him. In the background Caroline smiled at my embarrassment.

We went to the party in Caroline's car, the battered Mini that she used in the city. Jamie drove. From the exalted heights of university, he quizzed me about school, offered me advice, suggested where I might go next, advised me against places that were no good. He talked about the climbing he'd been doing, the Scottish winter routes, the ice climbing that was far ahead of anything anywhere else in the world. He seemed a generation different from me, driving through London like this, in command of the traffic, in command of his own life. After a pause he glanced across. 'How did you get on with my mother last weekend?'

I didn't know what to answer. I didn't know how you could deal with a thing like that, your mother opening her legs to a mere kid who was supposed to be some kind of friend of yours. I looked away, out of the window at the passing streets. 'All right.' The city was dark and wet and awash with Christmas lights. Swinging London, they might be calling it, but it was a tawdry place.

'She's lonely,' he said. 'Ever since my father died, I guess. Well, she has boyfriends, of course. But never to substitute him. Sometimes I feel . . .'

'What?' I dared to glance at him, and saw in his face contours that I perceived as hints of Caroline – her mouth transformed into something male and hard, her brow given weight and bluntness, his eyes that, in some intangible way, were hers.

'Oh, I don't know. She's searching for him all the time.'

'What was he like?'

'My old man? I hardly remember him. He was my father and I was just a kid.' He smiled. 'Anyway, you're almost in the same boat, aren't you? How often do you see your father?'

I shrugged. He was somewhere in Scotland, with another wife and three children. 'Never. My mother and he are estranged.' *Estranged.* I'd learnt the useful word. I'd even looked it up in the dictionary and found that it fitted, almost every meaning that the dictionary gave fitted this particular case, including the obsolete ones. 'I get a Christmas card from him, that kind of thing. At least, I used to.'

The house where the party was being held was in Hampstead. The front door was open and there were figures silhouetted against the light. The noise of people and music spilled out into the evening. Someone shouted, 'Here's Jamie!' as we got out of the car, and people came out to see whether it was so. He appeared at ease in all this confusion, at ease and vaguely distracted, as though none of it mattered. I was introduced to people and handed an open bottle of beer. There were bottles littered around the floor inside the house and a pall of cigarette smoke in the sitting room. One of the bedrooms reeked with the exotic scent of marijuana. The bathroom contained a large bath with a similarly large girl asleep in six inches of water. People wandered in and peed and pressed the flush and wandered out without taking any notice of her. 'Letitia is cooling down,' someone remarked airily. It seemed ever such a good joke.

I soon lost Jamie, of course. I pushed among the bodies and tried to pretend that I wasn't a solitary sixteen-year-old among people who all seemed older. The music all around us was the Beatles; but there was something else in the air, a sense that this kind of music, the jangling harmonies, the silly falsettos, was already passé. The harsh rhythms of the Rolling Stones and the Animals were taking its place. Someone had brought an LP by an American folk singer and in one of the upstairs rooms people were sitting round listening to a song called 'Oxford Town'. The voice of the singer was slurred and rough and tuneless, and he wasn't singing about Oxford, England. His Oxford was in Mississippi, a place of guns and clubs and tear gas. One of the girls was weeping. A girl in boots and miniskirt said to me, 'Oh, fuck, let's go and listen to some *music*,' and pushed her way out of the room, pulling me with her. Her name was Eve. She wore pale lipstick and heavy eye-shadow and had her hair cut short and sharp in what had once been an Eton crop and was now a Mary Quant. 'You're a friend of Jamie's, aren't you?' Eve asked me. 'You know, I fancy him like mad.' We stepped over people in the corridor, went on a search for beer. 'We went out for a while and then he dumped me.'

Downstairs we began to dance. The music there was something fast, but she put her arms around my neck and swayed from side to side as though it were slow, and I didn't mind. I thought of Caroline. Eve was bigger and softer, her breasts pushing against the thin stuff of her dress. Her belly pressed against me. 'You're all right,' she said vaguely, as though she wasn't sure whether I'd asked her opinion or not. 'But Jamie's better.'

'Better how?'

'Looking,' she said bluntly. 'And older. How old are you?'

'Eighteen,' I lied.

'You don't look it.'

We shuffled around each other. At one point she lifted her face to be kissed. There was the taste of tobacco. Her tongue coiled round mine. Slugs mating, I thought. There was much debate about whether a girl should have her eyes closed or open when kissing. Open seemed ill-mannered. Closed seemed as though she might be thinking of someone else. John Lennon, maybe. Like a diver underwater, I opened my eyes to look and discovered Eve's eyes wide open, hard and blue and looking directly back at me. She pulled away and frowned, as though I had done something wrong. 'I always keep my eyes on a man,' she said.

'Don't you trust them?'

'Do you think you're trustworthy?'

'No.'

'Well, then.'

We danced, shuffled, a bit more. 'You know he tried to take me climbing?' she said.

'Who?'

'Jamie, of course.'

'He took you *climbing*?'

'He tried. Some grotty place in Sussex, I ask you. He goes on about climbing all the time. All hearty, shinning up rockfaces or something. What's the point? You've only got to come down again. Hey, d'you smoke?'

I didn't.

'Shame,' she said. We kissed again. 'You know,' she said, pushing her belly against me, 'you should *ask* a girl before you go getting an erection against her.' And with that she slipped her arms from around my neck and wandered off to find a smoke. Later I saw her in another room sitting cross-legged with a joint in her hand and a fatuous expression on her face. She waved. I wandered off among the litter of bodies and bottles and thought of Caroline. In the room upstairs the folk singer with the lousy voice was advising his girl not to think twice; but I just couldn't help it.

The next day a group of us piled into cars and drove into the country. It was the place that Eve had mentioned during the party – a sandstone escarpment hidden away in some wooded corner of Sussex where climbers from London went if they couldn't get away to Wales or the Lake District. Eve herself, dressed in a battered pair of jeans and an Arran sweater several sizes too big for her, was one of the group.

'In God's name, why do I put up with it?' she complained.

'Because you're chasing Jamie?'

She eyed me thoughtfully through a haze of cigarette smoke. 'I don't chase men, they chase me,' she said.

The climbing crag was no more than a twenty-foot-high shelf of dirty rock buried in a scrappy piece of woodland. The ground beneath it was beaten into hardpan by the passage of thousands of city-bound rock climbers desperate for somewhere to practise near the capital. Harrison's Rocks. Anyone in the climbing world will tell you. ''Ard, scruffy little climbs,' one world authority has described them. The group of us gathered at the bottom and watched Jamie wander up a few routes where other people struggled. I remembered him in the quarry, the easy flow of his body up the rock. There was laughter and shouts of derision, the competitive banter he seemed to love.

'Come on, young Dewar,' he called, holding the end of the rope for me to tie on. 'Give it a go.' The rope ran up from the belayer at the foot of the cliff to a sling looped round a tree at the top, then back down to the climber: a kind of pulley effect. Someone tied me on and I tried a few climbs myself. The rock bulged, holdless and awkward. It was like trying to climb up a rusty metal tank. Eve cheered me on, which was gratifying. Jamie stood at the foot of the rock holding the rope and shouting instructions.

I stalled on a sandy overhang.

'Come on, Dewar!' he called. I scrabbled and slithered. 'You've just got to reach over and use the crack above. You've just got to *do* it.'

It was the first time I heard that edge in his voice, the merciless tone of the torturer – the torturer who knows that he can stand more pain than you. 'I can't *reach* the fucking crack!' I yelled.

'Well, then, you'll fall off. That's all there is to it. You'll fall off, and I'll save your life.'

I duly did. My sweating fingers lost their grip and I slumped exhausted on the rope, and he held me tight and lowered me to the ground, then caught me awkwardly in his arms. The audience laughed, as you might laugh at a comedian doing a pratfall. 'That's not bad,' Jamie said, his arm round my shoulders comfortingly. 'Five B.'

I assumed it was a mark out of ten or something. It didn't sound very good. Eve held my hand when we all decamped to the nearest pub. 'I thought you did wonderfully,' she said. She sat beside me in the pub, smoking and sipping a gin and lime and toying with a sandwich. She was pale, like a plant grown under glass. The Arran sweater she wore was her brother's. 'Of course, you know about Jamie's father, don't you?' she asked.

'What about him?'

'He was some kind of English hero. Frozen to death on Mount Everest or something. He must have told you.'

'I know something. I think it was Kangchenjunga.'

'They're all the same. Great piles of rock.' She made a face – disparagement, disapproval, something like that – and glanced round to see who might overhear. But we were in a corner and the rest of the group were involved in a game of darts on the other side of the bar. 'Well, the thing is, he's trying to live up to his father's name. Trying to be the hero. And, after all, his mother . . .'

'What about his mother?'

She sniffed. Eve was a London girl, born and bred. She looked soft but she had a Londoner's hard edge and, despite private schooling, London vowels in her voice. 'Well,' she said, 'she's not much to live up to, is she? I mean, her knicker elastic is rather loose.'

'What's that supposed to mean?'

'They keep falling down, darling.' She noticed that I reddened. Of course she did. She was too sharp not to. But she was too sharp to mention it at the time. The occasion would arise, of course. She would store away that little piece of knowledge in

101

some dark recess of her mind where revenge and blackmail brewed, and one day she might use it. She was a barrister's daughter, with a barrister's gift for sensing the weaknesses in a witness's story.

That evening back at his house, Jamie and I talked about fathers and lack of fathers, just as we had all those years ago in North Wales. We seemed very close. We sat on his bed and drank beer from the bottle and conjured fathers out of the stuff of our imagination. You create a father in your own image if you haven't got one; I guess that's it. I had a father, although materially I never saw him and never really knew him. But still he was there, to dull my fantasy. Jamie, on the other hand, was able to create his own father out of fantasy and wishful thinking – his father was tough and forthright and noble and sensitive, the kind of man who wants to know what is over the next hill, in the next valley, the kind of man who lives on the edge of the inhabited world, pushing beyond the frontiers. 'I reckon somehow he's there, watching,' he said. 'Does that sound daft?'

'Yes, it does,' I told him. 'Bloody daft.'

He laughed and pushed me away. For a moment we struggled together, a play fight over the absurdity of Jamie's father watching over him. But in a sense he *was* there, in Jamie's room: he looked out at you from a dozen framed photographs. He was there among a group of climbers standing at the snout of the Rongbuk Glacier; he was poised with apparent ease on a rockface somewhere in Wales, a rope hanging from his waist; he was sitting on a boulder in the sun, smoking a cigarette and dressed in tattered breeches and a collarless shirt, looking for all the world like a manual worker taking a tea break. The mountain that formed the backdrop to that photograph was dark and forbidding, a great triangular mass cast in shadow, with ice and snow cascading down its flank. 'That's in the Alps,' Jamie said. 'It's got it on the back. It says, "After the Lauper, June 1939". That's the Eiger.'

I looked at this mountain that had the reputation of a killer, and Jamie's father sitting in front of it with the casual smile of the invincible. Except that he wasn't invincible. The mountains had finally got him, hadn't they?

'Do you want to see his notebook? It's a log book of all his climbs. Mother found it.'

I'd seen it, of course, but I didn't tell Jamie that. The notebook had made its journey down from Gilead House and was now kept in a desk in the sitting room, like the relic of a saint tucked away in an altar. Jamie opened it.

<u>CIC hut, Ben Nevis, Easter 1939</u>
Thurs. 6th April: Comb Gully (in the wet). 2nd ascent?
Good Fri. with MacPhee et al: a new gully between Observatory Buttress and the Indicator Wall. A fine achievement.
Saturday: 8th: A wash out.
Sunday 2nd April. Tower Ridge. Solo, under blue skies!
Monday and Tuesday: prospecting on the Orion Face, without success . . .

'See what he did? All his climbs. Scotland, Wales and the Lake District.' I was sitting at the desk to read it. He stood behind me with his hand on my shoulder, reaching over to turn the pages.

<u>Fri. 9th August 1940</u>: Columnar Cliffs – Spiral Stairs and Flying Buttress (Difficult). DS 2nd.
<u>Sat. 10th</u>: Milestone Buttress – Direct (Difficult); Tryfan E Face – Grooved Arête (Very D). DS 2nd.
<u>Sun 11th</u>: Glyder Main Cliff – Direct Route (Severe). Diana 2nd.

He moved to turn them again but I stopped him. 'What's this?' I asked. Behind us the door opened. Caroline came in and walked over to see what we were doing. 'That's not to be touched,' she said. 'Anyway, Robert's already seen it.'

'Seen it?' said Jamie.

'At Gilead House, when he was helping me clear out. When I found it.'

She reached over to take the book, but I kept my finger on the page. 'What's this?' I repeated, looking round at her. 'Who's DS? It says Diana. Who's Diana?'

Caroline stopped. Her expression was an untidy blend of amusement and embarrassment. 'Diana?'

'Yes.' I pointed. And somehow I felt angry, a diffuse, confused sort of anger. As though things had been kept from me. 'It says DS here. And then Diana.'

There was a silence, Jamie and I looking round at his mother, and she looking back at us with something like anxiety in her expression. 'Diana's your mother,' she said flatly.

'*My mother?*'

'Yes. Didn't she ever tell you?' She tried to sound careless about it, as though it were obvious, really. 'She climbed with Guy.'

'She *climbed* with him?'

'They met in Wales, before I knew him. They climbed together.'

'I can't believe it.'

'It's true.'

'She never told me. I never knew.'

Caroline took the book and closed it. 'What child ever knows his parents?' she asked. It sounded like a quotation. Something from the Book of Proverbs, perhaps.

A couple of weeks later I was invited to stay at Eve's house. Her parents were away. It wasn't clear whether they knew about me being there or not but, then, I suppose Caroline's aphorism works both ways: there was quite a lot these parents didn't know about their daughter. She had got hold of some pot, and I doubt they knew about that. 'Do you want to try?' she asked. 'Or doesn't it fit in with your Welsh Methodist upbringing?'

'I'm not a Welsh Methodist. I'm not even Welsh. My father is Scottish.'

She made a face. 'That's even worse. Wee free or something. Does he beat you with a tawse?'

'He left home years ago.'

'Lucky you,' she said.

We spent most of the Saturday sitting on the floor of the sitting room, giggling and smoking and listening to records. She held the joint between her last two fingers and cupped her hand to her mouth to inhale. The musty scent filled the air. 'Are we very depraved?' she asked.

'Just slightly.' We giggled at being only slightly depraved. She passed me the joint. Her mind was unsteady, lighting on things at random. She spoke a bit about Jamie. 'I don't think he fancies women, do you?'

I laughed. 'You think he's queer?'

She had that trick of ignoring what you had said, just going on with her own line of thought. 'He doesn't fancy *you*, does he?'

'Me?'

'He always talks about you.'

'That doesn't mean he's queer.'

'It does if he fancies you and he doesn't fancy me.' She looked at me with her head on one side and her eyes ill-focused. I remember the size of her pupils, black and shining, rimmed with that startling blue. 'Do *you* fancy me?'

I did.

'Then you'd better *show* it,' she said.

8

The rain came in over the Irish Sea, thin and mean and grey. It rattled at the windows of my room as though trying to get in. 'Where did you get these things?' my mother asked, unpacking my suitcase and finding a shirt and a wide, flowery tie from a boutique in the King's Road. They seemed symbolic of all that London had to offer: bright and brash against the self-pitying grey of Wales.

'Jamie's mother bought them for me. They're Christmas presents.'

'First a watch and now these. What's Meg trying to do, take you over?'

'It's *Caroline*, now, Mum. She's Caroline.'

'What do you care?'

'It's just what she's called.'

'She was always Meg. It's a silly, pretentious affectation of hers to change her name. Typical of her type.'

'What *is* her type, Mum?'

'You tell me.'

We stood glaring at each other across the litter of unpacked clothes. I suppose she wanted to know the truth, but you can't ask directly, can you? In case you get the answer you don't want to hear. What if I had told her? Yes, Caroline and I have slept together: we're lovers. What if I had said that? But I didn't. I just shrugged instead. 'I don't know what you mean. She's just Jamie's mother. A bit of a laugh at times . . . different from most people her age.'

'What do you mean by that? She's no older than I am.'

'That's what I meant by it.'

We found that funny. She laughed and I laughed with her. 'Maybe I should start wearing miniskirts. Can you imagine what they'd say round here? And call myself Jezebel or something.'

It was when she laughed that I could see the woman who was in those wedding photos, the woman my father had married. I told her about Eve. 'She's all right,' I said. 'Her old man's a barrister.'

'That sounds very respectable.'

'You mean, she'd make a suitable daughter-in-law?'

She smiled at my teasing. 'You know what I mean.'

'And we all went to this place in Sussex where you climb. I had a go. Jamie said I can go climbing with him. Maybe when he comes here at Easter. He says we can go to the Llanberis Pass and he'll show me.'

The amusement slid clumsily from her face. 'What do you want to do that for?'

'For fun. He's says it's great. Scary and exciting.'

'It's dangerous. Look what happened to his father.'

I had known she was going to say that. I had the response ready. 'But *you*'ve done it. You went climbing with him, didn't you?'

'How on earth do you know that? Did Meg—'

'Caroline didn't say anything. We found his notebook, that's all. Jamie's father's. There's your name in it.'

Mother took a careful breath. It seemed to be difficult for her, as though breathing had become something that you had to learn and she needed practice. 'What did it say?'

'Just your name against a couple of climbs, that's all. "Second: Diana Sheridan", that kind of thing. Is it true?'

Her expression was difficult to read – guarded, puzzled, underpinned by something approaching fear. 'Of course it's true,' she said quietly. 'It was before Meg ever knew him.'

'You never said.'

'Why should I say?'

'What's the problem, Mum?'

'Nothing's the problem. Nothing at all.' She looked round my room as though for distraction, and found none. 'Just that I think, perhaps . . .'

'Perhaps what?'

'Perhaps I was in love with him.'

I felt embarrassed, awkward in the presence of adult emotion. Emotion was foreign to her, and her display of it a shock. 'It doesn't matter, Mum,' I said.

She nodded. 'It does matter,' she whispered. 'It *does* matter.'

And I had the sudden and terrible thought that she was still in love with him and had always been in love with him – this man who had married someone else and, anyway, was long dead on some distant mountain. Love was an emotion I had laid claim to with Caroline, but in truth it seemed to be something I could pick up or leave aside as I wished. I thought perhaps I loved Eve now. And yet here was an adult who seemed scarred by love, almost literally so, the tissue still growing over the wound and giving her the stiff, expressionless face of a burn victim.

She gave a fugitive smile, as though trying to show that it was all of no account. 'It was so long ago now I barely remember. We spent a whole weekend climbing together. He taught me how. How to use a rope and all that kind of thing. And on the Sunday he dragged me up a climb that was too difficult, really. We had a bit of a struggle getting up. But ' There was a cast to her eyes, as though she were looking somewhere else, somewhere beyond the narrow confines of our hotel, of the kitchen where she prepared breakfast and afternoon tea with the assistance of Mrs Jones from the council houses nearby, of the interminable lists, of shopping, of repairs, of things to do and things to be done.

'But?'

She shrugged. 'It was fun. Funny. We laughed a lot. But the war had just begun and after that I went down to London to join an ambulance unit and he went back to Manchester. He was, you see, a conscientious objector. He had to face some kind of tribunal.'

'And then . . . ?'

'And then.' She shook her head and looked around for something to do, some chore to bring things back down to earth. 'Then the laughing stopped,' she said.

II
North Wales, 1940

9

'You're Guy Matthewson, aren't you?' she said, as the descending climber approached her. She had been watching him coming down the rough path from the cliffs for some minutes, but had only recognized him as he got nearer.

He looked startled at being spoken to. 'Yes, that's right,' he said.

She blushed. 'I'm Diana Sheridan. A bit like the actress,' she added. 'Only she's Dinah.'

'What actress?' he asked.

She reddened. Was it ridiculous to expect that anyone might make the connection? 'It doesn't matter,' she said, and held out her hand towards him. For a dreadful moment he looked at it as though he was not going to take it, as though he might leave it there, thrust out into the space between them. Then he clasped it solemnly and shook it, and looked at what he had done and apologized for making her hand dirty. 'I've just been wrestling with a muddy groove, I'm afraid.'

'Oh, that's all right. Where?'

He gestured vaguely up the hill, up the grey rocks and green rakes of grass. 'Up there.'

'Were you on your own?'

'I tend to be these days. I'm a conchie, you see. Not popular.'

She blushed again. She wished he hadn't mentioned the matter of his being a conscientious objector, which was embarrassing, like having scabies or something. You wanted not to have to talk about it. Almost, she smiled and walked on. Almost, he merely nodded at her and passed her down the narrow path. But she screwed up her courage and asked the question, and on reflection she told herself that it was only because he was at a disadvantage, crippled by objecting to the war, that she had dared. 'Would you take me climbing?' she asked. 'Up there?'

He looked at her with curiosity. 'If you wish. Surely *you're* not on your own . . .'

'I'm at the youth hostel. I've got friends coming up tomorrow, but . . .'

'But?'

'They'll just want to go walking.'

'And you—'

'Would rather do some proper climbing.'

He smiled for the first time. It was just a momentary thing, so quick that she thought perhaps she had imagined it. His whole face was transformed by this smile. At rest it was rather reserved, private, a bit awkward. 'Why not?' he said.

So they agreed to meet the next morning. He would come for her with his motorbike – she didn't mind riding pillion? – and she would be ready on the road outside the hostel. At seven o'clock. They'd go round to the Llanberis Pass on the other side of the mountains.

'Why there?' she asked.

'Why not?' He was looking at her thoughtfully. He was head and shoulders taller than she and he was looking her up and down as though making some kind of assessment. Could you tell whether someone would make a climber just by looking at them? 'I hope you've got some slacks,' he said. 'Don't want you climbing cliffs in a skirt, do we?'

The very idea made her blush. 'Breeches. I've got breeches.'

He nodded. That was all right, then. 'And boots,' he added. 'Good stiff boots.'

The next morning she left a note with the hostel warden for her companions when they got there. 'Gone climbing,' she wrote. 'See you this evening.' And she was waiting there in the cool dawn – mist skulking over the waters of the lake, shreds of cloud hanging across the mountainside opposite like dirty washing on a line – when his bike came into view, roaring along the lakeside, then puttering to a halt at the turning to the hostel where she was standing. He pushed up his goggles and waved, and she hurried over to him, feeling suddenly shy at making this early-morning assignation with a man.

'How are you?' he shouted, above the noise of the engine. Somehow the question seemed a bit ridiculous. She was what she was. Couldn't he see that for himself? A tallish, awkward girl with lacklustre, mouse-brown hair, crooked teeth and a diffident smile. There were no secrets here, no mysteries to unravel. 'Fine,' she said.

He edged the bike round so that it faced the way he had come. 'Hop on, then.' She swung her leg over and settled herself behind him. He had a canvas rucksack on his back so she was spared the problem of how to hold on – she could grab the rucksack instead of having to grab hold of him. 'Ever ridden pillion?' he shouted.

'No!'

'Just go with it. It's instinctive, like riding a bike. Hold tight!' He twisted the throttle and the machine roared away. For an awful moment it seemed almost to pull itself from under her so that she had to cling on for dear life. That's what she'd tell them when she got back that evening. Clinging on for dear life.

'You all right?' he called over his shoulder.

The wind made her breathless. 'Fine,' she cried, and she *was* fine: exhilarated, excited, ecstatic, she was all of those things. The lake was still and lucid in the morning air as they drove along the shore. You could see the reflection of the valley wall inverted into its depth. Tryfan lay ahead, a mass of grey rock like a giant dinosaur laid across their path, with its tail flung out towards the lake and its head butting into the mountain plateau on the right. Stegosaurus, she thought, recalling a visit to a museum in Oxford where dusty skeletons had stood, it seemed, like mountains in a cold and milky light.

They passed the Climbers' Club hut at Helyg among its grove of trees – the only trees in the whole blighted mountain landscape – and turned southwards at the little village of Capel Curig to speed along the empty Mymbyr valley, Dyffryn Mymbyr, with its two glacial lakes and the Snowdon massif blocking the far end. There was something unreal about the drive, something fantastic, daring, as wild as any climbing expedition. They battered along, and the road branched off to the right and began to climb towards the head of the pass. At the top they skidded to a halt, with a small shower of loose stones, in the car park of the hotel.

'That was fun,' she said.

He shrugged. 'Let's get some breakfast. I assume you haven't had anything?'

They went through into the warm fug of the hotel. The place was wood-panelled, hung with old photographs of bearded men wearing tweed jackets and nailed boots and holding coils of rope. There was the sensation of ancient ritual and tradition. They ate breakfast in a front room looking out at the narrow roadway and the mountain rising up on the far side. 'That's Crib Goch. You know that?'

'I climbed it last summer,' she told him. 'We did the Snowdon Horseshoe.' He listened to her account of her adventure as though it were a great mountaineering achievement. She suddenly felt a bit of a fool, talking like this about something that Guy Matthewson would surely find no more than an easy stroll. This was a man who had been to the Himalayas, climbed on Everest with F. S. Smythe. He'd even known Leigh Mallory, so the story went, had climbed with him when he was still at school. What could he care about her account of a summer day walking round the Snowdon ridge? And yet he listened and nodded and seemed impressed. 'Jolly good,' he said. 'Jolly good.'

'I must pay my share,' she said, when the bill came, but he brushed aside her suggestion and paid the whole thing himself. They went back out into the morning just as the sun came over the mass of the Glyders at the back of the hotel and flooded its light across the top of the valley. It was magical, like an omen. She felt an absurd happiness as they remounted the motorbike.

There wasn't much further to go. Guy kicked the engine into life and let the machine free-wheel down the road for a few hundred yards before coming to a halt at a narrow bridge. The valley they were in was flat-floored and steep-sided, ground out by the passage of a glacier at some immeasurable time in the past. Brown slopes of grass and bracken rose up on either side, with outcrops of rock like broken teeth embedded in an ancient, fossilized jawbone.

He pointed up the hillside above them. 'The Columnar Cliffs. Aren't they fine? They have another name, of course, some Welsh name, all hack and spit. But we call them the Columnar Cliffs.'

Diana looked where he was pointing. They were square-cut crags, like huge cenotaphs carved out of the side of the mountain by a gargantuan stonemason. You thought of the Cenotaph in London, of course, where the soldiers paraded on 11 November to commemorate the Great War; but you also thought of things more distant, ancient, mysterious and druidic – dolmens, menhirs, cromlechs. The centre of the crag was split open like a book, a right-angled vertical corner soaring upwards for, what? Hundreds of feet? More than one hundred, surely. It seemed to lean over, hang right over them as though it might suddenly release its hold on the mountainside and come crashing down right on to them. 'We're not going to climb *that*?'

He laughed when he saw where she was pointing. 'The corner? Not that.'

'Can it be climbed?'

'It hasn't been yet. I'd say it was impossible, wouldn't you? It seems to overhang, but in fact it is just plumb vertical. We've sniffed round it. Someone will probably make it go one day, I dare say. You'd need rubbers, though, and a feeling for suicide.'

He humped the rucksack on to his shoulders and led off up the hillside with Diana struggling along in his wake. They stumbled over scree. His boots were nailed and the nails scraped at the rocks as though trying to tear them. The path led them up towards the right, away from the terrible corner. They settled at the far end of the cliff where a buttress of rock stood proud of the main mass. 'That is where we will conduct our lessons,' he said, and there was something absurdly pedantic about his tone, as though he were a schoolmaster. He unpacked the rope and uncoiled it on to the ground. 'Flaked it out' was the term he used. The bottom end he had thrown out to one side so that he could tie her on. 'Do you know your knots?'

'Not really.' She laughed nervously at the pun. And, thank God, Guy laughed too. She thought of him as Guy although she hadn't dared use his Christian name – or any name at all, come to that. She wondered how she would address him, how he would *expect* to be addressed. Mr Matthewson? Was that right? He must be, what? Thirty, thirty-one? And she was a mere nineteen, and the difference was all the difference in the world.

'We'll use the bowline,' he said. He looped the rope over her like a lasso, and then came and stood close behind her, his arms round her front, his body not touching her, *carefully* not touching her. She was painfully conscious of his closeness there on the morning hillside with the ground unsteady beneath her feet and the rocks rising up in front of her and his arms round her, trapping her with the rope.

He made a loop. 'Remember the rabbit.'

'Rabbit?'

She felt the breath of laughter on her neck. 'You're a rabbit, aren't you? A tyro, a beginner. So' – he shook the end of the rope to show her – 'the rabbit comes up out of the hole, goes around the tree, and then goes back down the hole.' And, in his hands, the end of the rope did just that, went up through the loop, went round behind the rope, and then went back down into its hole. He pulled the knot tight against her belly, and there was a moment of contact, his hands against her stomach, his thighs against her backside. Then he pulled the knot to pieces and stepped back.

'Now you do it.'

They spent a few minutes practising. He showed her how to hold the rope while he was climbing and explained how he would tie on at the first ledge that he reached – 'belay' was the word he used – and then she would come up to him. And the calls he would use and she would use so that they would each know what the other was doing. 'That's it, really. I climb, belay at a suitable place, bring you up, and then you belay and I climb up to the next stance. All right?'

It was all right. It was perfectly all right. He gave a brief smile, turned to the rock and began to climb. She watched the way he moved, the careful placement of his feet, sometimes using the nails – blade-like things along the side of the soles – to bite on to a lip of rock. There was barely a scrape, never an uncertain move. 'You keep your hands as low as possible,' he called down, in his schoolmasterly manner. 'Use them for balance, not to pull yourself up. That's good technique, always in balance if you can. And always with three points in contact with the rock at any one time.'

'What if you slip?' she called up. She didn't want to use the word 'fall'. To say the word 'fall' would surely bring bad luck. Like mentioning *Macbeth* in the theatre. He looked down at her. 'Do you mean, if I *fall*? If I fall, I hit the ground just beside you. Unless you try to catch me.'

Her heart gave a small leap of anxiety. 'You'd die.'

'That's why the leader never falls. Of course, once we get further up the climb there's a chance that you might hold me on the rope. I'd fall past you, but if we were sufficiently high, the rope would come tight before I hit the ground.' There was laughter and irony in his tone. He seemed absurdly courageous up there on the steep ridge with nothing between him and certain death if he were to fall. And they called conchies cowards!

He had reached a ledge. 'I'll tie on here and bring you up,' he called. 'It's really not hard. You game?'

'Whenever you're ready.'

There was a moment's delay and then he called, 'Taking in!' and the rope began to snake up out of her hands, the rough fibre almost burning her as it ran. 'You can let it go!' he shouted. The rope came tight at her waist. 'That's me!' she cried, delighted to remember the call.

'Climb when you're ready.'

'Climbing!' She stepped up to the foot of the wall. Like a diver stepping to the edge of the diving board. No, that analogy didn't work at all. The victim of a firing squad stepping up to the post. That was more like it. There was something thick and obstructive in her throat, a pulsing of fear behind her breastbone. She began to move up, keeping her hands as low as she reasonably could. As she climbed, the rope crept magically upwards too, so that there was always a slight slack before her but the feeling that at any moment she could cry out, 'Tight!' and he would snatch the rope against her and she would be safe.

'You're doing fine.'

She glanced up and saw that he was grinning down at her – she'd not seen him smile like that before.

'A few more moves and you're there.' His voice was nearer now, and when she looked down there was space beneath her, fifty, sixty feet of air. As high as a house. 'My gosh!' she cried.

'Don't look down if you haven't a head for heights.'

She climbed up towards him with a small spurt of exultation somewhere inside her chest. 'It's breathtaking,' she said. It was, literally, so. Breathlessly she reached him, and he leant forward and put his arm around her waist to pull her up on to his narrow perch.

'Was that good?'

She assured him, with that absurd sense of elation, that, yes, it *was* good. It was, in fact, wonderful. 'Where do we go from here?'

'Straight up.'

They edged around each other on the small platform. There was that clumsy intimacy, like dancing with someone, when convention allows you a closeness of contact that under other circumstances would clearly be forbidden. His hands on her hips for a moment, her hands on his shoulders as she moved across him. He tied her on to the rock just as he had been tied, then paid out the rope so that his end was coming from the top – these little details were important, he explained; you had to get them right or you got into the most frightful mess – and then he showed her how to hold the rope round the back of her waist.

'Now, are you ready?'

'I'm ready,' she assured him, and felt a great thrill that in some small way he was going to be dependent on her for his security, that, in a sense, he would be in her hands.

'Climbing.'

She paid out the rope as he went. He climbed straight up above her head, moving quickly and surely, without any pause or any uncertainty, until he disappeared from sight. She looked out over the valley, down to the road where the bike was parked, across to the other side where there was a crag rather like theirs (she thought of it as *their* crag, although goodness knows she could hardly claim any kind of joint ownership). Two birds were circling around up there: ravens, maybe, or perhaps choughs. Above them the mountainside went on upwards to the rocky ridges of Crib Goch, along which she had clambered with Meg and the others only last summer. Little had she dreamt that within a year she would be climbing up the vertical rocks in this place with Guy Matthewson; or that Britain would be at war. Both thoughts gave her a shiver of fright.

His cry brought her up with a start: 'Taking in!' The rope began to move rapidly upwards until it came tight once again at her waist.

'That's me!' she cried, and her voice seemed absurdly high and feeble among this wilderness of grey rock. Had he heard? She began to undo the belay, thinking what a satisfactory nautical sound 'belay' had to it, as though they were doing something as serious as sailing, which perhaps they were, sailing and rock climbing having things in common – ropes and knots, of course, but also the application of strength and the use of balance, and those distant views of wilderness, here the mountains, there the wilderness of ocean.

She heard his call – 'Ready when you are!' – and she shook the rope so that he took it in a bit more. Then she cried, 'Climbing!' and set off after him, feeling rather solitary, although she knew by the steady intake of the rope that he was there, out of sight but not out of mind. There was something wonderful about this progression up the rock, the two of them linked by the strange intimacy of the rope, separated and yet united. Something organic, an umbilical cord. The thought made her blush. 'You're doing wonderfully,' he said, as she joined him at the next stance. 'Really wonderfully.'

It took only a few minutes to swap over the belays and for Guy to start up the next stretch. Pitch, she reminded herself. 'Pitch' was what it was called. 'This one's pretty straightforward,' he called. 'The sting's in the tail.'

He began to traverse out towards the left, out across the wall, and then upwards above her head. When she followed she discovered a vast space beneath her, the whole height of the cliff down to the distant scree slopes and the narrow snake of the road along the valley floor. 'We'll make a mountaineer of you yet,' he called down to her, and she grinned up at him with fright and fight, both those things deliciously blended into what she assumed was the total experience of rock climbing. They belayed at a narrow ledge and the next pitch went further up, so that they seemed to be flying now – and, indeed, that was the name of the route, wasn't it? Flying Buttress, Guy had said. Finally they came to a narrow ledge. The rock above was split by a gash, like a knife-cut still choked with bits of flesh. It was a gruesome, elemental wound, rising up and opening out so that at the top it was almost wide enough to admit a human body.

'Up there?'

'The chimney. That's the sting in the tail.'

On the ledge there was only room for two of them if they were prepared to be rather closer than might be proper on a first day's acquaintance. He helped her tie on to some stones that were jammed in the bottom of the gash. 'It's a thread belay. It'd hold a falling horse.'

She looked up where he had to go. 'You're not going to fall, are you?'

'I hope not.'

'Have you ever?'

He smiled at her and shook his head. 'But keep it quiet or you may tempt the Fates. Now, you watch me carefully and see how I do it.' He scrabbled up directly above her with his boot nails scraping on the rock until, awkwardly, he was inside the shallow chimney and thrutching upwards. 'Thrutch' was the word he had used. It was a fine, evocative word, with elements of clutch and thrust to it. Diana loved it, just as she loved the sight of Guy (she hadn't yet called him that, hadn't yet called him anything) actually doing it, grunting, shoving and pulling – *thrutching* – and suddenly clambering cleanly free on to the ledge above.

'Phew!' He wiped metaphoric sweat from his brow. 'Let's see how you manage it.'

And she managed it well, that was the wonderful thing. In a way, perhaps because she was smaller, she managed it better than he had. But there was a moment when things got awkward and she was just about to cry 'Tight!' as he had taught her, and then she found something to grab on the left wall and that got her past the difficulties and the rest was easy. When she reached the summit of their crag she found him sitting on the edge with the rope piled to one side of him. She came up to him with a broad smile – her first climb completed, for God's sake! – and sat down beside him and he put his arm round her shoulders and shook her gently. 'That's well done,' he said. 'Well done, indeed. You seconded that better than many an expert I've seen.'

'Thank you, Guy,' she replied, and hated it when he took his arm from round her shoulders and stood up to coil the rope, for it almost seemed that he was offended that she had addressed him by his Christian name.

They walked down the screes and back to the foot of the crag. 'I've got some lunch for the two of us,' he said.

'Oh, I never thought—'

'You're my guest. It wasn't for you to think about things like that.'

'But I invited myself.'

'No, you didn't. I could just as easily have said that I hadn't any time to spare for teaching a beginner, but I didn't. So I invited you, and I'll provide the picnic lunch.' He unwrapped a packet of sandwiches and handed her one.

'Ham!' she cried. 'How on earth did you get *ham*? Oh, this is unfair. You cannot do this.'

He grinned. 'I'm well known at the hotel.' There were also two bottles of India Pale Ale. 'You do drink beer, don't you? There are no glasses so you can't be very ladylike.'

'Are you making fun of me?' she asked sharply. She didn't know why she said it. Perhaps it was because she had suddenly thought how unsuitable this encounter was and wondered what her parents might think if they knew about it: their daughter out for the day on her own with a man of over thirty – and a conchie at that. Whatever the reason, she had said it, and he looked embarrassed. 'Of course not.'

'I'm sorry,' she said. 'I didn't mean to snap. I just . . . Oh, I don't know what I just.' And she felt every one of those years that stood between her age and his, the difference between being a girl and being a woman. She desperately wanted to be a woman so she would know what to say to him and how exactly to say it. She ate in silence. Maybe the whole day had been spoilt.

Below them a car ran down the road from the head of the pass, almost the only car they had seen. War was returning the mountains to their primeval desolation. As if to confirm that, an aircraft flew over, the drumbeat of its engines rising and falling, the sun flashing on its fuselage. 'A Flying Pencil!' she cried.

He looked round. 'What?'

'That aeroplane. A Flying Pencil, that's what they call them. A Dornier. Oh, my goodness, it's the first I've seen. A German.'

The aircraft disappeared southwards over Crib Goch and Snowdon. Where were the fighters, the Hurricanes and Spitfires? she wondered.

'How on earth do you know that?'

'What?'

'The name of that aeroplane.'

She smiled apologetically. 'I did a course with the Observer Corps. At home.'

'Where's home?'

'Chester. Near Chester, anyway. A little village. We had someone come round and give a lecture about how we could tell enemy aircraft and that sort of thing.' The attempt at conversation seemed to die away. He ate his ham sandwich and drank from his bottle of beer while she contemplated, with fear and something close to excitement, the question that she wanted to ask. Maybe fear and excitement were almost the same thing anyway: they certainly seemed to be when you were rock climbing, the fear of slipping, of falling, of swinging off the cliff on the end of the rope being inseparable from the excitement of moving in the vertical plane, using holds that you never imagined could support you, making moves that seemed absurd. She took a breath. 'Why are you a conscientious objector?' she asked.

There: it was out in the open now. For better or for worse.

Had he heard? He kept chewing, kept staring out over the green and grey valley, almost as though he hadn't. 'Because of the last time,' he said finally. 'The last war, the so-called war to end all wars. I grew up in that. I've thought about it a lot and I decided that it wasn't a war between two peoples. It was a war between the governing classes of two countries, between the politicians. Nothing's changed.'

'Except for Hitler and the Nazis.'

'They're just politicians. Nothing more. The German people have never been allowed their say, not under fair conditions.'

'They seem pretty enthusiastic about it all. If you listen to the news.'

He laughed humourlessly. 'But whose news do you listen to?'

'And if they invade? What then?'

He picked distractedly at a tuft of grass. Suddenly he no longer seemed the confident mountaineer, the man who could breach precipices by skill and courage. Rather, he seemed confused and anxious. 'I don't know what then. For God's sake, I don't have all the answers any more than anyone else. But I'll not fight. I don't believe in it and I won't do it. Wars will cease only when men stop fighting.' The speech seemed to have upset him. He turned away from her and looked up across the mountainside, towards the skyline of rocks.

'I respect you for it,' she said. 'Don't think I don't.'

He laughed. 'You don't have to be polite.'

'I'm not being polite. I mean what I say.'

'But you should say what you mean.'

'I do. That's the same thing, you know.'

He looked round at her. She saw that his look was something else, not just the look of polite amusement that it might have been. 'Not the same thing a bit,' he said.

A small bubble of laughter lodged somewhere behind her sternum. She waited expectantly for him to continue.

'Why,' he said, smiling, 'you might just as well say that "I see what I like" is the same thing as "I like what I see".'

It was as though they had exchanged passwords, recognized each other in the dark. She released the laughter, and blushed at the same time. 'But do you?' she asked.

'Do I what?' His gaze was very steady, as though he was examining her blush and trying to judge the reason for it.

'Do you like what you see?'

'Very much,' he said; and turned away again and began to clear up the scraps of litter from their lunch. 'Now, what do you want to do next? Are you game for another climb? I'd thought we might try the Spiral Stairs.'

'Fine,' she said. 'The Spiral Stairs sound fine.'

So they climbed the Spiral Stairs, which had originally, so Guy explained, been named Sodom, but someone in the Climbers' Club had objected so another title had had to be chosen. They laughed at that, at the idea of a stuffy old Blimp objecting to such a name; but it *was* rather rude, she thought, although she was uncertain exactly what it meant. The climb itself was at the left-hand end of the Columnar Cliffs. It started from the foot of that awful corner, the corner that had never been climbed but might be one day, and it went out leftwards on small holds, out over empty air. Guy called to her to be careful, for if she came off there she'd swing like a pendulum below him.

'Thanks for the warning,' she called back, sarcastically. She was beginning to get the measure of him.

'You've got a head for these things,' he shouted. 'You're okay.'

'You like what you see, is that it?' Somehow being there on the crag, with the wind blowing around them and the rough rock beneath her fingers, gave her the courage to say it.

'And I see what I like,' he called back.

They finished the climb up easy slabs to the top of the crag and, as though to greet their triumph, the sun broke through the cloud and illuminated the litter of scree and the crags of rock. They sat together in the sunshine for a while and she knew what she wanted him to do: it was what he had done when she had completed the first climb, put his arm round her. Just that would have been fine. Nothing more. But he didn't. He just sat there for a while, then stood up and said, 'Well, perhaps I should be getting you back to your friends.'

'Not especially,' she said. 'They'll be all right by themselves. I left them a note.'

'Still,' he said, and she thought that perhaps he wanted to get rid of her. It wasn't until they were down at the road and about to get on the bike that he asked whether she was interested in doing some more climbing, and she answered that, yes, of course she was.

'How long are you here?' he asked.

'Tomorrow and Sunday.'

He kicked the engine into life. 'Tomorrow, then?' he yelled, above the noise.

'Tomorrow's fine.'

He left her on the road and she walked up the drive to where the youth hostel lay in its small grove of trees. Her friends weren't there. They'd gone to the Carneddau, the whaleback mountains on the far side of the valley, and they didn't get back until the evening. 'Where were you?' they cried, when they tramped in and found her there waiting for them. 'What's all this "gone climbing"?'

'That's what I did: I went rock climbing.'

'*Rock* climbing?'

'With Guy Matthewson. And he's taking me again tomorrow.'

'*Is* he indeed?' said Meg.

They sat down to their meal, laughing and joking, eager to hear about the day's adventures. In retrospect, it was a poignant evening. Did they know it at the time? Perhaps they sensed it. Innocence had only a few more weeks to run. Already the boys had their call-up papers – one was already in uniform. Already the girls had volunteered for the WAAF or the WRNS or

130

something. The war was about to stir them up in its wanton manner, send two of them off to die, one of them to be captured, all of them to grow up and into a different world. But for the moment they sat round the supper table and talked and laughed as though the future didn't matter, while Diana regaled them with stories of minute holds and vertical precipices, and they laughed and joked and quizzed her about Mr Guy Matthewson. Was she hot on him?

'He's about fifteen years older than me, for goodness' sake,' she protested.

'And a conchie,' added Meg.

The barbed comment put Diana on the defensive. 'That's not the point, is it? He's hardly a coward, if he climbs like that. It's just what he believes.'

'So what *does* he believe?'

But she didn't really know.

'He's a Commie, isn't he?' Eric said. 'That's what I've heard.'

'I've no idea. I only met him yesterday and we spent most of today fifty feet apart on either end of a rope. We didn't get to discuss politics. You don't do that kind of thing on a rock climb.'

'But you must be able to say what he's *like*. Is he – for God's sake, let's stop beating about the bush – is he *good-looking*?' It was Meg asking, of course.

'He's . . . interesting. Rather austere.'

'God, that's a bit of a put-down.'

'Can I come with you tomorrow?'

'Go *with* her?' Hilda cried. 'Oh, for goodness' sake, Meg, you'd be a real *gooseberry!*'

The high-pitched and excited voices, the soon-to-date slang, the ceremony of innocence, soon to be drowned. Within two months Diana would be pulling the headless body of a woman from the rubble of a bombed house in Stepney. Within a few months Eric would be stumbling through the dark and smoke of a stricken Whitley bomber to grab his parachute pack and throw himself out into the Arctic night above the city of Duisberg. Within a year Martin would be posted missing in the North Atlantic; Hilda, would be killed by a V1 in 1944 in south London.

'I'm not sure that we should leave you alone with him, Miss Diana Sheridan,' Meg said with a wicked smile. 'How do we know he's not a rotter?'

Diana laughed at the absurdity of the warning.

10

The next day the cloud was low and there was drizzle in the air. Surely they wouldn't be able to climb. Most of the others set off up the north ridge of Tryfan, but Meg decided to stay behind. She didn't feel all that good. Perhaps it was something she had eaten – that bully-beef, maybe.

'Oh, Meg, don't be such a spoilsport!' Hilda had cried, but Meg could not be persuaded.

'I'll be able to check out this man of Diana's,' she said. 'We don't want her falling into the wrong hands, do we?'

So the two of them stood together at the roadside huddled into their anoraks, waiting for Guy Matthewson. He might not even come, Diana decided. She was surprised, and a little annoyed, to discover how disappointed she was at the thought; she was also surprised, and a little afraid, to discover how angry she was that Meg was standing there beside her.

But he did come. Of course he did. First there was his bike far in the distance and then the sound of it tearing through the fabric of the cold, damp morning. She was amazed that she could ever have doubted him. 'Good morning, Miss Sheridan,' he shouted, above the engine noise, as he drew up beside the two girls.

'Good morning, Mr Matthewson,' she replied formally. Bantering. *Arch*, her mother would have said.

He pushed his goggles up on to his forehead. They had made red marks round his eyes. 'And who's your friend? Will you introduce me?'

'Margaret York,' Meg said quickly. 'Pleased to meet you.'

'Margaret York? It sounds like someone out of the Wars of the Roses.' He grinned as they shook hands, and Diana felt a small, treacherous throb of jealousy, as though that smile and the shaking of hands implied some sort of complicity between the two of them. 'What are we planning to do?' she asked.

'Is your friend coming with us?'

'Meg's not well,' Diana said quickly. 'The others have gone on but Meg wasn't feeling up to it.'

'I'm not that bad—'

He looked disappointed. 'But it'd be a bit tricky with a rope of three,' he said. 'The weather's not up to much and I was planning a pretty long route. Maybe some other time?' He smiled. It was quite disarming, his smile.

Meg had no option but to smile back. 'Maybe,' she agreed.

Guy looked at Diana. 'So, is Miss Sheridan ready?'

Yes, she was ready. She climbed on behind him and grabbed his rucksack just as she had done the day before. The sensation of jealousy dissolved. She felt almost sorry for Meg standing there alone in the mean morning. 'See you later,' she called, and Meg waved a hand and tried a smile and shouted back, 'Bye-bye darling. Be good.'

'Hold tight!' Guy called, and they accelerated away along the lakeside. The steep rocks of Tryfan's north ridge drew nearer. The others were somewhere up there, stumping towards the top. Perhaps they'd catch sight of them. 'I thought we'd stick nearer to home this time,' he shouted, and drew the bike to a halt just where the rocks of Tryfan reached the valley floor, where there was a milestone at the roadside marking the tenth mile. Ten miles from where? She looked up the steep slopes of the mountain, where the ridge rose up towards the clouds. Her eyes followed the skyline, then moved down through the rakes of grass and heather and the litter of scree. There was a line of tiny figures trudging up among the boulders, like soldiers setting off to the front. 'There they are!' she cried, pointing. She counted six. Two of them paused and looked round. She waved, and one of them – was it Hilda? – waved back.

'I hope your friends know what they're doing up there in the mist,' Guy said.

'They've done a lot of walking.'

'Margaret's a pretty girl,' he said, apropos of nothing.

'That's what everyone says.'

'Is it? I'm sorry to seem just one of the pack.'

What did he mean by that? They climbed over the drystone wall that bordered the road and set off up the beaten path towards the rocks. Guy climbed quickly, with a long, easy gait. He had climbed in the Alps, climbed in the Himalayas, been up to twenty-six thousand feet. Beside that the Welsh mountains must be mere hills. Diana was thrilled to be in his presence, let alone actually to be setting out on a climb with him, *another* climb. He was almost – she hardly dared express the thought to herself – a friend. And Meg was back at the youth hostel.

The path steepened and began to thread its way upwards through the rocks, round to the east side of the mountain where the major climbs were. He looked at her as she scrambled after him. His expression suggested that her opinion might mean something. 'I thought we might give Grooved Arête a try. It's on the east face and it'll take us right up to the summit. What do you think?'

'You're the leader.'

'It's a real mountaineering route, that's the thing. We couldn't have managed it safely with a rope of three, and certainly not with a total novice like your friend Meg. Are you up to it? There's a good breeze, which should keep it dry, and I don't think the weather's going to get any worse. I say we give it a go. Grooved Arête is tricky in the damp but not desperate. Except for the slab.'

'What slab?' she asked anxiously.

He smiled. He was teasing her and she knew it: delighted in it, in fact. He had changed from the day before: she felt that he had allowed her through his outer defences into some kind of familiarity. 'Ah,' he said, 'the slab.'

'What slab?' The slab became the great threat as they clambered up through the chaos of rocks that formed the lower part of the mountain; a threat and a joke, like something she had both laughed and trembled at when she was a child, a ghoul or a ghost in a story or something. They gained height, over great boulders that were jumbled together as though thrown down in a heap by a petulant child. There were short steps to climb, and he watched her with attention at these points, almost as though he were an examiner and she some kind of student. 'You're doing all right,' he said. 'You've a good sense of balance.'

'I insist you tell me about the slab,' she said, as she caught up with him. They had reached an angled terrace that ran along under the base of the main cliffs. Guy had halted where someone had scratched the letters GA on the rock. The cliff rose directly upwards from here, like the wall of a Gothic cathedral, fluted and ribbed. You expected gargoyles and groins and Quasimodo skulking around the misty heights above. 'If you don't tell me, I won't do it.'

He laughed, as though he understood that it was an empty threat. 'It's called the Knight's Move.'

'That sounds like something from *Alice*.'

He agreed. 'It's a very *Looking-Glass* business, climbing. You climb up in order to go back down, and very often you have to run as fast as you can merely to stay in the same place. You'll see soon enough. The slab is a sort of angled checkerboard, if you've got a bit of imagination. And to climb it you move up a bit and then sideways, just like the White Knight.'

'And you fall off?'

He laughed again. He was so different today, so relaxed and familiar. 'Occasionally. Unlike the White Knight, *very* occasionally, we hope.'

Diana peered upwards. 'I can't see any slab,' she said. 'Where is it?'

'Oh, the slab's a long way up. You can't see it from here.' He took the rope from her and paid it out on to the ground – what was the term he had used? *Flaked*. Another of those nautical expressions. He flaked out the rope and handed her the bottom end to tie on. 'You remember everything from yesterday?'

'I hope so.' And she *did* remember, the rabbit coming up through the hole and going around the tree and disappearing back down, and it was absurdly gratifying to be congratulated on getting such a small thing right.

'Now, are you ready?' She was. He nodded approvingly, turned to the rock and began to climb, and, watching him make his careful way up in his tattered flannel trousers and patched jacket, Diana thought what a wonderful thing it was to have discovered him, as wonderful as the discovery of climbing itself. After a while he settled on a ledge and called her up, and the thrill of yesterday repeated itself as she climbed towards him – a sensation of detachment, a release from things, from this bloody war that was swirling all around her and pulling herself and her friends and the whole world into it: a rendering of all the complexities of life down to this simple problem of progression upwards into the unknown.

'How's it going?' he called.

'Wonderful,' she shouted back. A *transport*, she thought: that strange, utilitarian word that applied to other things than getting from A to B; something that lifted you out of yourself, carried you into a world of delight. Surprised by joy, she felt. The words ran through her mind as she climbed. 'Surprised by joy – impatient as the wind, I turned to share the transport . . .'

She found him waiting for her, up there among the drifts of vapour. Far below them in Cwm Tryfan there were sheep grazing, like lice against the worn fabric of the hillside. This was a real mountain, not an outcrop like the day before. A real mountain, and they mere parasites on the great, grey body of it.

'How did you find it?' he asked.

'Wonderful,' she repeated. 'Just wonderful.'

They went on up, another pitch or two, Guy going first, tying on and bringing her up after him on the end of the rope, the whole progress like the movement of a strangely articulated animal, a worm, perhaps, or a leech. Hours were telescoped into minutes. There was a dirty blanket of cloud beneath their feet now. Occasionally the wind tore a ragged hole in the pall and allowed a glimpse down on to the scree slopes below the mountain. Otherwise they were alone on the cliff with only the rope between them as they climbed.

'How far up are we?' she asked, at one stance, and he paused and thought, as though calculating it all. 'About four hundred feet, I'd say.'

'And the slab?'

'Just up ahead there. The next pitch.' He went on up and as he climbed the words came back, a sonnet she had learnt for her Higher School Certificate, when she had intentions to go on to university, intentions that the war had cast aside:

> Surprised by joy – impatient as the wind
> I turned to share the transport – Oh! with whom
> But thee?

Wordsworth, wasn't it? What was the rhyme for *whom*?

'Taking in!' he shouted down.

She let go the rope and watched it snake upwards until it snatched tight against her waist. She called up, 'That's me!' just as she had been taught; and as she climbed up to him the memory returned:

> . . . With whom
> But thee, deep buried in the silent tomb . . .

Wordsworth writing about his dead daughter. The words brought a sudden chill, so that she was relieved to reach Guy once again, sitting on an ample grass ledge, pulling in the rope as she came up to him, and grinning. 'This,' he announced, as he tied her on, 'is your slab.'

She looked up. There was a short wall and then a stretch of canted rock, like a piece of old and battered boiler-plate, slanting up to an evil-looking roof, a real overhang, as black and menacing as a frown. It was as though they had reached the eaves of the cathedral, with the gargoyles seen close to, and the leads slick with rain, and no way out.

'But where do we *go*, for heaven's sake?'

'Oh, up and rightwards,' he said airily. 'That's your knight's move: up and across the slab and out round at the top. It's quite exposed.'

'I don't think I want to be exposed.'

He laughed. 'Nothing to put your honour at risk.'

How long had they been going? Her watch told her almost four hours; it felt like a few minutes. The ledge was comfortable enough, but beyond its edge the cliffs plunged downwards and all she could see were the lower slopes bellying out hundreds of feet below. And above, that horrid black roof blocking their way. For the first time she felt uneasy. 'I'm frightened, Guy,' she said.

'No, you're not, not really,' he said, as though he knew her feelings better than she. 'Climbing is a matter of mood. If the sun were shining now we'd be all sweetness and light. As it is, we feel as though we are standing at the portals to Hades. But there's really nothing to worry about. The slab's thinnish, but it'll go with a bit of care. You'll love it, and the next pitch. Are you ready?'

'Might you fall?'

'My goodness, *of course* I might fall. And I'd probably hit the ledge with a most frightful thump and you'd have to pull me back on board. Think you can do that?'

'You're teasing.'

'I hope so.' He stood, and waited for her to take the rope round her back as she had been taught. 'My life is in your hands,' he said, as he pulled himself up a crack directly above her, and although he had said it in the tone of a joke she suddenly understood that it was so: if only for a few moments, this man had committed his life to her care. Should he fall it would be she who had to stop him bowling over the edge of their platform and going down the cliff, maybe to his death. She felt a surge of affection for him.

He paused at a large rock bollard and looked down on her. The slab lay to his right, tilted slightly, criss-crossed with veins and cracks, twenty-five, thirty feet across. From where Diana stood there was nothing beyond it: a space, a void, the cloudy air. 'Straightforward up to here,' he said. 'From here you can get a good look at the crux before you commit yourself. Climbing's brain as well as brawn.' Cautiously, he moved upwards and across on to the sloping rock. 'Give me a bit more rope,' he called. 'Don't want to pull me off, do you?' He didn't look down as he spoke. It was almost as though his words were an afterthought, of no real consequence. She paid out a few feet, and thought of him slipping, thought of the sudden slither of feet and a dreadful plummet through the air and the rope coming tight around her waist, almost cutting her in two, pulling her against her anchor and almost tearing her from the cliff.

He moved on, two, three moves. She paid out more rope. There was a moment when he paused, and a moment when a foot seemed to slip downwards at the same speed as he moved up so the sum total was no movement at all; and then he'd found a side pull and a couple more footholds and he was well above her now and seemed to have a good handhold so that when his feet slid a second time he could steady himself. She could hear him grunt with the effort.

'How is it?' she called nervously. He didn't reply, but made another couple of moves and was suddenly on the very lip of the slab, over on the right, and he could turn back and look down on her.

'Oh, it's pretty,' he called.

'What is?'

'You are.'

'I'm not interested in silly compliments at a moment like this.'

That mocking laugh. 'The slab, then. Pretty greasy. Remember what I told you earlier: the important thing is not to lean into the rock. You'll want to, you'll want to hug it to you for comfort, but you mustn't. If you lean in, all you do is push your feet out. And that's not what's needed because it'll push them off the holds. I'll just be round the corner here, but very safe, so don't worry if you slip. And I'll be able to hear everything you say . . .'

She felt a sudden spurt of panic, standing there below the slab, with him at the top and nothing between them but the thin line of the rope. 'You mean I won't be able to *see* you?'

'You'll be all right. You saw the way I went. Just follow my line.'

'But I won't see you.'

'It's all right, Diana, you don't need to see me. You have your own instincts to follow.' And with that he had disappeared round the corner and a moment later was calling to her that he was tied on and the rope was hissing through her hands and up the slab. She scrabbled to undo her anchor as the rope came tight. 'That's me!' she called.

'Okay!' He sounded distant, detached, like someone going far away for a long time. 'Climb when you're ready.'

She began. She clambered up easily enough at first, then paused at the bollard and surveyed the next passage. The rope ran diagonally away from her towards the far corner where Guy had vanished. Surely this was the hardest thing she had done, and yet, so he said, it was not hard. This was merely Very

Difficult; but not 'hard'. Hard was Severe, or even – whisper it – Very Severe; and she certainly wasn't ready for anything like that yet.

'How are you doing?' he called.

Up to now there had been holds to grab and steps where you could place your foot, or at least part of your foot: hand and foot, you felt that you were secure. And now there was this stretch of cracked and lined rock without any of those things, just ripples and unevenness, and a thin slick of grease on them. 'I'm looking.'

'You don't climb by looking. Give it a go.'

She felt a small start of anger. 'Don't rush me!'

'I'm not. You just take your time.'

She moved. Her heart was in her mouth. Never had she felt the meaning of the expression so vividly. If not her heart, then something else organic: something thick and pulsating up there in her throat trying to force its way into her mouth.

His voice came from beyond the edge: 'Remember, don't lean into the rock. Stay in balance on your feet.'

'I don't need bloody instructions!' she shouted, and heard his distant, infuriating laughter in reply. 'Damn him,' she muttered. There were finger holds. Her fingers hurt on them, taking her weight, taking the load off her feet, which were clumsy and heavy and would surely slip. Don't lean inwards, she thought; whatever you do, *don't lean inwards*. She glanced down to check her footholds and, as she looked, the clouds opened up and there was air below her, hundreds of feet of cool damp air. She knew both fear and elation, those two sensations that were the Janus faces of climbing. She pulled on her fingers and stepped up, reached out her right boot on to a sloping ledge and eased her weight across on to it. The rope shifted until it was almost tight again, not pulling her, but there like a ready hand. Except that it went up and across in a diagonal and she felt that if something came unstuck, if one of her feet slipped on this greasy slope, she would swing like a pendulum across the slab and disappear round the edge.

'You're doing well,' his voice called.

'You don't know how I'm damn well doing,' she shouted back. 'You can't even *see* me.'

'But I can *feel* you. It's like playing a fish.' The line gave a little twitch so that it tugged gently at her waist. 'You see?'

'Let me be.'

'Like a fish. A whiting. "Will you walk a little faster, said the whiting to the snail—"?'

'For God's sake, shut up!'

He shut up. She stepped up and across again and discovered the same side pull that he had used, and went on without a skid, with the rope just moving up in front of her, with the edge of the slab coming nearer and the angle easing off slightly so that suddenly she no longer felt uneasy but instead confident and relaxed. And as though it were an echo of her mood, the sun shone through a break in the cloud, threw bright light on to the grey rock and kissed the back of her neck with a moment's fleeting warmth.

'"There's a porpoise close behind me,"' he called out, nearer to hand now, '"and it's treading on my tail."'

She reached the edge and there he was around the corner taking in the rope as she moved on to his exiguous ledge. He was smiling at her as though he were as proud of her as she was of herself. 'And here's my little porpoise,' he said. She came right up to where he was belayed and he reached out his right hand and brushed the damp hair from her eyes and there was a moment of startling intimacy. 'Did I make you cross?'

144

'A bit. I'm sorry I swore.'

'You're a marvel.'

'Was it all right?'

'You were wonderful.' They stood on that tiny sloping ledge, stood looking at one another. It was one of those difficult moments when you are afraid to be the first to move your eyes, like playing a childhood game but playing it seriously, playing it as though it really mattered. His eyes, she noticed, were an indeterminate green-brown colour, paler towards the pupils.

It was he who glanced away first. 'You haven't noticed the view.'

It was only then that she looked round. The cloud base had lifted to discover a great ocean of space below their tiny perch. The glimpse of sunshine had left them and gone chasing across the far hills. She watched it go, picking out a slope of grass, a brown patch of heather, a grey outcrop of rock, lighting on things as though by intention, as though to show her what was of interest. The wind battered at her ears. Everything was below, the whole world was below. 'Wonderful,' she said. 'Language doesn't do it justice.'

'Then don't say anything.'

So they stood there together in silence, and it was natural that his arm was round her shoulders as it had been the day before when she had reached the top of the first climb. What was that called? Flying Buttress. A mere scramble compared with this. And his arm had been round her then.

They reached the top by three o'clock. By that time the cloud had come down again and the day was suddenly dark. They clambered up on to the twin blocks – Adam and Eve – that marked the summit of the mountain and ate their sandwiches sheltering in the lee of them, but when they set off down the

North Ridge back to the valley their luck deserted them and the rain came down, real rain, hard and cold. Guy pulled a waterproof cape out of his rucksack. 'Will this help?'

'But that's yours.'

'And I'm offering it to you.'

'We'll share it.'

So they did, and the thing was ridiculous, really, for neither of them kept dry and it was almost impossible to descend over the rocky ground together with the cape like a tent over the two of them, and by the time they reached the motorbike they were both soaking wet, shivering with cold and laughter.

'What Miss Sheridan needs is a hot bath and a decent afternoon tea,' he said.

'But she's unlikely to get either.'

'Then pick up a change of clothes at the hostel and I'll take you to the hotel, where you most certainly can get both.'

'Oh, I couldn't.'

He wiped the saddle of the bike and climbed astride it. 'Why on earth not? Hop on.'

Why on earth not? It was difficult to formulate an answer, really. There were many reasons, but they all seemed paltry as she thought of them. He kicked the engine into life and manoeuvred round to face down the valley towards the youth hostel. 'Well, what's keeping you?'

So she climbed on behind him and the racket of the engine drowned any answer she might have had.

The hostel was deserted, the rooms silent and cool. She breathed a sigh of relief. Thank God Meg wasn't there. Even the warden seemed to have gone somewhere. She went to the dormitory to fetch some dry clothes, then scribbled a note and pinned it to the board by the desk: 'Meg. Climbed our mountain and safely down. Be back later. Diana.'

Guy was waiting on the gravel outside, the engine of the bike idling. She ran across, swung her leg over the pillion seat and settled into the familiar position behind him. Gravel skittered out from under the wheel and they roared away up to the road. The deed, if it was a deed, was done. *Fait accompli.* Which she had long thought to be something to do with *fate* until she had looked it up in the dictionary.

Tea in the lounge of the Royal Hotel, Capel Curig, looking down the twin lakes of the Dyffryn valley towards the pall of cloud that covered the mountains. She had had a bath just down the corridor from his bedroom, and changed into dry clothes, and now they sat in wicker chairs, facing the view. There were other guests. One or two were in uniform but most were people who had moved out of the suburbs of Manchester or Liverpool in order to avoid the bombing that everyone expected. Conversation was subdued, as though they were all shocked by the enforced move, by the whole damned inconvenient war. The tinkle of teacups provided a percussion accompaniment to tales of reduced services and unobtainable foods.

'What do you do?' she asked him. She knew nothing much about him at all, although they had shared two days together. Shared and not shared: separated often by a hundred feet of rope, sometimes out of sight of one another, sometimes as close together on a stance as though they were dancing.

He looked awkward. 'There's a family business,' he said. 'Shoes. Not very glamorous, I'm afraid.'

'What, the shoes?'

'No, you goose. Having a factory.'

She laughed. It was so easy to laugh. 'At least it's useful. And they'll want lots of shoes now, won't they? Boots.'

He shrugged. 'That's a problem, isn't it? Should the family firm contribute to the war effort if one of the directors refuses?'

She'd quite forgotten about his being a conscientious objector. 'Will you resign?'

'I don't know. I don't know what I'll do. My main concern is the tribunal, though.'

'When's that?'

'This autumn. The date is not decided. Perhaps I'll volunteer for something – the fire service, maybe. Perhaps they can use my skills.' He looked at her. 'And you?'

'I'm a nurse. Only an auxiliary, but it's better than nothing. There'll be a need for nurses one way or another. I was going up to university, Liverpool University, to read English. But—'

'You could still do that.'

'Not with the war on, I couldn't. So I trained as a nurse. I'm going to London next week. I'll be working in Clerkenwell.'

He nodded. She felt awkward. Perhaps she should be away from here, back in the hostel down the valley with her friends. 'Will you have more tea?' he asked, and the question seemed to her absurdly important, laden with significance quite beyond any matter of thirst, as though 'No' meant leaving immediately and going back to the hostel and 'Yes' meant staying; as though 'No' meant never seeing him again and 'Yes' meant the opposite, whatever the opposite might be. 'Yes, please,' she said.

He leant forward. As he lifted the pot one of the other guests, a tweed-jacketed, grey-haired gentleman, came over. 'Excuse my disturbing you,' he said, 'but aren't you Guy Matthewson?'

Guy half rose from his chair. 'That's right.'

'Struthwick. I was on the 'twenty-eight Everest expedition.'

'Of course.' Guy carefully replaced the pot and shook the man's hand. 'This is a friend of mine. Miss Sheridan. Diana Sheridan.'

Struthwick raised his eyebrows. 'Not the actress?'

She blushed. 'I'm afraid not. She's Dinah. It's quite close, though, isn't it?'

'Just as charming,' the man said, bowing towards her and taking her hand. He turned back to Guy. 'Gather you were planning to go to Everest yourself when this nonsense all blew up.'

'There was talk. With Shipton.'

'D'you know the German expedition to Nanga Parbat got trapped by the outbreak? Did you hear about that? The whole lot of them interned in India.' The two men laughed at the absurdity of it all, and talked of mountains for a while. 'Be a while before anyone can get back to the Himalaya,' the man said regretfully. 'I hear you've registered as a CO.'

Guy seemed to brace himself. She saw the flesh tighten round his mouth, the skin go white. 'As a matter of fact I have.'

Struthwick grunted. 'Can't be through lack of guts, can it? Not in your case.'

'It's a matter of conviction.'

The man didn't look persuaded. 'I fought in the Great War. Don't imagine you did. Can't say I found it a very edifying experience. But still, there's a matter of duty, isn't there? Duty to one's countrymen, I mean, not to the bloody politicians.'

'Perhaps we see our duty in different ways.'

'Perhaps.' Struthwick nodded towards Diana. 'Well, I must leave you to your tête-à-tête. Delighted, I'm sure.'

The man moved back to his table and Guy relaxed. It was as though he had been holding his breath throughout the encounter and now he could breathe. His voice was low and angry. 'You know what's happened, don't you? You know what this bloody war's done? It's made me frightened of people, that's what.'

There was an awkward silence. An intense discussion was going on at Struthwick's table. Voices were lowered, eyes darted across to where Guy Matthewson and Diana sat.

'You've no reason,' she said softly, 'no reason to be frightened.'

He reached out to where her hand lay on the arm of her chair. 'I'm sorry, Diana. That was an unforgivable outburst.' Slowly, lest his be frightened away, she turned her own hand over so that, for a blessed moment, they were actually holding hands, there in the lounge of the Royal Hotel in Capel Curig as the rain dashed against the windows like a handful of hurled pebbles. 'Understandable,' she replied, 'not unforgivable.'

'The thing is, everyone I know seems to have joined up or been called up. And I'm out on my own with this personal war to fight. I feel so much alone.'

'Is there no one else?'

He contemplated the view through the windows, saying nothing.

'Shouldn't I have asked that?'

He released her hand and leant forward to take up his cup and sip from it. With care he replaced it on the tray. 'There *was* someone else. There was my wife.'

She felt a jolt of emotion. It was like a slip while climbing, a sudden spasm of fear. 'Do you want to tell me about her?'

He smiled. 'In America I could plead the Fifth Amendment.'

'What's that?'

'It gives you the right not to testify against yourself.'

'Then say nothing.'

'Would you be happy with that?'

'What does *my* happiness have to do with it?'

He laughed faintly. 'That's what I'm trying to work out.' Then, as though he had come to a decision, he reached out and took her hand again. 'She was called Greta. We'd been married five years.'

Diana waited. He was under more strain than ever he was when climbing, under more strain even than when talking to that Struthwick fellow. She could see that. She could read the patterns in his face, the minute tensions, the whiteness at the wings of his nose, the tightness at the corners of his mouth.

'And after those five years she left me,' he said flatly. 'And took our daughter with her. Charlotte. Lotty, we called her. She took Lotty with her.' He reached into his jacket and took out a leather wallet. 'I have a photograph, if you'd like to see.'

'Of course.'

He passed across a crumpled snapshot. From within its deckle-edged frame a little girl smiled for the camera: pale hair, gap-toothed, four, maybe five years old.

'She's lovely.'

'It's immaterial whether she's lovely or not. She's my daughter.'

She flinched. 'But she's lovely just the same,' she insisted.

He closed his eyes. 'I apologize, Diana. I'm sorry.'

'It doesn't matter, really it doesn't.'

'Oh, but it does.'

She felt emboldened by his apology. 'When did all this happen?'

'Oh, 'thirty-eight, I suppose. Can you put a date on that kind of thing? She left me in 'thirty-eight. We seemed happy enough during those five years, you might say intensely happy at times. Of course she didn't like me going off to climb, but does that explain how she could just leave? Perhaps she really just didn't *like* me. Who knows? Who knows but her, I mean.'

'She never said? She never told you, talked to you, explained?'

'No. She just went. One day she was there, and the next day the house was empty, just a letter waiting for me when I got home.'

'How terrible.'

He looked at her, his face drawn and somehow suddenly old. 'Terrible, yes.'

'Did she love anyone else?' How did she dare ask such a question? And yet she felt a curious sense of power over the man, power without responsibility, which seemed to her a dangerous combination.

'Other than herself?'

'And Lotty, presumably.'

He smiled. 'I think perhaps she had a lover. But I don't know for certain.'

'And you?'

Guy shook his head, looking away from her and out of the window. The clouds seemed to be breaking up after the last rain. There was a hint of pale sky in the west. Perhaps the weather was improving. 'I was never unfaithful to her,' he said, with quiet emphasis. 'Never.'

'I'm sorry. I shouldn't expect you to talk of these things with me.'

He ignored her. 'I haven't heard anything of her for more than a year. She used to send the occasional letter telling me about Lotty.'

'An occasional *letter*?' Diana was appalled, outraged. 'Why don't you *see* her? She's your daughter, your own daughter, for God's sake! Don't you have every right to see her?'

He laughed. Whether he was laughing at himself or at her wasn't clear. But he laughed, and the sound was loud among the subdued conversation of the hotel lounge so that guests looked round in disapproval. 'Because Greta's in Germany, Diana. Didn't you realize? From her name, I mean. She's German. My daughter is now German, a child of the Third Reich. They live somewhere near Frankfurt.' He shrugged. 'Perhaps everything should be in the past tense: *was*, *lived*. God alone knows where they are now.'

'I'm sorry,' she whispered.

'You've got nothing to apologize about. Nothing at all.'

'I'm just . . .' She hesitated, blushing, feeling like a foolish child in the face of this adult disaster. Whatever she was about to say, she changed her mind. 'Do you love her still?' she asked instead, and she didn't really know what the question meant. She didn't really understand what love was, wasn't even sure whether it was a unitary thing that you could have and diagnose, like measles or the flu, or whether it was a whole complex of things, one of those syndromes, that ate into your body and left you helpless.

He shrugged aside her question. 'So, what do you think of me now? How does the noble Guy Matthewson add up? I've certainly given you a motive for my being a conchie, haven't I?'

'I'm not adding you up, Guy.'

'No?'

'No.' Her eyes stung. It was ridiculous. They stung with tears.

Then he asked unexpectedly, 'Would you be happy to keep in touch once we go away from here? Maybe we could exchange letters.'

'Of course.'

'Thank you. That'd be good. We can share quotations from *Alice in Wonderland* or something.'

'Maybe there'll be a bit more to write about.'

He nodded. 'Maybe.' He leant forward and busied himself

with the tea things, though the tea itself was cold and the cakes, such as they were, had long been abandoned. 'You wouldn't,' he said, 'like to have dinner with me this evening, would you?'

'I don't really—'

'Of course not.' He looked up with a quick smile. 'It doesn't matter. You want to be with your friends.'

'I don't have anything to wear. That's what I was going to say. I've only got these things.'

'Well, that doesn't matter at all.'

'Then I'd love to.'

'Perhaps . . .' He poured some tea. She noticed that his hand was unsteady. 'Perhaps you would like to keep me company—'

'Company?'

'Here at the hotel. If we're dining together. I thought perhaps you might book in. If they have a room free . . .'

'But—'

'You would be my guest, of course. It might seem a bit irregular, but—'

'Yes,' she said.

'I'm sorry. It was foolish of me to ask . . .'

She turned away from him. 'I said yes.'

'It's just that I feel rather lonely, these days,' he was saying, 'and with your going to London and my tribunal and things. However much I wish it, it might be difficult to keep contact and I thought we might spend this time together . . .'

'Yes,' she said again, quietly, looking not at him but out through the windows up the valley. The sky was clearing. Behind the outline of the mountains the sun was setting amid a battlefield of broken cloud, the whole scene red and black and grey, like a vision of war, a bombed city, the gaunt ruins silhouetted against flame. 'Yes,' she repeated. 'If you can run me back to the hostel, I can get my things. Perhaps it would be easier if we did it immediately, before my friends get in. It'd be easier if I didn't have to explain.'

'Yes. Yes, certainly.'

But they were there, of course. As she came in at the front door of the hostel she heard their voices in the dining room. She paused and listened. Hilda's voice was raised in some kind of criticism of Eric. His navigation: she was accusing him of having got them lost on the summit plateau and there was laughter and denial, and someone else was leaping to his defence. Diana crept past and went up the stairs. She thought she heard someone call out, but no one came to look. It was a matter of moments to gather up her few things and stuff them into her rucksack. Guy had assured her that they wouldn't turn a hair at the hotel, not at someone coming in with boots and rucksack and little else other than sweaters and things. They were used to climbers and walkers, had been for over half a century.

She paused to listen. The sound of voices still came up from the room below; but when she crept back down the stairs with her rucksack over one shoulder there was Meg standing in the hallway waiting for her. She had her hands on her hips, almost as though she was looking for an argument. 'Di, it *was* you. We thought we heard a bike. Where the devil are you going? I read your little *billet doux*, but . . .'

Diana shrugged. She knew she was blushing. 'I'm taking a room at a hotel in the village.'

'A *hotel*? What's wrong? Isn't the hostel luxurious enough?' And then understanding dawned in Meg's expression. 'It's your new friend Mr Matthewson, isn't it?'

'I'm having dinner with him.'

'Di, are you about to do something very silly?'

'I'm taking a room by myself, if that's what you're asking. A single room. I'm not selling either my body or my soul. It just seemed the most convenient thing to do, given that it will be pitch dark and with the blackout he couldn't possibly . . .'

'Oh, *Di*.' Sorrow and disappointment were carefully blended in Meg's expression.

Diana felt a glimmer of anger. 'Look, Meg. You can say what you like, think what you like, do what you like. But I'm nineteen years old and next week I'm going to London and God alone knows what is going to happen to me, or to you, or to him, if it comes to that. So I'm going to do this thing now because he has asked me to be his guest and that's that.'

'What a very dramatic little speech, darling. Have you been rehearsing it very hard?'

'Oh, for God's sake!' She tried to push past, but Meg held her arm.

'Diana, this might be very silly.'

'Meg, darling, please let me go.'

Meg released her hold and followed her out to the car park. Guy was there, astride the bike. Meg gave him a long, cool look; she was good at long, cool looks. 'Di has been most unfair keeping you entirely to herself.'

He looked embarrassed. 'She's a promising climber.'

'No doubt she's having expert tuition.'

There was a pause, one of those loaded silences, while people looked and measured and considered. Like playing bridge. Meg was good at bridge. She was good at most things. 'Well,' she said, 'remember that her friends are here.' She turned and went back inside.

Guy breathed out sharply, as though he had been holding his breath. 'She's very protective of you.'

'No, she's not. She's just jealous. Or envious. I'm not sure which.'

He laughed as he kicked the starter. The bike roared into life. It was a familiar sound now, and strangely comforting. 'Hop on.' The headlight threw a thin and inadequate slice of light on to the road ahead. 'Bloody blackout,' he shouted, as they moved off down the road. 'Bloody blackout, bloody war, bloody everything. Everything but you.'

11

Her room was a small, bare place up in the attic of the hotel. The ceiling sloped, the floor creaked, the window was difficult to open. Perhaps the room had been used by one of the maids and was only let to guests when no others were available. There was a single bed against one wall, a bedside table with a lamp shaped like the Eiffel Tower, a wardrobe with one door jammed shut, and a chest of drawers with a mirror so that it could double as a dressing-table. In one corner was a wooden washstand with a china bowl on the top shelf and a large jug of cold water below. She had never been in a hotel room before but if this was typical then she saw little difference from the boarding-houses where she had stayed when on holiday with her parents. There was that same sense of impermanence and indifference. On one wall hung an engraving of a fearsome mountain – Snowdon, it said. There were sheep in the picture, but no climbers.

As she turned from the picture she caught sight of herself in the mirror, almost as one might catch sight of an acquaintance in the street. 'Diana Sheridan, what on earth are you *doing* here?' she asked her reflection. The face in the mirror gave a little grimace but offered no reply. It didn't really have a reply, that was the truth of the matter. She was here on a whim. Nothing more, but that was plenty. Never before had caprice so ruled her life. Perhaps war, or the threat of war, did that to you. What on earth would her parents think about this? Would they ever know? Anxiety as a counterpoise to anticipation. Anxiety is to fear as anticipation is to excitement. Had someone said that? Perhaps it was original. Was it clever? she wondered.

She unpacked her paltry things, laying out her only skirt on the bed, and above it the blouse she had been saving to wear on the journey home. They'd have to do. She picked up the blouse and held it against her to see how it looked. It was pale blue and had a pleasing frill down the front, and it suited her, she thought. Among the rest of her things there was a cardigan that wasn't entirely disgraceful. But she hadn't brought any stockings with her. Stockings were too precious, now that there was talk of clothes being rationed. All she had was a pair of ankle socks. And she didn't even have a decent pair of high-heeled shoes, just lace-up walking shoes that might have been part of a school uniform. But, then, she could hardly have worn ankle socks with heels. She dressed, and tried to see herself in the mirror. No *Looking-Glass* world there: just the selfsame one she inhabited, ordinary and dull, except for the remarkable fact of the war and the curious fact of Mr Guy Matthewson. She leant towards the glass to examine her face. No Alice, either: just plain Diana Sheridan. Oh, people were always complimentary, always saying things like 'What lovely eyes you've got' and 'There's character in that mouth.' Meg was a great one for reassuring her like that. But

Diana knew well enough that praising the parts was merely damning the whole. She was, she thought, plain – honest, decent, and plain. The Americans had a term for it: homely. She had heard it in the cinema. She was homely. It had a fine, old-fashioned sound to it. Nothing to be ashamed of, she told herself.

She wished she had some makeup with her. She rubbed her cheeks to bring a bit of blood to them and licked her lips to make them shine. Temporary measures. She loosened her hair and shook it out in an attempt to bring it to life, then brushed it through twenty times each side, turning her head to change sides, brushing it back from her forehead. She tried a smile, the awkward smile that never showed the humour that she felt; then she grimaced again at her reflection and went downstairs to find Guy.

There were people in the bar. She was afraid of them. One of them rose and came over to her, and it was Guy, changed into grey flannels and blazer. 'What'll you have?' he asked, and she was afraid of that too, having never been in a bar, never really drunk alcohol except the occasional glass of wine at weddings and Christmas and things. 'Mine's a gin and tonic,' he said helpfully, so hers was too and she held it carefully in her hand in case it should escape and fall giggling to the floor.

Did she smoke?

She didn't.

Did she mind if he did?

She didn't.

'And here's the menu.' He presented her with a large leather folder that looked like something you might find in a solicitor's office.

'How grand,' she remarked. But the page inside was small and badly typed and told a sorry tale of Brown Windsor Soup and potatoes and carrots and something called brisket. They

carried the menu through into the dining room and sat opposite each other at a small table by the window. Struthwick
nodded and smiled at them from a table nearby. Diana blushed.
She ordered a small glass of beer with her food, and Guy a
pint, there being, he had explained, little chance of wine these
days. He raised his glass to her and proposed a toast that was
almost a question: 'To us?'

'If you like,' she said, with a shrug. 'To us.'

They talked, about the day they had had, about what they
might do tomorrow. They talked about where she had been to
school and where he had been to university and whether she
should have taken up her place at Liverpool or not. They talked
about where they lived and had lived, of their parents and their
families. They even talked a bit about Lotty; but nothing about
Guy's wife. And when they had finished their meal and had
their coffee he suggested that they go out for a stroll – 'if it's not
too chilly' – so they went out into the gardens, down to the
edge of the lake, which was black and gleaming like obsidian.
They were scrupulous about the blackout even here and there
wasn't a glimmer of light from the hotel, but the sky still glowed
with a backwash of light from the sun. A crescent moon was
held in the frame of the Gwynant valley. Further west, above
the dark pyramid that was Snowdon, hung a single brilliant star.

'Arcturus,' Guy said, when she pointed. How did he know
these things? Perhaps for mountaineering you needed to know
the stars. Perhaps you navigated by them. She looked for Orion:
the familiar shape of the constellation somehow made up for
the terrifying coldness and distance of the stars. Sometimes she
hated the stars, beautiful though they might be. But Orion
wasn't there, nothing that she could recognize was there. It was
as though she found herself in a foreign country without any
familiar points of reference. Guy laughed when she explained.

'Look, there's the Plough,' he said, turning her and pointing upwards. 'You'll always see the Plough. But I'm afraid that Orion's below the horizon now. We're probably standing directly on top of him.'

'Standing on Orion?' The thought chilled her, that the constellation of Orion could be below their feet, that the universe was all around them, below them as well as above; that they were suspended in its vastness, that the stars, the planets, the nebulae were all around them. For a moment she was dizzy with the thought. 'That's frightening, isn't it?'

He took her by the hand. 'You mustn't be frightened. You were brave enough on the mountain today not to be frightened by anything.'

For a moment they stood like that, close together, with her hand in his, and then he moved a step towards her and kissed her.

She had been expecting it, of course. She wasn't a fool, or naïve, or anything like that. And it certainly wasn't the first time she'd been kissed. There had been a couple of boys already, one only the month before who had gone off to join the Army and was now somewhere in Scotland and still wrote letters to her. Andy, his name was. She'd met him at a Ramblers' gathering in the Lake District. But this was the first time that she had ever been kissed by a *man*. That was how she thought of it. Andy and the others had been her own age, more or less, but Guy Matthewson was a man, with a man's confidence, a man's strength, a man's fragile self-sufficiency. When he kissed her he held her firmly in the small of her back, just like they did in the films, and his mouth was open for a moment. Hesitantly, his tongue touched her closed lips.

He let her go. 'Didn't you want that?' he said.

She didn't quite know what to say. 'It's fine.'

'I'm sorry if I took advantage . . .'

'No, not at all.'

'I don't really understand what's happened.'

'I'll tell you if you like.'

He laughed softly. 'Tell me, then.'

'You've met a nice young girl in the mountains who's shown a bit of sympathy towards you . . .'

'Is that all?'

'And she's got a bit of a crush on you, I suppose. And, given those two things, we both might make fools of ourselves if we're not careful.'

He took up her hand and held it in both of his. 'If you want it all to end here, then I'll honour that.'

The word 'honour' sounded very grand, rather loud, the kind of thing one said shortly before acting most dishonourably. Adolf Hitler used the word 'honour' rather a lot. 'Forget about honour,' she said. 'I don't think honour has done very well recently.'

He laughed again. There was enough light to see the gleam of his teeth. 'You really are a most remarkable girl, Diana Sheridan. Is that what you think?'

'It's not what I *think*. It's the fact of the matter.'

'This sounds like *Through the Looking-Glass* again. So: if that's the fact of the matter, what do you *think*?'

She turned away from him, putting up a hand to straighten her hair, making those little gestures of anxiety. For God's sake, what *did* she think? 'I don't really know what I think, Guy. I think that we might never see each other again. I'm off to London shortly and goodness knows what'll happen there. And you've got your blessed tribunal to face.'

She felt him grow tense beside her. She understood suddenly that he had forgotten all about the tribunal, as though their being together like this had achieved what climbing also seemed

163

to bring: forgetfulness. She looked round at him. 'I think perhaps I'm quite happy to make a fool of myself,' she said.

'That sounds very calculating.'

'Oh, I can calculate. I'm quite a mathematician.'

'Does that reduce me to the level of a problem?'

'A conundrum, maybe.'

'What's the answer, then?'

'Oh, there's no *answer*. If there were, it wouldn't be a conundrum.'

Once in her room Diana changed into her nightdress. She pulled back the bedclothes and placed a clean handkerchief on the bedside table. It felt as though she was preparing for something medical, something that she might have done in her nurse's training. Then she cleaned her teeth and climbed into bed and lay on her back staring at the slope of the ceiling, at the cracks in the plaster and the irregular stain where damp must have seeped in. She could taste the mint in her mouth and feel the grit of the toothpaste when she ran her tongue across her teeth. She felt like a child again, waiting in bed for something to happen – an illness to leave her, her father to come back from working late, some family crisis to reach its head.

The sounds of the hotel – the banging of air in the water-pipes, the closing of doors, people talking to one another in muffled tones – settled down. It must have been about half an hour later that she heard footsteps on the stairs and the creak of a floorboard in the corridor outside. There was a fingernail tap on her door, a tiny mouse-like sound. It might almost have been that, an animal in the wainscot.

She turned off the bedside light and called softly, 'Come in.'

The door opened. For a moment pale light spilled into the room and she could see the silhouette of his figure. Then the door closed and there was just his presence in the blackness and his footsteps crossing the floorboards. His voice was just above her. 'Where are you?'

'Here.'

A hand reached through the darkness and touched her face. She took hold of it, felt the sinew and the bone and the hard edge of his nails. There was the same physical sensation that she had experienced while climbing, the same sense of fear and excitement so mingled together that neither could be distinguished from the other. She pushed aside the bedclothes and made what room she could for him. He was shaking as he lay alongside her. 'You're cold,' she said softly.

'Not cold, no. Afraid, maybe.' She could feel his breath against her neck, as though words had a weight, a substance to them.

'Not of me.' She laughed at the idea. 'Surely not of me.'

'I'm afraid for both of us, I think. Of what might happen.'

'Does it matter, if it's what we both want?'

He laughed, and kissed her face very softly, as though tasting the different textures – her eyelids, her cheekbones, her nose, the faint down on her upper lip, the soft membranes of the lips themselves – as though trying to understand her by touch alone. He had drawn up her nightdress. It was round her waist now, and his hand was on her belly, stroking her.

'Guy.' There was a hint of uncertainty in her tone. His name was still strange to her, still new and foreign. 'Guy?'

'Diana,' he whispered, and again, 'Diana,' and the mere exchange of their names seemed an intimacy as great as anything that was happening now, as great as the shameless opening of her legs, and the sudden, startling presence of his hand there.

She arched herself against him. Delight flooded the basin of her body, like a flash of light in the darkness. 'Guy,' she whispered, as though there was some kind of danger and she was trying to warn him, 'Guy, be careful.' But then it was too late to do anything about it, for they were falling. She cried out with the shock of it, the feeling of release and the thrill of fear. It would stop, she knew that – a fall must always come to a stop eventually – but for the moment she didn't care: there was just the sensation of falling, and the shock, and Guy clinging to her.

The next morning was cool and clear. He had left her alone in the early hours and they had slept on apart. Now there was a strange mixture of shyness and intimacy between them as they met in the corridor before going downstairs together. 'How are you this morning?' was all he said. 'Are you all right?' He bent towards her and kissed her cheek almost as an afterthought, as an uncle might kiss a favoured niece. Had she wanted anything more? Certainly she felt that there ought to *be* something more, some celebration of her rite of passage, some acknowledgement that something now linked them more securely than any hundred-foot length of hemp rope.

They were the first in to breakfast. It was a blessing that there was no one else to see them enter the dining room together, and whisper about them. She picked up a newspaper as a distraction. It reported a quiet day. Bombs had fallen on Norwich but casualties were light. There were no losses of air-craft, either by the enemy or by the RAF.

'On a day like this we can do something challenging,' Guy said, as he ate his toast.

Did she want a challenge? She remembered him naked against her and blushed at the recollection, there in the dining room with the ancient waiter moving among the tables. It was a strange memory, a tactile one, a memory such as someone blind might have, composed of touch and pressure and delight, and that sensation of falling, and the sudden halt. She possessed a part of him and she wanted to talk about it; and yet she was held back by this apparent indifference, this businesslike discussion of where they should go and what they should do. She had expected him to be changed somehow, and yet he appeared the same – brisk, reserved, slightly impersonal.

'I think we'll go to Bochlwyd. We can do something on the Glyder Main Cliff. The Direct Route, that's what we'll do. You'll love the Direct Route.'

So they spent that final morning up in the hills, clambering about on more rock and manoeuvring the rope and calling down cliffs to one another. They climbed the route he had chosen and she couldn't follow him on one passage and had to go by a detour over on the left. The Rectangular Excursion, he called it. Every feature in the crags seemed to have a name – the Capstan, the Veranda, the Chasm. There was a facetious tone to them, the spirit of enforced jollity and deliberate understatement, the spirit of the past. She panicked when she had to traverse back to the original line of the route. She was expected to cross a smooth slab of rock using sharp handholds alone, her feet just scraping on the holdless rock below, and half-way across her strength gave out. It seemed a sudden thing, like fluid draining from a tank. 'I'm going to fall!' she shouted up at him. 'Guy, I'm going to fall!'

The rope ran diagonally up the cliff away from her. If she let go there she would make a great swing across the cliff beneath him.

'I'm going to fall!' she screamed at him, and his voice came back quite relaxed about it all, quite calm and collected.

'No, you're not, Porpoise. Just get your left leg up into the crack to help you. It's not very elegant but it's safe.'

She hung on with weakening hands and scrabbled on the rock with her feet and finally, blessedly, managed to cock her leg upwards, almost as though she was mounting a man's bicycle. It was a bit better like that.

'But how the hell do I move?' she cried.

'It's Sunday,' came the reply. 'Such language is inappropriate.'

'Damn Sunday! I want to get out of here.'

'Then you must sort of shuffle along.'

'I can't.'

'Well, darling, you haven't really got an option. Unless you wish to become another fixture of this famous cliff. Perhaps we'll call you the Porpoise. I can just see it in the guidebook – "an interesting feature that commemorates an epic attempt during the early nineteen forties".'

'Oh, shut up!' His facetious comments spurred her to anger. Somewhere deep inside she found reserves of strength and was able to push herself along, with her left foot up in the crack and her hands pulling as best they could and her free leg doing nothing more than scrape at the smooth rock below. Eventually she reached the ledge where Guy was belayed. He pulled her to him and kissed her. 'Darling,' he said, 'you were marvellous.' And stupidly she burst into tears.

At the top of the climb they scrambled up to look at the view. The summit plateau was a desolate wasteland of broken rock, mottled with sunshine, battered by the wind. They looked out across half of North Wales, across the ranks of mountains, as far as the sea, glimmering in the distance. It was an ancient and weary landscape. For all the play of sunshine and cloud shadow across the slopes she thought it a sad and defeated place.

Guy was talking of the tribunal. He was talking of the men who would read through his haphazard explanation of why he would not fight and would ask him pointed, probing questions, and shake their heads at fumbled answers. 'If they put me in prison,' he said, 'I think I'll kill myself.'

'They don't imprison people,' she protested. 'Surely they don't imprison people. Not this time.'

'Who knows? If I claimed religious objections it would be easy. Quakers and the like. But someone like me, with no faith, no belief at all . . . and a wife and child who are German . . .'

It grew cold in the wind. They scrambled back down a gully and ate their picnic lunch at the foot of the crag, beside a boulder that was called, appropriately, the Luncheon Stone. Out of the wind the sun was warm. Diana lay back in the grass and looked up at high, broken clouds where an aircraft, a mere silver crucifix, drew out a long white line across the sky. The sound of its engines came down to them almost as an afterthought, almost as though it was nothing to do with the machine.

'What happens next, Guy?' she asked.

He laughed. 'My dear Porpoise, we've had the most intensive three days. We've met, fallen in love—'

'Have we?'

'Haven't we?' He ticked them off on his fingers, and ran out of fingers: 'We've fallen in love, made love, ascended four rock climbs, had breakfast, lunch and supper, argued, shouted, laughed and cried. It's been pretty exhausting. And you want to know what happens *next*?'

She laughed, wondering whether he did love her and whether she did love him, and what the point was of talking about it when the war was there, just beyond the horizon? She was no fool. She knew that happiness was transient, blown away by death, by illness, by a dozen lesser things. But for that moment, lying on a Welsh hillside in the sun, she was happy.

12

On Thursday evenings people gathered in the White Horse pub off Theobalds Road. They gathered to plot, as though they were participants in a clandestine war – terrorists or guerrillas of some kind. There was the sharing of an arcane language, the secret whispering in corners of the bar over some plan, some new discovery. Men and women from all backgrounds and all social classes: a strange democracy united in the pursuit of the absurd. They called themselves the City Climbing Club. It was an eclectic group of people, with almost as many women as men, as many bad climbers as good. You found your own level. Two of the members had just returned from Pakistan where they had failed, in a Himalayan storm, to climb the Trango Tower. Others struggled up sedate V Diffs like Grooved Arête or Flying Buttress in North Wales. One of the members denied that it was even a climbing club at all. 'Not in the usual sense of the word, at any rate,' he said thoughtfully. 'More a knocking shop.'

It was Jamie who introduced me. He was doing a Master's degree at the LSE at the time, some confection of sociology and economics that was popular in those days. This was the period when he underwent that metamorphosis: Jamie becoming *Jim*, his voice acquiring an edge, the glottal truncations of the capital city. At the same time he was moving up in the firmament of climbing, putting up new routes, seeking out unexplored crags, laying plans. People noticed him, watched him, listened to what he had to say, asked his advice, deferred to him. Voices hushed when he came into the pub.

'This is Robert Dewar,' he announced, putting his arm round my shoulders. 'Rob's an old friend of mine. In fact, he was my very first climbing partner. Isn't that right, Rob? When we were kids.'

People looked up from their beer and their discussions and greeted me in that incurious manner climbers have because the only thing that matters is what you have done and what you are planning to do. 'Hi, Rob,' they said, and allowed me into the conversation and the drinking, and the margins of their plans.

For a couple of months that summer I climbed with different partners, whoever happened to need a second. Jamie was away in the Alps; but when he got back he suggested that we try something together. His regular partner had just taken up a post at Glasgow University on their return from France, so Jamie was more or less on his own. By that time I'd been up to Wales and done some routes in the pass, and had an epic on the West Buttress of Cloggy, which became something of a legend in the club. It hadn't been my fault. We were climbing a route called the Sheaf and the guy who was leading went off-route on

to the much harder White Slab, then got gripped. He was
moving neither up nor down, just standing on tiptoe with his
knees shaking and his fingers locked. I took some credit for
managing to climb a pitch unprotected to find a belay so that I
could get the rope down to him from above. Others had been
on the cliff to see the farce, and Jamie had heard with glee lurid
tales of brown trousers and white faces. 'Sounds as though
you've got a head for this sort of thing,' he said. 'Let's see how
it goes.'

'Why not?' I said. 'If you'll make allowances for me   '

'You don't need allowances.'

And so I began to climb with him. Most Friday evenings
after work we would dump our rucksacks in his Volkswagen
camper and flee the city – up the M1 in the gathering dusk and
across the sprawl of Birmingham to the A5 and the mountains
of North Wales. We shared the driving, we shared the food, we
shared almost everything. We developed a routine, a way of
talking with minimum words, a way of being together and tol-
erating each other's defects. I slept beside him, cooked meals
with him, drank with him, prepared the gear with him, and
stumped up dull hillsides with him to the foot of the crags; and
then watched him move up some obscure stretch of vertical
rock with the easy, almost derisive grace of a cat.

'Come on, youth!' he would call down, when I had to follow.
'You can if you *think* you can. There's nothing about climbing
that isn't in the head.'

There is, in a sense, a male and a female side to a climbing partnership: the lead climber is the active member, the demonstrative
one, the risk-taker; his second is passive, supportive, there when
needed; and although the climbing world is a promiscuous
society, there are such partnerships that acquire something of
the permanence of marriage. Ours became like that. When,

for some reason, one of us couldn't manage the Friday-evening appointment, the other felt his temporary partnership with someone else to be like a brief and shameful adulterous affair.

I began to see the world through his eyes, spot the lines up a cliff just like him, learn to anticipate the excitement of discovery as he did, the pure sensual joy of movement in the vertical dimension, the sensation of bending the body to your will, the almost sexual conquest of rock. There was a sense of the elemental about Jamie's progress up rock, of his being at one with the mountain. He climbed so much better than I did. He always climbed better. I was what they called solid and reliable, while Jamie was brilliant, gifted. I relied on strength and a grim determination, but Jamie used his bodyweight to advantage, knew the limits of balance, the limits of holds, the subtle dynamics of movement in the vertical and horizontal dimensions; he understood instinctively the physics of vectors and the mathematics of triangles of force. He thought with his body. I remember the assurance of his movements, the quiet method with which he attacked the difficult pitches, the speed with which he moved, his sureness on glazed rock. 'We can do it, youth,' was his call.

Together we did the big, hard routes on Cloggy and on the Anglesey sea cliffs. There was the odd new route – Jupiter on Dinas Mot, for one – and a raid in late autumn on Scotland when we stole a choice line on Carn Dearg that Scots climbers had been looking at and falling off. Ambition burgeoned.

Eve and I still saw each other. It was a nervous relationship, held together by mutual attraction, undermined by memories, fragmented by my absences in the hills. She was part of some political group, with a badly printed weekly news-sheet called *Red Rag*. They were anti-bourgeois, anti-imperialist, anti-Communist, anti-war, anti-peace. 'What the fuck are you *for*?' I shouted at her, during one argument.

And she just smiled at me and turned the question round. 'What are *you* for, Rob?'

I knew she had other boyfriends besides me; I could imagine exactly what she did with them, that was the trouble. 'If you're going to go off with Jamie Matthewson all the time,' she said, 'why don't you look for another girl – someone with hairy legs and BO who enjoys slogging up mountains?'

I protested. What exactly I protested wasn't clear – devotion, fondness, fascination, desire; all the components of love without the thing itself, perhaps. She was a wonderful blend of contradictions, sometimes almost apologetic about her beauty, as though to look like she did was a counter-revolutionary act. 'Why don't you come along with us?' I suggested.

'A *ménage à trois*? You've got to be joking.'

'Well, you used to fancy him.'

'And then I met you. Remember? And in my eternal stupidity I fell for you.'

'That's a very bourgeois sentiment.'

'I know. I spend all my time fighting it.'

We used to laugh at things like that. They were careless days, bereft of the personal anxieties that accumulate over time like those mutations that gather in your cells as you age. Her infidelities and my trips to the mountains seemed to pose little threat. Eve and I could break up after a row; and then we could pick up again and apologize tearfully and carnally, and the damage done never seemed terminal. Everything that happened was curable – time was the universal balm and we had plenty of it.

After the New Year the Scottish winter settled in. Jamie and I began to commute between London and the far north. During the week we saw little of each other – we lived in different parts of the city – but on Friday afternoon we would meet for the long drag up the motorway. Memories are of the journey as much as the climbing. Is there some mechanism in the brain that achieves this? At the time the climbing was what mattered and the journey was incidental, a tiresome interlude. But now what I hear is the clattering of that air-cooled engine somewhere behind us, and the radio hammering out pop music, and the road signs going past, Birmingham, Manchester, Penrith, Carlisle, Jamie at the wheel, his body leaning slightly forward so that he could peer through the windscreen down the shafts of light, his face under-lit from the instrument panel.

The Borders were desolate spaces of black, the northern slopes streaked with snow; the city of Glasgow was some kind of haven where we'd stop at the house of Jamie's old climbing partner David Cattenach, who'd have food ready for us, and whisky, and news of whether the mountains were in condition and who had climbed what and what the latest unsolved problem was. 'Here come the bloody Sassenachs!' Davie would shout, as we tumbled out of the van, stunned by noise and imperfect sleep. 'Come to sully the virgin Scottish hills with their greasy English hands.' And for an hour we'd be drawn into the subculture of Scottish climbing, an underworld with its own cant, its own rituals, its own coteries and hierarchies.

After that it was back into the van, sometimes with Davie as well, and more hours to travel, past the black stretch of Loch Lomond, past Crianlarich and the Bridge of Orchy, with the big hills looming out of the night. When the windows were down you could feel the breath of snow on the air, and if you peered upwards into the blackness you could see the upper slopes gleaming white beneath the moon. Where the road turned westward on the Moor of Rannoch we'd stop the van and get out and look, at the jaws of Glencoe ahead of us, with the blunt mass of the Buchaille Etive Mor like a great broken tooth beneath the night sky. It was a monochrome world, a world in negative where the snow shone white and the rock was a deep absence of light, an absorbing void. The winter climbs beckoned, the treacherous ridges and the desolate snowbound corries, the steep snow gullies and the vertical ribbons of ice.

They found Jamie's father in the spring. I think that he had been expecting it to happen. The possibility, the *probability* of his father being found loomed over his childhood and youth like the threat of congenital disease. He had always known that his father was there somewhere, encased in a glacier possibly, but equally possibly just preserved by the cold, dry air. Sooner or later some expedition would come across him.

He rang me early one morning. 'Have you seen?'

'Have I seen what?'

'Go out and buy *The Times*.'

I did as I was told, wandered blearily along to the nearest newsagent's and bought the latest edition. It wasn't on the front page, of course, but it featured prominently in the international section. It seemed an appropriate story for *The Times* – British, slightly absurd, replete with heroism and failure. 'From our correspondent in Kathmandu.' There was a grainy photo of a slope of snow and an outcrop of rock and a humped figure propped against it. Beside the figure was a pole, bearing what looked like shreds of washing drying in the wind. 'Americans plant Buddhist prayer flags as tribute,' the caption said. There was a diagram that showed where the body had been found – an approximate drawing of the Yalung face of the mountain and the height marked in: 26,500 feet.

'The team is bringing down certain items found on Mr Matthewson's body,' the story explained. 'These are believed to include a final note addressed to his wife.'

Later that morning I phoned my mother. 'Did you see about Jamie's father?'

'Of course I saw.'

'Apparently he was just sitting,' I said.

'Yes . . .'

'Covered in snow, of course, but just sitting against a rock. Frozen.'

'Yes, I saw . . .' Her voice faded away. She made a little sound at the other end of the line, a small cat-like sound, a mewing. She was shivering: it dawned on me that my mother was *shivering* there on the end of the telephone line, shivering with fear or misery or plain, imagined cold. 'Poor Guy,' she whispered. 'He would have hated all this attention.'

That evening Eve and I met Jamie for a drink. He'd been dealing with the press all day and now he seemed nervous, as though he was uncertain how to behave, as though a tragedy was being staged and he wasn't sure of his lines.

'Are they bringing him down?' I asked.

'It's too dangerous. Apparently they sort of buried him. Covered him with some rocks, conducted a ceremony. Prayers and things. A kind of funeral.' He hesitated, sipping his beer and looking round the bar as though someone might be watching. 'You know, I've always felt that he was kind of alive, looking over my shoulder, you know what I mean? I could discuss things with him, ask him things and get some kind of answer. It was a comfort.' He smiled, as though at the absurdity of the idea. 'But now, suddenly, he's really dead.'

Eve took his hand. I remember feeling a small thrill of jealousy at the sight of her pale, almost translucent fingers gripping his. She was solicitous and comforting with him, but after we left him her sympathy vanished. She seemed angry with the pair of us, as though somehow we were responsible for a distant death on a Himalayan mountain. 'Climbers have some kind of death-wish,' she said accusingly. 'They court it. It's the ultimate escapism. I mean, you don't want to die like my grandmother did, going gaga in an old people's home. But who the hell wants to be freeze-dried at the age of forty-five?'

To my surprise I saw that there were tears in her eyes. 'No one,' I assured her. 'No one wants that.'

'Then why do you pursue such a fucking silly pastime?' I put out a hand to touch her cheek, but she brushed it away. 'I don't want to be the brave widow fending off the press when you get killed,' she said. 'Are you so stupid that you can't see that?'

'Is that a marriage proposal?' I asked, but she wasn't amused.

Weeks later the things that the American climbers brought down from the mountain were duly delivered to the Matthewson household. Caroline had fled to North Wales to escape further attention from the press. Jamie rang me. 'Do you want to come and see, Rob?'

I hesitated. 'Isn't it a bit ghoulish?'

'I'd like you to see.'

So I went round and we stood in the sitting room, in front of a little heap of possessions that might have come from the pockets of a road-accident victim. Jamie picked through them vaguely. There was a cigarette lighter inscribed 'with love M', an old leather wallet, a bunch of keys, even two tickets for a London theatre, relics of a life snapped off without warning. 'I guess they were the keys to Gilead House,' Jamie said, holding up the key-ring. He seemed distracted, as though these traces of his father had awoken old, blurred memories and he was trying to sort through them without success. 'I hardly remember him. Just as though I had seen snapshots of him. In black and white. Isn't that strange? I don't remember him in colour.'

Along with the relics, there were some photographs that the American climbers had taken. One just showed mountains, peaks I recognized from books and magazines – Jannu like a fang in the foreground, and beyond, in the pearl blue distance, Makalu and Everest. Below the peaks, clouds floated like scum on a pool. Someone had written on the back of the photo: 'View from the last bivouac'. Then there was the same picture that had appeared in monochrome in the newspaper: a shot of a hunched figure at the top of a slope of white. The figure had its back to a brownish rock. Beside it was that stick with prayer flags flying in the Himalayan gale like scraps of tattered underwear on a clothes line.

The final photo showed a mask. It looked like a tribal mask, designed to frighten away demons. It appeared to have been made of ivory, with two ebony discs for eyes and a roughly cut triangular nose, with two holes for nostrils. There was a crudely carved mouth, with shrunken lips and long teeth like a herbivore's. Distinct moments after Jamie had shown it to me, I realized I had been looking at Guy Matthewson's face.

'Not very pretty, is it?' Jamie said. He gave a small and unconvincing laugh, then made an ineffectual movement with his lips, as though trying to formulate words and finding that he had lost the knack. There was a glaze of emotion in his eyes. 'And there's this,' he said, unfolding a battered scrap of paper that had been torn out of a notebook.

It was Guy Matthewson's last will and testament, written in pencil, the letters untidy and ill-formed like a child's first attempt at writing – a strange missive, part valedictory, largely unintelligible. The taller letters stood out like peaks from the plateau of undulating scrawl, and for the most part it was illegible. Jamie pointed out the words 'all right', the word 'cold', the phrase 'my dear boy'. But it was not clear what, if anything, was expected of his dear boy. He was to be looked after, perhaps. 'Look after my dear boy.' Did it say that? There was no real means of telling. Jamie tried to convince me that the final words were 'all love, Guy'. Except you couldn't read the Guy. It was just an approximate circle and a tail, like a spermatozoon.

A bitter irony, I thought, to make all that effort while you are dying – to hold the pad with one heavy mitt and clutch a pencil in blistered, frozen, wooden fingers, and try to get your mind focused on the task – only to have the resulting message impossible to read.

'Your mother,' Jamie said. 'She knew him, didn't she? What does she think?'

I shrugged noncommittally. 'It was a long time ago. Before the war.'

He nodded. 'There's something . . .' Then he hesitated. He looked confused, almost distraught, as though to formulate his idea in words would be some kind of betrayal.

'Something what?'

He cast around for the right words. 'I don't know. Something . . . almost deliberate about it, don't you think? Do you think he wanted to escape?'

'Escape?'

'I don't know, really. From my mother, maybe. They can't have been very compatible. And . . .' he hesitated, looking at the small heap of possessions '. . . I think she had lovers even then. Something she said the other day . . .'

I felt a small knot of guilt somewhere inside me, a visceral thing like a lump in my chest. What, I wondered, did he know? I tried to laugh away the suggestion. 'Surely you don't think he intended to die? Don't be daft.'

He shook his head. 'It's not difficult. He was high up above the rest of the expedition. On his own, short of oxygen. It's not difficult to push yourself beyond the point of no return.'

'Come off it, Jamie,' I said. 'Don't be idiotic.' But I admit that the thought had crossed my own mind. Climbing itself is an escape, and death the ultimate one. And it would have been an easy death. That sounds callous, but it's true. Hypothermia *is* an easy death. Contrary to his appearance in that photograph, Guy Matthewson did not die in some kind of agony. His body would have cooled down from the outside inwards: first the extremities, the fingers and the toes, the tip of the nose and the ears and cheeks, then the hands and the feet, and then the limbs themselves; finally, the core. He would simply have slowed down. Drowsiness. At about 33°C he would have begun to lose a true sense of where he was, of what the dangers were, of what he ought to do. He would have drifted in and out of consciousness. Sleep, he would have wanted to sleep more than anything else, more than life itself. So that's what he'd have done: at about 30°C. There would have been no pain. He would have just drifted off to sleep, dreaming, no doubt. Dreams and hallucinations would have been more real to him than any view out across the Himalayas, or any concerns about his wife back in England. A few more degrees down the icy slope and that would have been it – he would have been dead. And a hero.

That year Jamie seemed driven to greater things. It was like catching the right moment when you're surfing, catching the big wave, going with the mass of water that is so much greater than you, but using it to your own ends. 'Matthewson and Dewar,' they said, in the climbing pubs, in the bars and the huts and the bothies. 'Heard of them. Doing some good stuff. Isn't he the son of Guy Matthewson, the one they found on Kangchenjunga? Like father like son.'

That summer we went to the Alps. We lived in medieval squalor in a muddy campsite in the Chamonix valley. For a few days we joined up with a couple of Australian girls who appeared one evening and pitched their tent alongside ours, but for most of the time we led a monastic life, fitted to the rhythm of the days and the exigencies of climbing. The weather settled into one of its rare spells of calm. We divided our days between the valley and the high huts, between intense physical activity and indolence. There was the simplicity of unquestioning faith about what we did. Everything in the mountains could be explained, everything could be understood, every dilemma resolved. It was almost as though we were on a pilgrimage and searching for revelation and, like any pilgrimage, the journey was more important than reaching the goal.

'I don't want this to end, Rob,' Jamie told me on one occasion. We were huddled together on a bivouac ledge two thousand feet above the Frêney glacier, with the gas stove roaring in the dusk, and the stars scattered like ice crystals across a darkening sky. He might have been talking of a love affair. And if love is what people need to explain the world, to make it rational and comprehensible, then I guess that he was.

'It will end, though,' I warned him. 'When we run out of money.'

He laughed in the darkness. 'You're a bloody cynic, Dewar.'

'An idealist needs a cynic. It's the only thing that keeps him within the bounds of reality.'

'But does a cynic need an idealist?' he asked.

'Probably not. A cynic can usually get by well enough on his own – he just doesn't climb so high, or so hard.'

That season we did, among other things, the North East Spur of the Droites, the North Face of the Grand Dru and the Central Pillar on the Frêney Face of Mont Blanc; and we retreated from high up on the Brouillard Face in a storm that rampaged across the range for five days, killing four other climbers in the same area. Storms are like that: frenzied monsters that devour the pilgrims with complete indifference. When we finally emerged from the blizzard and staggered into the Monzino hut we were greeted with amazement by the climbers who had been stranded there. It was as though we had come back from the dead.

13

On my return from the Alps I holed up in my flat in London to try to pick up some pieces of my vagrant life. I had to earn some money, I had to catch up with my university work, there was Eve to see. Jamie's call a few weeks later seemed an intrusion on an existence that was, in some way, returning to normality. 'I've made a discovery, Rob. You've got to come up and have a look.'

'I can't get away that easily.'

'Take the weekend off.'

'Weekends are the most difficult time.'

'Midweek, then. Just come and have a look, Rob. Don't let me down.'

I argued a bit but I knew from the start that it was no good. Jamie was committed and there was no respite. So I hitchhiked up the A5 to North Wales and we met up that same evening at a pub in Llanberis. He was sitting alone in a corner of the bar nursing a pint of beer and wearing a secretive smile. The daft thing was that I was pleased to see him, pleased to see that conspiratorial grin, those hooded, thoughtful eyes, the hands that were never still.

'What's it all about?' I asked. 'It'd better be good. Eve thinks I'm crazy. I'm not sure I don't agree with her.'

'You are, Rob. Crazy. We both of us are.' He glanced round to see that we weren't overheard, then leant forward and spoke in a whisper: 'I've found a cliff. A sea cliff. Virgin. It's fucking marvellous.'

I laughed. I felt angry at being dragged back into his plans so soon, but still I laughed, at the sheer bloody-mindedness of the man. Even after our campaign in the Alps he could still find delight in the diminutive British crags. It was a measure of his obsession.

So we drove to see. The place was away from the mountains and over the bridge to the island of Mona, where once the Druids had reigned. We wound through narrow lanes and past undistinguished villages, out on to the deserted clifftop. There was an empty car park and a notice warning walkers about 'Dangerous Cliffs'. Beyond the rim of the world was Ireland.

Jamie pulled on the brake. The wind rocked the van on its suspension. 'Here we are. No one around, no climbers, no one shitting behind a rock, no sardine tins, no orange peel, nothing. Virgin.'

Ducking our heads against the gale we left the van and climbed over a fence. Noise was all around us, the distant abstract noise of the waves and the closer noise of the wind, which is not the wind's noise at all but your own noise, the wind rushing past your ears, roaring and gusting against your mind. The bull-roar of nature. And, above it all, the crying of sea birds – a desolate, anguished sound.

A slope of coarse grass led down to the edge of the cliffs. 'Watch out!' I yelled, against the racket. 'The grass is wet.' We slithered down, grabbing at each other's hands, clutching at rocks, clutching at straws. Herring-gulls and kittiwakes shrugged their shoulders at our arrival on the top of the cliff, leaning and tilting into the updraught and jeering at us as we peered over the edge. A precipice of pink gneiss fell away from blistered lips of grass and stone; at its base the sea dashed upwards in clouds of spray.

'What do you reckon?' he shouted.

'It looks promising.'

'Promising? It's bloody brilliant.'

'How the hell do we get down?'

'Abseil.'

'And if we can't climb out? I mean, what's the rock like, for God's sake? What happens if it just comes to pieces in our hands?'

Jamie laughed, his expression a mixture of the delighted and the demonic. 'We swim, youth, we swim.'

We clambered back up the slope to the car park. The wind was less here and we could talk without shouting. 'When can we start?' Jamie was asking. 'We don't want some other bastards coming along and stealing it, do we?'

'I've got the job to think about.' I was working for a security firm as a guard at various depots in the London suburbs. It was night work and the idea was that I could catch up on my university studies and earn a bit of money at the same time.

'Fuck the job,' Jamie said. 'I'll lend you some money.'

'I can't always be cadging off you.'

'Yes, you can.'

So I rang them to tell them I wouldn't be available for a week or two, and Eve to say that I was staying up in Wales for a while, and for the next few days Jamie and I lived in his camper van once again, among the usual litter of sleeping-bags, canned food and ironmongery. They were days of high wind and sun, careless days imbued with the strange freedom that climbing brings, where the only rules are the physics of friction and the only law is the law of gravity. Each morning we made some kind of breakfast of tea and bread and jam, before shouldering our gear like workmen – plumbers, maybe, or stonemasons – and tramping across the rough meadows to the nearby edge where the land finished. Gulls circled in the updraught as we climbed, complaining at our presence and shouting derision at our puny efforts.

'What a place!' Jamie yelled into the wind as he lowered down to the tidemark. 'What a fantastic fucking *place!*' That's how I remember him, grinning like that, a cross between the beautiful and the malicious, pale hair, blue eyes like the pale sky towards the horizon, his sunburned lips that were somehow like his mother's, his face still scorched from the Alps, alight with whatever it was he and I searched for in any kind of climbing: something sensual, something almost sexual, a physical charge that would find its echo in memory and give us something to recall just as someone in the shadows of age recalls a past love.

Not far from the cliff we found a pub where we could drink in the evenings. There were just the old boys from the village and the occasional motorcyclist in greasy leathers. 'What you lads doin', then?' the landlord asked, as he drew our pints.

'Climbing.'

'Climbing *what*? There's no mountains here.'

'The sea cliffs.'

'Messin' about on the cliffs? That's dangerous. You want to watch it.'

He was called Arthur. Each evening he'd listen patiently to our account of the day's work. 'Seems daft to me,' was his opinion, but as time went on and we didn't drown and didn't fall and didn't need rescue, his respect seemed to grow. 'Clever bastards, I suppose,' he admitted.

One evening Arthur's daughter was there, pulling at the beer taps and listening with half an ear to what we said, but saying nothing herself. She wore her hair ragged and tied into a bandanna, and her blouse had a tattered, gypsy look to it. 'I guess she's got a man,' Jamie suggested. When she came round the bar to clear away empty glasses you could see her calf-length skirt and narrow feet in leather sandals. There was a thin gold chain round one ankle.

'What's a girl like you doing here?' he asked. He reddened as he asked it. He always did that, blushed when first talking to a girl.

'Biding my time,' she said, taking little notice of him.

'Till what?'

'Till a knight in shining armour comes along.' She had just come back from Egypt and wore an ankh on a leather thong round her neck to prove it. Judging by what came over the speakers she liked the Stones and the Incredible String Band and Leonard Cohen. She had a tough face, sharp-featured. Scorched faintly by the sun. Maybe that was Egypt.

'Why you boys lookin' so pleased with yourselves, then?' she asked, when we came in the next evening.

'We've just done a new route.'

She placed the glasses in front of us. 'What's the *point*? Going down to the bottom just to come back up. What's the point?' Her accent made her words seem mocking.

Jamie eyed her. 'What do you enjoy?' he asked. I knew that belligerent tone. A challenge, like when he slagged me off when

I was climbing: 'Finding it *difficult*, then, Dewar? You're not *resting* on that runner, are you, youth?'

She returned his look without flinching. 'I enjoy smoking,' she said. She paused. 'And sex.'

There was no one else in the pub. Her old man was out at the back fixing something. Electrics, he was always messing about with the electrics. We reckoned he'd bypassed the meter or something and was taking the power direct from the mains. So, her old man was out at the back and there weren't any other customers that early, and this girl called Ruth had just told two almost strangers that she enjoyed smoking and sex.

'Well, climbing's rather like both of those,' Jamie said evenly. His cheeks were flushed, but he kept his tone level. 'Smoking *and* sex, both at the same time. You should try it.'

'Tell me when.'

'Tomorrow.'

She took the money for our pints and clocked it up on the till. 'My day off,' she said.

She came despite my protests. Perhaps because of them. Ruth had a hard core of belligerence, just like Jamie. If she thought she was being belittled, or her sex was being belittled, you saw that light come into her eyes, the smile that wasn't a smile so much as a challenge. 'Fuck you, Dewar,' she said, when I suggested that taking a novice down the cliff was a daft thing to be doing.

She'd found an old pair of plimsolls, black plimsolls that she had last worn when she was at school. 'They'll do,' Jamie had said.

'But how the hell is she expected to climb an XS route wearing pumps and never having climbed before in her life? I mean, there's no other way out. We'd have to get her off by boat if she can't climb out.'

'If you two can do it, Dewar, then so can I.'

'Like hell you can.'

It was only by threatening a strike that I persuaded them to be a bit sensible. 'Rob is like a father to me,' said Jamie sarcastically. So we drove to Llanberis to buy her a pair of rock boots and we got her to try them out on a couple of routes in the pass – Carreg Wastad and the Grochan, that kind of thing. Ruth was, it was clear, a natural. 'This is great,' she cried, startled to find such an experience on her doorstep, a thrill that you didn't have to travel half-way round the world for. Jamie was enjoying himself, delighted with having this strange, ragged girl at the end of his rope – 'at the end of my tether', as he put it. Other climbers stopped to watch. They knew Jamie, of course, but it wasn't him they were looking at, it was Ruth: her limbs cat-like on the rock, her spine drawn taut like a bow as she leant back to see the next moves, the mane of hair hanging down her back like some kind of medieval banner. Oh, you noticed Ruth, all right.

Afterwards we took her to one of the pubs in Llanberis. The bar roared like a storm. A cloud of cigarette smoke shifted above the heads and the room was humid with damp wool and slopped beer. The talk was of climbing, of grades and grips and plans for the future, of new routes that were desperate and old routes that had been found a piece of piss. Ruth was amused by the place and its subculture, almost as though it might be something encountered on one of her expeditions: a yak drivers' tavern, perhaps. 'So, how long have you guys been doing this?' she asked.

Jamie laughed. 'Rob and me? Climbing? For ever, off and on. From when we were kids mucking about.'

I watched how she looked at him; and how he returned her gaze – the same amused and analytical examination that he gave a pitch he was about to climb, as though he knew all the trouble it would bring, and that was part of the entertainment.

'And what are your plans?'

He feigned incomprehension. 'Plans?'

'You must have plans of some kind.'

'You mean finish my degree, find a wife, get a mortgage, those sorts of plans?'

'I mean climbing plans.'

'Oh, those.' He glanced round at the crowd in the bar and lowered his voice conspiratorially. 'Climb out this new cliff before the rest of these bastards get on to it, that's the first one.'

'That seems pretty limited.'

He laughed. 'There are other ideas. We've been doing good stuff in the Alps as well, big routes: the Central Pillar of Frêney, the Dru, things like that.'

'Doesn't mean anything to me.'

'Maybe it doesn't. Anyway, we're ready for something really major. The Eiger, perhaps.'

'I've heard of that . . .'

'And then . . .' His voice drifted away. 'Who knows? The Himalayas, maybe. What about the Himalayas? What do you reckon, Rob?'

I shrugged, caught up by the fantasy. 'Why not?'

He nodded, sitting there behind a small barricade of beer glasses, with Ruth listening to him in that way she had, a sharp interest blended with an air of detachment, as though she was listening, yes, and taking you seriously, but laughing at your small conceits, your boasting, your sense of importance. 'Maybe Kangchenjunga,' he said. 'Maybe Kangchenjunga.'

She had something, did Ruth. Nerve. Bottle. The next morning she stood at the edge of the cliff and gritted her teeth and held on to the abseil rope while Jamie screamed instructions at her, how to let the rope run gently, and how to slow it down; and she got it, more or less, this slight figure in wide flares and some old fisherman's smock that she had found in a second-hand sale, and her hair tied back in a bandanna but flying in the wind just the same. She went down the rope screaming with delight – a banshee scream that frightened even the gulls: 'This is *fantastic*, Jamie! Fantastic!'

There was laughter and a strange tension underlying that morning. You could tell what was happening. You could see the looks Jamie gave her and the way she returned them, that level, thoughtful gaze. You could tell, all right. It hadn't been like this with the Australian girls in Chamonix.

'How the hell are we going to get out of here if I can't climb it?' she asked, as we stood on the wave-washed rocks at the foot of the cliff. There was a steep wall directly above us, and then an over-hang that guarded the way on to a slab of pink gneiss. The slab was polished by the elements to a geometrical smoothness, but you couldn't see that from below. That was what you discovered when you were up there, clinging to small flake holds and looking to move left on to the slab, while the cliff was leaning into you as though trying to prise you off. I resisted the temptation to say that I had warned her, but she didn't really seem to care anyway. 'We'll find a way,' Jamie assured her. 'Even if we have to haul you up.'

She looked up at the line we had chosen, shielding her eyes with her arm. I noticed the dark hair on her arm, the suntan, the female angles that mollified her tough muscles, the novel *presence* of her in the midst of my partnership with Jamie. 'So, what are we waiting for?' she said. 'Let's go.'

She climbed it. Of course she did. I led to the first stance, then brought her up, giving her a tight rope on the hard moves and landing her like a gasping fish on the ledge beside me.

195

'Wow,' she said.

'You wait for the next pitch, my darling,' I warned her.

'Don't you darling me,' she replied.

Jamie followed her up. There was a tight squeeze on the ledge, so Jamie went straight through to climb the second pitch. His hair blew in the wind, plastered across his forehead. 'All right, kids?' he asked, as he left the ledge and set off up the rock, climbing easily, going up with that casual, fluid grace. There was something of the circus performer about him, something of the ballet dancer, something of the mountebank with bells and ribbons, something of the plain fact of the manual labourer. We watched him move upwards methodically, the gear jangling at his waist, his fingers feeling into narrow spaces, his body laying away from his holds, his toes smeared against the rock.

'He's all right, isn't he?' Ruth said.

I wondered about her, wondered about her vagrant manner, the undercurrents of aggression, the glances she gave him. 'Yes,' I agreed. 'He's all right.'

'You jealous?' she asked.

'Jealous? What do you mean?'

'Of him.'

'Why should I be?'

'You like him a lot, don't you?' she said, and her expression said 'more than like'.

'Of course I do. We've known each other for years. As kids. Sometimes,' I added unnecessarily, 'I love him.' And I was angry at the momentary lowering of the barrier, the moment's vulnerability.

'Is that so?'

'Not what you're thinking. Not that.' I was looking upwards, following Jamie on the crux moves, paying out the rope as he moved, ready to hold him if he came off, ready to save his *life*, for God's sake. I watched the swaying of his body, the outrageous way he moved up as easily as if he were climbing a ladder. He found a sweet combination of holds and almost danced across on to the slab, then vanished from our sight.

Ruth touched my arm. 'I'm sorry.'

'It's okay,' I replied. 'It's okay.' I wasn't sure what she was apologizing for.

Jamie began taking in the rope. His voice came to us above the sound of the sea and the laughing of the gulls: 'I'll keep it tight!' he yelled. 'Ruth! Climb when Rob tells you and I'll keep the rope tight.'

I turned my attention to the ropes and explained to her how she was to do it. 'He's got a runner up above the hard moves so that you'll be held from above. But you're going to find it damned difficult.'

She ran her tongue over her lips. She was nervous, however much she might have tried not to show it. 'I'll manage.'

I held her shoulders as she shuffled past me. There was the sudden breath of some perfume she was wearing, a dark, exotic smell. Patchouli oil. She glanced at me mere inches from my face, and gave me a faint smile. Then moved a fraction forward and kissed my cheek.

'I'm climbing,' she called out, just as we had taught her. And she began to pull herself up the rock. Her ascent wasn't the most beautiful thing in the climbing world; nor was it the purest. She took a tight rope some of the way and once or twice she came adrift and hung back on it. But she never gave up, never surrendered to panic or fear or any of those things. 'Take a pull on the rope!' Jamie's voice called out at one point, and she was game enough to shout back to him to piss off, and to scrabble up unaided. 'Christ alive!' she yelled, when she was once again in balance. I could see her knees shaking. 'Christ alive! That was scary, Jamie. That was fucking scary!'

I couldn't see from where I was, but I could imagine him smiling across at her as she came up towards him, that watchful, thoughtful smile that was just like his mother's. I could imagine his expression as he eased her across on the end of the rope like a fisherman landing a catch after playing it to exhaustion. 'You're doing all right,' I heard him call. And when she reached his stance on the slab, I could imagine him grabbing her by the arm and pulling her to safety and kissing her full on the mouth as she came towards him.

14

It was Ruth who gave the climb its name. We had toyed with one or two – The Pink Panther, Floating Rib – but nothing that we were happy with. Naming a route was important, we explained to her. It sets the character. It establishes your ownership.

'But it's not yours,' she protested. 'It's nature's. It's a piece of geology.'

'The cliff belongs to nature,' Jamie said, 'but the route is ours.'

She nodded. 'Okay. You need something Welsh, something with resonance. Pendragon, that's what you should call it. Pendragon.'

Pendragon: Dragon Head, the banner that the legendary kings of Britain carried into war. It sounded good.

That evening she sat us down in the kitchen of the pub and cooked supper. It was a Tunisian dish – something with fish and couscous. She'd been to Tunisia, all along the North African coast, in fact; and into the desert. 'To the Aïr.' Neither Jamie nor I knew where the Aïr was. We'd never heard of it, in fact. Before that there'd been that year at the Slade when she thought she might be an artist, and a year in Israel on a kibbutz when she thought she might marry a Sabra.

'But you didn't?'

'I didn't.' Now she was thinking of going back to university. Celtic literature it would be this time, the Mabinogion and the Arthurian cycle. But, of course, she was still painting and sculpting. Ruth Phoenix. Her work had attracted interest – there had been an exhibition of sculpture in Liverpool. She had a piece at the Institute of Contemporary Art in London. Her studio was in a converted stable at the back of the pub but she wouldn't show it to us, not yet. There was something personal and inviolate about it, she said.

So we ate and listened, and looked at each other and at her; and we guessed, both of us at the same time, that something new had happened in our lives.

'And all you two guys do is climb?' she asked.

'More or less,' Jamie agreed. He was amused. There was the light of mockery in his eyes as he glanced at me. 'Do you do anything else, Rob?'

I didn't.

'I don't think so. We just climb.'

'Jamie's got a father to live up to,' I said, 'but I just do it because I can't think of anything else to do.'

'What about his father?' Ruth asked.

'Jamie's father?' I glanced at him. 'His father was a mountaineer. Didn't you see? You must have been abroad. It was all over the papers. The discovery of his body, I mean.'

'His *body*?'

'He died years ago,' Jamie said. I could tell by his tone that he didn't want to talk about it. 'Nineteen fifty-four, on Kangchenjunga. Some climbers found him just this spring.'

There was the way that Ruth was looking at him. You remembered her looks. There was a cast in her eye, a curious reflective value that made you wonder what she was thinking. 'It must have been dreadful.'

Jamie shrugged. 'I hardly remember him. Just a sort of shadow in the background of my childhood.'

'And you climb to live up to his reputation?'

'That's just Rob fooling about,' he replied impatiently. 'I climb because I love it. Perhaps it's in the blood.'

'Do you know something else?' I said. I suppose I was a bit pissed. I suppose we both were. The euphoria of the day's climbing had evaporated. 'Do you know something else about Jamie's father? My mother was in love with him. Did you know that?' I looked from one to the other. Surely they had understood what I was saying. 'My own mother,' I repeated to make it clear, 'was in love with Jamie's father. Jamie's mother and my mother were rivals in love.'

He laughed dismissively. 'It was a schoolgirl crush, Rob. Mother told me about it. It was at the start of the war, years before she married my father.'

I think it was his laughing that annoyed me. I'd seen my mother close to tears, I'd seen her life blighted by marriage to my father, a man whom she hadn't really loved. I'd felt something of her pain. For a few moments I felt absurdly protective of her. I turned to Ruth. 'Jamie's mother stole him from her. My mother always felt that.'

He laughed again. 'Caroline's good at stealing men, isn't she?' he said. 'Doesn't stop at young boys, either.'

'What do you mean by that?'

There was the sound of the kitchen around us, the murmur of the refrigerator, something cooking on the stove, noise from the bar coming through the hatch, but there was silence between the three of us. Ruth sensed the undercurrents. She had no way of knowing what was going on but she was a clever reader of people's emotions; she knew when the stakes were high. Jamie took a sip of beer and placed the glass down with care beside his plate. Then he looked straight at me with an equivocal smile, two smiles, the sardonic and the faintly amused. 'I think you know exactly what I mean.'

How do you measure the shifts in a relationship? Certainly my friendship with Jamie changed after that, although the change was subtle and hard to define. And then I wonder, Why should it have changed? Before that outburst we had both known about Caroline and me; the only thing new was that the knowledge was now out in the open – I knew that he knew. Ridiculous, really; a kind of puzzle, a tongue-twister. He knew that I knew that he knew. But consider how many relationships survive sewn together with tacit complicity and mutual deception. It's the cold light of discovery that's so dangerous. Better live with the lies.

We said no more about it. The next day we were out on the cliffs again, talking occasionally about Ruth and saying nothing about Caroline. Ruth came with us when she could get away from the pub. I watched Jamie and her together and sensed the bond between them growing from mere attraction and curiosity into something else. Love? Did either of them surrender themselves enough for that? Was there ever that extinction of self in their relationship?

On the third evening he didn't sleep in the van at all. I lay alone in the darkness. If I sat up and pulled aside the curtains I could see down the hill to the pub, and the vague, glow-worm light in one of the upstairs rooms, the room that was hers, the room where she lay with Jamie.

Next day the weather broke. Grey cloud slid over the sea from Ireland and shrouded the coast. There was a thin drizzle in the wind with the promise of worse. Towards the south, the bulk of Cader Idris was shut away from human gaze. Jamie and I discussed what we should do, but there was another person in the equation now and we had that gulf between us, a gulf that was not a void but was filled with things – the detritus that comes with knowing each other too well and for too long, from knowing too many secrets. And it seemed that he and Ruth had conceived an idea. They'd been discussing it together, apparently. Just a fantasy. Something for a rainy day. 'What the hell are you talking about?' I asked.

'A business.'

'A *business?*'

'We thought of setting up a business.'

'What the hell do you mean, a business?'

'Climbing and trekking, something like that.'

I laughed. 'Don't be ridiculous.'

'What's so ridiculous? We could open a trekking and mountaineering centre. Maybe even do some climbing gear.'

'Matthewson Mountain Boots?' I suppose my tone was mocking. Anyway it angered him.

'Why not, Rob? Why the hell not? Christ, what's wrong with you?'

'Nothing's wrong with me.'

'Well, you sound pissed off.' While the rain pattered on the roof we sat there in the van wavering on the edge of a pointless argument, like kids.

Later that day they dropped me home. There was no more climbing to be done, and the spaces in our friendship had suddenly become too narrow for me to fit in. 'I should see my mother,' I said, 'and maybe do something to earn my keep.' They tried to persuade me to stay with them, but there was little conviction in their arguments.

The place wasn't far away, but it always seemed like returning to another country: the familiar road, the familiar hill with its view over the estuary, the familiar Victorian house that had the sign saying 'Homeleigh – Private Hotel' because my mother couldn't bear the word 'guesthouse'. Jamie parked the van in the road outside and came in to say hello. He gave her a kiss that she clearly didn't expect, and the assurance that, yes, Caroline was fine. He used her Christian name. *Caroline* sent her love. Mother smiled tightly and nodded, but didn't, I noticed, offer hers in return. And then he clapped me on the shoulder and climbed back into the van, and Ruth and he were gone, the old Volkswagen clattering away down the hill towards the coast road that led through a litter of seaside resorts to England.

'I rue the day that you ever started climbing,' Mother said, as we watched the van depart. I liked that. Rue. It had a fine, old-fashioned sound to it. 'Come on, Mum,' I told her, 'when you were my age you were pulling Blitz victims from the rubble. You've told me yourself. It was a damned sight more dangerous than climbing.'

'But there was a war on.'

'You could always have been a Land Girl and spent the war picking potatoes in safety.'

'And with Guy and Meg's son. How strangely things work out.' She seemed puzzled, as though Jamie's brief visit had confused her, as though there were things she might say and think, and she wasn't sure about any of them. 'It's all water under the bridge now, I suppose. At least he's not taken after his mother.'

What on earth did she mean by that? Yes, he *had* taken after her. I saw shadows of her in his every expression, the hint that beneath the edges of masculine toughness there lurked the ghost of that supple female strength. I saw Caroline in his petulance and his thoughtful reserve. I had never got near to the quick of her; and I had never really got close to Jamie, either.

'Is that his girlfriend?' Mother asked.

'I suppose that's what she's becoming. We met her a few days ago.'

'Looks like a gypsy.'

Those were dull, wasted days of rain. I sat at the reception desk of the hotel and tried to do some studying. I rang Eve and suggested she might like to come up and stay, but she was just about to go away with her parents, to France where her family owned a small, dilapidated farmhouse. 'I told you we might be going. What do you expect? You could have come.'

I noticed her use of the past tense. Whatever might once have been on offer now seemed to be lost. 'Well, give me a ring when you get back.'

'All right.'

Ridiculously I found myself hoping that she hadn't really gone, or perhaps that she would come back early. When the phone rang one morning a week later, I even lifted the receiver in the faint hope that it might be her.

It was a woman's voice on the line, but it wasn't Eve. Did we have a room for the night? I glanced disconsolately through the register and found two rooms free. 'Would you like a single or a double, madam?' I asked.

There was a hint of laughter in my ear. 'Madam? I like that. Madam's name is Phoenix. *Miss* Phoenix to you, Mr Dewar.'

I felt a small stir of delight. 'Ruth.'

'Can I come and see you?'

'To stay?'

'If you have a room.'

'Of course we have a room. I've just told you.'

'Well, then.'

'What about Jamie?'

There was a moment's pause. 'What *about* Jamie?' she asked.

She came that afternoon in her battered long-wheelbase Land Rover, the one that she had driven to the Aïr, the one with a double roof to insulate the passengers against the sun, and the winch between the front wheels so that you could drag the vehicle out of ditches or up steep inclines. She seemed an exotic creature as she climbed down from the driver's seat of this altogether improbable vehicle: long skirt and sandals, a silk waistcoat embroidered with sinuous forms like the organic patterns of a Persian carpet, her wrists with silver bangles, her ragged hair stained with henna. All these things were trophies from her travels in North Africa and the Middle East, and they conspired to give her the air of a hybrid being, half bird, half human, wholly unpredictable. What my mother had dismissed as 'gypsy'.

We kissed hesitantly, amused at seeing each other in this unexpected manner. Had Jamie and she quarrelled? Had their little relationship died at birth? Reluctant to ask anything, I led the way upstairs. I felt the need to apologize, for the bareness of the room, for the inadequacy of the whole place. The millstone round the family neck, was how I described it.

She looked round at the narrow space. 'It's fine,' she said. 'For God's sake, stop apologizing. It's perfect.' And, as though to stake her claim, she flung her bag – a red leather shoulder-bag incised with some Oriental design – on to the bed.

That evening we went out for a meal. We ate at a Chinese restaurant, one of those places with plastic lanterns and flock wallpaper. There were rubber plants in the window and chop suey on the menu. 'You know there's a painting by Hopper called *Chop Suey?*' Ruth asked. 'A woman sitting alone in a restaurant and through the window you can see the sign – "sue", it says. The other bits are hidden. It's a purely American dish, chop suey. You don't find it in China.'

Had she been to China?

Not yet.

We laughed. We talked, we discussed art and her art, and her travels and climbing and a whole lot of things. She knew more than I did, she'd done more, she understood more. 'Tell me about Jamie,' I said to her.

And she looked at me carefully, as though reading things in my face. '*You* tell me about Jamie. You know him better than I do. According to him you practically grew up together. And now you practically live together.'

'I wasn't talking about Jamie and me.'

'So what *were* you talking about?'

'I was talking about Jamie and *you*.'

She looked at me quizzically. 'Are you jealous?'

'I just want to know where we all stand. Tell me.'

She didn't. She was evasive and equivocal, neither admitting nor denying. She'd had some kind of disagreement with him. He seemed to want a kind of female carpet, to beat at intervals, that's what she claimed. 'He's childish. In the worst way. Spoilt child. He'll learn. If he wants me like he says he does, he'll have to learn.' She paused, to give her words weight. 'Perhaps it's something to do with his mother.'

I tried to shrug away the comment. I tried not to seem awkward and embarrassed beneath her gaze. 'Did you meet her?'

'Yes. She was charming.'

'She is.'

'Distant and detached, but charming.' A pause, a smile of something like complicity. 'But I understand what you saw in her.' She phrased it in the past tense – quite deliberately, I thought, as though challenging me to reveal whether my affair with Caroline was quite over.

We got back to the house at eleven and my mother was there, more or less waiting for us. Ruth was friendly and disarming. She could be that when she wanted. She smiled and asked the right questions and gave the right answers. Having a father who ran a pub gave her some sort of advantage, I suppose. The two of them ended up having coffee together and talking about all sorts of nonsense while I went to bed and left them to it. Some time later I heard them go up to their rooms. Ruth's room was above mine and I could hear her moving around above me. I lay in bed, staring at the ceiling, conscious of her presence there almost as though she was in the same room as me, as though I could sense her stirring in her sleep, as though her perfume filled my own room on the floor below. I didn't know whether she was on my side or not, or whether she had been sent by Jamie as some kind of emissary. I didn't even know if there *were* sides.

The next day was heavy and still, with the promise of thunder. Ruth decided to stay another day. I felt honoured by her presence, uncertain of her motives. We spent the morning going round the castle at the mouth of the river, one of the great fortresses that Edward I had built for the subjugation of the Welsh. In the afternoon we drove into the hills. We drove at random, turning on to the first side-road that took our fancy because it seemed to be narrow and winding and deserted. The road climbed past the occasional farmhouse. There were pastures marked out by drystone walls behind which sheep grazed. I had to climb down to open gates for the Land Rover to pass through. Its wheels rattled over cattle grids and the sound was an intrusion, something metallic and harsh in a soft, pacific valley. On one side of the road the remains of an abandoned lead mine emerged from the bracken. Beyond the ruins, a narrow, silent lake lay like a steel blade thrust into the hills.

Ruth parked near the water and reached over into the back for her bag. 'Let's get out and have a look.'

I followed her down through reeds to the water's edge. There was a wooden landing-stage, but no boats, no people, nothing to break the sultry weight of the afternoon. She dropped her bag and kicked off her sandals and walked out to the end of the stage to look. Out in the middle of the lake two cormorants were sliding through the water like snakes. We watched the birds for a while, until, with a fluid motion, they vanished beneath the surface. For a long while – how long could they stay submerged? – there was nothing but Ruth standing there on the edge looking out over the hard steel of the lake. When the birds eventually emerged, they were somewhere else, somewhere far away that you had not expected, as though there had been a disjunction in the fabric of time and space within the water and what had been in one place at one moment had appeared suddenly in another.

Ruth called over her shoulder, 'Shall we swim?'

'We haven't brought our things.'

'There's a rug in the back.' I went and searched in the back of the vehicle among a spare wheel and a jack and what appeared to be the components of an ancient tent. When I came back with the rug, Ruth had unbuttoned her shirt and tossed it on to the landing-stage. She stood there in only her skirt, the snake of her spine clearly visible, her ribs like ripples across the sandy skin. I felt something sticking in my throat. 'Ruth,' I called, 'there might be someone . . .'

She ignored me. I watched her undo a cord at her waist, then drop her skirt round her feet and bend to pull down her briefs. As she pulled the scrap of cotton over her foot some part of me recognized that awkward arabesque: a Degas bronze of a dancer bending to examine her right foot, the shape of a drawn bow, a taut spring, the tension transmitted through the substance of the afternoon like the vibration from a stretched skin. She threw her briefs on to the wooden planks of the landing-stage and for a moment she stood there, lean and naked, a figure of pale surprise there at the water's edge, an exclamation mark, raising herself on to her toes to punctuate the still afternoon. Far beyond her, the cormorants moved like two question marks on the even surface of the lake. Then she dived, curving up and over and vanishing with a liquid grace.

I went to the edge. I could see her shape, elusive, distorted by the undulations of the water, moving away from the landing-stage. Far out she broke the surface and turned back to the shore with her mouth open in something that was half-way between a laugh and a scream – delight, pain, triumph, protest. 'Are you coming in or not?' she called.

'It looks cold.'

'It *is* cold. Perishing. You're a coward.'

What to make of this? What to make of her? There was something swimming beneath all this like the secret, silent movement of a cormorant below the surface. I felt disquiet, a blend of anticipation and unease and plain guilt – the guilt of nakedness out there in the open air, the guilt of betrayal: that I would betray her by my refusal to join her and betray Jamie if I did. 'Do you need courage to be cold?' I called back.

She swam back towards the landing-stage in a slow crawl and reached out to grab the planks at my feet. White knuckles. Glittering drops of water ran down her puckered forehead. Her lips were mauve, her eyelashes matted by the wet. 'You do, Dewar. A great deal of courage.'

Then she pushed away and swam back into the deep, to turn and look back, treading water and watching me, no more than a head out there on the surface, her hair plastered against her skull like wet paint. I glanced round, but the valley was empty: no people underneath the livid clouds. I half turned away from her – a fleeting modesty, I suppose – and undressed hurriedly. But I had to face her when I went to the edge.

'Brave enough?' I called.

'Dive,' she cried. 'Dive!'

I didn't. Instead I lowered myself gingerly into the icy water and pushed out towards her. 'You *are* a coward, Dewar,' she cried in delight.

We swam cautiously round each other, careful not to touch, breathless with laughter and cold, our feet searching down into the dark, tarnished depths and finding nothing beneath us. There was a disturbing intimacy swimming together like this, bathed in a shared liquid like foetuses in the same amniotic fluid. Her legs shivered and gleamed in the shadows. I could see the paleness of her breasts and the darkness of her hair. Our legs touched, and then, for a moment, our hands. 'Maybe there's a monster,' I suggested.

'Oh, there is,' she agreed. 'And it's green-eyed.'

The water was too cold to stay in for long. When we climbed out it was with a sudden modesty, turning away from each other, glancing aslant to see and not be seen: a glimpse of her dripping flank and the side of one loose breast – a nipple as brown as chocolate. We only had the rug to dry us and keep us warm. We crept beneath it and pulled it over us in a tent and huddled against each other, shivering with cold.

'Ruth . . .' I said. She hushed me to silence, but I insisted: 'What about Jamie?'

She shook her head, clinging to me and shaking. Her teeth chattered. 'Don't ask,' she whispered. 'Don't ask. If you ask, then it will all vanish in a puff of smoke.'

So I didn't ask. There on the hard wood of the landing-stage, we huddled together while I rubbed her flanks to get warmth into her spare flesh. I touched my mouth against her shoulder; I touched her cold breasts; I felt the hardness of her nipples and the chill of her thighs. Occasionally we kissed. And slowly the warmth came back into her body. And when my hand found the rough patch of wet hair she shifted herself against me and said, 'Yes,' very softly into my ear, 'yes, do that. Yes.' And after a while she came to some kind of climax, very mild, without anything but that whispered word in my ear: *yes, yes, yes*, repeated over and over.

We didn't speak on the way back home – almost like one of those silences that you have after a quarrel, when you are each picking over the ruins of the argument like survivors looking through rubble for something worth preserving. But there had been no quarrel. There had been only compliance. Mrs Jones, the woman who helped out at the reception desk, watched us suspiciously as we came into the hotel.

'Where's my mother?' I asked.

'She's out, Mr Robert. And the boiler needs looking at. I didn't know what to do.'

'I'll ring the man later.' We climbed the stairs to Ruth's room. Once there, we talked. Sitting side by side on the bed we had one of those absurd, intense conversations that you have when you are young: analytical, emotional, confessional, mendacious. She had the power to destroy me and Jamie, we both knew that. Possibly herself as well. 'What do you want, Ruth?' I asked her.

'I don't know,' she whispered. 'I just don't know. Jamie, you, I don't know. Sometimes I think I want all the men in the world, and all the women too.'

'And what does Jamie want?'

She laughed at that, but never answered the question.

Ruth at work in her studio at the back of the pub: she worked barefooted, wearing torn jeans and an old cotton smock. Her hair was dusty with plaster. The studio was two rooms of an outhouse knocked into one. It was whitewashed and slate-floored, lit by wide windows that faced northward towards the Hebrides. There was an old stained sink, broken cupboards with paper and card, jugs and vases full of brushes. The air reeked of the organic smell of solvents. Piled against one wall were canvases and in the centre of the room was a block of slate on which she was working. She showed me the work, pointing out the fractures, the designs she had etched. 'It's a bloody awful stone to work with,' she complained. 'Tough, splintery and difficult. Like the Welsh. But look at the texture, look at the sheen!' She passed her fingers over the surface. 'Like a seal's skin.'

Near one wall there was a canvas on a heavy easel. It was large – five feet by four – primed with white and blocked in with masses of colour: hard edges of grey and slopes of moss green. Across the middle was a great swathe the colour of steel. This paint was laid on thick and smooth. It gleamed lucidly, like wet slate. In the midst of this grey Ruth had painted two black question marks. And then, on the bottom edge where there was green again, there was a tall, thin blade of white, its arm raised up to form the letter Y.

Did she have a name for the work?

She smiled. *Why?*

15

We didn't tell Jamie. Our intimacy was our secret. We shared it in a look, through a touch, by a secret and treacherous smile. Perhaps we were ashamed of what we had done, but shame is an emotion that can sit happily alongside others: desire, excitement, the palpitating thrill of the forbidden and the unknown. Was Jamie the innocent dupe, the victim of our deceit? At times I felt that he knew something. I would feel his eyes on me when we were all three together, and when I looked round he would flush faintly and look away, as though to suspect me was to do me an injustice.

Ruth never moved into his flat in London, but whenever she was in the city that was where she stayed. She was what he called his migratory bird – a joke that had more than a grain of truth in it, because there was something birdlike about her movements, but a splendid bird, an eagle or an osprey: her sudden arrivals in London, having hitchhiked down from Wales with nothing more than a leather bag thrown over one shoulder; her rapid, excited presence in our London life for a few days; her equally sudden and mysterious departures. I often wondered whether there was another man, or maybe men, elsewhere in her life. I think now that there might have been many, and some of them quite casual. Possibly the men she won lifts from on the A5 that led the way to the mountains. Possibly as part of her pursuit of what she liked to call self-knowledge.

'She's all right, isn't she?' Jamie asked me.

'She's great, Jamie,' I reassured him, although I wasn't sure myself.

That winter Jamie and Ruth spent much time in North Wales. His idea for a mountain centre had taken off with a surprising momentum. I remember the first sight of the place he finally bought. It was up a rough track behind Llanberis, past rows of slate-workers' cottages. There was an old sign that announced 'Bryn Derw', and a long, low house, and a building in the background that might once have been a miners' bunkhouse. It was raining when we got there, of course. The place was grey and dank, glistening in the wet. We climbed out of the van and Ruth took Jamie's hand and the three of us stood there looking at it as one might look over some famous archaeological ruins. Ruth translated the name: 'Oak Hill'.

'Where are the oaks?' I asked.

'We'll plant them,' Jamie said. His tone was sharp, as though I had been offering a criticism. 'Can't you imagine it? Done up, I mean. Matthewson Trekking and Climbing. Cottage industry sort of thing. Just imagine bringing a bit of economic life back to this area.'

He had some money and it cost nothing to buy the cottages. The slate mines were dead or dying, the owners desperate to sell and no one desperate to buy. So Bryn Derw passed into the ownership of Jamie Matthewson, or maybe the family firm itself, and he set about converting the property. Ruth was often there. Once Eve came up with me from London and all four of us had a ridiculous drunken weekend camping in one of the outhouses while builders were at work on the roof of the main house. The path to Cloggy was near by and when the weather was dry – which wasn't often – we could make our way up to that gloomy and atmospheric cliff and climb one of the easier routes in the damp cold.

And one day Caroline came up to look things over. She drove over from Gilead House on a raw December morning, when all the colours were tones of grey and the mountains skulked beneath a bruised sky. Beyond the roofs of the town, Llyn Padarn was like an ingot of polished pewter pressed into the valley floor. When I discovered that Caroline was expected I had suggested that it might be better for me to go, but Jamie turned on me as though I had insulted him. 'You'll bloody stay,' he insisted. Perhaps my being present would amount to some kind of penance, retribution for the damage I had done. Or perhaps it would be an exorcism of adolescent jealousies. So, feeling vulnerable and foolish, like a child caught out in some shameful wrongdoing, I hung back in the doorway to the main building as the white Mercedes turned in at the gate.

I hadn't seen Caroline for a couple of years and I had wondered how she would be. I wasn't disappointed. She had gained some of the lineaments of age, but still she wore her beauty and her sexuality in that explicit and defiant way, as someone might wear a fine but slightly out-of-date dress. 'Robert,' she said, with a faint complicit smile after she had greeted Jamie and Ruth. 'I haven't seen you in ages.' She placed her hands on my shoulders and rested her cheek against mine, and then, as though confirming that her memories and mine were indeed all true, whispered my name again. 'Robert.' Over her shoulder I saw Jamie's expression. It was a look of mingled pain and satisfaction, as though all this were necessary to extirpate some malignant growth in the body of our friendship. Ruth watched us thoughtfully, perhaps conscious of the power of this emissary from an older generation.

We went round the property, Caroline picking over it as though looking for bargains. She was a great cynic. I hadn't understood this when I had first known her, but I saw it now, cynicism sliding beneath the surface of her beauty like a treacherous current in a placid lake. 'But, darling, who's going to spend *money* on climbing?' she asked, when he outlined the project. 'People spend money on things that are sensual. Clothes, food, that kind of thing. Sex. But who the hell's going to spend money on slogging up mountains in the rain? Your father invested a small fortune in climbing and he didn't earn a penny.' She laughed. I remember her laughter, I remember her smiling at me to see if I was still stirred by her presence; and I remember the disturbing sensation of seeing the two women together in the same room – Ruth and Caroline, both of whom I had loved. Ruth knew it, that was the disturbing thing. Neither Jamie nor Caroline knew the whole; but Ruth did. Ruth and I held the whole delicate construct of my betrayal in our hands.

When the Scottish mountains came into winter condition, plans for Bryn Derw were shelved. Once again we began to commute between London and Scotland, Ruth often coming with us, taking her turn at the wheel. And once, just once, I stopped off in Glasgow to visit my father. When I asked my mother for the address I was surprised that she even knew it. 'I suppose I can't stop you,' she said.

'Why should you wish to?'

She only shook her head, as though shaking away the question and with it the whole matter of her failed marriage. So I wrote him a letter, a cautious, impersonal letter, explaining that I was often in his part of the world and would like to meet him. I mulled over how to address him, and settled for 'Dear Father'. Somehow I was faintly surprised even to receive a reply: 'I will be willing to see you,' he wrote, 'as long as you come on Saturday afternoon.' He was, it seemed, quite specific about the timing. 'You'll lose a whole day on the hill,' Jamie protested.

'You go ahead and do a route with Ruth,' I told him. 'Get her wielding an ice axe. I'll see you in the evening.'

The house was outside Glasgow, on the north side of the Firth of Clyde: a solemn, solid Victorian building with views over the water. Davie had agreed to drive me. He dropped me off and promised to wait outside until I emerged. 'I'll come running if I hear gunshots,' he assured me.

A sign saying 'Surgery' pointed to a side entrance, but I went up the front path and rang the doorbell. I didn't have long to wait before the door was opened. He stood there, looking at me. He was sandy-haired, stout and balding, older than I had pictured him, but that was only because I had imagined him absurdly young, frozen at the age he was in the few photos my mother had kept.

'I'm Robert,' I said.

He thought about this. It was almost as though he was making up his mind as to whether I was telling the truth or whether I was some kind of impostor. 'It's good to see you, Robert,' he said finally, holding out his hand. As I grasped it I felt an absurd wave of emotion, as though physical contact had established some other kind of communication, the subtle one you were meant to feel for flesh and blood. Ruth would have given it some spiritual gloss. Eve would have denied it all: pure sentimentality, she would have said.

'You'd best come in, my lad,' he said, laying his hand on my shoulder. 'You'd best come in.'

The hallway was stuffy and dark. There was evidence of his second family: coat hooks with raincoats of all sizes; an umbrella stand that held tennis rackets and a cricket bat besides a walking-stick and a couple of umbrellas. The sitting room was decked about with photographs of smiling children, smiling wife, smiling dog.

'They're out for the moment,' he explained. 'I thought it'd be for the best if . . .'

'If what?'

'If they weren't here. The family, I mean. It's just that the wife is Catholic.'

I was, I confess, confused. 'Catholic?'

'Aye. The, ah, situation has been a wee bit trying in the past. The fact is that there are those at her church who consider that she is living in sin.'

'Sin?'

'Aye,' he said.

'I'm sorry, I don't understand.'

'I daresay things are different in London, but in this part of the world there's still a finely developed sense of sin. She's living with a divorced man, you see.'

I wasn't sure whether he was joking. I found that I couldn't read either his expression or his tone. 'Now, would you like a good cup of tea?' he asked, as though tea might make everything clear. I accepted the offer, and he busied himself in the kitchen. He'd got things ready, a tray with mugs, a plate of ginger biscuits. We sat opposite one another, as though conducting negotiations, perhaps for the alleviating of some of this burden of guilt that he and his family appeared to carry. I think he was expecting me to make the next move but I kept my silence like a true Scot.

'Have ye come far?' he asked eventually.

'From London.'

'Of course. From London. And how's your mother?'

'She's fine.'

'That's good. And yourself, what are you doing now?'

'I'm at university in London. Reading English. But mainly I climb. I mean, climbing seems to take up most of my time at the moment. That's why I come up to Scotland quite a bit.'

Did he seem surprised by this? Interested, certainly. 'Is that right? I did some climbing myself, when I was younger and fitter. I was quite a Munro bagger in my time.'

'Perhaps it runs in the blood.'

'Your mother loved the mountains, you know that? I see that you're her child, clear enough.'

'That's what people say.'

'Aye, it's there plain enough. And what are you doing now?'

'I said. I'm at university.'

'Of course, you said . . .'

The conversation was one of those stop-start affairs where no one topic has the energy to keep things going for more than two or three exchanges. It was this fact that awoke the anger in me, the fact that I couldn't even hold a decent conversation with him. 'Did you never want to find out about me?' I asked suddenly. 'Did you never *care*?'

He almost flinched. '*Care?*'

'About the fact that you had a son, for heaven's sake!'

'Of course I cared, Robert. But this was the way your mother wanted it. Diana wanted no help, no sympathy, no apologies. She's a determined woman. Might be a Scot herself.' There was a faint flicker of amusement when he said that; even, I fancied, a

221

glimmer of remembered affection. 'She said to me, "There's a life to get on with. I've got to begin right away." That's what she said.'

'But *why*?' I asked. 'Why did you break up?'

He paused, looking at me with a pinched expression. 'Does she never speak of it?'

'Never.'

'Then how could I? I mean, there are things that are private between two people, aren't there?'

'But there are three people here.'

He smiled, and again there was that small hint that he might have a sense of humour buried somewhere beneath the Scottish Presbyterian exterior. 'At least three,' he said.

'So who are the others?'

'My family for a start.' He shook his head. 'Look, what's done is done and there's no use crying over spilt milk—'

'That sounds like the kind of thing she'd say.'

'Is it, now? You know, it's that long ago I hardly remember. But I do remember that she would quote from poems and that kind of thing. *Alice in Wonderland* was a special favourite. And Wordsworth.' The conversation seemed to have reached safer ground. 'She always wished that she'd read English at university. If the war hadn't come along she'd have gone to Liverpool University, did you know that? She had a place.'

I didn't. I confessed that I was surprised.

'Aye, so she did,' he said. 'She was a clever woman, cleverer than I deserved. Anyways, I'm sorry about it all, laddie, but really there's nothing more to be said. Raking over the past does no one any good.' We spoke a bit more, hedged round other issues, resolved nothing. Finally he clapped his hands on his knees and pushed himself up from his chair. 'Well, I'll not be keeping you, Robert. But it's been good to see you again. You've grown into a fine man, even though your hair's a wee bit too long.' And this time he did smile, and I could see that there was a sense of humour lurking beneath the dour exterior.

I followed him into the hall. For a moment he tried to show something like fatherly affection, patting me awkwardly on the shoulder. 'To have grown up without a father must have been a difficult thing, Robbie.'

I stood there in the open doorway looking at him. 'I don't know. I've nothing to compare it with.'

And then he did something strange, something that seemed right out of character, if you can read a man's character by a mere half-hour's meeting: he embraced me. It was an awkward, clumsy gesture and all the more moving for that. 'God go with you, Robert,' he whispered. 'God go with you.'

Davie was waiting for me outside. 'How did it go?' he asked, as I climbed into the car. I attempted a grin. 'I don't really know. I've nothing to compare it with.'

That amused him, but I was serious. It's hard to know what you feel if the emotion is new. I had thought I was in love with Caroline. I had thought that I hated my father. Experience had taught me that both emotions were false, or at least that they only told part of the story at a particular part of the time. 'Come on,' Davie said. 'If we get a move on we'll make the Fort before the pubs close.'

That Sunday Jamie and I made the first winter ascent of a route on the Orion face of Ben Nevis. It was a complex mixed route that wound its way up icefalls and over verglassed rock for over a thousand feet, a piece of route-finding that owed everything to Jamie's genius for moving in a vertical world. Sometimes it was easy, chopping our way up compact snow-ice; sometimes we teetered up heaped crystals that had the texture of potato crisps; sometimes we were climbing iced-up rock pitches with crampons and ice axes. The sunlight glittered from diamonds all around us. There was space below our heels and the sensation of flight in our hearts. We could never fall. Almost, for those breathless hours, we felt that we might fly.

When we finally emerged into an Arctic whiteness on the summit plateau the sun was setting in a welter of red and black over the Isle of Mull and the distant Atlantic. Jamie's yell of triumph was puny against the roaring wind, no more than a sparrow's cry. We stumped across the plateau to find the path down. Orion the Hunter hung in the gathering blackness overhead as we descended. Below us, in the shadows of Glen Nevis, were the lights of the van where Ruth and Davie were waiting.

'Bloody Sassenachs,' Davie protested, when he heard what we had done, 'coming here and stealing our routes.' He had to get back home, for an appointment first thing in the morning. We waved him off, then clambered into the warm fug of the van and threw off our gear. Ruth had a kettle on the boil for tea and a bottle of whisky opened.

'How was your old man?' Jamie asked. It was the first time the visit to my father had been mentioned. I really didn't want to speak about it.

'He's just that: an old man,' I replied.

'But he's your *father*, for God's sake,' Ruth said.

'I don't really know what that means,' I told her. 'Don't you see? Never having had one, I don't understand.'

The next morning we woke early. We said little, but packed away the things and prepared to leave. We took turns in driving during the long journey south.

During the next week a warm front moved in from the Atlantic. Rain swept across the British Isles, bringing a halt to any possibility of decent climbing and forcing us to stay in London.

Our lives were like that, predicated on the vagaries of the weather or the rhythms of the tides. Ruth had got tickets for a concert – the Incredible String Band, two guys with long hair and beads and flared trousers who sat cross-legged on cushions up on the stage, and plucked one-string fiddles and blew kazoos. Eve joined us. Afterwards the four of us had dinner in a Chinese restaurant off Gerrard Street. There was laughter, and a bit of an argument about politics and personal philoso phy. Scientology had started it all. The ISB were Scientologists. Scientology suddenly seemed to be Ruth's thing, probably because it wasn't Eve's. The two women were two different faces of the times, the mystical and the political in uneasy juxtaposi-tion. When we got back to Jamie's flat the argument continued: music on the record-player – the aimless psychedelics of the later Stones – and the four of us arguing and smoking and drinking, laughing often, sometimes swearing.

'Know thyself,' Ruth said. 'That's the key to happiness. Who you are and where you're going. It's the old Buddhist thing.'

'Bourgeois crap,' Eve retorted. 'A luxury.' She had climbed behind her street barricades and was waving the red flag and firing at will. 'Most people in the world can't afford to know themselves. They can't even afford a decent meal.'

'But I've seen them. In India, for example. They might not afford what you call a decent meal, but they're happier than we'll ever be. They know themselves, understand their place in nature.'

'Oh, for God's sake! That's just feeding them religion instead of feeding them food. The opium of the people.'

'*Opiate*, the word is *opiate*.'

'It's the same fucking thing! It's in translation anyway. Opium will do. Hashish, if you like. The hashish of the people. Just a bloody religious drug.'

'It's not a drug. It's searching for the truth. Accepting who you are. Like what Rob was doing when he went to see his father.'

'When he did *what*?' Eve turned on me. 'You went looking for the bastard who abandoned your mother?'

I hadn't mentioned it to her, that was the trouble. 'It wasn't quite like that . . .'

'But that's *exactly* what it was. You see? More bloody opium.'

'His father, for God's sake,' said Ruth. 'Why shouldn't he go looking for him?'

'Because he's a bastard, that's why. Because the bastard abandoned his responsibilities, that's why.'

'But he's Rob's own flesh and blood.'

'It's not flesh and blood,' Eve retorted. 'It's just a teaspoonful of sperm.'

Later Ruth and Jamie went off to his bedroom, leaving Eve and me alone. She sprawled on the sofa, smoking and eyeing me through the haze. 'Why didn't you say?' she demanded.

'Because I didn't really want to talk about it.'

'But you told *her*.'

'I didn't tell her. She just happened to be there.'

There was a pause. Eve inhaled some of her own personal opiate. 'You fancy her, don't you? The way you were looking at her this evening. I think—'

'*What* do you think?' I retorted. 'What the *hell* do you think?'

She smiled in quiet triumph. 'I think you've slept with her, haven't you?'

I tried to laugh the whole thing off, edge the conversation on to safer ground, but Eve was persistent. 'Does Jamie know? I'll bet he doesn't. Christ alive: first his mother and now his girlfriend. What kind of bastard are you, Rob?'

'Forget it, Eve. You're talking nonsense.'

'Oh, no, I'm not. I can read you like a book. She's dangerous, that's what Ruth is, and you're a fool.'

'Why a fool?'

'Not to see the danger.'

I shrugged away her fears. Jamie and I never spoke about danger. Climbers don't very much. There are two sorts of danger: objective and subjective. Objective danger is the type you can't control – avalanche, stonefall, that kind of thing. You try to minimize it: start early in the day when the loose rocks high up the cliff are still frozen into the ice; beware of fresh snow on old snowfields; avoid places prone to stonefall. But it'll get you if your number is up. Subjective danger is the type you can do something about: you can minimize it by using protection and by not climbing above your standard; you can eliminate it by not doing the climb in the first place. But then you might get hit by a bus on the way to the pub. A bus is objective danger. The fact that you stepped off the pavement without looking is subjective.

Which kind of danger was Ruth?

An evening in some Highland pub – the Kingshouse? The Clachaig? I can't remember. What I do recall, as so often, is the inconsequential and the essential but nothing whatever in between: certainly not the mediocre matters of geography or topography. The noise, certainly, I remember the noise. And the great press of damp bodies, figures reaching over shoulders to get their glasses to the bar. Puddles of beer or meltwater on the floor. And outside, the complaints of a typical Scottish night: a belligerent wind and the thrash of rain or sleet against the windows, like stones thrown by a gang of delinquent kids.

Ruth was there, but no Eve, of course: just Jamie, Ruth and me bivouacked round a tiny circular table, with people pressing behind us and someone leaning over and asking, 'What yer done, Jimmy?' and Jamie looking up and saying, 'Point Five Gully.' Which is internal evidence of a kind. Point Five Gully – a smear of ice one thousand feet high – is on Ben Nevis, so we must have been in Fort William.

After he had exchanged a few words with the other climber, I remember Jamie leaning forward across his beer and saying softly, 'I think we ought to do the Eiger, Rob. What do you reckon?'

We had talked about getting over to the Bernese Oberland the previous summer but had never made it. I ran my mind over the standard routes on the mountain: the Mittelegi Ridge, maybe even the Lauper Route up the north-east flank. We'd got some good Alpine routes behind us and we could burn off any Scottish winter route. So why not the Lauper, which was one of the great ice climbs of the Alps? 'Why not? If I can get away next summer—'

'I was thinking more like this spring,' Jamie said. 'As long as there's not too much snow. It's colder, the mountain stays in better condition. Less stonefall.'

His concern about stonefall was the first hint. 'What route are you thinking about?'

He sniffed. Sniffing was one of the proletarian mannerisms he had adopted. He kept his voice low, although no one was too likely to overhear in that scrum of bodies. 'The North Face,' he said.

There was a silence. The noise of the pub was all around us, but detached from the silent implications of what he had just suggested. 'The Eigerwand?' I whispered. 'You're joking.'

It wasn't the kind of plan you broadcast around the place in those days. Not unless you wanted to be left looking a bloody fool. It was still the great threat, still one of those routes you dreamt about during the day and had nightmares about when you slept. Not nowadays, I don't suppose. Nowadays they climb the thing in a few hours; nowadays there are as many routes up it as there are up a typical Welsh outcrop. They've even given them silly names – the Sanction, after the film; Yeti; Symphony of Freedom; names like that. They've televised an ascent live. The face has been soloed and descended. It's probably even been ski'd down. Nowadays it's probably climbed by Japanese tourists in sandals. But in those days it still possessed weight. There were still only two routes up it: the classic 1938 route and the 1966 *direttissima*, the one from which the American John Harlin had plummeted five thousand feet before he hit the ground at the bottom. Oh, yes, in those days the North Face was still something that could get your name in the papers, alive or dead.

'Not joking at all, mate. I reckon it's on.'

'But are we?'

He grinned. He had all the obsession that you needed, the focus, the artist's determination and the politician's conviction. 'Of course we are.'

What did we do the next day? Probably something on the Orion Face again, some mixed route or other that took the line of a summer VS. Orion Direct, maybe, with a variant line out of the Basin half-way up. I have only the vaguest memory: his climbing above me, the little showers of splintered ice coming down, the impact of his ice axe and the scrape and grab of his crampons, and all the time his voice muttering silly things like 'Brittle Edges' or 'Traverse of the Sods' or 'The White Cockroach' – all of them jokey Eigerwand references. I recognized the symptoms, the growing obsession, the sense that, like an inmate of a mental hospital, he was going to be muttering about the Eiger all the time, contemplating it, mulling it over in his mind, staring at photos, doing all those repetitive-obsessive things of the mentally disturbed.

Back in London we leafed through a book he had borrowed from the library – Heinrich Harrer's *The White Spider*. It was full of overblown prose and heroics on a mythic scale, but it was the pictures Jamie wanted, especially the photograph that unfolded from the centre to show the Face in more detail than any other, with little labels against all the famous features: the Shattered Pillar, the Difficult Crack, the Flatiron, Death Bivouac, the Ramp, the Traverse of the Gods. Then there were shots of the original ascent in 1938, huddled figures plastered against the ice-encrusted rock trying to shelter from the blizzard.

'Looks like a Scottish winter route,' he said.

'It's over five thousand feet,' I retorted. 'That's not like any-thing in Scotland.'

At the end of the book there was a full route description. We went over and over it, consigning it to memory, imagining our-selves in the midst of the tilting plane of the second icefield, working our way up towards the rotting cliffs that shut off the upper part of the Face. We struggled up the Ramp and teetered across the Traverse of the Gods with three thousand feet of space beneath us. 'It's nothing technical, Rob,' he insisted. 'There's nothing as hard as what we did last weekend in Scotland.'

'But it's over five thousand feet,' I repeated.

And there was something else, a hand reaching out from the past to tap him on the shoulder. 'Look at this.' He held out a school exercise book, a thing with a faded grey cover and stapled pages. 'Just have a *look*.'

The pages inside were brown with age. I glanced at the lines of faded ink in that vaguely familiar hand that had once written my mother's name against some rock climbs in Wales. 'Where did you find it?'

'In an old trunk at Gilead House. It's a log of his Alpine climbs.'

Grindelwald, summer 1939

June 12th Mittelegi ridge, 4 hours from the hut. Fine weather and views. Descent by West Flank. Eigergletscher 5 p.m.

June 16th The North-East Face (Lauper's route). 16 hours. Descent to Mittelegi Hut. Pretty fine!

June 19th Inspected N face (N for Nazi?) to Stollenloch. Looks plausible (pace Alpine Club!), need better weather. Next yr?

Jamie was watching for my reaction. He was like someone who has given a present and wants to see joy and gratitude in the recipient's face. 'See?' he said, in case I hadn't. 'My old man practically did the North Face just a year after the first ascent. When all the old farts in England were calling it unjustifiable.'

I smiled at his enthusiasm. 'He only got as far as the Stollenloch. That's the railway window, isn't it? About a third of the way up and before the real difficulties. Plenty of people must have done that, even then.'

'But look' – he pointed – 'next year, it says, next year.'

'And look what had happened by next year.'

'Exactly. But what if, eh? *What if?*'

I laughed. I knew that the only way to drive the demons from his mind would be to climb the thing, beat his father in this at least. And then set his sights on Kangchenjunga.

It was Jamie's birthday a few weeks later. I gave him a book: *The Devils of Loudun* – a book about madness and possession.

IV
London, 1940

16

Diana was billeted in Kentish Town, in a terraced house belonging to a Mr and Mrs Warren. Mrs Warren was vast and pallid. She looked as though she had been assembled out of suet by the Ministry of Food in order to advertise an arcane aspect of austerity or rationing: Mrs Lard the Greedy-guts or something. Her husband was a narrow, mean man with the reek of stale clothes about him. He lived off some kind of indemnity and passed most of his time at home in the kitchen, working on the kitchen table. He was always repairing things – bits of greasy machinery, cogs and cams and sprockets, parts of bicycles or motorcycles. Grease was ingrained in the surface of the table, giving it a dark patina of age and filth. 'Course, 'e knows what 'e's doin',' Mrs Warren would say proudly as he worked. 'An engineer, 'e was. In the mines.'

'The mines?'

'Coal mines, dearie.'

Diana hadn't associated coal mines with London. Mines were South Wales, or Nottingham, or places further north and even more foreign to her. '*Kent*, darlin',' said Mrs Warren, with heavy sarcasm. 'Coal mines in *Kent*. Where you bin livin' all this time? It's not just hopfields and thatch cottages them planes are fighting over. It's bloody coal mines an' all.'

Warren's lungs were bad from the mines, so he said. He coughed and wheezed to prove it. And he complained. Complaint seemed to be his natural state. He complained about the war, he complained about the rationing, he complained about the inconveniences, he complained about the regulations, particularly the regulation that had planted Diana Sheridan on him. His wife shivered and wobbled around her husband and applauded his complaints. 'Isn't he a caution?' she would say. 'Course, he fought in the last war so he knows what it's all about, don't you, dearie?'

Diana occupied the back room upstairs, the room that had belonged to the Warrens' son, who was in North Africa with the army – 'Sittin' on 'is arse and playin' wiv 'imself,' was how Warren put it. The room looked out over the exiguous garden with its Anderson shelter and its rows of vegetables, and, beyond that, other gardens and the backs of the neighbouring terrace. Two of those houses had been hit in one of the early raids so there was a surprising gap in the row, with a view through to a tiny park where an anti-aircraft gun was hunkered down behind sandbags.

She worked twelve-hour shifts. When she was on the night shifts her life was inverted, a mirror world in which she was awake in a time of dark and flashing light, of noise and screams; and asleep in the full light of day, in the back room of the Warrens' house, amid quotidian noises – footsteps on the pavements, people talking, voices calling across the garden fences, dogs barking, the occasional vehicle grinding past – and dreams of burning houses and shattered bodies.

Her ambulance unit was based in Clerkenwell in what had once been commercial garages and an underground meat store. The first-aid post was next door in a converted butcher's shop. She travelled back and forth to the unit by tube – the Northern Line, one of the deepest and therefore one of the safest. In the afternoon there were long queues of people waiting outside the station for four o'clock, when they were allowed down to find shelter. When she travelled back in the morning from the night shift, they were there on the platforms, rows of them huddled beneath blankets. You had to step over them. It was like walking over a ploughed field, trying not to muddy your shoes.

'Oi, mind where you're putting those dainty feet, miss,' people called.

'Can't you mind where you're fucking walking?'

'Can't you see we're fucking sleeping?'

The smell was almost unbearable at times, the stench of unwashed bodies, the smell of damp and dirty clothing, the stink of urine, the stink of faeces. They used the tunnels as lavatories, shitting in the darkness and wiping themselves with bits of newspaper. Man reduced to the level of a beast, living in caves, soiling himself, not caring. Promiscuity was rife, that was what Meg said. And the tube wasn't even safe from the bombs, not all of it. The station at Bank suffered a direct hit and rumours put the deaths at over a hundred. A high-explosive bomb could go fifty feet down through solid ground, that's what people said.

If she was lucky she would get back to the Warrens' by nine o'clock in the morning. She'd let herself in with the key they'd given her, call out, 'It's me!' and go straight upstairs to her room. Often she fell asleep on the bed there and then in her clothes. Exhaustion was like a dense liquid flowing in her veins, deadening her mind and her limbs, pulling her down into a world where she rehearsed the nightmare of the night's work, the burning houses, the shattered bodies, a world picked out by the orange glow of flame and the play of searchlights against the sky, like swathes of chalk drawn across a school blackboard. Only sometimes did she find the energy to get undressed and have a wash first. The bathroom was a shack tacked on to the back of the house and accessible only through the kitchen. She would knock on the kitchen door for politeness, and Mr Warren would call out, 'It's all right, it's quite safe to come in. I'm tied up.' The same damn joke, every day.

'You want to watch him, dearie,' Mrs Warren warned her proudly. 'He fancies the girls, he does. Now, how about a spot of breakfast?'

But she never felt hungry: faintly sick usually, faintly revolted. 'No, thank you, Mrs Warren. Just a cup of tea will do fine, thank you.'

'Got to feed yourself up, you know. Mustn't go without. Looking peaky, you are.'

'I don't really feel very well.'

The woman examined her closely. Her eyes were tiny, like currants embedded in dough. But not shining and friendly: calculating and suspicious. 'You all right?'

'I'm fine.'

'It's that muck you eat at the canteen, I shouldn't wonder.'

'Probably.'

Occasionally she thought of Guy, but life in London was so different from what she had known before, so stark in its contrasts, that she found it hard to conjure up any images of

238

home or friends or countryside. She'd had letters from him, letters from another world. '*My darling Porpoise,*' he wrote, '*when will we see each other again?*' In her mind he was wedded to the mountains, whereas now she inhabited an urban landscape where the cliffs were gutted buildings and the hills were piles of rubble; where plants were alien, intrusive things that sprouted between the paving stones or in the wreckage of bombed houses. She was not wedded to this new existence – that would be altogether too pure a relationship, too sanctified: she was living in sin with it. That'd do. In this new, fallen world the choughs were starlings and the doves were pigeons and the soughing of the wind was the wail of the air-raid siren. Guy Matthewson seemed too distant, in time and space and in another dimension that she could not quite identify – relevance, perhaps.

Dear Porpoise, my tribunal has turned me down. So I'm appealing, because it's an outrage. If they had accepted my registration I would have been happy to volunteer for something useful. I mentioned the fire brigade . . .

I think about you a great deal. I am sure you are very brave there under the bombs; but, oh, it is such a terrible thing to put you and the whole country through. My own battle sometimes seems paltry. Take care of yourself, my sweet. With love, Guy.

What did she think of that? She couldn't really tell. Sometimes she thought the whole world of him, but at other times he just seemed a dream in this new, twilight nightmare that she inhabited.

Sometimes she was on duty at the first-aid post itself, but often during a raid she went out with one of the crews. It all depended on what was needed. Besides the driver, each vehicle carried two stretcher-bearers and, occasionally, a nurse. At the start the nurse had been in full uniform: skirt and apron and stupid starched cap that you had to fold in a special way out of a semicircle of linen. It was damn silly trying to clamber over rubble in a skirt and black stockings, so the idea of traditional uniform had been abandoned soon enough. Now they wore overalls, with just a red cross armband to show what they were.

Night duty varied. Things might be pretty quiet when all the activity was in another sector. They didn't commit ambulances from one sector to another if they could help it because you never knew what was coming next in your own area; some nights you just spent a whole watch talking or playing cards and listening to the bombers over someone else's head, and the cough of distant anti-aircraft fire. On nights like that Diana learnt a new skill: to talk about nothing. It was a knack people had, to talk about nothing, to exchange one anecdote for another, none of them of interest, each designed to prove a point that was, in itself, of no interest either. Families, friends, enemies, *he* did this, *she* did that, why don't they do the other? A whole night's conversation that left no imprint on the mind. It was a kind of anaesthetic, dulling the sensibilities to other issues, other cares, other needs.

But when the call was in their sector chaos barged into their lives. Phones would ring, orders would be shouted, sirens would scream, and the vehicles would drive out of the garages to the latest incident. They would pick their way through the streets, make detours down side-roads to get round obstructions, ease their way past rubble, crunch with painful slowness over shards of broken glass, bump over fire hoses that writhed across the roadway like snakes in a demented, nightmare jungle. And end up in some forgotten street where flames roared and buildings collapsed and people died.

The driver she liked working with best was called Bert. She had expected almost everyone in London to be called Bert, but in fact he was the only Bert she encountered. 'Albert Jones, Esquire,' he said, giving her a look. 'But if you're very good to me, you can call me Bert.' Because he had been a taxi driver in peace-time, Bert could always find a way round obstructions. 'I got the Knowledge, 'en' I?' he would explain mysteriously, and the Knowledge took on extraordinary proportions in Diana's mind, as though it were a great philosophy – the secret of life or something. He would peer through the windscreen into the dust of an explosion, and say, 'Just like a fucking pea soup fog, if you'll forgive my French,' but he always seemed to know where he was. The vehicle – a Ford V-8 motor-car converted into an ambulance – would creep round corners and down alleyways and somehow it would always find its way to their incident.

They always called them 'incidents'. It was a bureaucratic euphemism. At first it had been 'occurrence', but then 'incident' had caught on. The etymology of disaster. It might be high-explosive, in which case there would be collapsed buildings and people buried, and the injuries were contusions and fractures and internal haemorrhaging. Or it might be landmines, parachuted gently down through the night sky to explode at street level and blast people and buildings into unrecognizable fragments. Or it might be oil bombs and incendiaries, in which case the casualties would be burns. The burns were the most terrible, with whole bodies charred and scorched and the skin peeling off to show fiery red beneath. The pulse would flutter away into oblivion beneath the anxious press of her middle finger; and what had been a face was torn open to the whole world like one almighty scream, life itself evaporating from the gaping mouth.

In her memory one incident merged into another, a confusion of sight and smell and sound. Above all, sound. The concussion of high-explosive and the crack of the anti-aircraft batteries, the rattle of incendiaries falling on roofs and pavements, the throbbing of the pumps and the rhythmic droning of the bombers, high up and invisible above the underlit, ochre clouds. She scrambled over scree slopes of rubble, carrying splints, bottles of saline drip, bandages, tourniquets. 'Nurse! Nurse, over here!' was the call. She stumbled and struggled, she wriggled into tunnels cleared through the rubble to get to buried bodies and deliver shots of morphine, she helped ease shattered limbs from beneath house beams, she applied splints as they lifted bodies out, and tourniquets to staunch the bleeding. Sometimes they dispensed with the splints and they just tied ankles and legs together, sometimes the only tourniquet was her own thumbs, pressed deep into the slime of a bloody thigh. The wounded were often coated in a fine powder of dust. With blood it turned into a kind of mud. The stench of drains enveloped her, the stench of gas from broken mains, the stench of damp from old cellars, the stench of unwashed bodies, and the hard, sulphurous smell of high-explosive. Sometimes a burning gas pipe lit up the scene with a hellish light. Sometimes a whole backdrop would be a burning building, smuts flying high into the lurid orange cloud, the flames the colour of burns: a crimson tainted with black, a bone whiteness at the heart. Hell was the obvious metaphor. Dante's inferno, a medieval world of plague and torment, with devils silhouetted against the light playing whips of water into the heat. Overhead the drone of invisible aircraft and the barrage balloons like maggots against the putrid flesh of the clouds, and the great rush of sound that was a falling bomb, falling through four miles of air, rising in pitch to a shriek before it vanished somewhere over the rooftops and there was the gust of an explosion and the tremor of the ground shock. You never had time to hear the one that got you, that was what people said. Bert explained it to her, and his explanation carried some kind of weight: 'Them bombs travel at something near the speed of sound, see? Which means they sort of, like, catch their own sound up, see? So you don't hear it. Not until the last second anyways.'

It never happened to her. It seemed strange. You felt so vulnerable down there on the ground with the bombers sliding across above the clouds and the bombs coming down like a celestial lottery, yet always falling somewhere else. Did it mean that she was somehow chosen? Or was she, perhaps, excluded?

'Just fucking lucky, darling,' said Bert, touching wood. 'Let's hope it lasts.'

And then the all-clear sounded its long lament, and a chill dawn seeped into the littered streets of the city like lymph leaking into a wound. The heavy-rescue teams would be at work throughout the daylight hours, pulling aside the rubble with their hands, shifting beams, tunnelling in towards the distant murmur or the muffled cry or the stifled appeal for help, for light, for life. The ambulance would pick its way through the streets to drop its burden of wounded wherever it was convenient, or wherever there were beds, or just wherever they could actually reach – Bart's or the Royal Free or the London Hospital in the Mile End Road, anywhere – and then make its way back to the unit in silence.

The day shift would be waiting for their return. Reports were to be written and handed over. There was a washroom in the ambulance station where you could rinse your face. And a gas ring for boiling a kettle. And home was the room at the back of the Warrens' house, fifteen minutes on the tube, if it was running.

Darling Porpoise, Today I heard from the appeal board and the news seems a bit better. I have to appear before them next week . . . I am sure you will think of me and wish me luck . . .

On one occasion Warren was evidently not tied up when she knocked on the kitchen door. 'Come in,' he called, and when she opened the door he stood up and blocked her way. Mrs Warren was nowhere to be seen. 'Gone to the shops,' he explained, with a grin. 'They say there's a shipment of fruit just in. *Bananas.*'

Diana attempted a smile. 'May I pass, please? I need the bathroom.'

But Warren didn't move. 'Wouldn't you like a banana, dear?' he asked. 'Long and thick and with a bit of a curve to it. Bit pointy at the end so it slips in your mouth easy. How does that sound?'

'I want a bath more than anything,' she replied, not really understanding, not hearing either his words or even his tone. He was standing right in front of her, his head at the level of her chest, his weasel face peering up into hers. Before she could step back, before she could even flinch, he put his left hand up and grabbed her shoulder. He was smaller than she, but far stronger. And quicker too, seeing that she had been on duty for the last twelve hours and was stunned with exhaustion. As he grabbed her with one hand, he slid the other inside her dressing-gown.

She froze. She was naked underneath. She shouldn't have been, but she was. He sucked in his breath when he discovered the fact: surprise, perhaps. Maybe it was as much a shock to him as it was to her. Perhaps he had expected to find that she was wearing a petticoat or something underneath the dressing-gown. Maybe he hadn't intended the violation to be so brutal. Perhaps he expected her to wriggle and giggle and say how awful he was, perhaps he expected her to take it as a kind of game: not a very nice one, but a game nevertheless. Anyway, she was naked, and she froze, and his hand was motionless.

'Nice bit of fur you've got there,' he said quietly. His tone was almost conversational. He swallowed and moistened his lips and smiled at her. 'Off the ration, is it?'

She would have screamed, but no scream came. She did actually open her mouth but nothing at all came out. She just stood there immobile, with his hands on her and her mouth half open. Warren shifted his fingers gently. 'Don't scream, darling,' he whispered. 'Just be quiet and you'll be all right.'

She could smell his breath. It had the sour, flat smell of town gas, the stench that often hung around the streets after a raid. She closed her eyes. Breathe in deeply. That's what she told the injured to do. 'Take a deep breath,' she would say, cradling their broken limbs, their broken bodies, trying to keep a grip on slippery, bloody pressure points. 'Breathe deeply. In,' pause, 'out,' pause; 'in,' pause, 'out,' pause. It's what you do to try to reduce hyperventilation and ameliorate the effects of shock. Shock is a big killer, people didn't seem to realize that. One minute the victim might seem quite all right, talking to you, smiling, responding normally; next minute they were dead.

'No harm intended, no harm done, eh?' Warren whispered. 'Just a bit of fun, dear; just a bit of a giggle.'

Finally, mercifully, she found her voice. Very quietly she said, 'If you let me go immediately, I won't say anything about this. Nothing at all. I promise you that.'

Perhaps it was the calmness that surprised him, her matter-of-fact tone. It certainly surprised her. Slowly, reluctantly, he slid out his hand from inside her dressing-gown and let her go. 'Just a bit of fun, eh?' he repeated. He lifted his hand to his nose and sniffed his finger. 'Nice,' he said.

She pulled the dressing-gown tight around her and pushed past to the bathroom. 'I can get you things,' he called after her. 'Chocolate and stuff. If you like. If you're good to me.'

She slammed the door behind her, locked it, and bunged up the keyhole with a piece of lavatory paper. Then she opened the hot tap and sat down on the edge of the bath, and wept.

She tried to change her billet after that, but things were difficult and if you couldn't find anywhere better you had to put up with it. So she put up with it. The motto of the whole bloody country: 'Put up and shut up.' They might as well have put it as a slogan on posters, along with 'Be Like Dad: Keep Mum.' Every morning she returned to the house, hoping to discover that the place had been hit by a stick of bombs and reduced to a heap of rubble. With Mr Warren underneath it all. But every morning the house was still there.

'You should have kneed him in the balls, darling,' Meg said, when Diana told her. 'What an odious little creep. Do you want me to come and sort him out?'

Meg seemed to enjoy the war. Austerity became her. She had blossomed. With her hair piled up and pinned, and her shoulders military broad, and her legs carefully balanced on high heels, and her lips blood red, she drew men's eyes the way a Dornier drew searchlights. The simile was hers. She was living and working somewhere near Croydon and occasionally they met in town. Usually they went to a Lyons Corner House, or sometimes a tea dance at one of the hotels. She had joined the WAAF and was doing something with radio, something she couldn't talk about, although how Meg could do anything worth not talking about seemed ridiculous. She was full of talk about other matters, of course. She knew people, she heard things. Apparently clothes rationing was going to be introduced, but they weren't going to ration makeup because Churchill liked to see girls with makeup. Apparently the American ambassador was a Nazi sympathizer and believed that the British would surrender within weeks. Apparently the factories were running out of rubber for condoms, and there was going to be the most frightful increase in the birthrate. Apparently.

Diana could talk freely about her work, of course; but she didn't much. 'You should see what it's like in the East End,' she said quietly. 'It's terrible, Meg. They've got no shelters, no proper shelters at all. They're using the tube stations and the authorities even tried to stop them doing that. And railway arches. There's fifteen thousand using the Tilbury arches under the Commercial Road. *Fifteen thousand*, Meg. They're living like animals, half the time.'

Meg sighed. 'Oh, for goodness' sake, don't give me the suffering-working-class nonsense. It's just as bad in the West End. We've even been hit in Croydon.'

Diana shook her head. 'Nothing like Stepney or Poplar or any of those areas. Really.' She felt sullen and depressed. What fact did she want to convey? She didn't know herself.

'My dear, we've all got our bomb stories. The whole bloody city has got its bomb stories. It's becoming the great social bore. Guess who's in Egypt?'

'Who?'

'Hilda, the lucky girl. I'd love to be posted to the exotic Orient. Anything rather than bloody London. Have you heard from any of the old gang? I got a letter from Eric.'

'Eric?' Diana found it difficult to remember him. It was absurd, this forgetfulness, this detachment from the past. As though it didn't exist.

'Yes, Eric, you chump. Remember Eric? Eric the airman. God, you two were together for a couple of months.'

They were in the ballroom of the Albion Hotel, the Royal Albion Hotel, featuring Jerry Rollo and His Music. There were half a dozen couples already on the floor, dancing the cha-cha. Jerry Rollo was shouting '*Olé!*' from time to time just to make it clear what was expected.

'Of course I remember Eric.'

'Well, he's training in Canada. Bombers, apparently. Says all it does is snow.'

Outside, the sirens began to sound, that awful switchback wail, that swooping up and down that brought a fluttering of panic, and the beads of sweat on your forehead and under your arms. The warbler, that's what some people called it. 'Oh, my God, what a bore,' said Meg, in her world-weary voice.

Jerry Rollo paused the music for a moment and turned to the hesitating dancers with a smile of pure Brylcreem. 'Ladies and gentlemen, it seems that we have visitors, and I don't think they're here to tango. If you care to avail yourselves of the hotel's shelter facilities in the basement, you are most welcome. The band, however, will soldier on.'

There was some laughter. People looked at one another nervously, as though to move would be to commit a solecism. One or two couples got up to leave, but maybe they'd have left anyway. Strangely enough, it was easier when you were on duty, actually out there in the streets, rather than sitting like this at a table on the edge of the dance floor pretending there was nothing wrong.

The music struck up again and drowned the distant sound of

the ack-ack guns. 'It sounds as though it's miles away, thank God,' said Meg. She lit a cigarette and blew a self-conscious stream of smoke towards the ceiling. Behind the music you could hear the crump of bombs far away in the docks. Someone else was getting it, not the hotels and clubs and cinemas in the West End, not this time. 'What about you, darling? Heard from that Guy?'

'As a matter of fact, I have.'

The cha-cha finished and some nigger minstrels came on and sang 'If I Didn't Care'. They swayed and warbled and rolled their eyes.

'Still battling for peace and civilization, is he? Guy, I mean.'

'The tribunal rejected his application. It's gone to appeal.'

'I can't say I'm surprised. Isn't he some kind of Communist? No wonder the board turned him down. Religious conviction can get you registered straight away, so I believe. Look, there are a couple of fellows over there. They're watching us. Come on, show your best profile.'

'Meg, I'm pregnant.'

'Hey, look, I think they're coming over.' She hadn't heard; hadn't been listening, hadn't heard.

'Meg.'

'Yes, darling?' They *were* coming over. One of them was in uniform, the other in civvies. They looked all right.

'Would you lovely ladies care for a dance?' the uniformed one asked.

Meg turned to Diana, feigning indifference. 'What about it, darling?'

Diana shrugged. 'All right by me.' They got up to dance. The floor was half empty or half full, depending on how you saw it. Meg would have seen it half full; Diana had no doubt that it was half empty. She shuffled round a bit and when the number was over she thanked her partner very much and said she was feeling slightly headachy and needed to sit the next one out if he didn't mind, and of course he didn't. He followed her back to the table and tried to engage her in conversation. He was something in the Ministry of Food. A reserved occupation, so he hadn't been called up. He could get her things if she wanted.

'Things?'

He looked furtive, a bit like Warren. 'You know, off the ration . . .'

The singers broke into 'The Java Jive'. They liked coffee, they liked tea, but these days, presumably, they couldn't always get it unless they knew this louche young man with the plausible manner. A Warren in the making. Diana had a vision of him in the next war, fifty years old and groping young girls billeted in his house. 'You mean black-market, do you?'

'Ssh! For Gawd's sake, you'll get me into trouble.'

Meg was hanging on to her partner's arm as they came back to the table.

'Meg?'

'Yes, what is it? Look, darling, Dan here—'

'Don.'

'*Don*, then.' She laughed at her mistake. It was easy for her. 'Don thinks we ought to go on to a place he knows off Shaftesbury Avenue, a kind of club. When do you have to be back on duty, darling?'

'Meg, I want to tell you something'

'Tell away, darling, tell away.'

'In private.'

Somewhere outside there was a louder explosion. The ground reverberated gently. Glasses and crockery trembled. They could hear the anti-aircraft guns going off nearer now, in St James's

Park probably. And perhaps there was even the sound of aero engines above the music of Mr Jerry Rollo. Meg smiled and asked whether the boys minded just letting them be alone for a sec. 'Just a sec. Girl talk. We'll be right with you.' Meg took out a cigarette, tapped it impatiently on the packet and struck a match. 'Well, what is it, darling? Tell.'

'Meg, I'm pregnant.'

Meg stopped. She looked almost comic sitting there across the table with her eyebrows up and her mouth half open. Bright red lips, with the cigarette hanging limp between them. The match burned down and she shook it out. '*Pregnant?* My God, darling, are you *sure?*'

'Keep your voice down—'

'Pregnant? Oh, my God, Di, this is awful! Who was it? How long have you *known?*'

'I've missed my third period.'

'God, that's *three months.*' Somehow three months made it seem worse. 'Di, you really are awfully silly not to have told me earlier. I mean, trying to keep a pregnancy secret is the most ridiculous thing, if you think about it. Who on earth *was* it?' It was plain from her expression that Meg was calculating, running twelve weeks back through her mind, and ending up in North Wales, in the Ogwen valley, on an August weekend. 'Oh, my goodness,' she said, 'not Mr Conscientious himself?'

Diana nodded.

'God, darling, he's about twice your age.'

'What's that got to do with it?'

'Well, he should have known better, that's what. I mean, didn't he *use* anything, darling? Apart from you, I mean.'

Diana shrugged and stared away across the dance floor, seeing the dancers through a blur of tears. Meg struck another match and lit her cigarette. The band played and the minstrels sang. The two young men who had been dancing with them hovered by the bar, glancing over from time to time and wondering whether the whole thing was pointless, and whether there were other fish to catch. Or fry. Meg spoke through exhaled smoke, a cloud of fashionable grey that emerged from mouth and nostrils and floated towards the ceiling like a chiffon scarf tossed up in the air: 'So what are you going to do, Di? Have you told your parents?'

'I've not told anyone but you.'

'And what about him? I mean, if he's got such a powerful conscience he ought to do the decent thing and make an honest woman of you. How would you fancy being Mrs Guy Matthewson?'

'I wouldn't fancy it at all.'

'Well, neither would I at the moment. I mean, Guy's a good-looking fellow, of course, but . . .'

'I haven't told him, anyway.'

'He doesn't even *know*?'

'Meg,' Diana said quietly, 'I want to get rid of it.'

Dear Guy,

Thank you for your last letter. I'm glad to hear that your position seems to be better. Here things go on as usual, which you will know from reading the papers. London is a sad place, half empty, drab and damaged; but not yet destroyed.

I am sorry to write this letter, but it is to tell you that I wish to stop this correspondence. The world is changing sharply and so, surely, are we. I enjoyed meeting you and enjoyed our brief friendship, but now I think it is time to look to the future. Although my experience here convinces me that you are misguided, my decision has

nothing to do with your stand against participating in the war effort.
   Yours, with respect,
     Diana S

She wrote and rewrote the letter, not substantially but in the detail. She tried 'Yours affectionately' rather than 'Yours, with respect'. She originally wrote 'joining up', rather than 'participating in the war effort'. Things like that. She shifted it from the familiar and faintly regretful to the formal and indifferent. It surprised her to discover how she could manipulate words to achieve a subtlety of effect. It surprised her to discover how readily she could consign Guy Matthewson to her past. There was within her a hard kernel of rationality that she had never expected to be there. Emotion had always been something that she claimed as hers: in her personal ladder of beliefs the affective response counted high above the rational one; and now there was this cold centre of logic and reason that she had discovered at the core of her personality.

17

Meg found the man, of course. Meg knew people, who would themselves know other people. 'It's not cheap, darling,' she warned.

'How much?'

'Fifty.'

'*Fifty pounds?*'

'Actually, darling, I think it's guineas.'

Diana felt sick. Was it real nausea, the sickness that she had been feeling so often these days, or the shock of the cost? 'I haven't *got* that kind of money,' she whispered. 'I only earn six pounds a month, for God's sake. Meg, what'll I do?'

'Look, we'll go and see. We'll go and talk about it. I'm told that the man is very good. A friend of a friend knew someone who had it done by him. Perhaps we can get him to reduce the fee. I can lend you some. We can work it out.'

'Is he . . . ?'

'Is he what?'

'You know. Is he a *doctor*?'

Meg smiled reassuringly. She should have been the nurse, with that lovely reassuring smile. 'Of course he is, Di. That's why it's guineas. Don't worry, I'm not going to put you in the hands of some dreadful back-street abortionist. Actually, he's much more than just a plain old doctor, he's a gynaecologist and a surgeon. A Mr Mandeville. Harley Street, no less.'

'Harley Street? But I thought this kind of thing was, well, illegal.'

Meg patted her hand. 'There are,' she explained, in her knowing manner, 'ways and means.'

They had to wait a few days for the appointment. It was in the early afternoon, so it wasn't difficult to get there as long as she was back on watch by six. Apparently there would be an examination. Meg came up from Croydon and they met at the station, then took the tube to Bond Street and walked from there. It was a cold and leaden day, the clouds lying low over the city and a thin drizzle brushing the air. Meg had her issue greatcoat, so she was all right; but Diana's coat was threadbare and did little to keep her warm. And there was something else: the chill of expectation. That was internal, not external, the icy anticipation of what was to happen to her, of how she would lie on her back with her legs up in stirrups while some strange man poked around inside her. No amount of outside insulation could dispel that cold.

Harley Street was forbidding in its restrained splendour, the impassive frontages in dark brick, the doors and windows and railings picked out in white, the brass plaques announcing arcane specializations and recondite qualifications.

255

Mr Humphrey Mandeville
FRCS, FRCOG

There was a nurse in starched white, and a receptionist whose disapproving expression suggested that she understood the purpose of their visit all too well. They waited in a drawing room, with copies of the *Tatler* for diversion. The pictures on the wall were reproductions of paintings by Stubbs: horses – stud mares, no doubt – with their grooms.

Mandeville himself was a tall man with a stiff collar and pince-nez hanging from a chain round his neck. He had the aspect of a bird: part owl, part eagle, wholly predatory. He sat behind his expansive desk and glared at the two women with an expression of barely concealed ferocity. 'Which of you ladies is Miss Sheringham?'

'It's *Sheridan*,' said Diana. 'Diana Sheridan. A bit like the actress.'

'You are an *actress*?'

She blushed. 'No, not me. My name's a bit like the actress's. Dinah Sheridan. Diana Sheridan.'

The man frowned. In his stiff collar and pince-nez he seemed to be glaring at them as from another century, an era when even an actress was something disreputable, never mind a pregnant unmarried woman. 'What actress? Why are we talking about an actress if you are not one?'

Diana felt an unnerving mixture of emotion: part shame, part anger, part the embarrassment of a child made an object of ridicule by an adult. Sweat crawled like an insect down from her armpit into the fabric of her slip. 'It doesn't matter,' she mumbled. 'It really doesn't matter.'

'So if you are not an actress, what are you?'

'A nurse.'

'A *nurse*, indeed?'

'An auxiliary. I work with an ambulance unit in Clerkenwell.'

'An *auxiliary*. Is that so?' He rested his elbows on the arms of his chair and placed his fingers tip to tip and bounced them gently against each other. 'May I ask, Nurse Sheringham, how you came to be in your . . . ah . . . present circumstances?'

'Well, I wanted to do something for the war effort and nurses seemed likely to be needed, so I did a course—'

Mandeville's expression contracted as though with pain. 'I think you misunderstand me. I do not wish to hear reasons for your commendable efforts towards the defeat of Nazi Germany, I mean your being with child. How did your *pregnancy* come about, girl?'

Perhaps it was the use of the word *girl* that annoyed Meg so. She interrupted angrily: 'I'd have thought you'd have known that, seeing as pregnancy is your line. Di slept with a man. They made love. How else do you do it, Doctor?'

Mandeville turned the weapon of his eyes away from the blushing Diana and on to Meg. 'Thank you for that. You see, that is precisely the point, Miss . . . ?'

'York. Like the city. And I'm a lady, not a girl.'

'I'm delighted to hear it, Miss York. Well, you must understand . . . both of you must understand, that the circumstances surrounding the conception of this child are of immense importance. If Miss Sheridan did, as you have just suggested, *make love*, then it is difficult to see how one can justify the destruction of the child.'

The phrase hung in the air, reverberated from the windowpanes with their criss-cross of adhesive tape, echoed through Diana's skull. *Destruction of a child.*

'Do you have to put it so bluntly?' Meg demanded.

'But that is precisely what it is, Miss York. The abortion of a foetus is the destruction of a child, specifically outlawed under the Offences Against the Person Act of 1861. For carrying out an abortion, under the terms of paragraph fifty-eight of this Act, both Miss Sheridan and I might be liable to penal servitude for life.' He looked from one to the other of the two young women seated on the far side of his desk. '*Life,*' he repeated, as though he were saying 'death'. 'Even you, Miss York, for aiding and abetting, might be liable to up to three years in prison.'

There was a silence, like the silence of the court room. Outside a car drove past. You could hear the tyres cutting through the wet. Inside Mandeville's office Diana sat with her knees primly together and her hands clasped tight in her lap and her mind ringing with words: the word *life*, the word *destruction.*

'On the other hand,' Mandeville continued, 'the Infant Preservation Act of 1929 provides for the possibility of performing a lawful termination. But to be lawful, I would have to be satisfied that by ending the life of the child I was preserving the life of the mother.' He looked over his pince-nez at Diana. She appeared eminently healthy – bursting with health; and guilty – crawling with guilt. As though tasting her, tasting both health and guilt, the man passed his tongue over his lips. Then he sniffed, glanced down at his desk and went on with his legal dissertation: 'The Bourne Ruling of 1939 defines the life of the mother in rather broad terms.' He held up a sheet of paper as though reading it to the jury. 'Termination may be allowable if – and I quote – "the doctor is of the opinion on reasonable grounds and with adequate knowledge of the probable consequences, that continuing the pregnancy would be to make the woman a physical or mental wreck".'

He looked up from the page. 'Strong language, is it not? "a physical or mental *wreck*". In the Bourne case, the mother in question was a fourteen-year-old girl who had been raped. Dr Bourne performed the abortion and was acquitted at the subsequent trial. The question is this: can I be convinced that Miss Sheringham –'

'Sheridan.'

'– Miss *Sheridan* would be left a physical or mental wreck by proceeding with her pregnancy? If she, too, had suffered the misfortune of rape, then perhaps I could do so, even though she is clearly not fourteen. But Miss York has suggested that Miss Sheridan and her partner *made love*. And I see before me a perfectly healthy young woman who gives every indication of being able to bring an equally healthy child into the world. Of course, I haven't yet examined you, Miss Sheridan, but unless you have any marked physical problem, then all I can say is that you are asking me to perform an illegal act. An illegal act of the gravest kind. And, I might add, an immoral act. Which is not necessarily the same thing.'

Mandeville stood. His pince-nez fell from his aquiline nose and hung down his front like a dead mouse. 'I assume that any medical examination is superfluous – it would, in any case, incur costs for you – and I suggest that we bring this whole unpleasant meeting to a close. I further suggest that you go away and bring your child into the world and turn yourself into a decent mother. There is enough death and destruction at the moment. Why not take part in the creation of life, Miss Sheringham?'

They went out into the rain. Just down the terrace from Mandeville's consulting rooms a house had been bombed. There was only the shell left, looking like a tragic mask – empty sockets, vacant mouth, frowning brow and hollow cheeks. At the back there were charred wooden beams, like ruined bits of stage machinery. Outside this place, in the drizzle, Diana sat down on a low wall and wept. She wept for many things: for herself, for her child that would never be, for her fleeting, fractured love for Guy; but also for those nameless people she had seen broken by the bombs, the baby she had seen exploded on a pavement in Stepney, the pregnant woman she had helped extract from rubble in Clerkenwell and subsequently watched die, the bewildered, ragged East-Enders who picked through the debris to find what remained of their lives; and she wept also out of pure, unmitigated tiredness, for she was tired. Exhaustion was a cancer that ate away at her mind and her limbs, that eroded the arteries and dissolved the nerves. She sat and wept and Meg stood over her, and the drizzle came down like tears out of a cold grey sky, so that the wet on her cheeks and the smudged mascara might have been the one thing or the other, a mere meteorological phenomenon or a personal disaster.

That night they bombed Bethnal Green. A high-explosive bomb hit the cemetery and threw old coffins and tombstones around the place in unthinking irony. Bombs also hit residential streets, rows of houses that were little more than slums, two-up-two-down terraces with outside privies and inside squalor. High-explosive swept the houses into rubble and one scored a direct hit on a surface shelter, one of those death traps that the borough councils had erected in unseemly haste at the start of the war. Twenty-five people were killed in the shelter. Incendiaries clattered across the wreckage of the houses and started fires. They called in ambulances from other sectors, from Hackney and Holborn and Stepney, and fire tenders from all over the City. Hoses wrote black arabesques across the Tarmac and the pavements. Ladders slanted upwards against the smoke, exclamation marks and oblique strokes punctuating the flames.

The ambulance was called from Diana's post at three in the morning. A doctor climbed on board at the last minute as they left; they didn't usually carry a medic. 'Thought I might be more use in the front line,' he said. He was a Scotsman, called Dewar. He had pale ginger hair and freckles, and eyelashes so light they were almost transparent. Behind them, red-rimmed and innocent, were childlike blue eyes.

'You can drive the bloody thing if you're so keen,' Bert suggested.

'I'm sure we're safer with you.'

Anti-aircraft guns were firing from near Spitalfields market, their reports dull and flat against the heavy concussion of bombs. You could see the explosions up there in the sky, the smudged flash of the shells going off in the cloud, uselessly probably, probably quite without effect.

They drove through the black streets and the orange light of conflagration, Diana in the front between Bert and the doctor. It was strange, Diana thought, how the wreckage of an affluent middle-class home or a squalid working-class slum looked much the same: beams and joists and bricks and plaster and the thick fog of dust together achieving a kind of democracy. Like the way that a laid-out corpse is classless. 'We bring nothing into the world and we take nothing away from it.' Where were those words from? They rang in her mind as they drove. And another line: 'Man, thou art dust and to dust thou shalt return.' Bethnal Green was returning to dust that night.

Shrapnel clattered down on to the roadway. High above the clouds the bombers droned. There was that curious rise and fall to the sound of their engines, like an old car straining at a hill. 'Beats,' Bert told her 'Technical term, darling. They desynchronize their engines and that makes the sound go up and down. Interference. Know what I mean?'

She didn't. She didn't know what anything meant, really. She just thought of the babies dead within the rubble and the baby alive within her womb.

'I'll bet you fought that *interference* meant something else, didn't you?'

'*Thought*,' she corrected him.

'There you go again. Just 'cos I don't speak lah-di-dah. I'll bet yours is all put on, in' it? I'll bet if I woke you up in the middle of the night, you'd speak natural, like me.'

'You'll never get an opportunity to wake me in the middle of the night,' she said tartly.

'I can hope, though.'

The doctor looked away from them, out into the lurid night. There was a sound above the noise of the engine – like coal being dropped down a chute – and he flinched against Diana. 'Incendiaries,' said Bert, peering through the windscreen. He prided himself on deciphering the noises of the Blitz, the oil bombs, the high-explosive, the incendiaries, just as Diana had learnt to decipher the injuries.

A yellow diversion sign pointed them towards Commercial Road. 'We don't want to go that fucking way,' Bert protested. 'If we can get a bit further down Brick Lane we'll be all right.' He leant forward over the steering-wheel, looking for one of his short-cuts. The end of Brick Lane was obscured by a dense cloud of yellow fog. There were figures in the fog, vague shapes shifting through the murk like shadows dimly perceived in nightmare. 'Someone else's fucking problem,' he said, pulling the ambulance down a side-street. They passed a pub with its windows boarded up. There were vacant windows and open, empty doorways. Narrow, mean streets, shuttered against the world. Where had all the people gone? Diana wondered.

'Jack the Ripper country, this,' Bert said. 'D'you know that, Doc? Of course, the Ripper was a doctor like you, wasn't he?'

The doctor laughed at Bert's words. 'Was he indeed? Like me?'

'Well, he must have been a doctor, you see. Because he had an intimate knowledge of a woman's *innards*.' Bert gave the word emphasis, making it sound like something inside a chicken: giblets or gizzards.

'Perhaps he was just an enthusiastic amateur.'

Bert shook his head. 'All the indications are that *he knew what he was looking for*.' The ambulance trundled along, crunching over broken glass. There were railway arches on their left, with figures huddled against the cold and the bombs. 'How are you on women's innards, Doc?'

'Is this the kind of conversation one should have with Nurse Sheridan present?'

'Oh, she's used to it.'

'I'm not sure that I am. And I'm an orthopaedics man, not a gynaecologist.'

'That children, is it? Orthopaedics?'

The doctor laughed again. 'Rugby injuries, more like.'

'Rugby.' Bert's voice was laden with despite. 'Bloody typical. Rugby. Come the revolution we'll *ban* bloody rugby.' He peered ahead. 'Here we are. Just round the Jack Horner and we should be there.'

'Do you really say that?' Diana asked.

'What?'

'Jack Horner.'

Bert sniffed and glanced across at his passengers. 'Just for Scottish tourists,' he said. He turned the ambulance into a residential street and brought it to a halt beside a group of helmeted figures. On the other side of the road rubble had spilled out across the Tarmac like the spoil from mine workings.

A heavy-rescue squad was at work by the light of a burning warehouse in the street behind. Men clambered up and down the rubble, teetering on planks, lifting beams, pulling bricks away with their hands and passing baskets of debris down the line to the street. The scene was like something on a stage, complete with backdrop, apron and lighting. Despite the efforts of the wardens to get them away to the shelters there was even an audience of ragged extras watching from the other side of the street – half a dozen wide-hipped women, a few anaemic-looking children, a couple of old men.

Diana, Bert and the doctor climbed down from the ambulance. Pompous and puffing, an air-raid warden came up to them. He wore a blue cover over his helmet. 'It's *my* incident,' he said, as though the fact had been disputed. 'Where the hell have you been?'

'I had a fare for the Café de Paris,' Bert said.

'We don't need your lip, mate. We've got people trapped, about half a dozen by all accounts. And there are some walking wounded.'

At that moment someone shouted down from the pile of rubble: 'Silence!'

In view of the racket all around, the drone of bombers overhead, the concussion of the anti-aircraft fire, the roaring conflagration behind, the throb of the fire tenders' pumps, it was a ridiculous command. Nevertheless everyone on the heap of rubble stopped. They seemed like puppets whose strings had been abruptly cut. They didn't merely stop, they became inert, almost lifeless, their arms hanging. At the top of the heap a helmeted man was kneeling down and talking to someone out of sight below him. He looked back. 'Is that a doctor?'

'I'm right here. What's the problem?' The doctor's Scottish accent was incongruous among the sounds of London. As he scrambled up the narrow walkway that the rescue squad had constructed, Diana had an absurd image of him in a kilt, scrambling up some Scottish hillside.

The pile of rubble was a kind of cone, like a volcano. Standing on the lip, they could see down into the shallow crater. From the depths came a smell that was like the stink of a volcano, a smell of gas and drains and the sulphurous stench of explosive. 'We've got someone trapped down there,' the rescue man said. 'She's conscious, just about. Looks like we'll have her out soon. She's in a lot of pain. Something broken, probably.'

There was a stir of interest among the onlookers behind them. 'It's Ma Philips,' a child's voice called. 'That's who it is.'

It was impossible to relate the mess to the house it had once been, impossible to resolve the chaos of joists and pipes and bricks into walls and floors and window-frames; but down at the bottom of the crater was a leg. Diana recognized it with a start of surprise. It was the colour, exactly, of the dust that coated everything, but it was, nevertheless, a leg, with a slipper still on it. There was a wooden beam and a dark slot beneath the beam and the leg emerged from one end of this slot. One of the rescuers was crouched down beside it talking into the darkness. You couldn't hear his words, just the tone, a low murmuring, a comforting crooning such as a mother might use with her baby. And behind this sound was another, a moaning, inarticulate animal sound that was the sound of pain.

The doctor slithered down into the pit. 'Nurse, I'll need morphine,' he called.

Another rescuer was trying to manoeuvre a piece of wood into the hole, lying on his side and pushing and shoving. The wreckage shifted and the man stopped. 'Keep it steady, George,' his companion warned. He called into the darkness, 'Don't you worry, darling, we'll soon have you out.'

Diana loaded a syringe and went down to where the doctor crouched. There was a moment of awkward scrabbling, the cleaning of a patch of flesh somewhere on the vast and dusty thigh that belonged, it seemed, to Ma Philips. From within her tomb, the woman moaned. She was calling for someone, she was crying someone's name. Edith or Edie or someone. Maybe it was Eddy. The doctor took the syringe and held it upright, the liquid beading on the end of the needle. It was a moment of strange and ritual calm. Then he slid the needle into the exposed thigh and pushed home the plunger.

'Righto, Doc,' the rescuer said. His face was black with grime. In the light from the fire his eyes shone like those of a Hallowe'en mask. 'We'll get her out as quick as we can. Give us fifteen minutes.' He turned back to the task, reaching in to pull bricks out of the gap, his mate trying to work a prop into the space to take the load. Diana and the doctor climbed gingerly back to where Bert waited with the stretcher. The doctor held out his hand to help her up. 'Well done, Nurse,' he said.

That was the moment when there was noise at the heart of the wreckage below them. They looked round. There was a groan from the rubble, as though the pile of debris were an animate being breathing its last: it groaned and its ribcage deflated and a small cloud of dust spewed out of the narrow mouth like foam bubbling up from its lungs, and when the dust cleared nothing was there that had been before, neither the two heavy-rescue men, nor the narrow space, nor the single, dusty leg.

Someone shouted. The man in charge of the rescue began yelling orders. Men pushed their way past Diana and the doctor. Overhead, but somehow detached from all this movement, there

266

was the rushing wind of a falling bomb, the noise rising in pitch to a shriek, the thing landing three or four streets away, not with an explosion but in silence.

Diana made her way off the rubble. At one point she slipped on something and fell. Exhaustion covered her like a blanket. Perhaps she could just stay there in peace, lying on the wreckage of this anonymous house with the rescue men shouting and struggling down in the pit. Perhaps she could sleep.

Dr Dewar pulled her to her feet. 'Come on, Nurse, gird your loins.' He might have been calling the Picts to war. With his arm around her for support they went on down the pile of debris to the street, where injured people were waiting beside the ambulance. There was one old man lying on a stretcher and a few others with lesser wounds. It was like a scene from the First World War, like those photos you saw of shattered houses on the Western Front. Except these ragged figures were not soldiers who had just staggered back from the shelling, they were women and children and old men who had been pulled out of their own houses.

'Get this lot out,' the warden shouted. 'There's another ambulance on its way.'

They loaded the ambulance with the wounded. 'You'll be all right,' Diana assured them. 'We'll have you in hospital in no time.' She could hear the men tearing at the ruins of Ma Philips's house. Anti-aircraft guns were firing. Shrapnel clattered on the asphalt further down the street. She was trying to immobilize a woman's broken arm and bandage a child's gashed head. They smelt. The injured people smelt, a foul blend of sweat and urine and faeces. They probably had lice. They certainly had scabies. 'You don't look well, Nurse,' the doctor said, as he climbed in after her.

'I'm fine.' She smiled to show just how fine she was.

'Hold tight,' Bert called, and the ambulance moved off. Squeezed between the casualties and the doctor, Diana was overwhelmed by tiredness. She felt her head go over on to the doctor's shoulder and she didn't have the strength to lift it. The doctor didn't object, didn't shift, didn't seem to mind. The engine roared in her ears and the motion of the vehicle lulled her into a soporific state on the borderline between sleeping and waking. And all around her, crouched on the opposite bunk, jammed along the narrow passage between the stretchers, were the people of Bethnal Green.

They came off duty at dawn. As Diana went to the washroom, the doctor called, 'Nurse Sheridan.'

She stopped. 'Yes?' She was too tired to go over to him, too tired even to use his title. She wondered what she might have forgotten. The morphine had been returned to the poisons safe; the saline drips had been put away; she'd handed in the syringes for sterilization and placed the splints in the cupboard. All that kind of thing had been done. What was it now? For God's sake, was he going to criticize her for falling asleep in the ambulance? This was the first time he had been out with one of the crews, as far as she knew. Was he one of those idiots who threw their weight around?

'I was wondering . . .' That thick Scots accent. He looked awkward. He'd never addressed a word to her, really, outside what was necessary. Now he looked awkward and embarrassed. His freckles stood out against the flush of his skin. 'I was wondering whether you might have dinner with me some time. If it's no trouble.'

She tried to smile. She felt ill and she felt tired and she wanted to get home. Home wasn't the word. She wanted to get back to the Warrens', to some kind of bath, to her bed. She tried to smile. 'Really . . .'

'If it's any problem . . .'

'It's no problem. It's just that—'

'You're spoken for?'

Spoken for. What a quaint phrase. Scottish, perhaps. 'Not that.' She thought of Guy. She thought of the child growing within her. Absurdly – she found it easy to think absurd thoughts – she wondered whether the doctor might even be able to solve her present problem. *Sometimes I think three impossible thoughts before breakfast.* Who had said that? The White Queen. 'It's just that . . .' What was it *just*? 'I don't even know your name.'

He grinned with relief. Almost boyish. 'It's Alan. Does that remove all the obstacles?'

'No, not really.'

'How about Thursday?'

'That's my day off.'

He looked sheepish. 'I know that. I had a look at the duty roster.'

'But I'm busy on Thursday. I'm sorry.'

'Next week, then?'

'Maybe,' she said. 'Maybe.'

'Good,' he said, not quite crestfallen. 'Good.'

She walked away to wash her hands and face in tepid water and change from her overalls into her ordinary clothes. She thought about Dewar. Why had she rebuffed him? Many doctors had joined up but Dewar was medically unfit, so the rumour went: only one lung or something. 'One lung, one kidney, maybe only one ball,' was Bert's opinion. 'Like Adolf himself.' But she hadn't rebuffed him for a silly rumour like that, for God's sake. He was a pleasant enough man, and brave and dependable. She had rebuffed him because she was frightened, she had rebuffed him because she quite liked him, she had rebuffed him because she was carrying another man's child. It wasn't that she was spoken for: she was far worse than that.

The journey back on the tube was dreadful. The train stopped in a tunnel for half an hour with the lights low and her ghost face staring back at her through the glass from the black tunnel wall. Panic bubbled up in her throat like nausea. Eventually they moved on to the next station and the doors slid open to allow in a belch of foul air. The remnants of the night's sheltering was there for all to see, a litter of newspapers and cardboard boxes and other, nameless debris. The train waited there for a further twenty minutes. When finally she got back to the Warrens' house she had to rush to the bathroom to be sick. She came out to find Mrs Warren in the kitchen, watching her with a thoughtful expression.

'You all right, dear?' the woman asked.

'Quite all right, thank you.'

But Mrs Warren stood in her way. She had a cigarette in her mouth. She always had a cigarette, and she spoke through it, so that the thing wagged up and down with her words and the smoke formed a kind of veil before her face. 'You been pukin' in there?'

Diana blushed. 'I didn't make a mess or anything . . .'

'I'm sure you didn't. And I'm sure it weren't anything you ate, neither.'

'I expect it was, Mrs Warren. Those terrible sandwiches they give us at the post.' She tried to edge past, but the woman just stood there, her vast bulk filling the space between the table and the cupboards, her arms folded beneath her breasts as though they needed that extra support.

'There anything you want to tell me, young lady?'

'Tell you?'

'Yes, darlin', *tell me.*' Her voice was larded with sarcasm. 'You're in trouble, aren't you?'

Diana felt the fabric of her defences tremble beneath the woman's gaze. 'Trouble?'

'Yeah, trouble. Don't think I can't tell, pukin' like you are every morning, lookin' all weepy and everything. I'm not a bloody fool. You're in the club, aren't you?'

'I don't know what you mean ——'

'You know perfectly well what I mean. Up the spout, in the family way, whatever you want to call it.' The cigarette waggled. 'It weren't my Roland, was it?'

Who was Roland? Was her awful husband called Roland? Diana shook her head. Could the dreadful Mr Warren really be called Roland? The name was so ridiculous and the idea of his being the father so incongruous that she wanted to laugh, laugh or weep she wasn't sure which, the two being on either side of the same coin, which was the currency of misery.

'Well, that's a blessing, that is. So, what are you going to do about it, then? Does the father know? Does he even care? Or are you all on your own?'

And Diana's defence against tears or laughter finally fell to pieces, and she began to weep. She had managed greater control with Meg, except after that awful visit to the doctor called Mandeville; but now in Mrs Warren's kitchen she broke down and wept, and was powerless to do anything when the woman herself, still with that cigarette in her mouth, moved forward (she moved with a curious swaying motion, thrusting one massive hip forward first, following it with the other, as though she were wading through water) and embraced her. Mrs Warren smelt. It was a strong, rancid smell, of old frying oil and sweat. 'There, there, dearie,' she said, holding Diana to her huge breasts. 'You have a jolly good cry. That's what you need. And when the crying's over we'll see what we'll see.'

'You'll do nothing of the kind,' said Meg, on the phone. She was almost shouting. 'I'm not letting you get into the grips of some awful back-street abortionist. Look, I've told you I've got this other address. We'll go and see on Thursday.'

So Thursday came – the day she might have been going out with that Scottish doctor, the day she might have relaxed and slept in a bit, then enjoyed herself in the afternoon, going to the cinema maybe, going for a meal. Thursday came and she met up with Meg and they took a bus. The place was somewhere south of the river, somewhere out at Camberwell. 'He's a medical man, so it's all right,' Meg assured her.

'Medical man? What's that mean? Another doctor?'

Meg looked a bit nonplussed. 'Actually he's a dentist.'

'A *dentist*?' It seemed ridiculous. There was something comic about it, really, something downright absurd. 'What's a *dentist* got to do with it?' They began to giggle. Sitting there on the bus as it crossed the river and traipsed out through the dreary purlieus of Kennington, the giggling turned to laughter. 'What's so bloody funny?' asked the clippie. She spun tickets out of her machine with casual dexterity, like a conjuror producing flags-of-all nations from a top hat. She was older than them, somewhere in her forties, with lots of makeup and dyed blonde hair piled on her head.

'My friend's got to see the dentist,' Meg said.

'Don't see what's so bloody funny about the dentist. Dentist's a bloody tragedy, if you ask me. I'd rather be bombed out than have to face the dentist.'

They almost enjoyed the journey. Bomb damage seemed to finish at the Elephant and Castle, more or less. It was a cold November day, but the suburban streets were flooded in sunlight and gave an illusion of warmth from inside the bus. When they got off at Camberwell Green the conductress even gave them a wave. 'Hope you don't have to have any extractions,' she called. Which didn't seem very funny.

The road they were looking for was tucked behind a church. 'St Botolph's, Church of England', a board announced. It was almost like being in the country: the church with its spire and a stretch of green grass, the plane trees at the back, London planes with their bark patterned like camouflage. There were freshly dug graves in the churchyard, without headstones. Meg consulted a scrap of paper on which the address had been written. 'Tear it up and throw it away when you've finished with it,' the person who'd given it to her had said, as though they were spies and this was a secret contact, which it was in a way. 'Here we are. This is the street.'

It was a suburban road with semi-detached houses, each one a mirror image of its next-door neighbour. Bay windows picked out in white. Gardens with roses pruned back to mere sticks. They counted the numbers, even down one side, odd down the other. 'Twenty-five,' Meg said.

But there wasn't a twenty-five; there was neither twenty-five nor twenty-seven, which would have been its next-door neighbour, its mirror-image twin. There was just a pile of blackened rubble: a low wall, a gate and a path with crazy-paving leading up to a pile of bricks and plaster, and through the gap a twin garden with a fence down the middle and the twin humps of two Anderson shelters. On the gate of twenty-seven there was a scrap of faded, rain-washed paper with a new address. But on number twenty-five, nothing.

A woman was watching them from a nearby garden. She had been lifting potatoes and her hands were caked in mud. 'You want the dentist?' she called.

'Do you know where he is? My friend's got a terrible toothache.'

'I'm sure she has.' The woman laughed, but there wasn't much humour in the sound. 'I'm afraid you're too late.' She nodded towards the rubble. 'He was underneath it all. A week ago. Blew all my windows out, it did. If you want to pay your respects you'd better go back to St Botolph's.' She turned back to lifting potatoes. Overhead distant aircraft drew white contrails against the blue. The day was sunny and bright, but the wind was in the east and bitterly cold.

18

Mrs Warren's friend was called Maud. What her surname was, neither woman ever said. Just Maud. Diana had expected her to be large like Mrs Warren – the name Maud seemed to suit large and fat – but Maud was small and thin, with a slight squint and a slight limp and a cigarette hanging from the corner of her mouth. She had raw red hands as though from long hours spent in soap suds. 'You never seen me, right, dearie? Not only don't you know who I am, you never even *seen* me.'

A very experienced lady, so Mrs Warren said. And clean, she emphasized: clean.

'Ten quid,' Maud said. 'That's all. Special price for friends, right?' She waited, wearing a smile that she might have used for a simpleton. 'On the nail, dearie. OK?'

Diana didn't understand. There were many things she didn't understand. 'The nail?'

'In *advance*, love.'

'Oh, yes. My purse is up in my room.'

'I think we can wait while you run and get it.'

She would never forget this. As she climbed the creaking stairs, she knew that she would never forget all this – the two women in the kitchen, with their caustic politeness, the stairs creaking as they bore her weight, the wall of the stairwell with its grey flock wallpaper. This would be in her memory for ever, a part of her more certain than the baby inside her.

She returned with the money and handed it over for inspection. Had it been coin no doubt the woman would have bitten it. As it was she folded the large white notes and tucked them away down the front of her dress. 'That's lovely, dearie,' she said. 'Now, if you'll just make yourself ready . . .'

Diana smiled at her. She wanted to please, she wanted to like Maud, love her, even. She wanted the woman's voice to be mellifluous, flowing like honey, soothing and loving. But she didn't know what Maud meant. 'Ready?' she asked. 'How?'

Maud sighed. 'Knickers, dear. Take your knickers off and get on the table. You're a nurse, aren't you?'

'An auxiliary.'

'Well, you ought to know about it all, then. What is the modern generation coming to, Mrs Warren? That's what I want to know.'

Maud had an old leather shopping-bag. Her reticule, she called it. Out of it she took rubber tubing and a syringe and other pieces of apparatus: a cheese grater, a bar of Lifebuoy soap and a bottle of disinfectant. Dettol. A kettle whistled in the background. 'Hot water, please, dear,' said Maud to Mrs Warren. The big woman mixed hot and cold, and rolled up her sleeve to display a forearm as large as a ham and as white as dough. She dipped her elbow to test the water. Maud began to grate soap into the water, bright pink curls, like parings of living flesh. All the time she hummed, expelling air through her teeth in a breathy, toneless whistle – 'The Mountains of Mourne' over and over. The smell of carbolic filled the room. Never again was Diana able to hear the tune or smell carbolic soap or Dettol without conjuring up that moment in the kitchen of the Warrens' house, with fear plucking at her diaphragm and the scrawny woman grating pink soap into a dish.

'Right, dearie?' asked Maud, turning to her with the rubber tubing in her hand. 'Are we ready?'

Diana was determined to make no noise. She'd seen so many people, victims of the bombing, suffering in shocked silence. She would behave like them, almost as though none of this mattered, nothing mattered, neither the destruction of a house nor the destruction of a child. So she lay on her back on the kitchen table and looked upwards at the stained ceiling and the single, bare lightbulb, and made not a sound as Maud groped around between her legs and inserted her tubing. Diana's very soul seemed pierced by it. The fluid flooded her and the tide of pain flowed and ebbed and flowed again. It was an interior pain, the agony of her soul being damaged, maybe even destroyed. She closed her eyes and she thought, oh, she thought of dozens of things: her room at home, walking in the Yorkshire Dales, Meg and Eric and the others, her parents, her various family. She tried not to think of Guy Matthewson. She tried not to think of whatever it was that was inside her. She tried not to think of the death and destruction that was all about her.

'There we are, dearie. Just wait a few moments before you sit up.' Maud was coiling up the tubing and putting it away. Mrs Warren was mopping up.

'That's it?'

The woman gave a dry chuckle. 'No, dearie,' she said. 'That's *not* it. It's only just beginning.'

There was an ominous pause, a kind of truce, time enough for Diana to go on day watch at the post. 'If nothing happens we'll have to have another go,' Maud had said, before she left. Her tone was that of an adult warning a child not to be naughty.

Diana waited. Sensitive to every stirring within her body, she waited. It was like a pause in the raids, an unnatural silence in which no aircraft sounded in the air above and no bombs fell, but the all-clear hadn't sounded: it was peaceful, but you knew it wasn't peace. At the post they had to tend a few minor injuries, cuts and bruises gained in the aftermath of bombing: a couple of children who had hurt themselves playing with bits of shrapnel, a woman who had fallen while picking through the rubble of her house to salvage her paltry possessions.

When she went to the lavatory she passed a liquid that was stained pink with soap or blood, she couldn't tell.

'You don't look well, Nurse,' said Dr Dewar, when she emerged. There were two people waiting to be treated, one with a cut from trying to open a tin and another who had scalded herself. It seemed ridiculous that among all the deliberate damage you could suffer an accident in the kitchen.

Diana smiled vaguely at him. 'I'm all right. I think I'll be getting home, though, once we've got these done.'

There was some kind of pain now, like a period pain. And she felt like vomiting. What had nausea got to do with it, except by proximity? How were these things linked inside? How could one symptom spill over into another? As she put bottles of disinfectant back into the cupboards her head swam with the smell of phenol, the same smell that had pervaded the Warrens' kitchen, the smell of the carbolic soap that spread through her memory and etched itself like acid into her mind.

She collected the instruments that had been used and put them into the sterilizing kettle. Then she scrubbed down the sink and collected the bag of discarded dressings. You wore uniform when you were on duty at the post – the white apron and starched hat. As she went out with the bag to the incinerator she caught a glimpse of herself reflected in the glass of the medicine chest: an efficient, sterile figure looking older than her nineteen years.

There was a sudden stirring within her abdomen. She paused, and closed her eyes against the pain, and it suddenly seemed to her that her baby was in there, fighting for its life, drowning in carbolic. A shudder passed through her body and someone grabbed her arm.

'I say, are you all right, Nurse?'

The room moved. As though it had been hit by a bomb. They said that happened if you were near a blast – the walls would shift and sway like a ship in a storm. Often you never heard the sound of the explosion, so they said. 'I've got to get home,' she said.

'Not for the moment, you haven't.' A Scots voice. 'You'd best lie down.'

The post had once been a butcher's shop and the inner room was the cold store. Now there were half a dozen hospital beds with iron frames and bare mattresses, but there were still the pipes along the walls and the rails from which carcasses of beef had once hung. The doctor helped her on to one of the beds and bent to take off her shoes, a strange and touching gesture that almost made her weep. She'd a hole in her stocking, her big toe showing through. A potato, that's what her mother called holes like that. And thinking of her mother brought on the weeping, so that she lay there with her skirt pulled down primly and Dr Dewar taking her pulse and her big toe poking through her stocking, and the tears flowing. One of the other nurses was hovering uncertainly in the background. You didn't leave a woman patient alone with a male doctor. 'Is it your time of the month?' Dewar asked.

'Maybe that's it.'

He placed a hand on her forehead. His touch was cool and dry. 'Maybe. But we'll take your temperature and see if you're sickening for something. It's probably all brought on by exhaustion. I've seen you working, Diana, and it's enough to stop a man in his tracks.'

He'd never used her Christian name before. Among the waves of nausea flooding up from her abdomen, she noticed that fact. How did he even know it, she wondered. She closed her eyes and swallowed something. 'I think . . .'

'What is it?'

'I think I want the bathroom.'

He called the other nurse to help her. In the bathroom she vomited and she bled. Later she must have fainted, because when she came to she was sitting on the floor and someone was hammering on the door and she vaguely heard Dewar's voice coming through the wood panelling. He was saying something about taking the bloody locks off, it was bloody lethal to have locks on doors in a bloody clinic. She noticed the way he said *bloody*, the Scottish intonation. Shortly after that they broke the door open, but she was beyond caring by then. She heard a call for towels and felt hands picking her up and his voice telling them to go carefully, for God's sake. There was blood on her legs – to go with the *bloody* in his language, she thought. There was pressure on her stomach, someone leaning and pushing. Then they hurried her outside and there was the motion of the ambulance, and then a stretcher and doors banging and bright lights in a long corridor and a room with a sink and a sluice and a glass-fronted cabinet. There was more pain and the pushing on her abdomen and the sound of water flowing. And then they transferred her to a trolley and wheeled her into a ward full of women. 'Where am I?' she asked one of the nurses.

'The Royal Free.'

They put screens round her bed and a male face looked down at her. He reminded her of Mandeville. He had a stiff collar and a thin black tie. His hair sprouted grey wings above his ears, like a gull's. That was even his name, she discovered later: Dr Gull. 'Do you understand that you could face criminal charges for this, young woman? It ought to be reported to the police.'

'Have I lost it?' she asked. How was it possible to want the answer to be twofold, positive and negative at the same time? How was it possible to hold contradictory ideas like this, to want death and life, to feel both relief and pain, happiness and misery at the same time? The doctor looked down on her with the pinched and sententious expression of a priest. 'Yes, you've lost it. It was a girl,' he added, 'but I don't expect you care, do you?'

'Of course I care.'

'Then why did you do it?'

She turned away from him, to stare at the plain grey cloth of the screen. There was no answer to give, really. Dimly she was aware of the man rising from his chair. 'We'll have to do a small operation to clean things up,' he said, as he turned to go.

She felt a sudden panic, and turned to look at him, to grab his arm. 'Will it damage me?' she asked. 'I mean, will it stop me having babies?'

He paused, measuring his answer, wanting, no doubt, to be able to deliver worse news: 'Let's hope not.'

Later the ward sister looked in on her and asked if there was a number they could phone. 'You'll be out the day after tomorrow and you'll need looking after.' Diana gave Meg's number. There was no one else. There was a whole city out there, but her knowledge of it was limited to the ambulance unit and the first-aid post, and the Warrens, and Meg; fewer people than you'd know in a village.

The sirens went that evening. They had to evacuate the ward. Women in dressing-gowns and slippers trooped down to the basement. Those who couldn't walk were pushed in wheelchairs. One or two had to be taken down on their beds. They sat in the half-darkness beneath the central-heating pipes and the water-pipes and the ventilation ducts and listened to the distant concussion of high-explosive. Diana thought of the ambulance unit, imagined Bert driving through the littered streets and Dr Dewar at work with the wounded in the first-aid station. The all-clear sounded at three o'clock in the morning and everyone went back upstairs, grumbling and complaining.

Later that morning they did the operation. D and C, they called it. They gave the impression that she ought to know what the letters meant, but she didn't, and she was too afraid to ask. When she came round from the anaesthetic she was back in her bed. This time there were no screens: she was immersed in the noise of the public ward, people coming and going, trolleys trundling along, patients complaining, exchanging diagnoses, prognoses, disasters. Her next-door neighbour looked across at her with a wry expression. 'Up the spout were yer, love?' she said. 'Always the way. There's dozens of 'em in 'ere for that.'

She discovered her own nightdress and dressing-gown beside the bed. 'Who brought these?' she asked a nurse.

The girl swept past in a rustle of starched apron. 'Some doctor. Scotsman, I think. Never seen him before.'

Visiting time was in the afternoon. Diana sat up in bed and watched the people come in, the husbands with bunches of flowers, mothers with things to bring comfort, no visitors below the age of twelve. Sometimes you saw a young child being held up at the door of the ward, to wave at its mother in a distant bed. The noise in the ward got louder, a railway-station noise, the noise of the public. Only after the first rush were there two visitors for Diana, each eyeing the other warily, not knowing who the other was, how much the other knew. 'I've brought you chocs, darling,' Meg said. 'Black Magic. Cost a packet.'

Dewar had brought a bouquet of flowers. 'They're from the unit,' he was careful to explain. A note attached to them said, 'Knocked off from a bombed-out florist', and was signed 'Bert and the rest'. She smiled. She recognized it as the first smile since the loss of the baby, the first smile for days. The shadow, perhaps, of the baby's smile that would never be.

There was desultory, awkward conversation before Meg leant over and kissed her cheek. 'Must fly, darling, and I don't want to be a gooseberry. I'll give you a tinkle.'

They watched her clip her way down the ward. She managed to impart a measure of glamour to her WAAF uniform, even wearing issue stockings. Men followed her with their eyes, watched the swing of her slender legs and the movement of her backside. 'She's an attractive girl,' Dewar said. He rolled the R as though he was savouring the word.

'That's what they all say.' There was an awkward pause. 'Was it you who went round to get my things?'

He nodded. 'Aye, I did. And I met the lovely Mrs Warren.' There was another silence; *pregnant* this particular one, Diana thought. She surprised herself by almost smiling at the idea. Dewar kept his voice low so that he wouldn't be overheard: 'Did she do it?'

'Do what?'

'Whisht, Diana. You know very well what. When I knocked she was terrified that I was the police.' He made two syllables of the word – po-lis.

Diana shrugged. 'If you're going to interrogate me, you can go.'

'I don't want to interrogate you. But it was a terrible thing to do.'

'It's done,' she said. Her finality surprised her. 'There's no use looking back. And I'm not sure it's any of your business, Dr Dewar. You were very kind, you looked after me and all that, but that's only what any doctor would do.'

Dewar nodded. He picked at a button on his jacket. Harris tweed, the jacket, of course. There was even a gingery thread in the cloth to go with the ginger of his hair. 'I spoke to the sister. You'll be out tomorrow morning. Where will you go?'

'Back to the Warrens, of course. Back to the unit. Where else?'

'You should rest up a bit. Go home, maybe.'

'And brood about it? And have to evade my parents' questions? No thanks.'

'My invitation still stands,' he said.

She smiled. He seemed almost comic, with his Scottish manner and his Scottish turns of phrase – what the devil did 'whisht' mean? – and his awkward shyness. 'Maybe,' she said. 'Maybe.'

'That's the same answer as last time. Can't I have a more definite one?'

'I suppose you can,' she said. And suddenly she found herself overwhelmed by the fact that this man, who despised what she had just done, still wanted to see her. The understanding brought her to the brink of tears. Which wasn't hard in her present state. 'Yes,' she said.

V

19

I suggested to Eve that she come, but she refused. It was not an easy conversation.

'I don't want to go and I don't want *you* to go either. I don't want you to climb mountains and I don't want to be sitting there at the bottom when they bring your body down.'

'That's ridiculous—'

'Is it? How many has that bloody mountain killed? Thirty, forty?' Her eyes glistened. She didn't weep – she was too tough for that kind of thing – but she walked dangerously close to the edge of tears. One false step might have thrown her over the precipice. 'And then there'd be Ruth, wouldn't there?'

'Of course.'

'Well, can't you understand that I don't like her? Can't you get that into your head? Can't you grasp the fact that I hate to think of you and her fucking together?'

'That's past—'

'Is it? Is a thing like that ever past?' She managed a laugh. 'You'd like it, wouldn't you? The pair of you, I mean. You and Jamie. You'd like to have the little women waiting for you to come back from the war. Well, I'm not playing. I have other battles to fight.'

So there were just the three of us in Jamie's battered old camper van when we set off on the cross-Channel ferry to Calais. The vehicle had a 'Ban the Bomb' sign on the back and the slogan Make Love Not War across the front, and flowers painted by Ruth along the sides – gentians and edelweiss as well as daisies. It stuttered across Europe with the three of us taking turns at the wheel.

We spent the first night at a farm near Soissons, and in the morning we were woken up by the farmer's daughter standing at the door of the van and holding out a plate with three fresh eggs on it. '*Pour le petit déjeuner,*' she said. What did she make of the three inhabitants of the van, Ruth with her lean breasts and angular shoulders sitting between the two men – a tense little trio of jealousy and desire? Perhaps she thought nothing of it. Adults occupy a different world from the young, and foreigners a different one still.

That day we drove on to Switzerland and reached Interlaken in the afternoon. The weather was gloomy. Clouds hung down over the twin lakes and shrouded the mountains. The world beneath was grey and green. Ruth took the wheel for the final leg. I lay in the back on the pile of climbing gear and Jamie sat in the front because he knew the way. 'Used to come here on family skiing holidays,' he said.

The van clattered up the Lauterbrunnen valley, hemmed in by the mountain walls, winding between the cliffs. Waterfalls crashed down through the trees anywhere they pleased, as though the whole place had only recently been hastily slammed together and the fine detail still hadn't been worked out. Rain spattered against the windscreen and turned into sleet as we climbed. We debated how long it had been like this, how much longer it would last, the usual futile weather debate that climbers always have, as though talking about it might change it. 'Just as bad as bloody Wales,' I protested. Jamie reckoned we might as well turn round and go home, reckoned we might as well forget the whole fucking thing.

'You're just trying to tempt fortune,' Ruth said dismissively. 'What will be will be.'

'That's your bloody Welsh fatalism,' Jamie cried. 'That's why you ended up with all those English castles.' You could feel his energy, bound up and caged inside him by the mindless fact of weather and circumstance.

Ruth swung the van on to a side road where the sign pointed to Grindelwald. The engine clattered away at the back of the vehicle. We swung round curves, swerved to avoid a post bus, crawled behind a tourist coach; and then the narrow confines of the hillside opened out into the basin where Grindelwald sits, and there was the sensation that we were out of the claustrophobic ditch and could breathe again. The air was chill and there were streaks of old snow in the sheltered slopes. We pulled into a lay-by to get our bearings. The meadows above the town lapped up to the base of the rock, but the cloud was down to two thousand feet and you couldn't see anything of the mountain. 'Oh, damn you bastards!' Jamie shouted at the clouds.

Cows stood morosely in the damp like extras for a tourist postcard waiting for a photographer who hadn't bothered to turn up. A train grunted up through the meadows, past picturesque chalets. It was a brightly painted little thing, like something out of Toyland. Jamie turned on me as though I was the final court of appeal. 'You've not been here before. Believe me, Rob, believe me, up there' – he flung an arm upwards towards the grey pall directly overhead – 'is the whole north-east ridge of the Eiger. And there – just *there*, for crying out loud – is the dreaded, the ghastly, the murderous Nordwand itself, the Mordwand, the Murder Wall. Gets your blood up just to think about it.'

But amid the gathering dusk and the gathered cloud, there was nothing to be seen. He might have been crazy, standing on the side of the road and pointing out nothing at all with the conviction of a lunatic.

Invisibility brought a sense of detachment to our presence there beneath the Eiger, almost as though there were no mountains, there was no North Face to climb, there was no fear to overcome. We pitched a tent at the campsite and mooched around Grindelwald in the evening. The place was a front-line town in the tourist war, recently abandoned by the skiers and now occupied by a different army – Japanese, mainly. To Jamie's disgust Ruth even bought some souvenirs: a miniature ice axe with Grindelwald engraved down the shaft, and a little arrangement of artificial edelweiss under a plaster model of the Eiger. 'My parents will love them,' she said. 'I don't care what you say. I can just see this axe among the horse brasses over the bar.'

Next morning was no different. We dropped in at the guides' office in the main street to get a weather report. The man behind the desk was lean and tough-looking, his face burnished by sun and wind to the colour of polished oak. 'Not worry,' he said. 'The forecast is *gut*. This weather will clear and high pressure moves in.'

'I'll believe it when I see it,' Jamie said.

'You're just a pessimist,' Ruth remarked. She was the only one keeping a sense of balance, the only one who tried to get some enjoyment out of the situation.

'You know what a pessimist is? A pessimist is someone who's never disappointed.' Jamie smiled humourlessly at the guide. 'What are conditions like on the Face? Has there been a lot of snow? What's the freezing level? Is the whole thing going to be one big waterfall?'

The man frowned. 'What face?'

'How many are there? Christ alive, who is this guy? The Nordwand, of course.'

'You are going on the Nordwand?'

'Is it out of bounds? I thought that was in the nineteen thirties.'

Ruth tugged at his sleeve. 'Don't start a row,' she said.

The guide was being pointedly polite, the way a policeman might be with a drunk shortly before bundling him into the back of the squad car. 'You know what you're doing, sir?' he asked.

'I'm standing here having a nice conversation with you.'

The man's smile was like a split in a sheet of ice. 'I mean you are *able*? We are having problems with English climbers.'

'Nothing like the problems you're going to have with this one.'

Ruth smiled sympathetically at the guide, as though the man she had to deal with was some kind of nutcase. I suggested that Jamie shut up.

'I'm not going to shut up,' he said loudly. 'What's this guy want me to do? Sign an affidavit that we won't expect a rescue if we get into difficulties? The North Face is a *climb*. They talk about it as though it's their personal property.' He turned to the guide. 'Hey, youth, have *you* ever climbed it?'

The man looked nonplussed. 'I have been on it,' he said.

'But have you *climbed* it?'

'I help in rescues.' He added pointedly: 'The Englishmen called Brewster.'

'Sure.' Jamie's tone was full of contempt. It worked in any language. 'I'll bet you just went up on the train and nipped out through the railway window to throw them a packet of sandwiches. The fellows that rescued Brewster were another couple of Englishmen – Bonington and Whillans.'

We pulled him towards the door.

'Have you the adequate experience?' the man called. 'That is what I want to know. You have no mountains in your country.'

'Experience!' Jamie yelled back. 'The North Face is nothing more than Scottish winter grade five. Bloody hell, the hardest rock pitches are no more than Severe. I'd like to see you on the Orion Face!'

We pushed him out. 'Is he drunk?' the guide called.

'No, he's English,' Ruth answered.

'Is that not the same thing?'

The main street was a sanctuary of trinkets and souvenirs and expensive outdoor clothing, where Japanese tourist groups grazed like herds of herbivores. Ruth asked why he couldn't keep his mouth shut, but he just ignored her. 'That fucking guide probably spends all his time shepherding customers up the Mittelegi Ridge and thinking he's at the forefront of climbing,' he complained. 'Probably never leaves this bloody valley. The nearest he gets to any other mountains is when he goes to the supermarket at Interlaken.'

The cloud stayed down. We lay around the campsite and sorted out our gear and talked to a couple of climbers from Bradford, who wanted to know about the Mittelegi Ridge and where could you get some decent beer? 'All this lager piss,' they complained, 'gives us indigestion.'

They'd heard of Jamie, of course. 'Jim Matthewson? Done a lot of new routes in Scotland, haven't you? Didn't you do that variation of Orion Direct?'

'The pair of us,' said Jamie.

'And what are you planning to do here?'

'The North Face.'

They sniffed and looked slightly awkward, as you might at the funeral of someone you don't really know. 'What would that be?' one asked. There was the careful use of the conditional tense. 'The third British ascent?'

Jamie shrugged. 'I don't read record books.'

'Well, good luck,' they said.

There was a high wind and still the odd speck of sleet in the air. During the afternoon the cloud parted to show some ragged patches of the Face, but they were out of context, like parts of a room glimpsed through a keyhole. 'What about that bastard's weather forecast?' Jamie complained.

We waited. We were bored, and tightened by the tension of the coming climb and the foul weather. The mountain brooded up there behind the clouds and waited for us like the spider waiting for her prey. We laughed, we argued, we told stories and lies. We sat in the van and pored over the photos and climbed the various pitches in our minds yet again, and discussed the merits and demerits of making an early start and bivouacking on the Flatiron, or going up to the Swallow's Nest the afternoon before, so that we could start up the icefields as early in the morning as possible. We waited. There's even a name for it, that listless wait for the weather to settle, a wait made brittle and bad-tempered by anxiety: Eiger-watching. There's a name for everything: the Difficult Crack, Death Bivouac, the Traverse of the Gods, the Spider. The whole damn mountain is tied up with names, the names of the features of the Face and the names of the dead.

In the evening Ruth played her guitar – a plangent, mournful voice singing Celtic laments – and a few of the people in the campsite came over to listen. Above us the mountain lay back beneath its blanket of cloud and slept. We went for a few beers with the Bradford climbers – Jamie showed them where you could get *Dunkel* and *Heferweizen* – and when we got back to the van Ruth cooked a meal of rice and beef and vegetables. We killed two bottles of overpriced Swiss wine to go on top of the beer.

'That was a great meal,' Jamie said. 'What do you call it?'

'Chop suey.' She glanced in my direction. 'There's a painting called *Chop Suey*, do you know that, Rob? By Edward Hopper.'

'As a matter of fact—'

'Why does he always say that?' Jamie interrupted. '*As a matter of fact*. As though he was a lawyer in court or something.'

I ignored him. 'As a matter of fact, I do.'

'It shows a lonely lady in a Chinese restaurant.'

'I don't think she's on her own. I think she's got someone with her. There are two of them, one with her back to the viewer.'

Ruth smiled knowingly. We knew, that was the trouble. Ruth and I knew. That's always the trouble with betrayal: the betrayers know so much more than the betrayed. 'Maybe they were discussing a man,' she suggested. 'A man whom they both love.'

We laughed, but there was something beneath the laughter, undercurrents of knowledge and desire. She leant across and kissed me. Jamie didn't seem to care. She turned and kissed him; and then kissed us both with a fine indifference. When I made a move to go she put out her hand to stop me. 'Don't.'

So I stayed. Perhaps the whole thing was inevitable. The alcohol had something to do with it, of course. There was the promiscuity of shared tiredness and emotion, and the hot smell of our bodies. Our minds were clouded with alcohol and ideas of sexual freedom, our bodies were craving, our nerves were shredded by the wait and by the certain knowledge that hanging over us, invisible like all the best monsters, was the Eiger. Ruth laughed in the gaslight and put her arms round the two of us, accepting kisses from either. Jamie laughed too, but I couldn't read the tone of his amusement, whether there was complicity in it or mere acquiescence.

She was wearing a T-shirt. You snatch minor things out of the swamp of memory: I remember that T-shirt, the design. It was tie-dyed, a sunburst of white and orange across a black sky. I remember how she pushed us away and crossed her arms across her belly and grabbed the hem of the shirt and dragged it over her head. 'There,' she said, tossing it aside. From the waist up she was naked.

Jamie touched her. We were laughing. It was funny and shocking at the same time, seeing his hand on her breasts. There was a sense of trespass, the breathless trespass of children stepping past the signs that said, 'Perygl, Cadwch Allan – Danger, Keep Out'. We tiptoed into the unknown, touching, laughing, pulling apart, wondering how far this would go and where it would end. There was the pliant texture of her body, and the hard edges of Jamie's. And then the laughter died and we were mere movement, a triangle made of sinew and muscle and bone and nerve, bending awkwardly in the narrow space; a scalene triangle, shifting, flexing, the angles changing; but always Ruth at the narrow point of convergence. 'Yes,' I heard her say, very quietly in my ear or Jamie's, as though she were answering one of us alone, 'yes, yes, yes.'

The next morning no one said anything. It was the silence after the fall. We sat in the van and drank coffee and ate breakfast and peered out of the windows to see what was going on up there above us, and said nothing. Clouds shifted and swirled around the invisible mountain.

'What do we do?' I asked eventually. The question was there to be answered as anyone pleased. Ruth looked from me to Jamie. He sipped his coffee and looked thoughtfully at the two of us. 'Let's go up to Eigergletscher station and have a look at the West Flank. Get a bit of exercise.'

'Okay,' I agreed. 'Why not?'

Payment deferred, I think we knew that. We guessed there was something to pay. We had eaten the fruit of a particular species of the tree of knowledge, a rare and exotic species, one that was almost certainly poisonous. We wouldn't get away unscathed. So we took the train up to Eigergletscher and the momentary reprieve brought with it a certain light-heartedness. As the vehicle clattered up through the meadows there was a holiday mood between the three of us, a sense of relief.

Eigergletscher station is a brutal place, a ferro-concrete block-house nestling below the West Ridge of the mountain. It is the station before the tunnel, where the railway burrows into a black hole to climb up through the bowels of the mountain on its journey up to the Jungfraujoch. Directly behind the station, above the tunnel entrance, the West Flank rises up in great steps towards the summit five thousand feet above. To the left, deep in shadow, is the North Face.

That day the cloud base was barely above the station buildings. We left the platform and went round the back of the buildings, past official signs that warned us about the dangers of the mountains, on to the mountainside itself. Cliffs rose above in a desolation of rubble and scree. The route zigzagged upwards over sloping ledges and rock steps. There were cairns and, in places, a beaten path. Assuming everything went well with our climb, this was the way Jamie and I would come down from the summit. We paused at intervals to look around and try to get our bearings, but soon we were in cloud and bereft of all landmarks. We climbed apart, cocooned in our own worlds. At a snowfield we paused to put on crampons.

'How much higher do we go?' Ruth asked.

Jamie shrugged. The route slanted up to the foot of an icy gully. Cairns marked the way, and in places there were pitons that had been used for abseiling. The wind plucked at our sleeves, as though reminding us of something. And then we found ourselves on a knife-edge ridge, peering over into the ominous darkness of the North Face where the wind keened and no one moved. The cloud swirled past us, cold and silent, pouring into the shadows.

I looked at Ruth's face, pinched with cold, huddled into her hood. She looked ugly like that, wasted and shrivelled, like an old woman wearing a headscarf. I smiled. She smiled back, but her smile lacked conviction. We went up a bit further before turning back and picking our way down through the murk until the roof of the station loomed out of the mist below us.

There was a feeling of relief to be off the mountain, out of the darkness of the cloud and back in a place where there were people and lights. We got something to drink at the bar and then we walked side by side down the path below the station. The mood had changed. The Eiger has that quality. Civilization laps up to its very foot, so that you can step from the desolation of the mountain into the comforts of the human world in a few paces. We went on down the path like innocent friends out for a stroll. There was sunlight now, shafts of it breaking through the cloud. Where the path was wide enough, Ruth walked between the two of us, linking her arms through ours as though holding us together, laughing and talking as though nothing mattered. But someone was going to get damaged; perhaps all three of us. We sensed that, each in his own way. We had trespassed. There was, beneath our casual manner, the darkness of a deep hurt.

That evening we ate supper in near silence. Jamie and I talked of the weather, the prospects, the gear we should take, where we should bivouac, all assuming that the cloud would clear and the mountain would allow us a few days of decent weather. Ruth watched us and kept that dark Welsh expression of reserve and withdrawal, like the mountains looking down on the English castles there on the coast.

'So what about *us*?' she asked, when it seemed that we were finished, when the plates had been cleared away. 'Where do we go from here?'

So we talked. It was a long, rambling, circuitous conversation, not the kind of thing you recall in clear detail, perhaps because the detail was never clear at the time. In some ways it seemed unreal. We made assertions of eternal love, we made accusations of betrayal. I remember that she wept. I had never imagined that this might be possible. A remarkable event, her pallid face streaked with tears, her eyes and nose flushed. 'I want you both,' she cried. 'I want you both, I love you both, and you both love me and you love each other. Can't we leave it at that? We have something so special here. Can't we just do what the hell we like?' I think perhaps that in her mind we were playing Arthur and Lancelot to her Guinevere. Guinevere is

Welsh – Gwynhwyfar. The whole story of Arthur is Welsh, really, so I guess it suited her Celtic mysticism.

I sound cynical. Across the space of so many years it's difficult not to be. We were children of our time, eager to draw our lives against a background of a universal love that no one had really witnessed but everyone claimed. Eventually, with nothing resolved, we dozed. When I was next aware of the world around me, the luminous hands of my watch told me that it was three o'clock.

Something was different. I listened. The figures beside me shifted in their sleep. I sensed that something had changed in the world, some factor of wind and temperature and humidity. Cautiously I slid open a window to look out.

'What's that?' Jamie mumbled.

'Nothing. Sleep.'

Outside the van the night air was cold and dry. The cloud had vanished, as completely as though it had never been there. Craning upwards I could see stars, thousands of them scattered like crystals of ice across the luminous sky. And something else: a dense black wedge thrust up above us to cut out a third of the visible universe. For the first time I was looking at the North Face of the Eiger.

Two points of light gave some kind of perspective to the dark mass, like two lone stars in the midst of a great black nebula. They were the lights from the railway tunnel that lies buried in the heart of the mountain.

I shivered, not from cold but from anticipation and fear. There was a lot to be afraid of. There was fear for Jamie and Ruth and me. There was the irrational fear of the night and the rational fear of the Face itself. I slept in this fear, and dreams merged with memory so that when I finally awoke in daylight I was unsure what I had seen and what we had said and done, and what I had dreamt. Ruth was still beside me. I touched her, as though to confirm the reality of her presence there. She moaned and turned away, presenting the long snake of her spine towards me. But where Jamie had lain there was just a mess of sheets and sleeping-bags, and when I opened the door I found that he was standing beside the van, staring up at the North Face through binoculars. Without turning, he said, 'There it is.'

I pulled on some clothes and climbed out. The morning was cold and clear, brilliant with frost. I stood beside him, looking up at the Face. The features were familiar from a thousand photographs – the strata of the lower slopes, the rock bands, the slopes of white that are the icefields, the wedge of the Flatiron standing out from the Face like the prow of a ship; and high above all those, the funnel of white ice that is the Spider. From this angle the wall seemed to lean back from the vertical, its steepness mollified by the presence of that dimension that is always missing from the photographs – the dimension of depth. It looked almost as though it was inviting us in. A drift of vapour was wrapped round the West Ridge and across the summit rocks, like a chiffon scarf round the neck of an old, raddled woman. There was a flush of dawn pink on the summit.

'What'll we do, Jamie?' I asked.

He didn't take his eyes from the binoculars. 'Looks a piece of piss, doesn't it?'

'About Ruth, I mean.'

'Of course, if the weather holds up, technically the thing is precisely that: a piece of piss. *Technically.*'

'I asked about Ruth.'

'The second fact is that, seen from down here, it's foreshortened. What you've got to bear in mind is that the north-east face of the Ben would fit into that little number about four times. That's *four* times. So if you do the Orion Face in a day, then this is going to take you four days.'

'Jamie.'

He looked round from his binoculars. 'Mathematically speaking. The third point, of course, is that the weather won't hold up for four days in a row. It probably won't hold up for three. Not unless we're bloody lucky. Now, let's go and climb the fucking thing, Rob.'

So we had some breakfast and packed our gear. Ruth watched us silently as we went over what we would take and what we could leave. You want to take everything, just in case, but you have to compromise – only so much rope, only so many karabiners and pitons and ice screws, only so much fuel and so much food and so much water. Everything measured out, the sacks humped to feel their weight, sleeping-bags argued over, one stove left behind, one entire meal abandoned.

Later that morning we took the mountain train up to Kleine Scheidegg. On the train there were mothers with their babies, old men and women in their retirement and young men and women in the first years of their parenthood. Our rucksacks jammed the aisle and the Japanese smiled and nodded, as though somehow they understood. Jamie stared out of the window, trying to see up the hillside where bits of the Face could be seen through the trees. 'We should have walked,' he said. 'We should be out on the hill.'

At Kleine Scheidegg station we clambered out among the holiday crowd. There was a young man with an alpenhorn on the steps of the hotel. People stood beside him to have their pictures taken. Occasionally, as long as the price was right, he put the horn to his mouth and blew a few notes. 'Like a cow in labour,' Jamie remarked. There was a coin-operated telescope through which you could peer at the North Face, but at the moment there was no notice to tell the watchers that there were climbers in action. For the moment the greatest public stage in the whole theatre of climbing was empty.

The tourists headed for the cafés and the souvenir shops. We humped our sacks and set off to walk up the final stretch of the line to Eigergletscher. Ruth would come with us and then go back down to the bunkhouse at Kleine Scheidegg to wait. 'Just a day or two,' Jamie said. 'Or three,' he added, knowing that it might be four or five, but if it were any more than that, then it would be for ever.

The sky had that hard enamel blue that altitude gives it, a blue that promised what the forecast had claimed: three days of settled weather, maybe four. Enough. We said our farewells on the narrow platform as one of the trains dragged itself up and into the tunnel that burrows through the bowels of the mountain. Tourists stared out of the windows at us. 'Now, don't you cry,' Jamie told Ruth.

'I wasn't,' she replied.

He smiled a bitter little smile. 'We should be well into the Ramp by midday tomorrow. And we'll probably bivvy again before the Traverse of the Gods. Then we'll climb out the next day. See you back down here Thursday evening. Day after tomorrow. Could be late.'

What did she feel? Impossible to tell from her expression. She gave each of us a kiss, then turned back to go and get something from her bag. Her camera, that battered Nikon that had accompanied her to Egypt and Libya and the Aïr. 'A photo of the conquering heroes,' she said, with an ironical downturn of her mouth, and we stood there self-consciously while she aimed the lens. The shutter fired, once, twice, three times, a patter of metal leaves. She gave a little smile and tucked the camera away.

'You ready, Rob?' Jamie asked.

I agreed that I was, as ready as I'd ever be, and we turned away from her and went up the path that leads from the platform round the shoulder of the ridge. Just before we turned the corner into the shadow of the Face I glanced back. I'd made a bet with myself that she wouldn't be there, that she would have shrugged her shoulders and gone back to the café. But she was still standing there when I looked and when she saw me glancing round she waved. The gesture seemed almost hieratic, a mixture of farewell and blessing.

It was cold in the shadow of the North Face, with the deep cold of a place that has never seen the sun. I trudged along behind Jamie. Below us the meadows sloped steeply down to the chalets of Alpiglen. Above us rose the ragged vertical mile of snow and ice and rock that was the Eigerwand. On its far side the northeast ridge was picked out in sunlight, but the whole concave precipice of the Face itself was in shadow. Tamed by foreshortening, it leant back almost in welcome, like an old whore who knows her business and wants to make things as easy as possible at first, because the real experience, the seduction, the caresses and the climax, will not be as pleasurable as it might seem at the start.

There were some walkers on the path in front of us – a young couple with their two children. They stopped and watched as we branched off for the foot of the wall. The adults pointed and talked to each other and explained to the kids. They were telling a kind of fairytale no doubt, of heroes going off to pit themselves against the Ogre. One of the children waved. Perhaps he had been prompted by his parents. I raised a hand in acknowledgement, and the essential absurdity of the whole undertaking crowded in on me. That little family would stroll down to Alpiglen in the sunshine and catch the train back to the town far below. They'd return to their hotel, have dinner in comfort, sleep the sleep of the just. Their lives would not be any less fulfilled for not having climbed the Eigerwand. I felt a mixture of emotion, the logic of fear and the illogic of an absurd ebullience, as though there was nothing difficult ahead of us, no pain, no fear, nothing that would not succumb to Jamie's ability and my own brand of bloody-minded stubbornness. And Ruth was suddenly nowhere. It was going to be a piece of piss, Dewar.

At the first snow slope the going became easier and we began kicking our way up towards the first pillar and the first rocks. The family group had fallen into proportion now, become a cluster of tiny, irrelevant figures behind and below, creatures of another world. Ahead were the rising tiers of shattered rock and the swathes of white. We went on up, kicking steps in the old snow and pausing occasionally to get our breath, while the meadows fell below us. Without fuss, without any drama, the Face enveloped us, took us into its embrace, wrapped its cold arms around us, while the breeze whispered to us treacherous murmurs of reassurance.

'Over here!' Jamie called. He had found a boot. It was old and wrinkled, a relic of some distant and nameless disaster. It seemed to give him immense pleasure, this boot. '*Ist ein Boot!*' he exclaimed, in a ghastly imitation German accent.

'I think *Boot* is boat.'

'*Ist ein Boot von Bergführer tot!*' he cried. The idea – the boot of a dead mountain guide – seemed to bring him some kind of delight. For a moment he toyed with the idea of keeping his trophy – 'perhaps *ist der Boot von Hinterstoisser*' – but I persuaded him to throw it away. As we continued we came across other relics: old slings, a rusted tin can, an abandoned glove, an ancient canvas rucksack. We were on a haunted mountainside, surrounded by ghosts and tripping over their possessions.

At the Entry Chimney we put on helmets. The climbing was deceptively enjoyable and straightforward. 'You OK, Dewar?' Jamie called down. 'V Diff all right for you?' The ledges were littered with fragments of rock. There were stretches of scree up which we slithered and struggled. The Shattered Pillar passed easily and the runnels and gullies that led upwards. Everywhere there were the signs, the rusted pitons, the slings of bleached and brittle rope abandoned by climbers abseiling off the Face. Eventually we reached the tunnel window, a metal shutter sunk into the rock through which you could escape into the troglodyte world of Swiss railways. Below our heels empty space had appeared, unfolding itself out of green alpine meadows like a clever piece of trickery.

Jamie stood on the littered ledge and looked around with a thoughtful expression. 'This is it,' he said. 'This is where he turned back.'

He meant his father. I tried to picture Guy Matthewson there on that scrappy ledge, his nailed boots crunching over the shards of rock, thrilling to the situation and, no doubt, disappointed that he couldn't continue. Who had been his companion? A fellow Englishman? A German? What had held them back? It would have been the second ascent if he had been successful. Perhaps his partner hadn't been up to it. Perhaps the weather was too uncertain. Or had they just looked upwards at the rising tiers of rock above them, at the runnels of ice and the dark grooves going on and on above their heads, and thought that it was beyond them? Climbing is all in the head, Jamie used to say. Most of it, anyway. But not here, not on the Face of the Ogre.

Jamie shrugged and patted my shoulder, as though I were a kid, as though we were kids together once more and there was no Ruth. 'Come on, youth.'

So we went on: a traverse leftwards, then up a chimney and upwards over broken ledges. An old fixed rope hung down the so-called Difficult Crack. The crack was straightforward enough, like a climb in the Ogwen valley, no more than Severe. At the top, at the foot of the Rote Fluh, the Red Wall, we paused again to look. Below us the ground fell away to distant meadows where there was sunshine and warmth, and a vast slanting wedge of shadow – a mile of darkness cast down the hillside by the mountain itself. The incongruous sound of cowbells drifted up in the afternoon air. We could see the railway track descending towards the little station of Alpiglen, and then, far below to the right, in the very bottom of the valley, the buildings of Grindelwald. Directly above us was the Red Wall. It isn't red: it's only a pallid flesh colour, streaked and stained like dirt in grazed skin. From a distance it seems a tiny feature in the whole Face, a mere blemish, yet it rose vertically above us now for almost a thousand feet. You try to fix your own dimensions. You try to get things in some kind of perspective: the Red Wall alone is the height of the Orion Face of Ben Nevis; but it is a mere plague spot on the face of the Ogre.

'No one else around,' Jamie said with satisfaction. '*Wir* are *allein*!'

'Is that a good thing?'

'It means we won't have to fight over a bivvy site with a bunch of Krauts.'

'It might mean that everyone else thinks the Face is out of condition.'

He shrugged. 'Looks okay to me.' We turned back to the business of the climb, edging leftwards beneath the Rote Fluh towards the centre of the Face. There were pegs crammed into cracks, bunches of old, used slings, and then a rope in place, hanging in swags across a stretch of blank slab. The exposure was sudden and dramatic. The rock hung down in a smooth curtain, pale and compact; beneath it there was nothing.

'This the Hinterstoisser Traverse?'

'Must be.'

We paused on the brink and contemplated it. You can't avoid it. You can't avoid the story any more than you can avoid the traverse itself. In the summer of 1936 Andreas Hinterstoisser had tiptoed across this smooth slab, tensioning on a rope to balance, pulling sideways on the few holds that he found. It was the key pitch to get out from under the Rote Fluh and into the centre of the Face, the crux of the route that he was prospecting with his three companions. On the far side he fixed the rope and the others – Edi Rainer, Willy Angerer, Toni Kurz – followed across easily, using the rope as a handrail. Then they retrieved the rope and pushed on upwards. Three days later, when they were retreating in a storm with one of their number injured, they might have reversed this pitch had they left the rope in place. As it was, they couldn't. As it was, they died.

Kurz, he dead. And Rainer and Angerer and Hinterstoisser. And Sedlmayr and Mehringer. And fifty others. The Face is a playground, and a cemetery, and a memorial. Its history is an obituary.

I clipped into one of the pegs and belayed Jamie while he climbed down and grabbed the fixed rope. 'What's it look like?'

'Fairly good.' He swung out and down, his boots scuffing against the rock as he pulled himself along. It took only a few minutes to reach the other side and belay. The rope sagged like an old washing-line beneath my weight when I followed. I envisaged it snapping, I wondered about its age, I wondered about how hard the pitch would have been to climb free, wondered quite why I was there. Jamie grinned at me as I came across. 'Piece of piss, eh, Dewar?' He was tempting the gods that rule the place and I wished he wouldn't. They are pagan, Nordic gods and they kill without compunction.

Beyond the traverse a short chimney led up to a bivouac site: the Swallow's Nest, perched beneath the eaves of the mountain. Out of the shadows of the Rote Fluh, we were in the warmth of the afternoon sunshine. There was a fugitive sensation of safety and contentment. We could take off our helmets and rub our heads and sit in comfort to look at the view. We could brew a cup of tea and prepare for supper. We could smile round at the place – the plunging spaces, the shabby grey scaffolding of the mountain, the small splinters of rock that we kicked from beneath our feet – and, despite everything, feel a little bit in love with it and with each other. There is something old-fashioned about climbing. It lets in emotions that one does not readily admit to any longer: companionship, commitment, even love. I wondered how Jamie's father would have felt if he could have seen the two of us there, sitting at the Swallow's Nest, a third of the way up the Eigerwand. For an ephemeral moment, I thought how much I loved Jamie, and Ruth, and Eve, and the whole world.

We had some food, and when it was dark we flashed a torch in the direction of the lights of Kleine Scheidegg, hoping that Ruth would see us and know that we were okay; but whether there was an answering light we couldn't be sure. Then Jamie turned to me. He'd been thinking about her, just as I had. I suppose he'd been trying to find the right moment. It was easier in the dark. 'About Ruth.'

I swallowed something. 'What about her?'

He was silent for a moment, hunched in his down jacket,

smoking a cigarette. Apart from the soughing of the wind there was no sound up there on our stony ledge. Then he touched me. In the darkness he put out his hand and touched me on the shoulder almost as though to confirm my presence there on the ledge beside him. Perhaps he was even trying to comfort me, although surely it was he who needed comfort. And I felt like a child again, as we had been all those years ago with Bethan round the back of the garden shed. I felt the sympathy in his touch, the sympathy in his look, as though he were a parent to me. 'Are you in love with her?'

'Yes, I suppose I am.'

'And what about Eve?'

I shook my head. 'I don't know, Jamie. Eve as well. I just don't know.'

He nodded thoughtfully, silent for a while as he drew on his cigarette. The small point of fire flared. 'We've been through a lot together, haven't we?'

'Sure.'

'Bethan, that bastard in the quarry, things like that . . .'

'The Aussies.'

He laughed. 'The Aussies. The one who fancied me, what was her name?'

'Kerry.'

'Kerry. And now this.'

'Maybe we've shared too much.'

'Maybe. Shared my mother in a way, haven't we?' I watched the red fire of his cigarette flare in the darkness.

'You know how I found out about you and her?'

'Jamie, it's long over—'

'We had a row. I can't even remember what it was about. Maybe about one of her boyfriends. God knows. Shortly after you'd come up to London and we'd been to that party. You remember? And I asked her straight out about you, and she brandished it in my face. "Yes," she said. "Yes, I've had Robert. Yes, we've been lovers. Are you jealous or something?"'

He scuffed his feet in the stones that littered the ledge. I couldn't see him clearly, just the movement of his shadow. He picked a stone up and tossed it over the edge, like someone tossing a pebble into a well and listening for the sound of it hitting the water. But here there was nothing. No sound, nothing. 'I *was* jealous,' he went on. 'Jealous of both of you. Jealous that you had both been closer to each other than I ever could be.'

He paused again. He sounded confused. I wondered whether he was even in a fit state to be climbing this bloody mountain. I felt that I had to say something, anything to placate the gods of his unhappiness. 'I was just a kid, Jamie. And she was lonely . . .'

He turned to me, just his shadow in the luminous darkness of that frozen ledge. 'And now Ruth. Now I'm expected to share Ruth with you.' His voice was no more than a whisper above the sound of the wind. 'First you take my mother, and now you're taking Ruth.'

'*Taking* her? It was what she wanted, for God's sake. All three of us wanted it.'

In the faint backwash of light from the sky I could see him shaking his head. He drew on his cigarette and stared out into the darkness. When he spoke again his tone was bewildered: 'You practically own me, Rob, you know that?'

'I don't know what you mean, Jamie. I own precious little. A comprehensive collection of scratched Rolling Stones records, and a few books stolen from University College library. That's about it.' I paused. There was something hugely absurd about talking like this perched up there under the eaves of the mountain, absurd and dangerous. I wanted the conversation to go away, but it wouldn't any more than Jamie would go away. I was stuck here on the ledge with him, for better or worse, for richer for poorer, until death, possibly, did us part. 'We could toss for her,' I suggested. It was a joke, a hammer to break the tension, a clumsy weapon.

'Why not?'

'I wasn't being serious . . .'

'But why not? It gives you a chance, doesn't it? Fifty–fifty.'

'Oh, for Christ's sake—'

'Why not? There's that book, isn't there? What was it called? *The Dice Man*. The guy who decided everything by the throw of a dice?'

'It's *die*. Singular's a *die*.'

'Seems more appropriate. Let's do it.'

'Do what?'

'Toss a coin.'

'Jamie, it was a joke—'

'But let's do it.'

I didn't know whether he was serious or not. He was a mad bugger at times, shot through with a streak of anger and a seam of recklessness. 'For God's sake! What about Ruth?'

'But she'll not know. She'll never know. It'll be a secret between the two of us. You scared of doing it?'

'I'm not scared, it's just fucking silly. How can you toss for a woman?'

He searched in the pocket of his breeches and found a coin. 'Why not? Why the hell not?'

So we did. We settled ourselves to the absurd game like two drunks round a table. I suppose we *were* drunk, really, high on the drug of emotion and tension, nervous of the morning and the climb ahead.

I've often thought back to that moment and tried to decipher what it meant. I think I took it like that, as nothing more than a game. I thought that what happened wouldn't count in the final balance of things, that whatever there was between us would still be settled by human love and jealousy and prejudice. There was even a part of me that rehearsed how I would tell this story to Eve, how we would laugh together at the image of Jamie holding out the coin in the pale light of his head torch, as though to demonstrate that everything was above board. 'You ready?'

'Jamie, this is ridiculous—'

'You ready?'

'Okay,' I said. 'I'm ready. Whatever you say.'

'This is for serious, youth. Whoever loses gets out . . .'

'For God's sake, just get on with it.'

He flicked the coin. For a brief moment light flickered from its surfaces as it spun in the space between us. Then he snatched it from the air and held out his fist. 'You call.'

I looked at him. In the torchlight I could see the anxiety in his expression, a tension that was greater than in any climb. 'This is crazy, Jamie.'

'Just call.'

'Let things take their course, man.'

'Call, fuck you! Call!'

I thought he might hit me. For a moment I thought we might have a bar-room brawl up there on the narrow ledge of the Swallow's Nest. I was on the Eiger with a madman. Which was more dangerous, the mountain or the guy I was tied to with a rope? 'Tails,' I said resignedly. 'Seeing as that's what we're after. Tails.'

He didn't laugh at the joke. He just opened his fingers and showed the coin lying there in his palm, with the allegorical figure of Lady Helvetia, the patron saint of bankers, upper-most.

'I hope you're happy together,' I muttered.

After that we curled up and tried to sleep. We slept fitfully, the sleep of the damned, drawn out with dreams and nightmares into a kind of torture. I woke to the rattle of Jamie's alarm clock and his swearing and cursing in the darkness.

'What time is it?'

I peered at my watch. The luminous numbers were bright from the light that they had absorbed during the day. 'Almost four.'

'Where's my torch?'

A lamp snapped on, casting a puddle of pallid light into the dark. Exposed on our tiny ledge, we were enclosed by the fateful whisper of vapour. 'Shit, we're in cloud.'

'Mist.'

'Is that a good sign?'

'I suppose it means it's cold.'

Cold was good. Cold cemented loose stones into the ice and reduced the stonefall. Cold cements joints. We flexed our hands and elbows and our knees. The demons of the evening before had retreated, but they were there in the background laughing at us. We melted snow and made tea. We ate some biscuits and chocolate. Our breath measured the chill in clouds of vapour that swirled like cigarette smoke in the light of our head torches. We packed our things away and sorted out the ropes.

'All right, Rob?'

I held up my hand against the glare of his head torch. He looked like a miner standing in the darkness of a tunnel, his eyes bright white and his face darkened with shadow and stubble. Beyond him was a pale slope of ice. Nothing more. There was no depth to our surroundings, no exposure. 'Ready when you are.'

We humped our packs and looked round to make sure that nothing had been left. 'Let's go.' Jamie edged leftwards out on to the ice, his torch creating a pale womb of light around him, his crampons scraping on rock, then cutting into the hard névé of the first icefield. Axe and hammer swung in a growing rhythm as he warmed up. He moved up, running out the rope smoothly, with the ease of someone strolling up a hillside, his figure growing dim until it was little more than an opalescent blur in the mist above.

'I'll get an ice screw in here,' he called down. 'Just for form.'

An ice screw; a nice screw. One of his hackneyed jokes. The whole world was still. I heard the metallic click as he clipped a karabiner into the screw; and then the rhythmic chopping recommenced and he moved on up. I loved him; I hated him. I loved the sureness of his movements, the bloody-minded skills he showed, the courage of four o'clock in the morning when the spirits are lowest; and I hated him for loving Ruth. In the cold light of morning there was no doubt in my mind: she loved him and only him. I was just a game for her.

He belayed in the middle of the icefield on a pair of screws. I climbed up to him and led through. As I reached the top of the ice, dawn seeped round the north-east flank of the Face. The mist began to thin. We could see the features around us, the vertical pillars and walls, the icefields hanging like dirty washing on a line, all of these structures sketched out in the dissolving mist. Far above was a silver blue sky. The air was cold.

'Fantastic day!' Jamie called, as he led on past me. 'Fantastic day!'

Access from the first to the second icefield is cut off by a rock band. The Ice Hose is meant to provide the link, but it was no more than a smear that year. He fiddled around a bit trying to find a way up. His crampons scraped on the rock. I looked directly upwards at the underside of his boots and imagined him coming off and down towards me, the talons on his feet like an eagle's. He scraped and scratched rightwards and found the cold comfort of ice – a vertical smear of glaze among the grey rock. 'Fucking steep,' he muttered. The casual obscenities of the working man: they give a kind of satisfaction, the way that doing something hard and physical does: no thought, no reason, just the dull fact of action. He belayed precariously and brought me up. The ice was more or less continuous now and the axe and hammer bit home. There was little talk between us, just the unexpressed feeling that we had work to do, and quickly. You deliberately put yourself in an idiotic position and then you work as fast and efficiently as possible to get yourself out of it. You taunt danger and step aside.

I edged past Jamie. From far below came the sounds of another world: the first train grinding up through the meadows towards Kleine Scheidegg, the ringing of cowbells; and then a mournful echo like the cry of a cow in pain: the sound of the alpenhorn that some character in fancy dress blew outside the Bellevue Hotel every day.

I balanced on up to the rim of the second icefield, to a sudden change of perspective, a sudden opening, the great thousand-foot sweep of grey ice running upwards above me to the foot of blackened, rotting cliffs. The ice was pitted with gravel. The aspect was almost industrial, like some hideous mine-working, abandoned and dilapidated, littered with the bits of its decay – a quarry, an ancient quarry, haunted by ghosts. Over to the left and high above us, the rock of the Flatiron jutted out of the ice like the bows of a battleship.

Jamie joined me and we contemplated the future together. 'It's huge,' I muttered stupidly.

'Of course it's huge. That's the whole point of this route. Let's get on with it.'

For all its expanse the icefield was an oppressive place. We tiptoed up it, banging in ice pitons occasionally, aware of the fragility of our bodies and our skulls. This was the firing line. This was like stepping over the parapet and making your way across no man's land. We crept up as quietly as we could in case we might be noticed by snipers, wondering whether to move together and deciding against it because of the size of the place, the oppressive exposure, the vastness of the cliffs above.

The first stone came past with a mere whisper. It was so subdued that for a second I wondered what it was. 'Don't look up!' Jamie shouted. I was belayed in the middle of the slope and Jamie was below me, moving up fast, almost like a soldier trying to get into a shell-hole before the next missile. A second and a third stone came down, small explosions of anger. Something glanced off my helmet just as he reached me.

'Christ!'

'What is it?'

'Nothing. Just a stone. Tiny.'

'Just don't look up.'

It was the randomness that terrified. In climbing little is random: the rock is a puzzle set in three dimensions. It rarely changes. You can judge yourself against it. There are those who fail and those who succeed. But in the stonefall of the Eiger there is none of this. There is only pure untrammelled chance, the vagaries of luck, the casting of dice.

'Best keep moving,' Jamie said, and went on, almost running up the slope, pausing only to slam in an ice piton. Just for form's sake.

The stone hit him two pitches later, when we had another five hundred feet to go, when it was just beginning to feel endless, a kind of torment, a rack on which we were strung like torture victims. I glanced up to see how he was going and there were sudden black marks against the sky above him. He shouted something and flattened himself against the filthy ice and I heard him give a cry that was half pain and half expletive. He didn't fall, I'd have held him had he fallen – he had a couple of ice pitons in and he wasn't far above the top one and, anyway, the angle wasn't steep, just about fifty-five degrees – but somehow he managed to stay on. When the stones had passed and I could glance up safely, there he was, hunched against the snow.

Panic fluttered inside me. 'Jamie? Jamie! You okay?'

'Fuck and shit,' I heard him say. Something like that. Cursing the gods of the mountain.

'Where did it hit you?'

'Face.'

'Is it bad? Can you belay me? I'll come up.'

He moved. There was the hammering of metal on metal, and after a while, working like a navvy, swearing and cursing like a navvy, he began to pull in the rope. When I reached him, he had blood down one side of his face and an ugly broken bruise over his eye. 'I think it glanced off the rim of my helmet.'

I examined the wound, looked into his eyes to see him looking back from far away. 'How do you feel?'

'I'll be all right.'

'You sure?'

'We're not going down, if that's what you mean. We'd better get on, get out of the line of fire.'

'There's nothing coming down at the moment.'

319

'That's what they all say –'

'– shortly before they get hit.'

He laughed wryly, and closed his eyes.

'Hey, are you okay, Jamie?'

He took a deep breath. 'Come on, Rob,' he whispered. 'For fuck's sake, let's get a move on.'

So, after a moment's hesitation, we went on up, rope length after rope length, two soldiers crawling across no man's land, our passage marked by spots of blood from Jamie's injury and the clawmarks of our crampon points. When, finally, we gained the foot of the cliffs at the top of the icefield we felt that we had won a battle. But it was only a skirmish: the war would continue for a long while yet. I rummaged through my sack and found the first-aid kit that Ruth had put together. I cleaned Jamie's cut as best I could and stuck a plaster across it, then got out the camera and took a picture or two. 'You look like something just walked out of Stalingrad,' I told him. He grinned from beneath his helmet, like a soldier who had got away with it so far.

The traverse leftwards along the top of the icefield towards the Flatiron seemed interminable. We chopped sideways like crabs, finding the best line round rock outcrops, occasionally descending, occasionally slipping, sometimes glancing down and seeing the great sweep of ice below us, and below that the abstract, inaccessible meadows – Elysian fields, warm in the distant sunlight. I glanced at my watch. The early start had been eroded away and it was approaching midday by the time we reached the rocks at the foot of the Flatiron. I belayed while Jamie scratched and bridged his way up a shallow groove at the side of the buttress. It was an untidy blend of rock and ice, the kind of hard, mixed climbing that you might find on Ben Nevis. At the top was slabby rock leading up to a steep wall and a sheltered ledge. We paused there, at the Death Bivouac, where the first climbers to attempt the Face, the Germans Mehringer and Sedelmayr, had sat and frozen to death. 'Bloody graveyard,' Jamie muttered, as he picked over the place. There were pegs in the rock, bits of rope, a crushed tin, bits of frozen orange peel, all the fragments that mark the passage and temporary residence of man, like a Stone Age midden that might delight archaeologists. A few steps down there was even the stain of excrement in the snow. Above us were the great barriers of cliff that shut off the upper part of the Face.

Now that the sun had hit it, more stones were coming down, funnelled into the Spider above us and down the spout of the third icefield. For all its ghoulish name, Death Bivouac was a sanctuary of a kind, protected by the cliff overhead. We sat and ate some chocolate and looked at the view, the plunging spaces down to the chalets of Alpiglen. The hotel at Kleine Scheidegg was in the sun now – everything was in the sun except the mile of rock and ice that we were climbing. The sound of the train could be heard, and the mournful gong of cowbells. Away to the right, six thousand feet below us, were the buildings of Grindelwald, scattered like grains of coarse salt on a green baize cloth. There was the temptation to wait, to waste the after-noon secure in this spurious safety. I pulled out the camera and took photographs. The wide-angle lens: Jamie at Death Bivouac, his forehead plastered and a grimy streak of blood below his eye. *That* photo. He glanced at his watch. 'Better get a move on.'

Reluctantly we moved off the Flatiron to the edge of the ice-field. The ice was canted thirty degrees off the vertical, steeper than a roof, steeper than seemed reasonable. Below it was empty space. On the far side a great cliff of grey rock rose up like the side of a cathedral, split by the deep diagonal gash of the Ramp, the key to the whole route.

I hesitated on the margin of the ice, looking back at Jamie. 'Is it safe?' I called stupidly.

'Of course it's not fucking safe,' he shouted back. 'Where do you think we are? In a supermarket? You want me to lead? I'll take over if you want.'

It was a challenge, far more than mere banter on a British crag, something underscored with the matters that stood between us. 'No, thanks.'

'Then get a fucking move on.'

I edged out into the line of stonefall. My helmet felt as thin as an eggshell. I didn't dare look up in the same way that a child closes its eyes against fear: the object of your fear doesn't vanish, but not seeing it makes you feel better. Axe and hammer swinging, I chopped across the ice, crabbing leftwards, glancing across towards the refuge on the far side: the rock wall, the piton in place, the sham security of the fact that people had passed here before, some fifty of them since the first ascent in 1938. Chips of ice sprayed up into my face and skittered down the slope below. My feet slithered and scraped.

Finally I gained rock and the shelter of the cliff. Jamie followed me across. Things slithered down the ice beneath him and shot out into space – bits of ice, bits of the mountain – but he moved towards me with disturbing speed, as though things like height and space didn't matter, and indeed they don't, being nothing more than the constructs of the mind and contributing nothing rational to the difficulty of climbing. He reached me and passed by, making a downward traverse to the foot of the Ramp. He was quick, confident, assured, as though this were a natural place to be, a place where he could move at will, as though gravity was a dimension that did not concern him, as though the matter of Ruth didn't exist.

'Okay,' he called. 'There are pegs in place here. The whole fucking mountain is bristling with them. I should think it deflects compasses.'

Throughout that afternoon we climbed up the Ramp. It was narrow and awkward, a place of shadows and security even at the hard pitches, a gash cut into the mountain in which you can hide. The climbing was intricate and compelling, a puzzle in three dimensions, and for a while Ruth was a distant figure in both our minds, as small and insignificant as the tiny train that crawled up the line from Grindelwald to Kleine Scheidegg far below us. Imagine looking out of the window of an aircraft. That high.

The afternoon sun had come round the West Flank and spread its light and some fragile warmth around me as I led up the narrow funnel of ice at the top of the Ramp. 'We're okay,' I cried down. 'We've cracked it. We've bloody well cracked the bugger.' Something like that: the blind expletives that come with exhaustion.

We climbed out to the right, where the architecture of the mountain deteriorates into ledges and steps, a litter of broken fragments and rubble like the bombed ruins of a building. The Brittle Ledges. No poetry about that name, just plain fact, the mountain crumbling to pieces beneath our boots. There was a final steep, precarious pitch, which Jamie led with minimal protection, and then we tiptoed round to the right, with three thousand feet of air beyond the edge and old rope to show us the way, and found our next bivouac site. It was a wide, safe ledge, hung with ancient ropes and rusting pitons and bathed in the evening sunlight. We melted snow and laid out our sleeping-bags, while the sun set over the mountains in a gory mess of red and orange and grimy black. Jamie seemed distracted and clumsy.

'How's your head?'

He shrugged. 'I've got a bit of a headache. It's nothing.'

I changed the dressing. Was he all right? Was his mind clouded, or was this just the exertion, the altitude and the cold? We drank tea, as many mugs of tea as we could get water for. I cooked some kind of mess of rehydrated stew and potatoes and argued with Jamie when he didn't want to eat. We had retreated from the complexities of life to the fundamentals of a cave existence – drink, food, the need to piss, the need to huddle against each other for warmth and comfort.

'Ruth—' I said.

'Ruth's all right. She's tucked up in some warm bed. She's all right.'

We pulled the tent sack over our heads and lay down, but neither of us slept much. I felt the warmth from his body, the cold from the rock at my back. Mountain cold is like a vacuum, a great absence that draws everything into it, heat, light, life. It is as dark as the grave. 'I don't mind, Jamie. That's all.'

'Forget it, Rob. Try not to think, about her or about anything. Just try to sleep.'

But sleep was a fragmentary prize. We had climbed an entire day – some kind of lunch snatched at Death Bivouac – and were still only two-thirds of the way up the Face. Ahead of us was the traverse into the Spider, the highest of the icefields, a hanging glacier plastered three thousand feet up the Face. We had to climb that, and then we still had to find our way out through the headwall on to the summit snowfield. Another nine hundred feet of steep climbing on iced rock. There was all that to come. It was not an easy night. There were dreams and a sense of dread, the fear of the dark and the fear of the space beneath our ledge and the fear of the space that lay between us and was inhabited by Ruth.

I awoke some time in the small hours to find Jamie's arm around me. Outside our sack there was a muffled silence and a faint, threatening whisper from the gods of the mountain.

'What's that?' Jamie had woken as well. He pulled open the tent sack and peered out. Our head torches excavated pools of pallid yellow into which snow intruded, a thin scattering of flakes alighting with care and delicacy all over the sack, all over the ledge on which we sat, all over the great, sombre, rotting Face that crept out of the darkness all around us.

'Oh, shit,' he said.

We dozed until nearer dawn. By then the wind had got up and was grabbing the sack and shaking it like a dog with a rat. Snow swirled around us. The rock was glazed with ice. We muttered about taking care, and putting on crampons properly, and minding that fucking stove, and who'd got what gear. The terror is the fear of dropping something. Life depends on so many small things, the ice axe that hangs round your wrist, the crampons you buckle on with clumsy morning fingers, the gloves you must put on and take off, put on and take off. Drop any one of these things and you may well be dead. For want of a nail the kingdom of life may be lost.

Tiptoeing round each other, clumsy in our down jackets and gloves, we contemplated retreat. The argument went back and forth, my caution with Jamie's recklessness. 'A day descending this bloody pile of rock, or half a day to climb out?' That was what he said. 'If we were at the Flatiron, okay. But we're not going to descend the bloody Ramp. Not that. And then, what is this? A bit of snow. Have we ever climbed in snow in Scotland? Have we hell, and harder than this.'

'Or we stay here and sit it out.'

He laughed. 'How many people have died doing that? They're all there in the history books.'

He wasn't wrong; he wasn't right, either. That's the thing about the Eigerwand – wrong and right is judged by one thing only: the outcome. Climbers have retreated successfully from as high up as the Exit cracks. Others have attempted retreat from as low down as the Swallow's Nest and still they've died. Many have tried to sit out storms and ended up corpses, to be lowered down by rescuers months later.

'To go on is impossible, to retreat unthinkable!' he cried, in his guttural *bergführer* voice.

'Stop playing silly buggers. We could die getting this wrong.'

He grinned humourlessly. The snow settled on his helmet and on the rope that was draped across his chest like a bandoleer. 'On this fucking Face,' he said, 'we could die getting it right.'

We went on, rightwards across the Traverse of the Gods, which is a series of shelves, almost a path in good weather, that cuts across the top of vertical, unclimbed walls and leads into the bottom of the Spider, *der Spinne*, the arachnid that was spinning a web of spindrift when we got there – a white funnel with a maelstrom of snow swirling round in it. I tied on to an old peg and Jamie led out on to the ice. The rope was frozen stiff, like copper piping you have to bend round a corner. His figure was hunched against the wind and the sleet, only vaguely discernible as he chopped his way out into the icefield. I watched him blur into the murk. This, I remember thinking, is how disasters start.

20

How would it have looked, that day, to people on the ground, to the tourists making their way up the mountain railway to Kleine Scheidegg, to glimpse the edges of the high mountains, to the watchers at the hotel, to the railway workers or the shop-keepers down in Grindelwald? How did it look to Ruth? A reasonable spring day, a brisk and capricious cold breeze tearing rents in the cloud to let shafts of sunlight through, sudden and briefly warming. Occasionally the summit of the Eiger would emerge from the pall and be visible. The tourists came up on the train in their droves. They laughed and stamped their feet against the cold, and smiled and posed for photos beside the youth with the alpenhorn. They bought souvenirs and trinkets and generally congratulated themselves on the view.

But up there above their heads, above the roofs and the green slopes of Alpiglen, up there in the grey funnel that was the

North Face, it was different. Jamie and I crept upwards through swirling blizzard, running out no more than fifty feet of rope between us. Our shouts were pulverized by the wind, torn apart, battered and shredded into mere fragments of sound. It was cold waiting for the other to climb. Cold was a liquid diffusing into the bones, down to the marrow, down to the very core. In the normal way of things we might have moved together, keeping two or three runners between us for safety as we climbed the ice, but not in this.

Jamie shouted, his voice subtracted by the gale: 'Get . . . move . . . on!'

'I'm fucking moving as fast as I fucking can!'

'What? *What?*'

'Doesn't matter!'

Powder-snow avalanches spilled over the cliffs above and hissed like a snake down the ice. I stood in the flow and watched it course round my axes and over my boots. When the stream died away I continued climbing, through a world that was reduced to the limits of my body, a world contracted to this patch of grimy ice, this length of frozen rope, these thoughts of supplication and anger. The wind roared and stung. Beneath it was the sound of my breathing and the pain in my muffled hands. We kept to the right edge of the ice where there was some shelter. Grey cliffs loomed out of the murk above us, like quarry cliffs emerging from the shadows of a nightmare. Jamie was yelling into my face: 'Which is it?'

'Which is what?'

'Exit . . . Cracks,' he shouted against the wind. '*Which gully?*'

I looked up. The cliffs were there, just there: primeval and evil. 'Just get the fuck out of here!'

'Which bloody gully?!'

'Just follow the pegs. There must be pegs. The whole bloody mountain is littered with them. Pegs and corpses. Clip on to the pegs and climb over the corpses.'

We traversed leftwards, leftwards, leftwards, edging beneath rock, looking for a way out. Somewhere over the other side of the mountain, beyond the Jungfrau, there was a clap of thunder. At the foot of a possible gully we cut a stance in the ice and hammered in a piton, then Jamie began to lever his way up out of the Spider's clutches. Powder snow streamed down the rocks. I mouthed obscenities into the storm, pushing the rope upwards. The Spider was like a rubbish chute below us, dropping away to nothing, a grey void down which the snow flowed.

The rope tugged at my hands. I craned up to glimpse Jamie belaying and taking in. I climbed towards him, out of the Spider and into her web. The rock was glazed with ice. Crampon claws scraped and scratched. You try to find nicks, you try to find cracks, you lever the pick of your axe into any cavity that will do, you depend on millimetres.

'Piece of piss, is it, Rob?' he shouted, as I went past. There was ice encrusted in the stubble round his mouth and his eyebrows were rimed with it. He looked like someone made up as an old man for a play.

'Piece of shit, more like.'

'Think of the view we're missing!'

'Stuff the view.' I bridged up directly above him. There was a muddle of rock and ice above me, a variety of grooves, any one of which might have been the best line. Somewhere hereabouts Andreas Heckmair had come off during the first ascent in 1938. He'd hit his second twenty feet below and stabbed him with his crampons, but somehow they'd stayed on. Somehow. Otherwise it'd have been another of the Eiger's disasters, another four deaths. Somewhere here the Italian Corti had perched on his solitary ledge until they rescued him by lowering a man down from the summit. Corti's partner, Longhi, waiting lower down on another ledge, had died. The Eiger was a hungry beast.

I belayed on an old peg, brought Jamie up, and we went on. Snow hissed down the gullies around us and over us. I lost count of the pitches: somewhere there was a traverse across into another gully, but the Quartz Crack – if there was a quartz crack – we never saw. The rock was compact and treacherous – no place for pegs, no pegs in place, nothing. The grooves were smeared with ice and choked with snow. I led past Jamie, sweeping away snow to discover sloping holds with a thin glaze. There was the sense of eternity about the climb: like Sisyphus we'd done the same thing before, over and over, and still the mountain kept coming at us, as though someone were adding to it above us even as we got near the top. I remembered the joke: the light at the end of the tunnel is actually the torches of the management hastily building more tunnel. I remember laughing, laughing and crying at the same time, as I edged leftwards into the bottom of an open groove, ice in front of me, the angle about eighty degrees, my crampons grabbing at glazed rock, my axe hooked up above me somewhere where there was a nub of ice or rock, I couldn't really see; and laughing.

'This bloody thing must ease off soon,' I shouted down, but he couldn't hear me. I worked a piton into a crack, then hammered it in an inch or two. The sound began bright and firm and reassuring, and ended with a dull finality. It'd have to do. I tied it off with a sling and clipped the rope into the karabiner. Security of a kind. I looked down again and yelled: 'Reckon we're off route?'

His face was a pale rag amid the grey murk. '*What?*'

'Is this the route? Do you reckon we're—'

I paused. A stream of powder snow came down towards me. I waited, clinging. The snow swept down and over, a torrent of stinging crystals.

'*You reckon we're off route?*' I screamed.

I think he shrugged. I think he heard me, and he shrugged. I looked back above me, at the foreshortened stretch of rock where I was to go. Another stream of powder snow swept down towards me and I went up through it, the talons of my crampons clawing at the rock. There was a sense of release, as though I had been freed for the moment from the law of gravity. Reaching up I dug the axes into whatever cracks I could find, then pulled and straightened and went up on nothing at all.

And then the rope stopped.

'Slack!' I yelled. Maybe it had frozen in the karabiner below me. Maybe it was kinked, and the kink had jammed. Maybe. I screamed into the storm, 'Give me slack! Rope! Give me rope!' I was teetering on points, wobbling on knife edges. 'Jamie! Give me some fucking slack!'

There was wind sound and snow sound, the battering of air round the cliffs, the sweep of snow streaming over the rocks all around me. I tried to see down but Jamie was out of sight, round the angle of rock. 'The rope's jammed!' I screamed at his invisible figure.

The sky went dark. It was as though I had said something to offend the monster of the place. A stream of snow came down at me like a snake, hissing with cold. The snake grew, darkened, and engulfed me in its jaws. There was a tremor in the darkness like a great animal shaking itself. I prayed. Quite who I was praying to was not clear – the gods of the mountains, perhaps, the Ogre himself, maybe. Spreadeagled on the rock, perched feet above my fragile piton with the snow streaming over me, I prayed that I would stay on. Just that. I prayed that my picks would stay notched into the ice, that my claws would grip, and I would stay on. Prayer and fear are intimately linked. The snow pummelled me, swept over me, through me. 'Please let me stay on,' I prayed. 'Please,' I begged. 'Please.'

My left hand was snatched from the rock, and then my right. I went over backwards, into space, plummeted down, hitting the rock, slithering down a short slope, plunging free. I remember taking it as a blessed relief. I no longer needed to struggle, no longer needed to hope. There was the simple thought: All this will stop. Somewhere, somehow it will come to an end. And then I will find out.

No past flashed before my eyes, no revelation was bestowed on me, no truth was perceived. I just fell.

When I stopped, I was hanging upside-down with my face against the rock. The Hanging Man. I was clearly, and somehow not unexpectedly, alive. After the crazy motion of the fall, there was now a terrible stillness. I righted myself and scrabbled to some kind of ledge. I discovered that when I put weight on my left leg, it collapsed. There was no pain, but it wouldn't support any weight. I bent down, felt through my gaiters and found a swelling on the surface: a bruise, I thought.

'Jamie!'

I looked round – at the pall of cloud around me and the gloomy cliffs dropping down into darkness below and rising up above. Hell in shades of grey. My lifeline stretched above, woven red and yellow, disappearing upwards over my horizon of rock.

I wasn't frightened, but I knew that in all probability I was going to die.

'*Jamie!*'

The wind flung my voice back at me like an adult pushing away a child's punches.

'*Jamie!*'

There was pain now, emerging from the depths of shock, an exquisite agony deep in the marrow of my left leg.

'*Jamie!*'

But the only sound was the wind, battering against the edges of rock. Solitude was a substance all around me, a thing made of black rock and grey ice and the keening of the wind.

'*Jamie! Jamie!*' The sound of my voice was nothing: a mere breath in the midst of this orchestration of storm.

How long? Time is a malleable dimension, as plastic as Dali's ridiculous watches. It seemed like hours before movement came from above. A rope, weighted by two karabiners, clattered down towards me. Before he appeared I heard him shouting, his voice dismembered by the wind. And then he was there, blurred by the cloud, hanging fifty feet above me at the lip of rock, looking down. 'You all right?' he yelled. 'What the hell . . . Rob, are you all right?'

'I think so.'

'Then get the fuck up here!'

The pain in my leg had grown. It was a constructed, complex thing, with layers and meanings, with shades and colours. Sometimes it was strong enough to bring a moment's insensibility. More often it was mere agony. I shouted up, 'Something's wrong with my leg.'

'What?'

'*My leg!*'

He slid down the rope, his figure hardening as he came nearer, like an image being brought into focus. His crampon points bit and tore at the cliff. 'What's up?'

The pain came fully now, as though it had finally made up its mind: a swelling, burgeoning agony, something possessing me as though there was no room for anything else – no personality, no Robert Dewar, just the plain fact of pain. 'My leg. My fucking left leg.'

'What's wrong with it?'

'Bruised. Don't know. Just hurts. I can't put any weight on it.'

He came further down and was there beside me on what passed as my ledge, tying off the abseil rope and looking around. 'Well, we've got to get you up. Fucking hell, we've lost time. You'll have to prusik up.'

'Where are we?'

'God knows.' He leant out on the rope and craned to see down below us. 'Somewhere above the Traverse of the Gods, I think.' I could see him thinking, counting minutes and hours, estimating distances, looking for ways out.

'My leg,' I said. 'I can't use it. Can't bloody move it.' I think I said that. That's what I intended to say, but my mind was blurred by pain and the words came out mangled. He crouched down and pulled at my gaiter and my socks, and swore when I screamed. For a moment my shin was exposed, with a long swelling down the front of it, like a tumulus, a burial ground of all our hopes.

Jamie looked up at me and said the words that had been going through my mind but had never been allowed to come to the forefront, never allowed to take precedence over the pain: 'It's broken,' he said flatly.

I was cold after that. Could his words have brought the cold, or was it just the effects of shock? I was cold and shivering and tired at the same time, like someone with a fever. I wondered whether I could just crouch down here on this exiguous ledge and sleep.

'You've got to keep warm, Rob,' he said.

'How'll we get off?'

'You've got to keep warm. I'll try to get some pegs in.'

'How'll we get off?'

He began to search round for likely cracks, but the rock was friable and compact at the same time: a dangerous combination. He hammered and swore. Bits of rock splintered away and skittered down the cliff.

'How'll we get off, Jamie?'

'I don't know how the fuck we'll get off!' he shouted. 'I don't know, right? *I've no fucking idea!*'

I remember apologizing, as though the situation were my fault, as though I had willed the avalanche, as though it was a weakness of mine that my leg had snapped. 'I'm sorry, Jamie,' I whispered. 'I'm sorry.'

He ignored me, pulling bits of rock away from the cliff, trying to drive some pegs half-way home. Eventually he tied on, then began rifling through my rucksack to get out my down jacket. 'You've got to keep warm and keep awake. Put your duvet on and see if you can sit down.'

I struggled into the jacket. I was like a child in an adult's hands. Even sitting required his help, as though I hadn't learnt the trick properly. I screamed like a petulant child as he lowered me down. It was cold. My left leg was laid awkwardly across the uneven ledge. The right hung over the edge. Like a kid sitting on a window-ledge, one leg cocked up to the side, the other dangling in space. I shifted myself to get more comfortable. Pain shot up through my groin, like a fire, like a sword buried deep in the marrow and turned with exquisite skill. 'What'll we do, Jamie?' I asked, when the pain had subsided a bit. 'What'll we do?' I felt like a child asking an adult for words of wisdom.

He looked down at me. I couldn't read his expression. I think there was fear there, some kind of misery, and some kind of pain, but the overriding expression was one of fear. He crouched beside me. 'We've got a choice, Rob. We could try to get you down, but that would mean four thousand feet of abseiling. I don't know if you could manage that . . .'

'Or what?'

'Or you bivvy here and I climb out and get help.'

'Leave me?' There was a treacherous bubble of panic in my chest, a tremor of fear. 'Leave me alone?'

He licked his lips, like someone trying to formulate his words exactly. His lips were cracked and broken and he seemed to have difficulty getting them to move properly. 'I don't see much alternative, Rob.'

'You'd have to climb solo. It'd be safer to descend, wouldn't it? Abseil. Christ, Jamie, quicker, far quicker.'

'I could protect myself a bit. It's only a dozen more pitches to the snowfield . . .'

'Or we could both stay here.' There was pleading in my tone, the nagging of a child. 'Sit it out until there's a break in the weather. There's Ruth. She'll get help. They know we're up here. We could sit it out.' Ruth was suddenly no longer the object of our conflict: she had become our saviour.

'We could be here for days,' he said quietly. 'We'd die. We'd die like the others, like Longhi and Sedlmayr and all of that lot. Like Toni Kurz on the end of his rope.'

'You can't leave me, Jamie.'

But he was already going through the gear, portioning it out like a thief going through the swag after the getaway. 'It's our only hope, Rob. Our only hope. I'll leave you all the food. And the spare gas cylinder. I'll get help to you as quickly as I can. The sooner I get on with it the better. I'll leave the rope in place. It may help them see where you are—'

I begged. I can still hear the whine in my voice, the impre-cation. Some fragment of personality that was still left loathed the sound and the person who had uttered it. 'Jamie, please. For God's sake, don't leave me. Jamie, I beg you.'

He paused in his work. The wind battered around the edges of rock. A flurry of snow swirled into our faces. 'I'm not leaving you,' he said. 'I'm going to get help.'

He tried to arrange me as best he could. He slackened off the laces of my boot to allow the blood to circulate and tried to immobilize the leg, strapping my ice axe against it with nylon tape. He did that. Then he pulled the bivouac sack up round me, and attempted to fit my injured leg into it. It was awkward moving around on the tiny ledge, but he tried something.

'You must keep warm,' he kept saying. 'You must try to keep awake and try to keep warm. Massage yourself. Hug yourself. Try to get a brew going, can you do that? Keep your liquids up, keep your fingers warm. Keep awake.'

A few minutes later I was watching him going back up the rope above me, jerking up on prusik loops, his crampons grating against the rock like bone on bone. He reached the horizon of rock and turned and looked down. 'See you, youth!' he shouted. 'Just hang on there.' And then he had disappeared above the lip of rock. Bits skittered down for a while – stones, chips of ice – and then they, too, ceased. I was alone.

The question is, what should he have done? That was what was argued over in the press, mulled over in the bars and pubs, analysed in climbing huts and bothies, discussed in the journals. What should Jim Matthewson, son of the good and the great and the legendary, have done? And, what if . . . ? Always, *what if*? Because you don't just judge by outcome, do you? You judge by a whole plethora of other, less clearly defined things. Under the circumstances that held at the time, what was the right thing to do? Climb up to the summit and descend the West

Flank: or abseil down the whole Face below us: or just stay with me and wait?

Look, I survived. I wouldn't be telling the story if I hadn't. But Jamie didn't know I would at the time, and neither did I, sitting in agony on my miserable little ledge of rock with pain grinding in my leg, and the clouds swirling round me and the cliffs plunging down below me in precipices difficult to imagine for the non-climber. The solitude. Difficult to imagine that, too. The sense of isolation, desolation. It is the closest thing to death without actually dying. That's what I believe, anyway.

The cloud around me darkened. The wind had dropped and it was no longer snowing, but the cloud was still there, blanketing off the world. I struggled to stay alive. Trivial things matter: whether your fingers are cold, whether your boots are too tight to allow the blood to circulate. Better that you take them off so that you can massage the toes, but I couldn't reach my foot as it was and Jamie had left the boots on for insulation. I fiddled with the stove and managed to get it alight at the cost of taking off my gloves. My fingers stuck to the metal. You gain one thing and you lose another. There was some snow that I could melt, but it disappeared into almost nothing and I couldn't reach any more. I added some of my precious water, like a miser measuring out scruples, and then some soup powder, and made myself something lukewarm to drink. I fumbled some chocolate into my mouth. I lived with my fears. Pain was a constant percussion beneath the discord of my misery. When I looked at my watch the hands seemed to have stopped. Tissot. Twenty-one jewels. Swiss made. Time was no longer plastic: it was ice cold rock. I wondered where Jamie was, whether he had climbed out or whether he had been forced to bivouac, or whether, silenced by the wind and hidden by the cloud, he had fallen the five thousand feet of the whole

338

wall and lay now, crumpled and broken, on the scree slopes at the bottom of the Face. The stone of time eroded, crystal by crystal. Time and death are the great parameters of the Eigerwand.

In the late evening the cloud grew luminous with a pearly sunlight. There were rents in the vapour and for precious minutes I could see down to the ground. It was like looking through the wrong end of a telescope: a glimpse of green fields and dark trees far, far away; the snake path of the railway; a cluster of buildings throwing long shadows. For those few minutes I felt an absurd optimism, as though merely seeing the ground might somehow get me off this place. But optimism faded when the sun died. In the darkness I flashed my torch in the direction of the buildings, the six long flashes of the distress signal, but I doubted that anyone would notice such a feeble point of light up there among the cloud that swathed the Face. Hopelessness was as tangible as the cold. I pulled my balaclava over my nose and mouth, tucked my hands into my armpits and hunched against the rock as though it might give me some protection, but the mountain seemed to draw the heat out of me as though it were hungry for it, so that I had the feeling of sitting on a great void, a heat sink into which all the warmth in the world was being sucked.

Throughout that night I wandered along borderlines between waking and sleeping, between sleep and uncon- sciousness – sleep's deadly sister – between life and death. I dreamt. Where dreams ended and hallucination began was not clear. I struggled through a fantastic landscape of pinnacle and precipice. Sometimes I was with Jamie and sometimes, somewhere round about two in the morning, I was with Caroline. She was younger than I knew her, as young as Ruth. Maybe she *was* Ruth. And then she was Eve, naked beside me. And then she was Jamie, and Eve, and Ruth, and we were walking (gravity was suspended) up the easy pathways of the Eiger, laughing and tripping and falling, and picking ourselves up unhurt.

'You silly fucker,' Jamie said, and there was affection in his tone.

I emerged from my dreams to shadowy precipices and the whisper of cloud around my ledge, and the sensation that, if only I knew the trick, I might recapture that vanished dream happiness. I dozed fitfully and by morning I couldn't feel my left foot, or the toes of the right.

The cloud around me was thinner, torn apart by the breeze, cut open by knives of sunlight that flashed across in front of me but never touched me with their fire. I shivered and hunched and no longer thought much about anything, neither death nor survival, neither hope nor despair. Why was I there, dying on a sloping ledge of rock among a litter of scree and icy rock the colour of slate? Why was I still conscious? I didn't have the answer to any of these questions. Life was a faint warmth in the middle of a pile of dying embers. I dozed and shivered and dreamt, and some abstract part of me knew that this was my life ebbing away.

I heard the helicopter some time during that morning. It was a metallic muttering on the edge of awareness, the sound coming and going with the wind. I had to strain to hear it at first, had to persuade myself of what it was, and then what it might be doing. I only cared with half of my mind. The other half stumbled along behind, thinking of my discomforts, my pain, the need for sleep, the need for comfort. The sound came and went, ringing in my ears like tinnitus, sometimes there and sometimes only a kind of illusion. Then I saw down through a rent in the cloud, and there it was far below me, chuttering and jerking, dodging towards the Face. I waited and wondered.

And then, quite suddenly, without my knowing where it had come from, the helicopter was there, just near me. The concussion of the machine's rotors battered the air all around me. The fuselage was there, blood red and sterile white, standing away from the Face and glaring at me with a bulbous Perspex eye. I looked back into its gaze. The machine bucked and pitched in the swirling air. Inside the plastic bowl there was a figure. It waved and I waved back, like a child. From the open door a helmeted crew member with a vast metallic mouth shouted at me above the racket of the engine: 'INJURED?'

Hope came slowly, like a kind of warmth; and with it the return of fear.

'YOU – INJURED?' the voice asked again.

I shouted words against the noise and pointed to my leg. 'Broken!' I yelled. I suddenly had strength, the strength of fear and panic. 'Broken! I can't fucking stand on it!' But, of course, my words were feeble, paltry things that couldn't cross the gulf between us, couldn't beat against the hammering of that engine and the thrashing of the rotors.

The figure at the open doorway grinned, waved back and gave a thumbs-up sign, then made a swirling movement with his hand. Abruptly the helicopter lurched away and chuttered off into the distance. 'No!' I shouted after it. 'No, don't leave me! For Christ's sake, don't leave me!'

But the machine had gone. Alone on my ledge and afraid once more, I wept.

Wind spilled over the West Ridge into the hollow of the Face. Clouds materialized and vanished. I willed them to disperse. I harboured the illusion that the immediate future of the weather was under my control, if only I could learn the trick. If I could only work out how, the whole world was mine to redesign as I wished. I looked at my watch and noted the time and decided that I could speed things up or slow things down at will. I'd tried to gather my things together. I was going home. I wasn't sure how or when, but as long as I could keep the weather good I knew I was going home. Pain crept out of the shadows and showed itself in the bright light of consciousness, but I could stifle that. If I could command the clouds, surely I could control pain.

Two hours later the helicopter came back. This time it rose up towards me and went up above and rattled overhead, two hundred feet directly above me, the spinning disc of its rotors reaching out as though to touch the rock. Bits spun down around me – fragments of ice, swirls of snow, bits of rock. I saw the white cross of Switzerland and a figure hanging from the machine like a corpse from a gibbet. The rotors flogged the carpet of the air around me and the figure grew larger and larger until it was a hanging man mere yards away. He held a ski pole towards me, fishing.

'English?' he shouted, above the engine racket.

'Yes.'

'You have anchor?'

'Yes.'

'Take the pole. Pull me in. Okay? You hold me while I release. Okay? You got that? You hold me, okay? Then I clip on.'

It took a moment. He was talking all the time, not to me but into the microphone of his walkie-talkie, a rapid German in counterpoint to our crude, shouted English. He swung in and I grabbed the pole and pulled him on to my ledge. For a moment he floundered across me while I clung on to him. I would never let him go. I would hold him to me and love him dearly till the end of time. He grabbed at one of my slings, released the helicopter cable, then clipped himself on. '*Gott sei Dank*,' he muttered, in relief.

The helicopter moved away, clattering above our heads and dropping down to our level. It circled round in front of us, turning in that strange dragonfly manner, nose dipped and wings blurring.

'You may let me go now,' the man said.

I held him tight.

'You may let me go!'

I released him reluctantly, as though I might lose him even now. He clambered to his feet, pulling on one of the slings as though he trusted it not to come out. 'Siegfried,' he said, holding out his hand to me. He looked ridiculously young – even younger than me. 'You call me Sigi.'

We shook hands solemnly, as though at a business meeting. 'I'm Robert. Thanks for coming.'

Sigi frowned. 'You are hurt, Robert?'

'My leg. I think it's broken.'

'Pain?'

'Less than yesterday. I can't feel my foot.'

He examined the offending leg for a while, his fingers pressing through my gaiters so that I screamed in agony. 'Only your leg?' He straightened up and stared into my eyes as though hoping to find the truth there.

'Only my leg.'

'So.' He rummaged in his rucksack and pulled out a plastic ampoule. 'I give you a shot for the pain,' he said. He tugged at my breeches and exposed some pale flesh. 'It will stop your hurt.' For a moment I thought he said *heart*. I thought it would stop my heart, snatch life from me just as I had regained hope. I felt a moment's ridiculous panic as the needle went in, but Sigi was unconcerned. Apparently he was used to killing people, used to

343

speaking calmly with them as they died. He was checking the pitons that held us to the rock, glancing round at the plunging precipices, at the walls and cliffs above us, at the space below.

'You are alone?' he asked. It seemed a ridiculous question, as though there might be others hiding somewhere around the corner.

'Sure I'm alone.'

'Where is your friend?'

My mind stalled. 'My *friend*?'

'Where is he? Did he fall?'

'Jamie? No. He climbed out on his own. Didn't he call you out?'

'He *left* you?' He looked puzzled. 'He went *solo*?'

'Wasn't it he who called you out? Hasn't he got down?'

'It was your girl,' he explained. 'Your girl said you had an accident. It was your girl you must thank.'

So where the hell was Jamie? Whereabouts was he on this fucking mountain? I shouted at my rescuer, as though shouting would make him understand the importance of the question: 'Where, in Christ's name, *is* he?'

Sigi shrugged. 'We will see.' There was, it seemed, nothing more to be said. After a quick search in his rucksack he brought out a Thermos flask. He poured warm tea, and fed me pieces of chocolate. 'We keep your blood sugar up a bit, no?'

I ate the chocolate greedily, thinking of Jamie, thinking of Ruth, of survival and death, of jealousy and envy. Whatever it was that he had injected into me was having its effect. My heart still beat but pain was retreating fast, like a landscape left behind by a speeding car. Where the hell was Jamie?

'The chopper comes back in one hour,' Sigi said. He used the word 'chopper'. Maybe he had seen too many films. 'When it comes you go first. *Gut*?'

'Okay,' I agreed. 'Sounds fine to me.' But where was Jamie? This might be salvation, but it was salvation only for me. Where, in God's name, was Jamie?

'But first we do something for your leg, perhaps.' He crouched awkwardly, unstrapped the ice axe and pulled splints from his rucksack. 'How did you fall?'

'Avalanched. We were climbing out through lousy weather and I was hit by an avalanche.'

'Too bad.'

'You can say that again.'

He glanced up. 'Why?'

'Why what?'

'I say that again?'

I managed a laugh. 'An expression. Just an English expression. It means that I agree.'

He nodded and smiled. When he had finished splinting my leg he began arranging things, helping me strap into a harness, tying on my rucksack, bundling things away, tidying up the ledge, speaking occasionally into the radio. I had no idea what had happened to my leg. If there was pain it was something that affected someone else.

'Now we get ready,' he said.

'Ready?'

'For the chopper.' He grinned. 'I do not know if we succeed with this. We try for the first time.'

'The *first time*?'

'*Ja*. Is interesting, no?'

'That's one way of describing it.'

He arranged me on the ledge, facing outwards, perched over the void, held by a single piton. Then he stood over me, talking into the radio; and the radio chattered back at him, a furious, electronic voice.

'The wind is over limits,' Sigi said, with disappointment in his voice.

Only the wind? I thought. We waited. The clouds poured into the Face and the wind battered against us. I peered down into the funnel of the Spider. Below the ice there was nothing until the fields at the bottom, so far away as to be like a landscape seen from an aircraft. When the clouds parted briefly I could see the buildings of Kleine Scheidegg, the hotel, the railway station, and what looked like crowds gathering. A rescue on the Eiger: good for the tourist trade. The helicopter was circling around far from the Face, over the green slopes of Alpiglen.

'What happens if they can't get in?' I asked.

Sigi shrugged. 'If we cannot get off we do *abseil*. Maybe they get someone down to us from the summit. Maybe we get down on the – how do you say? *Bügeleisen*?'

'Flatiron.'

'Right. It is easier there. Let us hope it is not necessary.'

We waited. Time, the relative dimension, played its trick of moving at different speeds simultaneously: the wait seemed interminable, and yet the precious daylight hours sped by. What was happening? The helicopter stuttered away into the distance and alighted like an insect at the Männlichen station, which lies beyond and above Kleine Scheidegg. Were they refuelling? I think perhaps I prayed, but to what I am not sure. I thought about Jamie, of course. I thought about Ruth, and I thought about Eve. Somehow I needed Eve at that moment. She was detached from all this, cynical about it, an atheist confronted with the religion of climbing. And I was fast losing my own faith.

Sigi was talking to the radio, communing with salvation. We watched the helicopter take off again. I remember the elevation of hope like a physical sensation, as though I was being tossed high into the air, a transport. 'Is it coming?' I asked. 'Is it coming?' It might have been ecstasy, orgasm.

'Maybe. The wind is less, but with less wind the cloud comes down, maybe.'

'Let's hope not.'

Whether my prayers were answered or not I have no means of telling; one never does. But the wind must have dropped, for suddenly the helicopter rose up towards the Face, coming closer and closer until it was clattering above us, bucking and rocking. A shower of spindrift and ice came down. The racket was all around us and Sigi was shouting into his radio in rapid, staccato German. A cable descended, a thread that swirled in the down-draught from the rotor blades, a hairline between life and death. Sigi leant forward and fished with his ridiculous ski pole. '*Lose,*' he called. '*Lose.*' Some part of me, stunned with morphine and detached from all this, realized that he was calling for slack – 'Loose, loose,' he was saying.

And then he had fished the cable. He pulled it towards us. 'Release!' he shouted to me. 'Release!'

I fumbled at the single karabiner that held me. Somehow I snapped it open and unclipped it. For a dreadful moment I was detached from everything, sliding forward into space off our perch, tied neither to the mountain nor to the stuttering heli-copter. And then Sigi had clipped the cable on to my harness, and was shouting, '*Gehen wir!* Let's go!' and the cable sprang tight and I was snatched into the void, spinning up under the red underbelly of the helicopter as it tilted away from the rock. I saw down. I saw down on to my miserable little ledge, with its litter of slings and rope and Sigi standing there waving. Besides that detritus of climbing and that solitary rescuer, something else was left behind on that ledge, something less substantial: my love, precarious at best, of the whole business of mountaineering.

The cable whirred me upwards. The ledge shrank, so that it was no longer a discernible feature of the mountain, just a blemish on the grey fortress cliffs above the Traverse of the Gods. I saw the runnels and gullies below it, the great diagonal slash of the Ramp and the nameless cliffs beneath, down to the grey scree and the green fields where the cattle grazed. I felt no fear. This was surrender and surrender is beyond fear. The red underbelly of the helicopter came nearer and then hands were grabbing me and I was being bundled into the clattering coffin of the fuselage.

'Is *gut*, no?' someone yelled, above the racket of the engine. 'Is *gut*?'

'Is very good,' I cried, as they lifted me on to a stretcher and arranged my legs. 'What about Sigi?'

'We get him. Or maybe we leave him to climb down.' There was raucous laughter at the idea.

Memory gives little away beyond the sensations of sound and movement, the hands lifting me, the rattle of the helicopter. A few moments later the winch was whirring again and Sigi's face appeared at the lip of the door, grinning and shouting. I couldn't even hear what he said. I was barely aware of the motion of climb and descent and a leaden return to earth. I was half drugged, exhausted, let down by the sudden collapse of adrenaline. People leant over me. Ruth's face was pinned among them like a rag hung on a line. She was in tears. 'Where's Jamie?' she kept saying. 'Where's Jamie?' There was the thrashing sound of rain and wind, a clap of thunder.

Lights and faces and the clatter of feet on concrete, and the helicopter lifting off again, pitching and shuddering in the wind. There was a steep descent, down into the valley, down into the warmth of morphine-induced sleep.

21

I dreamt. Of hybrid beasts that were Ruth and Jamie, Eve and Eiger. I knew terror and contentment, and the third member of the triangle, which was metamorphosis, one thing transformed into another: fear into happiness, pain into ecstasy, ignorance into profound knowledge. I awoke to a white room and a view out of the window of forested slopes and lowering clouds, the colour, exactly, of a bruise. Rain was running down the window-pane. There was the dyspeptic grumble of thunder somewhere on the floor above.

'Where am I?'

A nurse looked up. 'You are awake,' she said, which wasn't exactly answering my question.

She was doing something at my feet. The blanket was raised over my leg by some sort of cage. 'Where am I?' Fragments of the last few days came back to me, sensations mainly: the cold and the noise of wind, a sense of desolation, hurrying the dreams away.

'You are in hospital.'

'Obviously.'

'Interlaken.'

Then memory came crowding back, a convulsion of memory, of noise and motion and fear. 'Where is my friend?'

'*Freund?*'

'Yes. Where is he?'

She shrugged. I watched her work for a moment. Above me was a stand holding an intravenous drip. A tube snaked down and into my arm. 'What have they done?'

'I will get the doctor.'

'Tell me what they've done. I want to know what they've done.'

She straightened up, a lumpish girl who, in another era, would have tended cows on some Swiss pasture. She frowned at not knowing the English. 'They have tried to make your leg good. And your . . .' She shrugged helplessly. '*Zehen.*'

'My what?'

'The fingers of your foot.'

'My toes?'

'You have frozen.'

The doctor came shortly afterwards. He was almost fluent in English, a small dark man who seemed faintly amused by the things he found around him. 'My brave almost-conqueror of the Eigerwand,' he greeted me.

'What happened to my friend?' I asked.

'They found him on the West Flank.'

'*Found him?*'

'Oh, he is living,' he said, with a laugh. As though survival was some kind of joke. 'He was living and coming down. He had made *Biwak.*'

'Bivouac?'

'Coming down he had made bivouac on the west side. He is all right. He is very brave.' The doctor smiled. 'The newspapers say so. Some of them.'

Jealousy crawled like vermin through my mind. I confess to impure thoughts, about death and survival, about revenge and retribution. I didn't admit it at the time, of course; not even to myself. 'My foot hurts,' I said.

'We have taken away the morphine. If it gets too bad . . .' I liked the morphine. I liked the comfort and the dreams. 'About your foot,' the doctor was saying. 'We will have to wait and see. We are treating the condition – it is important that you do not smoke – and we will just see how it goes.' He pulled aside the blanket and sheet to show my foot inside its cage. It was swollen and discoloured and blistered, the toes like rotting vegetables.

'Christ alive!'

'Perhaps it is not as bad as it looks. It is difficult to tell at the early stages. You are lucky that they got you off when they did. The weather has closed right down. You would still be up there now . . .'

'What'll happen?'

He shrugged, Gallic rather than German. 'We will see. The only real cure for frostbite is time. You were unlucky. The break affected the blood circulation in the foot, which did not help. But now you are perhaps in good hands.'

'Will I lose toes?'

'That we will see with time.'

'Time?'

'Weeks. Maybe as much as eight.'

'*Two months!* For Christ's sake! And my leg?'

'Oh, the fracture is nothing. For the moment we have immobilized, but once the oedema in the foot is down we can set the leg. Here we mend fractured legs like dentists fill teeth.' It was a practised joke. He had said it to hundreds, maybe thousands of skiing casualties.

Jamie came that afternoon, with Ruth. He looked rough – his face battered by ultra-violet and frost, his chin smeared with a four-day growth of stubble, his expression wary and suspicious. They stood at the foot of the bed and asked how the hell I was and thank God you're okay and that kind of thing.

I felt the aftershock of fear translated fluently into anger. 'You left me, Jamie,' I said. 'You fucking abandoned me to complete the fucking route.'

'I was going for help, Rob. You know that.'

I couldn't control what was inside me. It was like the anger of a little child, the stuff that comes up from inside you without your being able to control it, like vomit. 'You deserted me. You just up and left me.'

He shook his head. 'I had an epic climbing out, I can tell you, and I fucked up on the descent. It was almost dark and I went too far over to the left and ended up buggering around on the upper part of the glacier. And then I was avalanched and had to bivvy in a crevasse, for God's sake.'

As Sigi had said, it was Ruth who had called out the rescue. She'd seen my light on the Face, the six long flashes, the distress signal we'd mentioned to her in passing almost as though it was a joke, something that happened to other people. There'd been a rent in the cloud and she'd been looking up and had seen the light.

'If they hadn't got you off then, you'd still be up there,' Jamie said. 'They'd be bringing your body down next week. Ruth saved your life, Rob.'

She smiled wryly. 'Thanks,' I said to her, not finding much else to say. She came round the bed, bent down towards me and kissed me on the cheek. '*Cariad*,' she said. For some reason that I couldn't fathom out, I resented her. I had seen her standing naked against the lake and the hills. I had held her in my arms. I had loved her. Unexpressed emotion changes into something else, is that it? Love into hate, gratitude into resentment.

We talked about the whole thing for a bit, going round in circles that were bent and distorted and deformed; and then we fell silent, all three aware that something, some bond that had held us together as a trio, had snapped. Like a rope. Survival had destroyed us more surely than the spinning of some bloody silly coin. I wondered if she knew. I wondered if he had told her, or would tell her.

'Well, at least Jamie climbed the bloody Face,' I said.

'So would you have, Rob. You can't fight an avalanche. Think what would have happened if one like that had hit me afterwards.'

'They'd be scraping you off the scree at the bottom.'

'They'd be putting me in bags.'

We laughed, but there was nothing there any longer, no shared laughter, no shared affection – we just laughed at the same time. He had left me, that's what I felt; and no amount of reasoning could alter that.

Later a couple of the rescue team came to visit, Sigi and the helicopter pilot. Sigi grinned like a little boy. 'We were lucky,' he said. 'You don't know how lucky. Ueli here thought he wouldn't get back to us.'

Ueli smiled and nodded. '*Der Wind*,' he kept saying. '*Stark, stark*.' And making movements with his hand, like a child playing at aeroplanes.

'He thought the weather would close us in,' Sigi explained. 'You imagine down rope from that place in a storm? With your leg? You imagine . . .'

I didn't want to. After they had gone an English television camera crew came into my room. They peered at me through a blank, black lens and asked fatuous questions about fear and death. The journalist held out the carrot of a documentary film that might involve some climbing.

'I really couldn't give a fuck about a climbing film,' I told him. 'God knows whether I'll be able to climb again. God knows whether I'll want to.'

'Your mate is interested,' the man said.

'I'll bet he is.'

It was some time after they had gone that the phone beside my bed burbled. Or maybe it was the next day. Or the next. Time had little meaning in the context of that sterile prison cell. I reached over for the receiver and a distant voice sounded in my ear: 'Christ, I've had trouble getting hold of you,' it said. 'Are you there? How are you? You've been all over the papers, you know.'

The ridiculous thing was that I wept. I wept just to hear her voice.

'Are you there, Rob? Christ, has the bloody line gone? Robert, are you *there*?'

'I'm here,' I said. 'I'm all right, more or less.'

'And Jamie? Is he there? And Ruth?'

'I think they've gone home.'

'I'll bet they have. When are they going to let you out?'

'I don't know yet. Frostbite. I might lose toes.' I laughed bitterly. 'Nothing disfiguring, except when I take my clothes off.'

She laughed at the far end of the line, in London where I wanted to be. 'Don't worry about that. By that stage it's usually too late.' I loved the sound of her voice, even through the constricting wires of the telephones. I never realized until that moment how much I loved the sound. It had a roughness to it, as though she had borrowed it from an old drunk.

354

'Eve,' I whispered. 'Eve?'

'What's happened? Can't you speak up a bit? Christ, these bloody phone lines . . .'

'Eve, I love you,' I said.

There was a pause. 'We'll see about that later,' she said eventually. 'For the moment . . .' She stalled. Or the line went or something.

'Eve?'

'Just get better,' she said. 'For the moment, just get better. Then we'll see.'

After that she rang once or twice a week, I suppose from her parents' house. She wasn't so stupid as to run up her own phone bill on international calls.

I recall those hospital days as a kind of purgatory, underwritten with nagging pain and watched over by indifferent demons. Over and over again I climbed that final pitch. I climbed it in my thoughts and in my dreams. Perhaps I was trying to purge it from memory, but remembering it only stored it there, engraved it into the circuits of recall so that I could no longer tell the experience from the remembering, the facts of waking from the fantasies of dream. Sometimes I fell under the cold deluge of snow crystals; sometimes Jamie pulled on the rope and it was he who brought me down rather than the avalanche, a Jamie who laughed as I plummeted, a Jamie who was Ruth, who was Caroline, who was one thing and the other, male and female, friend and foe.

'You'll just have to be patient,' the medics told me, when I asked how long I would be stuck there. Time was the great healer, they assured me: time to re-establish the circulation and reduce the oedema, time to recover lost tissue. 'I am afraid that you need patience,' they told me.

I don't think patience is much of a virtue. For most virtues you have to do something, but for patience you only need to wait. I waited six weeks before they agreed I could go, and even then I was confined to a wheelchair like a geriatric case. They shuttled me through the airport on an electric golf cart and, despite my insistence that I could manage by myself, hoisted me up into the aircraft on a lift.

There was a blonde stewardess waiting for me at the door, as plastic as the food they served. 'Did you do it skiing?' she asked, as they manoeuvred me in.

'Not exactly. I fell off the North Face of the Eiger.'

She laughed. She thought I was joking.

The flight took a couple of hours and we flew high above any mountains, and at the other end, at Heathrow airport, among the waiting relatives and the tourists returning from the Maldives and the Seychelles, Eve was waiting.

They made the film later that summer on the Pendragon cliff, with a couple of cameramen hanging on ropes and Jamie drifting up the route in that derisory manner of his and talking climbing at the same time. He even paused at the crux to light a cigarette. 'The man who challenged and surmounted the Eiger's dreaded North Face now takes on a different challenge,' the voice-over said.

'Did you see it?' people asked. 'Did you see Jim on Pendragon?'

Yes, I saw it. I was sitting in the wheelchair once more, after having three toes amputated from my left foot. I saw it all right. Eve was with me, watching the film with a tense expression, her lips tightly pursed, as though she found it offensive and, if it continued like this, she was going to write to her MP about it.

She was there a lot in those days. She had an appealing matter-of-factness about her. She was unfazed by the sight of the two ruined, discoloured toes that were all that remained on my left foot. She even seemed happy about things, content with my anger and bitterness. She helped me up with the crutches and pushed me around the corridors of the hospital in the wheelchair, brought me books to read, things to do – cards, jigsaw puzzles, a silly game with blocks of wood that you had to build into the tallest possible tower. We played that game against each other for hours. The person who collapsed the tower was the loser. 'Rather like climbing,' Eve remarked drily. 'You don't really have winners, just losers.'

Jamie dropped in just once to see me. The pressure of work, he said in excuse. He was full of the television climb. 'They're talking bigger things. An alpine route, perhaps. Or even something in South America. And there's this international expedition to do the South-west Face of Everest. They want me to go along. I reckon this is it, youth. This could be the breakthrough.'

'How's Ruth?' I asked.

Ruth was fine. She sent her love. Something told me that all was not well between the two of them.

'She might have come to see me.'

He nodded. He was looking at me carefully, as though weighing up my possible reaction to what he might say. What would it be? Was it that they were no longer together? But when he did speak it was anodyne, something about being sorry, sorry about how it had panned out, sorry about the foot, sorry about everything.

'It's not your fault, Jamie.'

'Maybe not. But it's bloody awful luck, the whole thing. Still, you'll soon be back to normal.'

'The doctors say . . .'

'What do they say?'

I shrugged. What did I care any longer? 'The circulation will never fully recover. Apparently it never really does. It'll always give problems, always be sensitive to cold. That kind of thing.'

He looked concerned. 'It's tough, isn't it?'

Was it? I couldn't separate what had happened from what I wanted, that was the problem. I wouldn't be able to climb again, not properly; but on the other hand, I didn't really want to climb, not any longer. The fall had driven something out of me. I'd lost my sense of invulnerability, I suppose. And when you lose that, something else always takes its place: a disturbing sense of your own mortality.

So Jamie went away, to be a star, to be a hero, to be what his father had been, while I remained with Eve. She appeared happy to be with me when it didn't seem that I was really worth being with at all. I had no work, no degree, no toes worth the name on one foot, and no longer any desire to follow the only thing I had any talent for, which was the idiotic pursuit of trying to pick out the most difficult line up a piece of cliff, and then climb it. And there Eve was, showing some kind of devotion when all around were losing theirs and blaming it on me. So I moved into her flat when I was discharged from hospital. She was working for some left-wing magazine at the time. She was always working for a cause, always with the hard edge of cynicism about her, always with a deep-seated sense of real conviction. In those days it was the Vietnam war and the campaign for nuclear disarmament; later it would be ecology and animal rights and anti-fox-hunting. Maybe I became just one of her causes.

'Of course, I could always go home. My mother wants me to.'

'And run a guesthouse?'

'Private hotel,' I corrected her.

'You'd be mad. I can just see you by the time you're forty – fat and greasy and boring all the guests in the bar with stories of how you used to climb, how you were almost a hero—'

'There's no bar. We don't have a licence for a bar.'

'You'd soon get one. If I'm really going to save you, you've got to get a job here in London. But what can a guy like you do? Other than fuck his best friend's mother, I mean.' I remember the hard glare of her eyes, the kind of hard enamel blue that you see painted on water taps to show which one is cold. 'Don't pretend,' she said. 'I know perfectly well. Okay. She was probably a good lay – I'm certain she's had enough practice – but that kind of thing stops now, do you understand?'

'Or?'

'Or I do.' She smiled. It was a smile entirely without humour. 'Look, my father's got a friend who may be able to help you with a job . . .' She said *father*. If she'd said *Daddy* I'd probably have told her to get lost. 'It might be up your street . . .'

So I went round for an interview. 'Went' sounds as though there was speed and efficiency about it. I hobbled round, took a taxi, hobbled out of the cab and into the place that had once been a warehouse down at the far end of the King's Road. Nowadays it said PORTEUS FINE ART over the doorway, and the high, mean windows had been replaced by plate glass that gave the passer-by a privileged sight of expensive white space and large, abstract canvases. As we went in, a girl in a short geometric dress – something by Courrèges, no doubt – with cropped hair and ridiculous false eyelashes, clipped across the parquet flooring towards us.

'I have an appointment with Mr Porteus,' I said.

'Then you must be Mr Dewar.' She pronounced it 'Due-are'. She was that kind of girl. 'Would you walk this way, please?' she asked.

Eve said it. I thought it, or something like it, but Eve said it: 'If he could walk that way he wouldn't need toes.'

VI
London, 1945

22

The metamorphosis was complete: London had been a provincial city cringing beneath the bombs; it had become a metropolis, filled with uniforms and accents from all corners of the earth. Bomb damage was still evident – you still turned a corner and found a wasteland, with willowherb growing over the rubble – but the bombers had done their worst, and the flying bombs after them, and now the war had moved on.

'*How is Alan?*' Meg wrote. '*Do give him my love. He is awfully* nice *and really very* devoted *and I'm so happy to hear about your engagement. It makes me feel quite on the shelf. That's a joke: I'm having a* wonderful *time and marriage couldn't be further from my thoughts! You know what they say – go out with a Pole and come home with a Czech.*'

She carefully added 'cheque' in parentheses in case Diana didn't get the joke. Since she'd moved to the Air Ministry she'd got in with a fast set. It was the Café Royale and the Trocadero and places like that most nights. This evening, when she'd finished the letter to Di and had a bath and changed, it was going to be the Café Élysée. Elysian fields, all right. '*There's a rather dishy young colonel (my goodness, the colonels are only about thirty years old, these days!), who's something in Special Operations,*' she had written. '*Will I surrender my virtue yet again, I wonder?*'

The Café Élysée was off Leicester Square. The entrance was an inconspicuous door between a cinema and a tobacconist's. You went downstairs into the foyer where there was a bar on one side and doors ahead of you opening out on to the balcony. It was always a surprise to newcomers. First the shadowy foyer with people drinking at the bar, and then you pushed through the double doors and there was the café laid out below like a stage seen from the gods – gilt tables, red plush, the lights on each table almost like candles, the mirrors throwing the scene back at you from a dozen different directions. There always seemed to be a crowd there – men just back from the Middle East or Europe where they had risked life and limb; and with them women who were usually prepared to risk other things besides. The colonel – Colonel Tommy, she called him because that was what she'd heard his driver call him and she thought it rather fetching – had been delayed by some flap or other and telephoned her to go on ahead without him, and she was damned if she was going to worry about being a girl on her own, so there she was descending the stairs in style and making her way between the tables towards the one that had been booked by her own group; and there was this man, sitting at a table with four others – two men and a couple of girls – five in all; and Meg knew at once.

She paused. Someone from her group waved at her. The man looked up. He didn't recognize her. Of course he didn't. A strong face, sun-tanned, looking more mature than so many of the others. Army general service uniform with the rank badges of a major.

'Aren't you Guy?' she asked.

He got to his feet, looking faintly embarrassed. 'Yes . . . but I'm afraid . . .'

'Margaret York. Sounds like something out of the Wars of the Roses. That's what you said. People call me Meg, although I always think *that* sounds like a sheepdog.'

They shook hands, but he clearly still didn't remember. Behind them the band came on to the diminutive stage to scattered applause. 'I'm a friend of Diana Sheridan's,' she explained. 'We met in Wales . . .'

He reddened. Even in the subdued lighting of the Élysée you could see it. 'Oh, my goodness, yes,' he said, and sat down in his chair as though she had pushed him. 'Are you in touch with her? How is she? Look, won't you join us for a drink or something? Let me introduce you . . .' There was a shaking of hands with his friends and an exchange of brittle, instant smiles. Meg ordered a gin and tonic. Guy drew up a chair for her and she sat down, crossed her legs and looked at him thoughtfully. 'I didn't expect to see you in uniform,' she said. 'Well, I didn't expect to see you *at all*, come to that. But certainly not in uniform.'

He withered under her gaze. 'I changed my mind.'

'You did *what*? Good Lord, I thought you were immutable in your beliefs.'

'It does sound dreadfully feeble, doesn't it?' he admitted. 'But when that business about the concentration camps came out – when was it? two years ago now? that announcement in Parliament by Eden – I sat down and I thought about everything . . .' He shrugged and looked at her as though for help. 'You know what I mean?'

She gave him her withering look. 'Most people had worked that kind of thing out long before.'

'Maybe I'm a bit slow.' He laughed awkwardly. 'Anyway, they needed people with my skills to train squaddies not to fall off cliffs and that's more or less what I did – in North Wales. Arduous training, they call it. But now they've posted me to an office in Whitehall. Typical, isn't it?'

The band had started playing – some Benny Goodman number – and a few couples had got up to dance. 'So tell me about Diana,' Guy said. 'Is she well?'

'Haven't you heard from her?'

'We exchanged letters for a while, but she sort of . . . told me to stop. Actually, when I got to London I did try and find her. Went to the place where she had been billeted . . .'

'And?'

He looked distressed. 'Nothing. Bombed out. Well, of course I thought, oh, my God, Di . . . So I asked around, in the local pub, the corner shop, the ARP post, that kind of thing. But the owners were the only victims, apparently. A Mr and Mrs Wardle or something—'

'Warren.'

'You knew them?'

'I met them.'

'Both of them killed, poor devils. Last winter in fact, a doodle-bug, a direct hit. I must admit it's a bit of a relief to know for sure that Di's still . . . around.'

'Oh, yes, she's still around,' Meg said. She thought for a moment, sipping her gin and watching Guy's face with care. Clearly he didn't know: he didn't know a thing. 'As a matter of fact, she's married.'

'Married? Good Lord.'

'Yes, married. It does happen. In Di's case, to a doctor. He works in Liverpool general hospital, although they met when she was here in London. They're very happy.' It was hard to read the man's expression – sadness of some kind, but a nostalgic sort of sadness, as though he was regretting a whole lot of things that were not just Diana: his life before the war, the mountains perhaps, his vanished pacifist principles.

'Well, that's excellent, then,' he said. 'I'm glad she's happy.'

Meg glanced round. People were coming down the stairs from the balcony, her colonel among them. 'I'm afraid I have to go.'

Guy rose from his chair. 'Maybe I could get in touch with you some time?'

She thought for a moment, considering him carefully as one might consider the future and wonder what it had to offer. Then she opened her respirator case, found a pen and bent to scribble on the back of a bill. 'My phone number. There are three others in the flat, so someone's usually there to take a call. One of my flatmates is on nights, so try not to ring in the morning.' And then she had gone to join her friends, easing her hips round the other tables, waving to Tommy, who suddenly seemed rather obvious, gauche, even, loudmouthed and uninteresting beside Guy Matthewson. Guy's eyes followed her as she went, watching the sinuous line of the seam down the back of her stockings. She knew it.

He rang a few days later. They went out to the cinema together and to supper afterwards. It was hardly a passionate encounter: he was polite and withdrawn, as though Meg were some kind of relative, a distant cousin perhaps, and he was doing all this out of a sense of duty. She felt cross throughout the evening, cross that he was not making a pass at her, cross that he could presume to take her out without doing so, cross that Diana had broken through barriers that seemed, for the moment, impregnable to her.

When he dropped her back at her flat he got out of the cab, came round to her side and even accompanied her to the front door of the block but, no, he didn't think he ought to come in for a coffee or anything. He ought to be getting back – an early start tomorrow. He put out his hand and he actually expected her to *shake* it, shake his bloody hand, for God's sake. 'Don't I even get a kiss?' she asked.

He smiled wryly, and bent and kissed her gently on the cheek. Brother and bloody sister, she thought. She turned away and walked in through the door and didn't even glance round as the car started up and drew away. That was the last she would see of Mr Guy bloody Matthewson. She would consign him to the scrap heap of lousy dates.

23

Although it came shortly after VE Day, shortly after the end of the war in the West, shortly after those two days of cheering and laughing and herding rather aimlessly – and later, drunkenly – round the streets of London, Diana's wedding was a drab affair with little in the way of celebration. The uncles and aunts and cousins were there, of course, but so many old friends were still far away. Not that Meg minded that, really. Somehow the friends from before the war had lost their relevance: they seemed to belong to another person and another century.

'Darling, I'm wildly honoured,' Meg had said, when Diana asked her to be a bridesmaid, 'but I'm not sure that it's really appropriate, is it? Aren't bridesmaids meant to be just that?'

'Just what?'

'Well, *maids*, darling. You know, *virgo intacta*. Hardly the case, is it? Haven't you got some adorable little cousins who can look coy and be sick all over their dresses?'

'Well, it's hardly the case with me either, and I'm wearing white.'

'Maybe I could be a matron-of-honour,' Meg suggested, as a compromise. 'Mind you, that sounds as though I've got fifty-two-inch hips.'

Diana's wedding dress was adapted from her mother's. Rationing meant that a new one was out of the question but she looked pretty enough, if a little *passé*. Alan was solemn and rather fine in kilt and tight black jacket. He insisted on explaining the finer points of his kit – the skean-dhu, the type of tartan, all that kind of nonsense – to anyone who would listen. That was rather a bore. And, of course, the inevitable jokes were made – about sporrans, about what Scotsmen wear beneath the kilt – but not in front of the groom. The couple seemed happy – they *were* happy, according to Diana. 'He's very *kind*,' she assured Meg. 'Very *thoughtful*.'

The service was in the church in Diana's village and the reception was at a hotel in Chester. It was a rather dull affair and really a bit thin on champagne. Meg slipped away and went upstairs to find Diana in one of the bedrooms, where she was fussing over her going-away dress. She was standing in front of the mirror in her underwear with the dress held against her like a limp and recalcitrant child. It was in some kind of nondescript grey wool, but it had still cost, Diana claimed, twelve coupons.

'Darling, it's lovely,' Meg said. 'It makes you look positively *respectable*.'

'Trouble is . . .'

'What's the trouble, darling?'

'Alan knows I'm not.'

'Oh, don't be silly. Everyone's been in your position these days.'

'You haven't.'

'There've been a few close calls, I can tell you. Look, darling, there's no point in just standing there *posing*. You've got to put the damn thing *on*. By the way . . .' She said it casually, tossed it into the conversation like someone throwing a stone into a pond, just to watch the ripples. 'By the way, I came across your old flame the other day.'

'Who's that?' Di asked. 'Eric?'

'Don't be silly, darling. How on earth could it be Eric? He was posted missing in action three years ago. No, Guy Matthewson.'

Diana went pale. There she was, dressed in her underwear – parachute-silk knickers, Meg happened to know, having been instrumental in getting hold of the material – and hugging her dress to her and looking as though she was about to be sick all over it. She sat heavily on the bed. 'Oh, my God,' she whispered.

'Darling, what on earth's the matter?'

Diana shook her head. 'Don't say anything. To Alan, I mean. Not about Guy. For God's sake.'

'But, my dear, why should I?'

'Just don't, that's all.'

'Of course I won't.'

'Alan has been so understanding . . .'

'Of course he has.'

'But—'

There was a knock on the door and Diana's mother came in, wondering where she was, wondering what was keeping her, wondering whether she was feeling quite well. 'You're not having first-night nerves, are you, darling?'

'Don't be silly, Mummy. It's just the excitement.'

'Well, for goodness' sake, get a move on.'

She waited until her mother had gone. She was picking distractedly at things, her new dress, the counterpane, the top of her stockings where it looked as though there might be a ladder beginning. 'How is he?' she asked.

'Guy? You'll never guess . . .'

She looked round, her expression vulnerable, open, eager to hear. 'Never guess what?'

'That business about being a conchie. It's all over – he's in uniform just like everyone else, been in uniform for years, actually. I tell you what . . .'

'What?'

'Tell me you won't mind . . .'

'Won't mind what?'

'We went out together.'

Diana swallowed. Something, the heat, the nervous tension, made her head swim.

'Well, come on, darling. You haven't got property rights over him.'

'No,' she said. 'No rights at all . . .'

'And it wasn't as if . . .'

'What wasn't it as if, Meg?'

'Well, he wasn't a great love or anything. Just a weekend, for God's sake. A weekend that went a wee bit wrong.'

Diana stared at Meg. Her expression held within its compass elements of fear and amazement, and other things that Meg couldn't quite name but which she found rather frightening. 'But I *did* love him, Meg. I *did*.'

'Don't be silly.'

'I *did*,' Diana insisted. 'I have never been more certain of anything in my whole life.' She wasn't going to cry, that was the interesting thing. She was tough, was Diana. Maybe the Blitz had done that. She breathed in deeply and stood up. She'd got over that awful moment of shock and the nausea had died down. She stepped into her frock, pulling it up over her hips and wriggling her arms into the sleeves. 'Can you help with the buttons, darling?' She smoothed the dress over her hips where it was a bit tight, adjusted it over the shoulders, smiled at Meg's reflection in the mirror.

Meg fiddled around at Diana's back for a moment. 'So you'd rather I chucked him?' she asked.

'I never said that . . .'

'But that's what you were thinking.'

'All right, that's what I was thinking.'

'Isn't that being rather bitch-in-the-manger?'

'*I*'m not the bitch-in-the-manger,' Diana retorted.

'Who is, then?'

There was a pause. Diana examined her own reflection. How long, she wondered, can you keep a person in suspense like this? 'His wife is,' she said eventually, noting the widening of Meg's eyes, the faint flinch, the hasty effort at composure.

'His *wife*?'

'Yes, darling, his wife. You know, what I've just become and you haven't bothered.'

Meg ignored the taunt. 'My God, the bastard never said a word.'

24

A few days later Guy rang again. Could he speak to Flight
Officer York? She felt that little snatch of anticipation at the
sound of his voice, that was what was so damned infuriating.
'You already are,' she said tartly.

'It's Guy.'

'I know it's Guy.'

'How?'

'I recognized the tone of apology and evasion.' She took
delight in his laughter. He was, apparently, going to watch
some cricket at Lord's. He thought she might like to come, or
would it be a terrible bore? It was in aid of the Red Cross.
They were calling it the Victory Test Match. What did she
think?

What did she think? She toyed with the idea of turning him
down. She toyed with the idea of saying something extremely

unladylike, something like 'Fuck you, Mr Guy Matthewson; fuck you, with your cheerful ability to have a girl fall in love with you and then get her pregnant, all without even realizing it, and all despite the fact that you are married.' But she didn't. Instead she said, 'All right.' Just that. Nothing more than that. Nothing that would show he aroused any kind of emotion in her, be it solid anger or something more undermining: those shifting, unstable currents of desire that flowed beneath the surface of her personality, the desperate desire – she hardly dared say it even to herself – to have him inside her, there between her legs. So she said yes, and they arranged to meet outside the gates of the ground, and it transpired (but it was no great surprise) that Guy took her in through the members' gate, that he wore the hideous orange and yellow tie of the club, that stewards knew him by name.

There was a good crowd, people anxious to see such a peaceful thing as a cricket match after the years of war. Meg and Guy sat in the spring sunshine, watching distant white figures move around the pitch. She glanced uncomprehendingly at the score card, and asked him for explanation.

'You give me one,' he said. 'Why do you think I'm apologetic and evasive?' He must have been saving the question, waiting for the right moment.

'You have reason to be.'

'Is it about Diana?'

'Perhaps.' She was enjoying taunting him. The cricket could go hang.

'Does she know about us?'

'What is there to know?'

'That we're seeing each other?'

'Is that what we're doing?'

'Well, isn't it?'

Out in the field someone did something, took a wicket, reached fifty, something sufficient to evoke a round of applause from the spectators. Even Guy clapped – 'Well *done*, sir,' he cried, 'well done!' – before turning back to Meg. 'Look, I don't quite know how to deal with this. I feel that you may know things that—'

'That I shouldn't?'

'Perhaps.'

'Like the fact that you got Diana into bed with you within twenty-four hours of meeting her?'

He glanced round nervously to see if any of the other spectators was listening. 'If you want to put it crudely.'

'There's another way? Look, Guy, we're all much older and wiser now, aren't we? We've spent the last few years jumping in and out of each other's beds. Why not admit it?'

'You might have,' he said. 'I don't think that follows for most of the members of the MCC.' There was a silence. 'It was a particularly difficult time for me.'

'And for Diana.'

'But now it's resolved itself, hasn't it? At least for her.'

It was apparent that he had no idea, that was what was incredible, no idea at all about what had happened. Di hadn't told him and he had no idea. Meg wondered whether she should shatter once and for all the even surface of his complacency and tell him the whole story about the aborted baby, there and then, among the respectable spectators at this most respectable cricket match. 'But it hasn't resolved itself for you?' she asked.

He shook his head and turned back to the game. 'No, not for me.' A wicket must have fallen, for there was a new batsman taking guard. 'Edrich,' Guy said. 'Bill Edrich. Sounds German, doesn't it?' The crowd was silent while the bowler ran up to the wicket. There was the sudden trajectory of the ball and a flashing stroke from the new batsman, and, out of phase, the impact of ball and bat. Fielders were running, the batsmen crossed over, the ball was returned to the bowler.

'He's a squadron leader,' Guy said. 'Bomber pilot.'

'Who?'

'Edrich.'

'We weren't talking about Edrich,' Meg said. 'We were talking about you. And maybe even me.'

He nodded, sitting with his elbows resting on his knees and his hands clasped beneath his chin. The batsman called Edrich was crouched at the crease again, a small, compact figure waiting patiently for the next ball. The bowler ran in and this time the batsman rocked on to his back foot and hit the ball powerfully past cover point. There was a further burst of applause from the spectators. 'I'm probably going to join the Control Commission that they're setting up,' he told her. 'I'll probably be going to Germany.'

'Germany?'

He shrugged. 'It's my knowledge of the language, you see. They seem to find that more useful than the fact that I can climb mountains. Now that everything's over.'

'You know the language?'

Guy nodded. 'Didn't Diana tell you?'

'That you speak German?'

He looked round at her in surprise. 'No, Meg. That I'm *married*. That I have a wife and daughter. That they are German.' He corrected himself: 'At least, I *had* a German wife and daughter. I know nothing about them, I've heard nothing about them since 1939. I don't even know whether they are still alive.'

Meg shrugged. 'There are plenty of stories like that these days.'

'How do you feel about it?'

'What's it got to do with me?'

'I thought it might put you off. I thought perhaps that was why you seem so . . . hostile.'

Meg laughed. 'I think you're mixing hostility up with suspicion.'

'Are you suspicious of me? Is that what it is?'

'I was suspicious of a married man who was happily taking a girl out without mentioning the existence of his wife.'

'But I assumed you already knew . . .'

'I also suspect that you are still in love with her.'

Did he looked startled? 'Who?'

'The little wife, of course.'

He smiled, shaking his head. 'I doubt it. Maybe I'm in love with the idea of her, but I doubt I'd be in love with the reality. Not Greta. Not any longer.'

'And your daughter?'

His expression changed. Beneath the outward equanimity there was pain, like a splinter beneath the flesh. '"I have not seen thy sunny face",' he said quietly. '"Nor heard thy silver laughter."'

'What's that?'

'Alice. *Through the Looking-Glass.*' He looked at her and attempted a smile. 'It goes on . . .' But his voice faltered and he stared away towards the players out on the square. 'I'm sorry, I'm being sentimental.'

'No, tell me.'

A pause. There was a small battle with the balance of his voice, like someone trying to tune an instrument. He coughed and faltered and started again: '"No thought of me shall find a place, in thy young life's hereafter." That's how it goes on.'

'How sad. But you'll find her, and so it won't apply.'

'Perhaps.' He didn't sound convinced. 'I've tried to get news. I don't know how soon I'll hear anything . . .'

They watched for another hour, until the players came in for tea. 'Shall we go?' he asked. 'I'm sure you're bored by the game.'

'Let's go back to the flat,' she suggested. So they caught a bus that went down the Edgware Road and got off at Sussex Gardens. Meg's flat was in a modern block nearby, a red-brick building whose front was pockmarked by shrapnel from when bombs had fallen immediately across the street. They went in through the glass doors – suddenly no longer boarded up, suddenly blazingly transparent – and into the featureless hallway. The lift took them upwards. Apologizing for the mess, she let Guy into the flat, and they sat awkwardly on the worn sofa while one of her flatmates, the one who worked nights, went back and forth to the bathroom complaining all the time about the rationing, the shortages, the inconveniences of the tube, a whole gamut of things that made Guy smile and Meg frown, so that when the girl had eventually gone they suddenly had laughter in common, their shared impatience with this scatter-brained girl and her scattered possessions. And laughter did what laughter so often does – pushed aside the barrier that separated them, so that he put out his hand and touched her arm, and she, for a moment, allowed him to turn her head and kiss her (the strange fragility of his lips). Yet at that instant of contact she surprised herself by drawing away and putting up her hand against his chest to keep what little distance remained between them. 'No,' she said. She shook her head, not really understanding what she was denying. She had done this with a dozen other men, this and far more than this, for God's sake, sometimes with indecent haste, sometimes with a terrible burgeoning desire inside her. But this time she just shook her head and turned away from him. 'No, Guy, not now.' And she got up to clear away their tea things and run a bowl of hot water to do the washing-up, their own things and all the dishes that her flat-mate had left. 'I really don't know, Guy,' she said, when he came anxiously into the kitchen after her. 'It's just . . .' What was it just? 'It's just that you're still married and somehow that matters . . .'

But it never had before.

25

He heard a few weeks later. A letter finally came through the tortuous channels of the military machine that was now governing the wreckage of Germany – an envelope camouflaged by official stamps, one of which said OFFICIAL CENSOR in blue letters and bore the hieroglyphic scrawl of some nameless army captain. He rang Meg at work. His voice was unsteady, as though he didn't know quite how to pitch it, as if he had reverted to adolescence and his voice was breaking all over again. 'What is it, Guy?' she asked. 'What's the matter?'

'I've just heard about Greta and Charlotte.' He seemed to cough or clear his throat or something. 'I'm sorry,' he said. 'I'm sorry. I've just got a letter. From Greta's father.'

'Tell me.'

'They're both . . .'

There was another silence. 'Guy? Guy, are you there?'

There was a silence on the line for a moment, the silence the telephone brings, which is the silence of detachment, the silence of complete separation, as though the other person was not there at all.

'Guy?'

'In an air raid last year,' he whispered. 'They're dead.'

'Meet me,' she said. 'Can you? Now?'

'I suppose I can get away.'

'Of course you can. It's not as though there's a war on. Meet me outside Horse Guards Parade, ten minutes.'

He was waiting for her when she got there. The guards outside the gates were still in khaki, but there was a lorry parked inside and the sandbags that had barricaded the building for the last five and a half years were being removed. Things were changing, the country was loosening up. She waved from the other side of the street and crossed through the traffic, and when she reached Guy, she held his hands and stood on tiptoe to place her cheek against his for a moment. 'Darling Guy,' she whispered. 'Darling, darling Guy.'

They walked through the archway and into St James's Park. It was a warm day. There were people sitting on the grass, just as they used to in peace-time. This *was* peace-time, for God's sake. The country was still dominated by things military, but it was peace-time. A military band was playing from the band-stand and there were mothers pushing prams, and it *was* peace-time, and Meg was suddenly, unconscionably happy. She held Guy's hand tightly, as though to comfort him.

'They weren't in the city,' he was saying. 'Apparently they'd gone to relatives in the country – a market town south of Frankfurt. For safety,' he added, in case the point hadn't been taken, in case the irony had been missed. 'Something went

382

wrong, some bloody Pathfinder dropped the target markers in the wrong place, something like that, and the town got hit. Flattened. Five hundred bombers or something, all aiming for Frankfurt, all on the wrong target.'

They walked some more. The band played 'Land of Hope and Glory' and someone in the small crowd applauded. 'Fuck,' Guy said quietly, and the word was shocking on his lips, far more shocking than it would have been coming from her own. 'Fuck everything.' He said it loud enough for passers-by to overhear. A woman looked appalled and muttered something to her companion: 'shell-shock', maybe, or 'socialist'. Or perhaps it was just a complaint about how there was a different class of person in officer's uniform these days.

'I'm sorry,' he said to Meg, as the women walked on.

'Don't be.'

'It's Lotty. My daughter. Oh, yes, and Greta in a kind of abstract way. But Lotty . . .'

'Of course.' What does one say to the bereaved? There had been so much practice in recent years and yet no one had got much better at it.

'Poor little Lotty. It's what I said at the match, isn't it?'

'The match?'

'The cricket. That quotation from *Through the Looking-Glass* . . .'

'I never liked the Alice books,' Meg said.

They crossed the Mall. There was a small crowd outside the Palace, hoping to see a sign of the royal family. The sandbags had gone from there too, although the guards were still in khaki. 'Time,' she told him. 'That's what you need. Just time. Time cures everything.'

He tried a laugh. "But we haven't got time, have we? You've got to get back to work.'

383

It was a joke of a kind. She laughed encouragingly. 'I've got all the time in the world. I told my wing commander that I was taking the day off and he always agrees to what I say.'

'How do you manage that?'

'By not going to bed with him.'

They walked. They went almost entirely by parks, right across the city, from St James's to Green Park, then across the road at Hyde Park Corner and into Hyde Park itself. There were horse riders along Rotten Row and some boats on the Serpentine, all those peace-time things. At Speakers' Corner there were the usual orators and the usual hecklers. Someone was talking about famine in India and the dismemberment of the British Empire; another was preaching the end of the world. A man with one arm was arguing about the future of Europe, about how it was time to throw off the yoke of capitalism. Marble Arch was decked with Union flags, but the triumphalism of the city was half-hearted. The future held too many unknowns. Revolution hung on the coat-tails of war.

'What'll you do now?' Meg asked, as they crossed the Bayswater Road, their feet on pavement for almost the first time. 'Once you've been demobbed, I mean.'

'There's the family business. Shoes. Unfortunately it's not a very good time for shoes, but we'll muddle along.'

'Didn't you make army boots?'

He laughed. 'As a matter of fact, we did. But I don't think there will be much of a market for them now.' He fell silent. 'And I want to get back to the mountains, if I can. Before it's too late.'

Meg shivered, as though she was cold in this day of sunshine. 'I think I hate the mountains.'

'You were there in North Wales.'

'That was *then*,' she said. 'That was another person in another place. So much has happened since.'

They found themselves outside her flat. They hadn't planned anything, but that was the direction their walk had taken them and it seemed obvious. 'Anyone at home?' she called, as she opened the door to the apartment.

There was no reply. The wireless was chattering away to an empty sitting room, something about the new bomb that had been dropped on Japan. Atomic, that was what they were calling it. Splitting the atom, splitting the world apart, apparently. 'When will Deirdre learn?' Meg said, turning the thing off. She looked round. Guy suddenly seemed very miserable standing there in the middle of the untidy sitting room, somehow dwarfing the place, somehow ill-suited to the drab furniture, the tattered sofa and overstuffed armchairs. 'Do you want anything? A cup of tea? A drink? Whisky, gin? We've got stacks of stuff. Someone I know in the Ministry of Food . . .' There was a nervous haste to her words.

He shrugged.

'Guy,' she said. She went over to him and put her hands on his shoulders and lifted herself up on to her toes to kiss him on the mouth. He didn't move, didn't respond, let her press her lips to his and then look at him quizzically. 'Shouldn't I have done that?' she asked.

He cast around for something to say, as though he might find the right words lying around in that untidy room, among the cheap magazines and the scattered cushions. 'I'm sorry. I'm just . . . distracted. Confused.' And quite suddenly he was weeping, looking round the room for words, and weeping, and Meg was holding him, her arms round him clumsily as though to restrain him from doing himself harm.

Afternoon to evening. Sunlight coming through the windows of her bedroom like shards of glass, piercing discarded clothing and entangled limbs, crumpled faces and eyes that blinked against the dazzle. They talked, not of much but of the future: fanciful talk, high, wild talk of mountains and glaciers. He would go to the Alps, to the Himalayas; they would buy a house, in Wales; they would have children. He would live again, not in this limbo that he had occupied for so long. Her warm, moist body gave him hope; and he gave her hope that there was a contentment to come, not always striving after things that were intangible. Meg had never felt more optimistic. 'Darling,' she said, holding him there, in a way that Greta never had, 'do you want to do it again?'

They were married the next spring. It was a register-office affair in Kensington, where they had found a flat. Diana had promised that she would come down from Liverpool, but at the last minute she couldn't – some family thing up in Scotland – and there was only a telegram from the two of them: WISHING YOU BOTH VERY BEST FUTURE STOP MUCH LOVE DI ALAN. The register-office ceremony was a bit absurd, really, with the registrar trying to imbue the whole thing with a sense of ritual, as though he was a sort of secular priest. 'Marriage is a most solemn under-taking, before friends and relatives, and before the State itself, embodied in me.' That kind of thing. There was a lunch party afterwards. There was Guy's mother, old and fragile and disap-proving of Meg. There were half a dozen of his climbing friends, members of the Alpine Club with an air of Harris tweed about them. There were friends from their offices. Meg's colonel Tommy drank too much and told Guy that he was fucking lucky to have got her and a fucking bastard to have taken her away from him and did he know that she could do the most marvellous thing with her mouth and her fingers? 'Like this.' And the fool blew through his lips and ran his fingers over them at the same time so that he made a blabbering noise like a little baby. It was a joke. Through his laughter he asked, 'Weren't you a conchie once?'

Guy stiffened. 'As a matter of fact, I was.'

'Blue funk, was it? Bloody coward, are you?'

At which point Meg appeared at Guy's side as though she had been conjured out of the air. 'Tommy, you're drunk,' she said, leading Guy expertly away. 'When the doodle-bugs came over,' she said, 'Tommy spent the whole time in the shelter underneath the ministry. Something to do with secret planning, he used to say. I don't know what colour it was, but it was a funk sure enough.'

After the reception they climbed into Guy's old Riley. With cans clattering along the road behind them and a notice saying CLIMBER TYING THE KNOT hanging from the boot of the car, they set off out of the city along the Western Avenue. They paused in a lay-by to remove the decoration, then continued to Oxford, where they stayed at the Mitre. The next day they went on, up the A5 towards Wales. 'Somewhere rather special,' Guy said, when Meg asked where they were going. 'Somewhere I'll bet you've never been.'

And he was right. Meg never had been there before, never even imagined that such a place could exist in dull grey Wales, the strange little seaside village that they finally reached, a collection of buildings clinging to the cliffs of a headland and overlooking the estuary of a river. It was more like somewhere in Italy, the Amalfi coast, she thought, although she had never been there. There were cottages and follies in pink and yellow stucco. There were cobbled alleyways and little arches and a campanile; there were fountains and statues; there were pine and rhododendron and holm oak. It seemed a kind of dream, a transport out of the drab, monochrome post-war world. 'That was where Nöel Coward wrote *Blithe Spirit*,' Guy said, as they passed one of the cottages. And the whole place seemed appropriate to the creation of fantasies, the conjuring up of dreams. They lived in a small cottage with a bedroom and a sitting room that smelt vaguely of damp. From the low windows there was a view over the estuary south towards Harlech. In that cottage, for those five days, in the rather uncomfortable double bed, with the windows open and light reflected upwards against the low ceiling from the tidal flats, she felt happy.

VII

26

'Have you seen?' Eve said one day. This was not long after I'd started work at the gallery. We were renting a flat in Fulham and I'd got home early. She had come in later and was unloading shopping on to the kitchen sideboard and talking to the bags of vegetables and packets of tea. 'Have you seen?' It was the kind of thing she always said, always with the assumption that it would be obvious what she meant.

'Have I seen what?'

'You haven't, then?'

'How do I know until you tell me?'

So she said it, in her flat matter-of-fact voice, with the London vowels and glottal stops, the sound that drove her father mad: 'Jamie Matthewson's gett'n' married. To Ruth.' She noticed, of course. She wasn't even looking at me at the time, but still she noticed: my expression, my mood, the small shock

I felt – maybe I transmitted something through the air, some subtle hint of pheromone or some fractional electrical disturbance that emanated from my brain. She noticed everything.

'What happened, Rob?'

'What do you mean?'

'Between you and Jamie and her. In Switzerland. You've never said.'

'Oh, for God's sake . . .'

But she wasn't going to be deflected by mere anger. Eve had been in the front line in Grosvenor Square. She'd been charged by police horses and hit by batons. In Paris her eyes had run with tear gas. She wasn't going to be deflected by a bit of phoney anger. 'Well, what *did* happen?'

I felt the need to justify myself, like a witness being questioned by a prosecutor. 'We were cooped up together, facing the biggest climb of our lives . . .'

'And?'

'Things got out of hand,' I replied warily.

She smiled at my discomfiture. 'She likes that kind of thing, does she? Bit of a tart, really.'

'I thought those were the kind of morals you approve of.'

'In theory, darling, in theory.'

'Anyway, I owe her a lot. You know that. She saved my life.'

The smile faded into something close to regret. 'Well I'm afraid I can't *save* your life, Rob,' she said. 'But I can preserve it.'

I can't deny that she was right. She did preserve my life. Together we flourished. Our lives flourished, our family flourished. Two children, the first one born fashionably out of wedlock, the second shortly after a brief ceremony at the register office. And in the meantime Porteus Fine Art blossomed. The seventies and eighties were the right time to be selling works of art. Canvases of hard-edged acrylic were the perfect symbols of those years of brash money and emotional nihilism: the customers had one and aspired to the other. We pandered to the buyer's prodigality and the artist's greed, and made money on the margin. And the assistant employed reluctantly by Harold Porteus as a hopeless university drop-out with half a foot became an appreciated manager, and later a valued partner, thanks to an injection of cash, partly from Eve when an uncle died and partly from me when my mother finally retired and sold the hotel.

But we didn't go to Jamie and Ruth's wedding. An invitation did come, but we were abroad at the time, a long-standing trip to Eve's family cottage in France. Her father's sixtieth birthday. Something like that. So we didn't go to the wedding and we didn't talk about Ruth or Jamie again, and they remained outside our lives, figures of memory that we could do with as we pleased, but which we were never going to share.

We bought a house south of the river. It was just when the area was being discovered and exploited, the rundown terraces being tarted up like old whores finally admitted to polite society. Later we bought a second house in the country, with a paddock and a pair of ponies to go with the pair of daughters. Eve mellowed from New Left to New Labour, from throwing bricks at policemen to collecting money for the miners, to waving banners at the local fox hunt. We'd come home.

The relationship between gravity and acceleration has long been known; but what about the relationship between time and acceleration? Is there an equation to describe that? For the first few decades you are merely slithering down an incline, like kids playing around on a snow slope, laughing and joking. You can even pretend you're having fun. It happened to a group of schoolchildren near the summit of Snowdon one winter. I remember reading about it in the newspaper: a few of them slipped and down they went, laughing and shouting, slithering on the hard snow of the ridge, having fun. But, like life itself, the slope was convex: the further they went the steeper it got. They hadn't got ice axes and they weren't wearing crampons. It wasn't fun at all. At the bottom a cliff was waiting for them.

One day I was on the steeper slopes and wondering what had happened to the last two decades, when the receptionist at the gallery (no Courrèges dress any longer, a wide-shouldered black suit by now) buzzed through to my office. 'There's someone to see you. An *artist*, I think.' Her voice fell as she said this.

I sighed. One doesn't always want to meet artists. They are your lifeblood, but they are also your burden. 'Can't you deal with it?'

'Very insistent, Mr Dewar.'

'Can't you fix an appointment?'

'Apparently not.'

So I finished whatever I was doing and went through into the gallery, into the pure, whitewashed space where a Hockney Californian swimming-pool was hanging, a classic that we had on exhibit prior to its auction. There were one or two browsers shuffling round. There was that hushed muttering that you get with visitors in church: they know that something is going on but they don't really understand. They know there is meaning and intent, but they can't always grasp it. The artist, the inconvenient artist wearing regulation jeans and leather jacket, was standing in front of the Hockney. She turned to me at the sound of my footfall behind her.

Twenty years and a dozen Christmas cards between this moment, in front of a pool of blue acrylic on a sunny Californian day, and the last time I had seen her. A small avalanche of emotion swept through me, an icy rivulet, a glittering stream of crystals of memory: pretty enough, but dangerous.

Two decades amount almost to a lifetime, may be an entire lifetime if you happen to be unlucky. And there she was, turning from the painting and looking at me thoughtfully because she knew who she was about to see and was prepared for it, whereas for me it was all surprise.

'Ruth.'

She gave a wintry smile. She was good at those. 'You recognized me.' Her Welsh accent was still there, a flowing current beneath the even surface of her words, faintly mocking. She had aged, of course: her complexion was a parchment tempered by wind and sun. You could see the tendons in her neck, and in the hand that went up to brush a strand of hair from her forehead. There was some gold at her throat – a plain chain with a small, gold ankh. 'You're looking good,' I told her. She grimaced. She *was* looking good, though. She had the kind of looks that age well: a dry, angular structure to her face, a strong, lean body. Her hair was still hennaed, but she was no longer wearing those gypsy clothes my mother had once complained about. A black T-shirt beneath the bomber jacket. What was she now? Forty-seven?

We kissed. It was a hesitant, knowing kiss: knowing more than either of us was prepared to admit. We exchanged the usual banalities. How long it had been. How are you? How's Eve? How are the children? Goodness, they must have grown, all that kind of thing. How was Jamie?

'In Patagonia,' she said, carefully not answering my question. 'He'll be back in a couple of weeks.'

I had heard from him occasionally: a postcard, a phone call, those Christmas cards. For a couple of years I had even gone to the annual dinner of the City Climbing Club, and he had been there, and we had drunk a lot and reminisced a bit, and he had even suggested that we do something together. But he was already out on a limb by then, gasping and grunting his way up a succession of Himalayan peaks, risking cerebral oedema for the sake of the charge that he got from standing on a table-top of ice and rock with a three hundred and sixty-degree view of central Asia around him. K2, Annapurna and Everest, the latter two without oxygen. He was often above twenty-six thousand feet, the death zone from which only about half return. But he'd returned. He'd got big lungs, had Jamie, and a strong heart and tough arteries, a high lactate threshold and high hematocrit; all the physical and physiological qualities that you need to go high. And something else: the obsession. On one expedition he spent, so I heard from an acquaintance, an entire day over twenty-six thousand feet on the Yalung Face of Kangchenjunga, searching for his father's body. He never found it. Perhaps the mountain had shrugged away the relic, sent it down the snow slopes and over the cliffs, consigning the body of Guy Matthewson to the deep freeze of the Yalung glacier, to become an archaeological exhibit in a thousand years' time when finally it emerged from the snout. There must be scores of climbers encased in glacial ice like that, ready to come out into the light of day dressed in a motley variety of tweeds and down, leather and plastic. Or perhaps Jamie was just unlucky, and desiccated father and dehydrated son had failed to meet up by pure chance.

'Actually, I'm here on business,' Ruth explained. 'I know I should have made an appointment, but . . .' She wanted us to have a look at her work. She'd got some stuff in her van. 'Perhaps . . .' She gave a small, diffident, self-deprecatory laugh.

'Perhaps?'

'Perhaps it's good enough for Porteus-Dewar to consider?'

I smiled. I looked, at my watch, at Ruth, at the gallery, at the Hockney with its stark blue that was almost the colour of Eve's eyes. Swimming-pool blue. 'Why don't we . . .'

'Forget about it?'

'Have lunch first. Let me take you to lunch. Give things a bit of time to settle down.'

'Is that a brush-off?'

'It's realistic. You're asking me two things. One is to judge an old love –'

'Is that what I was?'

'– and the other is to judge a prospective client. I need to be able to separate one from the other.'

She laughed at my dissembling. 'Ever the bastard,' she said.

'Is that what I was?'

'And you didn't even realize it.'

We went to a wine bar near by. Amid the noise of the lunchtime crowd we exchanged lives across a diminutive table. I found myself talking too much, and laughing nervously at things that weren't that funny, and telling her things that I shouldn't have, things about Eve, for example. From her I learned little: she'd helped Jamie with his mountain centre, his photography and his expeditions. She'd even been on a few trips with him, the lightweight one to Makalu, another to Baffin Island. She'd spent some time in villages in Nepal, doing voluntary work. And they'd had a couple of years in the States, in California. 'And now I wonder where I've been for the last twenty years.'

'That's what we all feel. It's called age.'

'So I thought I'd start by trying to find out who I was twenty years ago.'

'And have you?'

She frowned at me, as though she was trying to remember where she'd met me, trying to recall my name. 'I'm here to check.'

'Does Jamie know about your coming to see me?'

She evaded the question with a sideways movement of her head, like someone seeing a falling stone out of the corner of her eye and just shifting her head to avoid it. 'He talks about you a lot, you know that? Always has.'

'What does he say?'

She seemed to wonder how to reply, whether to plunge into the past, her past, our past, or whether to stand aside. Eventually she said, 'He's a strange man, isn't he? I used to think it was something childish at first. When I first met the two of you, I thought, A couple of kids looking for a bit of childish adventure. A bit of fun. And then I realized that it was something more than that. I mean, at least kids come in when it's supper-time. But he never came in, or if he did it was just to snatch a bite to eat and then go out again. And the game was different. It wasn't pretend danger, cowboys and Indians or British and Germans or anything like that. Bang-bang, you're dead, count up to twenty. This was real danger and the guns were loaded. And still he keeps playing.' For a moment the defences were down. Her eyes were glistening. 'Did you know they brought him down from K2 after some kind of collapse? Cerebral oedema, or something. He was weeks in hospital. I mean, he's putting his *mind* on the line, his fucking mind, Rob. It's not just you with your wretched toes. It's his whole bloody *personality* that he's risking. And then I wonder, what else is there? Other than this obsession, I mean . . .'

After lunch she drove her van round to the back of the gallery, to the unloading bay. I could sense the tension in her. It was like the moment when the jury has filed back into court after a long deliberation, and the foreman is standing to deliver the verdict. Only here I was judge and prosecution as well as jury. She opened the doors of the van and I helped her out with a couple of carefully wrapped canvases. We carried them inside.

I knew. I guessed from the faint smile on her face as I untied the string and unwrapped the sheet that covered the first canvas. I stood back and looked at the painting I hadn't seen in over two decades, the painting that was, in some way, part of me. Questing cormorants cruising the pewter surface of the lake; the exclamation of her own body, as naked as a blade, poised to pierce the water.

She stood back, looking at me, trying to gauge my reaction. I nodded.

The next canvas was a work I had not seen: the same scene a second or two later, the cormorants arching down and a white flesh arrow stabbing through the surface – a Celtic *Big Splash*, the Californian sunshine modulated to a smudged and watery light the colour of pearl.

'What do you think?'

I tried not to laugh. 'How do you expect me to judge them? In God's name, Ruth, how do you expect me to be objective about *those*?'

'Then try these. They're recent ones.' They were abstracts which, on closer inspection, proved to be figurative – intricate and exact paintings of slabs of rock, of cracks and chimneys, ribs and walls and narrow, insidious ledges. One was called *Cap*, another *Dome*. 'Yosemite,' she said. 'Jamie was climbing, and I painted.' Her tone was almost apologetic, but there was nothing to apologize for. The paintings were intriguing, suspended between the purely abstract and the exactly figurative, things of texture and shade and subtle gradations of hue and tone, just like rock itself – rock architecture. There was another called *Pendragon*, a composition in pink and grey and lead white, a thing of flesh and bone and tendon, cut up the middle by an irregular dotted line. The line of our climb.

I laughed with pleasure.

'And this is what I'm doing now.' Smaller and more curious, they were what she called her slates, reliefs constructed in various shades and colours of rock, abstract compositions of texture and form that seemed like the mountains and hills the stone came from.

I felt her watching me for some hint of what I thought. 'Have you been selling locally?' I asked.

'A bit. My bread and butter is landscapes. You know the kind of thing.'

I smiled. 'They're our bread and butter too.' We talked a bit more, about the art market, about the chances and the possibilities. I wondered what she really wanted, and what I wanted, come to that. One of the larger canvases showed three human figures on what looked like a stage. They seemed naked, androgynous, devoid of face or features. Behind them loomed a great black triangle, as threatening as a vulture, as overwhelming as a mountain. The painting was entitled *Trinity*.

'It was dangerous, wasn't it?' I said, looking at this work. 'The three of us, I mean.'

She shrugged. 'It's happened before.'

'Will it happen again?'

She looked round at me with that smile, and shook her head. 'I don't think so, Rob, do you?'

'Why not?'

'Because after all this time the stakes are too high – children, homes, husbands and wives, all that. You don't just toss a coin for all that, do you?'

'You know about that?'

She gave a wry smile. 'When he told me I almost rang you up to tell you that you were the winner, after all.'

'When was that?'

'A few months after.'

'And why didn't you?'

She shrugged. 'Because of Eve, I suppose. Perhaps it was the only time I've acted selflessly. But I left Jamie just the same—'

'You *left* him?'

'Told him he was a male bastard and walked out on him.' She laughed. 'We were apart for over a year.'

'I never realized . . .'

'There were a lot of things you didn't realize . . .'

'About?'

She turned back to the painting, picked it up as though to take it back to the van. 'About Jamie. And me. We're pretty lousy together, but we're worse apart. It's that kind of relationship.'

'Leave it,' I said.

She stopped, the canvas held across her chest like a shield. 'Leave it?'

'The canvas,' I said. 'Leave the canvas. You want to try to sell the thing, don't you?'

And she looked down at the picture she was holding and laughed, perhaps with relief.

'Guess what,' I said to Eve, when I got home that evening.

She didn't look round from whatever it was she was doing, something on the computer, some case that one of her pressure groups was pursuing. 'That's *my* line,' she said.

'Guess who came to the gallery today.'

'Picasso?'

'He's dead.'

'How sad. Matisse, then. How do *I* know, for God's sake?'

'Ruth. Jamie Matthewson's Ruth. Ruth Phoenix.'

'I thought she was dead too.'

'Phoenix risen from the ashes. She wants us to represent her. Brought some of her work for me to look at. It's good.' I explained too quickly, I know I did.

'The ashes of what?' she said, looking round at me for the first time.

27

We showed one or two of Ruth's paintings in the London gallery and a few more in the new Birmingham one. It wasn't difficult to move them. The landscapes – reminiscent of Stanley Spencer, all slate fencing and barbed wire and scre bracken – were snapped up with some regularity. They allowed the purchaser to have a landscape on the sitting-room wall that was something better than pretty rolling hills and cows chewing the rural English cud. And then someone made an offer for the large canvas that I called the Celtic *Big Splash*, and he asked to see some other work by the same artist and then to meet her. He was an American with Welsh ancestry and he was just what Ruth needed, a collector with a desire to be a patron. 'He revolts me,' she said.

'But he loves your accent,' I told her.

So she found herself crossing the Atlantic in first class, and being met at Logan airport by a limousine sent by the Howell

Jones Foundation. She was photographed for an American art journal, standing in open white spaces like a Giacometti figure in a gallery. A one-woman exhibition was set up in a SoHo gallery. The media came, eager for novelty. She had, quite suddenly, arrived.

Jamie was no more than a figure in the background of all this. Ruth mentioned him occasionally when we met, told me what he was planning, where he was going, when he was returning. 'What does he think about all this?' I asked her, meaning her success as an artist.

She shrugged. 'He's hardly aware of it. He doesn't understand it so it doesn't really interest him. He thinks it's good for me, like exercise or a healthy diet or something.'

'And me? What does he think about your working with me?'

She gave that small laugh – part ironical, part bewildered. 'I'm not sure what he feels, Rob. I never have been. I don't think he knows either. I think . . .'

'What?'

'I think climbing is a substitute for feeling. It's an evasion. That's what I think.'

Perhaps she was right. Perhaps that was what climbing did for you, like cocaine for an addict: a snort of Technicolor excitement to take the place of the chiaroscuro of ordinary life. 'Anyway, give him my regards,' I told her.

'Of course.' But something in her tone told me that she wouldn't.

And then one day I saw posters somewhere in London, in a bookshop. They might even have been in the tube. *In the Death Zone*, was the title. *A life above 26,000 feet* was the subtitle; and behind it was the face of James Matthewson superimposed on a pyramid of ice and snow that might have been the Mustagh Tower, might have been Jannu. Somehow the picture gave the illusion that he was trapped inside the mountain, peering out like a caged animal. 'Jim Matthewson at the Royal Geographical Society' was written along the bottom of the poster, and times and dates and even a charge.

I wondered whether to go. I wondered whether to suggest it to Eve. But in the event I went along by myself, and queued with a motley collection of city-bound climbers to buy a ticket for what was billed as a multimedia presentation to take you beyond the surface of things into the real experience of climbing at altitude. Something like that. We filed into the hushed and reverential lecture theatre like worshippers into a modern church, to find ourselves confronted, from the screen above the lecture bench, with the same mountain as on the poster and the same face staring out at us. To one side was a table with copies of Jamie's book piled high, the glossy cover with the same photomontage, and the same title: *In the Death Zone.*

'He's amazing,' someone was saying beside me. 'The only British climber who ranks alongside Messner and Kukuczka.'

I'd heard of Messner, but I didn't know who Kukuczka was.

We took our seats. The lights dimmed and hushed us to silence and a voice came over the speakers explaining what we already knew, that the guest this evening had become a household word for daring and determination, that he had climbed in every continent in the world and stood on the top of six of the world's eight-thousand-metre peaks, that he had been described as the leading British climber of his generation. And then Jamie stepped up to the microphone, pinned in the spotlight like a circus performer.

Applause exploded round the theatre, a sudden, concerted rockfall of sound. He looked up at the audience with a faint cynical smile that reminded me powerfully of Caroline. His face appeared ragged and worn, as though it had been abraded too long by the wind and the sun, desiccated too often by altitude. I don't know whether he noticed me among the hundreds there. Probably not. Probably he was just enclosed in his globe of light and we were nothing but an anonymous mass beyond the limits of his small, circumscribed world on the stage.

'Climbing above twenty-six thousand feet,' he said, pausing to look at us, 'you are working in the death zone.'

Pictures of climbers appeared behind him. Colour seemed dominant. They wore brightly coloured down clothing – blue and red and orange. They struggled up slopes of white snow trailing brightly coloured rope, wielding brightly coloured axes and hammers, clipping brightly coloured karabiners into the only things that were not brightly coloured: steel grey pitons, silver-grey ice screws. The sky was the hard, enamel blue of altitude.

'Over half the people who have ever been over twenty-six thousand feet have died doing it,' Jamie said. A monochrome photograph of a climber appeared on the screen, a shot of a man sitting on a boulder in the sun and smoking a cigarette. He wore tattered breeches and a collarless shirt. The mountain that formed the backdrop was the Eiger, the North Face. 'My own father was among them,' Jamie said, and the monochrome photo faded into a colour one: a figure hunched at the top of a snow slope with its back against brownish rock and beside it a stick with prayer flags that fluttered in the Himalayan gale.

Oh, it was a fine and affecting performance, tugging alternately at heart-strings and sinews, mixing memory and fear with pure, untrammelled physical exhaustion. And at the end, after the sweat and the agony, with the summit conquered for a brief Nirvana of fifteen minutes, Jamie's own face appeared full-screen, fiery-red and ash-grey, hideous with the agonies of

406

high-altitude effort. There was tumultuous applause. People in the front row even stood, as though he were an opera diva or something.

'Fantastic,' my neighbours said to one another. 'Amazing.'

I joined the queue of admirers going up to shake his hand, to buy his book and get it autographed. He smiled distractedly at each supplicant, as though he had forgotten exactly why he was there and who all these people were. Perhaps his mind was still up in the high Himalayan valley. I wondered whether he would even recognize me. 'Hi, Jamie,' I said, when my own turn came.

He gripped my hand and smiled at me as though he were smiling at a distant view. 'Hi.'

'It's Robert,' I said.

'Robert,' he repeated, bending to write in the book.

'Robert Dewar,' I said. 'For God's sake, Jamie, it's me! Rob!'

People around us were staring. Someone behind said, 'Get a move on, you're not the only one.'

Jamie looked up from the book where he had already written 'To Robert'. I watched his gaze come into focus, his expression metamorphose from indifference through various stages of memory and regret to a kind of tired smile, the smile you might give someone who has done the wrong thing for the hundredth time, but you are willing to accept it yet again. The people around us had edged away, sensing that they were watching something more than a mere encounter, sensing the possibility of theatre. 'Rob,' he said, 'what on earth are you doing here?'

'I was wondering whether I was in the book.'

He glanced down at it, frowning slightly. 'I hope you didn't pay for it.'

'Of course I did.'

'Well, you must have your money back.' He turned to the girl at the table. 'Give him his money back. He's already paid for it. With his toes.'

Despite my protests I found notes being pressed into my hand. Someone edged me aside and thrust his own copy forward. But Jamie ignored him, putting his hand on my shoulder and moving us away from the table, away from the queue with its burden of books. Behind us there was a small disturbance of outrage. 'Rob,' he repeated. 'It's good to see you. I've heard all about you. From Ruth . . .'

I gestured to the disappointed queue. 'What about all them?'

He looked round distractedly. 'You wait here,' he said. 'You wait here and we'll go and find us a drink. How about that? I'll just do my duty and then we'll go and get a drink.'

'Don't forget we've got dinner arranged, Mr Matthewson,' the girl from the publishers said.

He looked at her and shrugged. 'It's just been cancelled.'

We found a pub down towards the Cromwell Road. There were tables on the pavement outside, put there in the hope that it might be a warm, sunny evening. I fought my way through a crowd of students to get to the bar. As I waited for the beers I wondered where all this might be leading. Surely Ruth and her art meant more to me now. Surely Jamie was no more than a curio, a thing one finds by chance when searching through one's memories. He didn't matter any longer.

When I took our drinks back to the table he was sitting there, staring across the street as though hoping that the buildings opposite might fade away and be replaced by something more desolate – a valley wall, perhaps, or a mound of moraine or the snout of a glacier. He had the manner of someone who lives in the wilderness and is awkward in the face of the rituals of city life, uncomfortable in ordinary clothes. I noticed how he patted his pockets and glanced round nervously before picking up his beer. He nodded at me, as though to reassure himself that we were really there, having a drink together in a pub in London. 'Your foot,' he said. 'How's your foot?'

'It gives me a bit of pain in winter. Nothing I can't put up with.'

'Of course. How long's it been, Rob?'

'Over twenty years.'

He nodded. 'A lifetime. You're looking all right. Bit paunchy, but all right.'

'It's all that walking round art galleries that I do.'

He laughed. 'Ruth said that. She said you were the predator of the galleries, tearing the unsuspecting artist limb from limb. You seem to have made her quite a name, Rob.'

'It's her merit, not mine.'

'But it's only through you that she's had this success. Only since you took her on.'

'Are you wondering whether she's one of my victims?' I wanted to make a joke of it, but he took my words seriously. Was it, I wondered, the effect of too much time spent too high, with too little oxygen? Perhaps all that work in the death zone had destroyed his sense of humour along with the millions of brain cells that it was supposed to. 'Perhaps,' he said. 'Perhaps that has something to do with it. Jealousy. You must know that.'

'You think we might have taken up where we left off all those years ago?'

'Perhaps.'

I shook my head. 'Things change, don't they, Jamie? People change. I've been married to Eve now for years. Fifteen, sixteen? I always forget, she always remembers. We were living together for a couple of years before that. We've got two kids, a dog, three cats, a pony and a budgerigar. I'm not going to throw all that away just for a memory. Especially not the budgie.'

Finally he laughed. 'I suppose you're right. They were good memories, though, weren't they?'

'They were all right. Like all memories, you can make of them what you want.'

He sipped his beer. 'You were lucky to get out when you did, you know that?'

'Why lucky?'

'To do something else.' He gestured at the tables around us, the purely urban sound of people in a crowd, of private conversations in public places. 'To get used to all this shit. You know I sweat when I come to the city? You know I feel more afraid than when I'm gripped on a mountain? Panic, can you imagine?'

'It's only what you're used to.'

'I'm not used to people.' He smiled into his beer. 'Or talk. Or anything very much. I mean, look at this bloody place. How do you bear it?'

I shrugged. 'You don't seem to spend much time here, not according to Ruth.'

'Sure. But it can't go on for ever, can it? I've felt the limits for years, now. And then, what is there?'

'Gentlemanly retirement in Wales. You've got the business, haven't you?'

He made a face. 'The business is crap. It's run by some twenty-year-old who climbs E7 when he's off form. All purple leotards and bulging pectorals and chalk bag. When he's not climbing he screws Ruth.' I protested at this, but he dismissed my doubts with a laugh. 'You know better than me? He'd be mad not to. There she is on her own, working away on her bloody paintings, and me half-way up some godforsaken mountain in the Karakoram. What else is there for her to do in the evenings? Or him, come to that. She probably likes it like that. She's always liked a bit more than she's entitled to, hasn't she?' He was watching me. That hooded, hounded look of his. I'd catch him watching me like that in the old days sometimes, look round and find that his gaze was on me.

'Ruth thinks the world of you,' I said.

He didn't respond directly, but smiled as though I were a child, exhibiting a child's naïvety. 'Remember Grindelwald? That time before we did the Eiger.'

'Of course I remember. How could I forget?'

And he laughed, a sudden harsh sound like a shout across a mountain valley, so that people at nearby tables glanced round as though expecting trouble. 'Tell me,' he said, 'what did you think?'

I didn't want to answer. I didn't want another of his bloody arguments. I'd avoided them for more than two decades and now we'd met up like this, pure chance, more or less, and here he was banging on about the same old thing. 'Do you want something to eat?' I asked. 'They've got reasonable food here, I think. Or we can find a restaurant.'

'You haven't answered my question.'

'We all three knew the score, Jamie,' I protested. 'We'd been drinking. We were nervous, charged up, waiting for the weather to break, keyed up to do the biggest climb of our lives . . .' Something welled up inside me that was close to anger. Maybe it was a kind of frustration, and a small pinch of fear and a touch of uncertainty, things that blend together to give a parody of anger. I looked round, as though planning an escape. At one table a group of French tourists were sipping halves of bitter with obvious distaste, and arguing about the cost of something;

at another, a couple of students from Imperial College sat conspiratorially over two pints. They had hair like something made in patent leather. I noticed that the girl had a lump of metal through her tongue and a row of rings round the rim of her ear, like tiny karabiners on a climbing rack. I turned back to Jamie. 'Christ, it was nearly thirty years ago, Jamie.'

He smiled, as though he knew a joke that I didn't. 'Haven't you ever talked about it with her? Between discussing her pictures?'

'We talk business, not childhood, Jamie. We talk exhibitions and contracts and percentages and that kind of crap. It's a business relationship.'

'Ruth knew right from the start, I think.'

'Knew what? In God's name, what the fuck are you talking about, Jamie?'

'Women know, don't they? They're more perceptive, that's what everyone reckons.'

'What the hell are you talking about?'

'Remember Bethan? Remember that afternoon, just the two of us?'

'Kids,' I said, 'messing about.'

He sat back in his chair. He wasn't looking at me any longer, but at the beer in front of him, at the beads of condensation that ran like tears down the glass. He wiped them away with a finger, smiling a tight smile, the kind of smile you give when you're in pain, the kind that signifies that it hurts but that you're going to put up with it, like you put up with the headaches and the pain in the lungs, the cerebral oedema, the diarrhoea, the vomiting, all those things of high altitude. Then he looked me directly in the eye. 'Thing is, my whole life has been an escape, Rob. Escape from Guy Matthewson, from my mother, but above all' – he nodded, as though the idea had just occurred to him – 'from you.'

I suppose I stared at him. It was like being struck – oh, lightning, stonefall, avalanche, anything you please. Or as if he had suddenly leant forward across the table and done the job himself – hit me across the face with his fist. And for that moment I felt as though the whole of our childhood was illuminated in a different light, the whole of our friendship rendered in different shades, new colours. I experienced, I think, something close to panic. 'Jamie . . .' I said, but I didn't say anything more. I couldn't think of the right words.

He picked up his glass and emptied it, then replaced it on the table between us. 'The trouble is, I've been wrong all the time. I think the person I've really been trying to escape is myself. That's why it's been so difficult.' And with that he got up from the table and walked away down the street, as though he had just remembered something but would be back in a moment. But he didn't come back. I called out to him, but he didn't even turn to look at me. Perhaps he didn't hear.

Behind me the French tourists had finished their beer and were leaving. The students still argued, in low, urgent voices. The city went on more or less as it always went on, unconcerned and uninterested.

28

The coroner's court was as solemn as a Welsh chapel – might have been a chapel once, in fact, with its ogive windows and steeply pitched roof. Outside there was a certain amount of pushing and shoving, the sparking of press flashlights, a crew from Harlech Television waving a boom mike above the crowd, that kind of thing. But inside it was as serious as a Methodist Sunday service. The coroner eyed Ruth over the top of his spectacles and expressed his sorrow at the untimely demise of her husband – he used the word 'demise', as though mere 'death' wouldn't do justice to the occasion – and the pathologist delivered his report in the tones of someone reading the lesson: 'Multiple fractures of the cranium and widespread internal injuries,' he said. 'Rupture of liver and spleen . . .'

In the narrow seat beside me Ruth stiffened. Her hand gripped mine.

'Death would have resulted from any one of these traumas,' the pathologist observed, as though inviting us to take our pick.

Then there was a pause and a shuffling of the cast and the offering of various testimonies: one of the mountain-rescue team and one of the walkers who had been witness to the whole thing, a schoolmasterly type with balding head and tweed jacket, the kind of guy you find in the Pen-y-Gwryd Hotel reminiscing about Hillary and Tenzing. 'He had no ropes,' this man said. 'Nothing at all. And then he just came off.'

'Did you see Mr Matthewson begin this climb?'

'Not really, no. We noticed him when he was some way up. One of my group said the climb was called the Master's Wall, one of these extremes—'

The coroner peered over his spectacles at the mountain-rescue man where he sat in the audience. 'Is that correct? The Master's Wall?'

The rescue man half stood, feeling awkward at being called out of turn, as though the ritual was being disturbed. 'I believe it was the Great Wall. A different route, a little to the left. The Master's Wall is considerably harder.'

'There are *harder* climbs than this one?' the coroner asked. 'Is this wall not vertical and holdless?' The elaborate negative was a fine touch. There followed a discussion over the terms 'vertical' and 'holdless', as though these were conceptual and philosophical rather than purely physical. 'The Master's Wall is graded E7,' the mountain-rescue man explained. 'Great Wall is E4.'

'E7, E4? They sound like food additives.' A mutter of amusement sounded round the room. Even Ruth smiled.

'E stands for Extremely Severe. Once upon a time it was called XS. E7 is high in the class. Great Wall is E4, considerably more straightforward.'

'Easier?'

'None of these climbs is easy. To a non-climber they would seem impossible.'

'To you?'

The rescue man smiled wryly. 'They are all beyond me.'

'Then perhaps "excess" is the correct way to describe them?' the coroner suggested.

'Well, they can be protected,' the rescue man said. He suddenly seemed to realize that climbing was under some sort of criticism. 'These days, you can use special equipment to protect yourself against a fall.'

'Ropes, you mean?'

'Ropes and a whole lot of other things. Nuts, friends, lots of different protection gear. Climbing can be very safe.'

'But Mr Matthewson is dead. It seems he lacked whatever you said. *Friends.*'

'Jim Matthewson wasn't using any protection. He was climbing solo.'

'And would he have expected to climb at that standard without any such . . .' the coroner glanced down at his notes '. . . protection?'

There was silence in the court room, a silence made all the more intense by the fact that it was not silent, that people strained forward in their chairs, that reporters' pens scratched at their notepads, that someone whispered something.

'I really don't know. He was a very experienced climber. I believe he used to climb at that standard—'

'Used to?'

'I don't really know what standard he would be expected to climb at now.'

'Mr Matthewson was fifty-three years old.'

The rescue man shrugged. 'Extreme climbing is a young man's sport.'

Ruth leant towards me. I felt her breath in my ear, the subtle intimacy of breath and memory: 'Is this some kind of trial?' she whispered. 'Can't they just sign the papers or whatever and let us go?'

But the coroner had called Dominic Lewis to give his view of events and she had to turn back to the intricacies of the inquiry, the small rituals, the barbed comments with their hidden poisons.

Lewis looked uneasy sitting up there by the coroner's desk. He fidgeted and fiddled, he moved his knees as though ready, at a moment's notice, to dash out of the court room. A callow youth in the guise of a man. I wondered about what Jamie had said to me of this young man and Ruth. She didn't move as Lewis talked; just sat there staring straight ahead with her expression set against the blizzard.

'I can't really say much,' Lewis said. 'I wasn't a direct witness.'

'But you were a friend of Mr Matthewson. And both his climbing and business partner.'

'Yes, I was that.'

'So you can tell us whether his behaviour was normal, the kind of thing you might expect of him?'

Lewis shrugged. 'It's the kind of thing I'd have done.'

'But you're not Mr Matthewson.'

'No.'

The coroner thought for a moment. 'And have you done it, Mr Lewis? Have you soloed the climb called Great Wall?'

Lewis sniffed. 'As a matter of fact, yeah. Summer before last.'

'So you would consider it a normal thing to do?'

'For someone with the right ability, with a lot of psychological preparation.'

'Does that include Mr Matthewson?'

'The other fellow just said it. Extreme climbing is a young man's sport.'

'And Mr Matthewson was not a young man.'

'It was above his standard. Quite frankly, for someone like him, it was suicidal.'

The word sounded loudly in the stuffy court room. Beside me, Ruth stiffened. Her nails dug into my hand. The coroner looked up from what he had been writing. 'To what standard did Mr Matthewson climb?' he asked.

'Oh, extreme, yeah. E2, E3 maybe, but roped. You know what I mean? Roped, not solo. HVS solo, maybe, but not Great Wall.'

'HVS?'

'Hard Very Severe.'

'But he tried Great Wall.'

'Yes.' Lewis shrugged. 'Who knows why? I can't explain it.'

The coroner pondered. The people in the audience shifted in their seats, uncertain where the inquiry was going. 'The business in which you and Mr Matthewson were partners,' he said. He never made a mistake, never used the present tense when referring to the dead man, never slipped on the treacherous slope of solecism. 'The . . . ah . . . Matthewson Mountain Centre. Has it been a success?'

'We've had our ups and downs. What business hasn't?'

'But recently?'

'It's okay. We've introduced a new line in plastic mountain boots, and there's the guiding business. It's been going all right. I mean, everyone seems to want to climb Everest, these days.'

The coroner nodded, looking at Lewis, glancing at Ruth sitting in the front row beside me. Abruptly he asked Lewis, 'Do you have any reason to think that Mr Matthewson might have done this climb deliberately? I mean deliberately chosen to climb something that he knew he would fail on?'

The fidgeting in the room stopped. There was traffic noise from outside. Ruth whispered something. It must have been 'Oh, my God.' God came into it, of that much I was certain.

'I don't get you,' Lewis said. 'Jim take the chop deliberately? You're joking.'

'I don't think this is the place for jokes, Mr Lewis.'

The court waited. Lewis flushed slightly. 'No,' he said. 'It would not have been in character for Jim to risk something like that.'

'And you don't see any grounds for his acting out of character on that occasion?'

'No. No, I don't.'

The coroner nodded. He thanked Lewis for his testimony. He looked round the assembled company, the journalists, the climbers, the curious public, and the incurious officials, and he decided that he had heard enough. 'I commiserate with Mrs Matthewson for the stress that all this has brought to her at a time when, doubtless, she needs to be left with the comfort of those close to her,' he said. And then he wrote something on a form in front of him. 'I return a verdict of death by misadventure.'

Wasn't it a foregone conclusion? What had anyone really expected? Jim Matthewson, climber, mountaineer, had come to the same sticky end as so many of his kind. You die frozen on some Himalayan ridge, starved of oxygen, starved of warmth; or you die in a crumpled mass of bone and muscle at the foot of some ridiculous lump of rock in the green and pleasant British countryside. You could think of it as a terminal illness, climbing.

We walked out into a thin drizzle, and flashlights fired like magnesium flares in our faces. Lewis and I had Ruth between us, covered in a raincoat like the victim's mother in a child-abduction case. We hurried her through the small crowd and

419

into the refuge of my car. 'I'll get back to the Centre, then,' Lewis said.

'You do that,' I told him. Ruth was weeping. Sitting in the passenger seat she was weeping silently, tears streaking her cheeks. She had made up that morning to look good in front of the cameras – she didn't often wear makeup – and now that the stuff was smearing her cheeks like dirt she looked dreadful. I climbed in beside her and slammed the door shut. 'He thought it, didn't he?' she whispered, as we pulled away from the reporters and photographers. 'He thought that Jamie might have done it deliberately. Climbed a route he knew he couldn't manage until he fell off. Suicide, that's what he thought whatever the verdict.'

The windscreen wipers swept back and forth, clearing a space in the chaos of rain. 'Why on earth would Jamie do a thing like that?'

I glanced across and saw Ruth's face set in pale stone. I knew. I knew it in my bones, or however it is you know such things. Guts. I felt it in my guts. How did people ever make the mistake of thinking that the heart is what rules the emotions, when it is so obviously the guts? I suppose I should have felt angry on his behalf or something. Can you do that, feel emotion for someone else?

We left the town and crossed over the bridge to the island. 'He loved you, you know that?' she said.

'I know. We talked about it. That time we met in London. He seemed confused.'

She said nothing, just stared through the windscreen at the familiar landscape. New highways were being built on the island to take the extra tourist traffic, but we found the familiar road, winding between small fields. There was the sense that you were climbing out of the villages, out of the settlements, up to the edge of something strange and wild. Nestled against a hillside was the pub her father had owned. Ruth made a small sound when the building came in sight – it might have been a sigh, might have been a small, ironic laugh.

'Who runs it now?' I asked.

'No idea. I think it belongs to one of the big breweries. There's a manager, I think.'

Beyond the pub, up towards the cliffs, there was now a proper car park. A notice signed by the Countryside Council for Wales explained what animals and plants you might see along the cliff path, species that you wouldn't see any longer if you didn't respect the environment. There were pictures of puffins, guillemots, and razorbills.

After I had parked the car Ruth sat still for a while as though gathering strength for the task to come. Then she reached over the seat and lifted the container out of the back. It was an urn made of a heavy grey plastic that was designed to look like ceramic. She held it with both hands, as though it was a great weight. 'Come on, let's get it over with.'

We left the car and went through a gate and along the cliff path. Over to our left the sea was as dull as lead, stretching away towards a pearly grey horizon. Gulls heaved their wings and cried at the sight of us, anxious that we would not interfere with their lives. There were flecks of drizzle in the air but it was no longer raining as it had been inland. That had always been one of the advantages of the place: often you could climb in sunshine when it was raining in the mountains.

The path was fenced where it ran near the edge. A sign issued its statutory warning: 'Dangerous Cliffs'. 'Ruth, be careful,' I called out. 'The grass is wet.' But she had already climbed the fence and was walking down the slope on inadequate town shoes.

Panic welled up inside me. 'Ruth! Be careful!' What did I think? That she might throw herself off? But she just stood as though she had not heard me, as though she had not registered the anxiety in my voice. I slithered down to her and took her elbow. 'I can't think of anything to say,' she murmured, more to herself than aloud to me. 'A poem or a prayer or something. I should say something.'

Abruptly she opened the lid, inverted the urn and shook the contents out into the air. There seemed to be a great deal of the stuff, a cloud of white and grey, a ghostly presence above the cliff, dispersing quickly into the breeze. 'Oh, God, how awful,' I heard her cry. The grass at her feet was smudged with grey. She replaced the lid and turned to me, weeping, the tears running down her cheeks like rain, her small body shaken by sobs. I held her against me.

'Do you remember that first climb?' she said, when she had calmed down. 'Here. Do you remember?'

'Of course I do.'

She nodded, as though the fact of remembering were good enough. 'I don't think we did very well by him, did we?'

I didn't reply. I didn't think it was the kind of comment that required a reply and, anyway, a full reply would have taken too long. I held her steady and together we climbed back up the slope to the path. Holding each other's hands tightly, we walked away from the cliffs towards the car park. 'Will you be going home, Rob?'

'Yes, of course.'

'Give Eve my love. She never liked me, did she? But give her my love just the same.'

'Of course I will.'

'And your mother,' she added, as we climbed into the car. 'You must give her my love too. I liked your mother.'

'You only met her that one time.'

'But I got to know her well. So give her my love.'

'She doesn't always remember, but I'll try.'

'Try your best.' She sat there in the passenger seat, staring ahead through the windscreen. There was something in her expression that made me wait, some quality of uncertainty or expectancy.

'Shall we go?' I asked, with my hand on the ignition key.

She took a deep breath, then exhaled slowly. 'There's this,' she said. She reached inside her jacket and took out an airmail envelope. 'I found it yesterday among his things.' It was battered and crumpled, and the flap was carefully slit open. For a moment I thought she had found the very thing that the coroner had been hinting at, a suicide note or something like it; but somehow it seemed too old to be anything that Jamie might have just written. I took it from her and turned it over to see how it was addressed. To Ruth, I assumed. Or to Caroline, perhaps. Or maybe even to me.

There was no address, just the name written in smudged ballpoint pen: *Mrs Diana Dewar*.

'What the hell's this? This is my *mother*, for God's sake.'

'Have a look,' Ruth said.

I pulled out two sheets of flimsy airmail paper. There was no sender address. The first line was simply 'Camp 4 – 23,000 feet, 15th April'. And then, 'Diana darling'.

They talk about your heart stopping. It's a cliché, but like all clichés it is grounded in experience. My heart stopped – seemed to stop, really stopped? I don't know. I felt a moment's suspension of time and emotion, a moment's void that was filled abruptly with a hurrying beat and something akin to anger. 'What, in God's name, *is* this?' I asked.

She shook her head helplessly. 'I told you. I found it when I was going through his things. I didn't really know what to do with it, Rob. Perhaps I should have just torn it up.'

I glanced over the writing and turned the page. The script ran half-way down the second page and ended with the looped signature: *Guy.*

'What is it?' My mind stumbled clumsily over the words. I felt a kind of panic, a feeling that things were running out of control. Like falling. 'I mean, what's this all about?'

Guy. A letter from the grave. It had been found on his body, of course, brought down with the other things, those relics Jamie had once shown me. I measured the time, in decades – two? three? Who had opened it? Jamie, of course. But when? And Caroline? Did she know? I tried to read the words, but it was difficult. My eyes had lost their focus; so had my mind. I looked across at Ruth and saw nothing but anguish there, no help and no comfort. I looked back at the pages of writing and I understood only that I had understood nothing, nothing about my mother, nothing about Jamie and Caroline; nothing about me. Nothing about who I was or who I might have been.

29

It was one of those climbing hotels, all low beams and wood panelling and an open log fire that was often burning well into spring. Sometimes they even had it lit during the summer. She sat over by the window, nursing a half-pint of beer and feeling rather self-conscious because these places were still male-dominated even though things had changed in that way since the war. There had been women heroes in the forces, women in the ambulances, women fighting in the occupied countries, women keeping the factories going. Fat lot that mattered now, mind, what with rationing still going on, and unemployment so high, and the Labour government, which everyone had put so much faith in, having such a difficult time. Somehow she couldn't bear the thought of Churchill getting back into power. It felt like taking a step backwards into the Blitz.

She sipped her beer and took a bite of her sandwich – Spam, of course – and glanced out of the window: a slope of grass and heather slanting up into the cloud, grey rocks like tombstones. Rain flecked the glass. The clouds were sagging with water, like a ceiling when the bath upstairs has overflowed. Will there be a sudden rupture? she wondered. The simile made her smile.

'Diana? Diana Sheridan?'

She looked round. Momentarily her eyes were dazzled from looking at the approximate daylight outside: she saw just a shape standing over her, a silhouette.

'Yes, I—'

'It's Guy.'

Panic, or something very near panic. Panic's little sister. As a girl she used to drink Peardrax and think herself ever so grown up. 'Cider's little sister', it was called. She looked past him towards the group at the bar, towards a shifting haze of cigarette smoke. 'Oh, goodness . . .'

'Do you mind . . .'

'What?'

He laughed softly. The sound of that laughter – faintly mocking, slightly self-deprecating – was so familiar. 'I just wondered if I might join you for a moment . . .'

Panic. Sweat on her forehead and breaking out in her armpits. She tried to smile at the shadow. 'Yes.'

Another little breath of amusement. 'Yes, you do, or yes, I may?'

'I'm sorry?' Was he laughing at her?

'Yes, you do mind, or yes, I may sit down?'

'Oh, goodness, yes, of course. Sit down. I'm sorry. You gave me quite a . . .' What did he give her? Quite a shock? Quite a surprise? Quite a turn, whatever that meant. It was the sort of thing her mother was always saying. Quite a turn. Turn for the worse, presumably. Or turning over of the heart, an unpleasant feeling, a reminder that the organic was only just there below the skin and quite beyond one's control. 'Start,' she decided. She moved over as though to make room for him on the banquette beside her, but he took the chair on the other side of her table, thus saving her the embarrassment of proximity. 'You gave me quite a start. I was day-dreaming.'

'A penny for your thoughts. But sixpence for your dreams.'

She smiled. The panic subsided. Absence of panic was something positive, a strange welling up of contentment. 'How strange to see you after all this time, Guy. Is Meg . . . ?'

'She's in London. With the baby . . .'

'Oh, yes, the baby. She sent me a snap. He looks lovely. You must be very proud.'

'Yes, of course.' He looked round. 'Your husband?'

'He's coming,' she said, as though Alan might literally be walking in through the door, heavy and dependable, with that Scottish reserve of his that so often made you wonder what he was really thinking. 'Later. He gets here later.'

'Well, what a surprise this is. How many years ago—?'

'Six,' she replied, too quickly.

He seemed amazed. 'Six. And you've been married now, for . . . ?'

'Three.'

'Any children?'

'Not yet, but we're hoping.' She sipped her beer, feeling herself blush. 'You and Meg have put us to shame. Why have you abandoned the new mother?'

'Preparation for an expedition. We've got our sights on Everest. There's quite a race on to get there first. Us. The Swiss. I think the Germans and the Italians are out of it for the moment.'

'Good luck.'

'Thanks.' He hesitated, as though he might be looking for a way to go.

'I'm sorry about Greta and Lotty,' she said. 'Meg told me in a letter.'

'Yes,' he said, as though mere affirmation was sufficient. 'It was a difficult time, but Meg was wonderful . . .'

'She's a great help when things are difficult.'

'Yes, she is.' He seemed to cast around for something further to say. 'Your husband . . . I'm sorry, it's awful of me but I've forgotten his name . . .'

'Alan.'

'Of course. Alan. Does Alan know? About us, I mean. Does he know about us?'

She turned away, almost as though he had struck her. 'Us?' She looked at the gloomy hillside and the spitting Welsh rain; at the rock, grey and shining in the wet like pewter. 'No, he doesn't,' she said, to the window.

'No regrets?'

'What about you?'

'You haven't told me about *you* yet. And I asked first.'

He doesn't know, she thought. He doesn't know about the baby, about the abortion, about the awful weight of guilt. He wouldn't be acting like this if he did. Meg hasn't told him. It must be the only secret she has ever kept in her whole life. She tried to laugh. 'Let's talk about other things, shall we? What are you doing now, other than climbing, of course? How are Meg and the baby? And the family business – wasn't it shoes? Tell me all those things.'

So he told her: the neutral things, although precious little was neutral when you came to think about it. He told her about the shoe factory, which was struggling with a depressed market and difficulties in getting trained staff, and he told her about the baby and Meg's failed attempts at breast-feeding and things

428

like that. 'Meg insists on staying in London, but I'm trying to persuade her that it's much better to bring up a child in the country. She has . . .' he hesitated '. . . her own friends in town. In fact, I've hatched a plot. Do you want to hear about it?'

Of course she wanted to hear. All these things were fragments she could cling to, like someone clinging to the wreckage long after the ship has gone down.

'Well, we're going to buy a house here.'

'Here in Wales? Oh, how wonderful.'

'I say *going to* but, actually, I already have. That's part of the reason for my coming here, to see the solicitor about the conveyancing. Got it all tied up only yesterday.'

'Where? Where is it? What's it like?' For a moment she toyed with the fantasy of owning a cottage somewhere here, in the Nant Gwynant valley, perhaps. Among the trees, with a view of Snowdon rising in the background. There'd be a baby, of course; and the father coming in from the hills in the evening, clumping up the path and pushing open the low cottage door and ducking his head as he stepped inside, and calling out a greeting. He was a silhouette against the light, so she couldn't see his face . . . 'Oh, what a marvellous idea, to have a house here . . .'

He laughed at her enthusiasm. 'But who knows if it will tempt Meg? We're renting a flat in London and that seems to be all she wants. "Buy something in town," she tells me. She doesn't seem to have any idea of the cost in London. But here things are different . . .' He paused. 'I tell you what . . .'

'What?'

'When does Alan get here? How'd you both like to come and have a look?'

'At what?'

'The house, Porpoise. The house.' He said that. *Porpoise*. Quite without thinking. He'd called her Porpoise that weekend;

and used it in his letters to her; and that was it. And yet now he used it almost as though he had been using it habitually, over and over for all those six years.

She blushed and looked away again, out of the window. 'It'll have to be another day. He's not joining me until the day after tomorrow. He's got some conference up in Edinburgh and I couldn't bear being stuck in the house all on my own so I came on ahead of him . . .'

'Oh.' There was a pause. He sipped his beer. 'That's that, then. I've got to get back to London by then.'

'Shame.'

There was another pause. She was expecting him to go. There was no reason for this awkward little conversation to continue and she was expecting him to end it, almost hoping, really. It would be so much easier. She smiled at him and put the last piece of her sandwich into her mouth and looked back out of the window.

'Look, why don't you come anyway?' Guy asked. 'This afternoon's a wash-out. Why don't we drive over and you can have a look? There are one or two things I have to do . . .'

'I'd love to.' She spoke softly, more to the window and the view of the sodden hillside than to him.

'I mean, if you've got any other plans, then fine . . .'

'I'd love to.'

'But it wouldn't take more than half an hour to get there. Well, forty minutes perhaps—'

She turned her head and looked at him. 'Guy, I'd love to,' she repeated.

They drove beneath the drab slopes of the Glyders. There were the twin lakes, lying along the valley floor like a smear of quicksilver in the palm of someone's hand. There was the Royal

Hotel, looking drab and run-down, as though it, too, had just been through a war. Guy seemed to read her thoughts. 'The Canadian army used it,' he said. 'Arduous training centre.'

She felt herself blush. 'I remember standing in the garden and looking at the stars. Looking for something familiar.'

'Orion.'

'And you said that it wasn't visible at the moment . . .'

'We were standing on it.'

'That's it. Standing on Orion. The thought terrified me.'

'You didn't seem terrified.'

'I never do,' she said.

The house was out of the mountains, in a softer valley. They drove across the river by a narrow stone bridge and picked their way through a town, then climbed up through the hills on the far side, through fields and woods, round narrow curves and into small, hidden valleys. He brought the car to a halt where there was barely room for two vehicles to pass, where there was a slate wall and a slope of grass on which sheep grazed. Always sheep in this country, their bleat like a perennial complaint. A gate, with a sign, the paint blistered and flaking, saying 'Gilead House'; a gravel drive with weeds growing down the middle, and then the house itself tucked back into the hillside against a patch of woodland – slate grey stones, and a slate roof and the windows and doors picked out in white. 'That's the place,' he said.

'It's lovely.'

'Needs a lot of work done.'

He got out to open the gate and they drove through on to the rough track and up to the front of the house. There were some breaks in the cloud, errant shafts of sunlight picking out features of the hillside, the fields of luminous green, the dark woods. 'Gilead,' she said. 'Isn't it biblical?'

'Part of it was some kind of chapel,' Guy said. 'Let me show you round.'

And then the words rose out of her memory from somewhere, a Sunday-school lesson, perhaps. She had this memory for words, for lines, for the oddments of literature. 'Is there no balm in Gilead? Is there no physician there?' And she thought of Alan, of course, who most assuredly was a physician *not* there.

'How very clever of you.' Guy was searching in his pockets for the key. 'Where's it from?'

'Isaiah, I think. Or maybe Jeremiah.'

The front door – wide and ponderous as a chapel door – opened on to a dark hallway. There was the sour, flinty smell of dust. They looked into desolate rooms, shuttered and dark. A few bits and pieces had been left by whoever had last lived there: a broken chair in a corner, a wicker table, a plank, a tea chest. The rooms still had gaslights on the walls, and bell-pulls to summon servants from behind the moth-eaten green baize door. The kitchen had slate flagstones on the floor and a large black range set into one wall. In the scullery there was an ancient mangle, like an instrument of medieval torture.

Guy worried about whether the place was too big, whether it would be possible to heat it, whether it would make a home.

'It will be wonderful,' she assured him.

'Do you think Meg will like it?'

Diana laughed. 'That's a different matter.'

A staircase led upwards into the shadows of the first floor. At the half-way landing was a tall window of painted glass: a knight and his lady, bordered with sinuous vines, dull with dust. 'Arthur and Guinevere,' Guy said.

'Why not Lancelot?'

'Maybe it is Lancelot.'

The treads creaked and flexed under their feet as they went upstairs. A long passage led past the bedrooms. There were cobwebs, dust, the minute scratchings of vermin in the wainscot. Inside the empty rooms shafts of light cut through cracks in the shutters and revealed swarms of dust motes. 'Are there ghosts?' she wondered aloud.

'There are always ghosts,' he assured her.

The house was set into the hillside and at the far end of the passage french windows looked on to some kind of upper garden. More words came to her. 'Down the passage that we did not take, towards the door we never opened.' Where were they from? The window-panes were bleary with grime. She cleaned a patch and peered out, on to weed-ridden gravel paths and low box hedges, an attempt at a formal Italian garden here in the cool Welsh summer. Guy struggled with the lock and finally got the key to turn. He pushed open the door with difficulty, and moved aside for her to go out. It was one of those moments of confusion: she stepped forward and halted in the doorway; he was following her out and bumped against her as she stopped. She stood still on the edge of the daylight, with him against her, his hands on her shoulders.

They remained like that for a while. She could feel him shivering, as though with cold. She remembered another occasion, that same tremor. She remembered so much that was compressed into so short a time. 'Guy,' she said. Her tone was neutral. She might have been doing no more than calling his attention to something out there in the watery sunlight of the garden, out there among the hedges and the gravel paths and the dark holm oaks on the hillside.

'Oh, Porpoise,' he said quietly, 'what have we done? What the hell have we done?'

She had a sudden sensation of something like nausea, something like panic – a sense of desolation so powerful that for a moment she wondered whether she would be able to bear it. She closed her eyes and put her hand up to her throat. She was going to fall. He gripped her shoulder as though to hold her steady. 'What shall we do, Porpoise?' he whispered in her ear. 'What the devil shall we do?'

Her hand moved from her throat to his cheek, to hold him against her. Things were plain: there was no way out, no escape, no solution. It was like a terminal disease. You tried to comfort the patient, of course, but you mustn't raise false hopes, you mustn't tell lies. She spoke to the empty garden, the rank box hedges, the weed-ridden paths: 'There's nothing we *can* do, is there?' she said.

'Why ever did you write me that letter? Why did you break things off?'

Whatever happens now will be irrevocable, she thought. Every error, even the tiniest slip, will have its consequences. It was like climbing, like that rock climbing she did with him all those years ago: the tiniest slip might be fatal. Carefully, so as not to disturb anything, she said, 'I had no choice. You were married. We couldn't go on. And now we both are, to different people.'

'So what do we do? Nothing?'

She turned to face him. 'What else do you suggest, Guy? We break up two marriages in order to try a third? And how long would that be, and what strain would it put on us, and would we even survive? You've even got a child . . .'

'We love each other, don't we?'

It seemed a childish question. 'I suppose we do,' she agreed. 'We must, mustn't we, after all this time?'

'Yes, we must.'

They stood there helplessly, facing each other, feeling peculiarly childish, for childhood is when you are helpless: adults are meant to act for themselves and know when to act. And paradoxically, amid all this helplessness, she felt contentment. The boundaries were precisely drawn and within those narrow boundaries, the boundaries of this moment, she was free. 'I suppose I've never not loved you. I suppose it was that ridiculous thing that they have in the films – love at first sight, that moment when I saw you coming down off the mountain towards me.'

'And me. The same.' He touched her face, as though to convince himself of the reality, to fix the memory in his mind. His finger traced the curve of her jaw, the subtle contours of her cheek and her lips. 'I've got my stuff in the car,' he said. 'I was going to camp here. Doss down in one of the rooms. For God's sake, there are enough of them.'

'I'm booked in at the hotel.'

'It doesn't matter, does it?'

'Not really.' She followed him down the stairs, out of the front door to collect things from the car. It didn't matter at all. They were like children having some kind of adventure, playing at camping, playing it for real but knowing that it was not serious, that it wouldn't last, that at the end the adults would call them in from play and they would have to dismantle the tent. From the boot of the car they got his Primus stove and some cooking pots and tins of food, and an old tartan travelling rug. Then they searched the house and discovered a couple of chairs and, in one of the back rooms, an old mattress, which they struggled with up the stairs. They chose a room on the first floor, looking out over the top garden. There was a broken sofa, an old table, some empty trunks and, with its baize torn and threadbare, an old snooker table. Most of the rooms had gas fires, but this one had an open fireplace with a black, cast-iron mantelpiece, something from the early years of the century with sinuous art-nouveau curves. 'Let's make a fire,' Diana suggested.

'We don't need a fire in this weather.'

'But let's have one anyway.'

Firewood was easy. They collected it along the edge of the wood at the back of the house. It was damp, but not sodden; and in one of the outhouses they found a pile of kindling, put aside by some previous occupant for a fire that had never been. 'Maybe the chimney's blocked,' Guy said. But the fire drew, the flames roared and crackled in the grate, and the dusty, desolate room suddenly acquired a warmth: ash-grey transformed into warm ochre. Vague disquiet transformed into happiness. He turned to her and put his arms round her. She didn't care what might happen. Alan might phone the hotel and discover that she was not yet in, but how could that matter? The remainder of her life might be a misery, but how would that stand against this fragment of joy snatched out of time and context?

When they made love later that evening, she did it with ease. She knew exactly how. She knew how to open herself for him, how to give every bit of herself to him, body and soul, without shame. It wasn't like when she was with Alan. With Alan she felt awkward, almost as though he were a stranger even after all these years. But this was different, a great, racking, consuming possession, physical sensation elevated to the spiritual, lust made love, her whole body penetrated by his, so that for those few moments they seemed not to be two people but one and the same.

Afterwards they lay together in front of the fire and he bent his head and kissed her, and she laughed with the impossibility of it all, with the excitement and the anticipation, and the sensation that she had somehow recovered Guy from the dead.

'What are you laughing at?' he asked.

'I'm not laughing *at* anything,' she retorted.

'That sounds like Alice.'

'It's not, you fool. It's just true. I'm laughing *with* something: happiness, to be precise. For the moment, I'm happy.'

'So am I,' he agreed. He lay back beside her, looking up at the ceiling. The firelight sculpted his face in shifting planes of gold and black. 'But then what?' he asked. 'What about tomorrow?'

'Tomorrow I'll be unhappy.'

'Unless we meet again, like this.'

She felt a small stirring of excitement, or something like excitement. Fear, perhaps. 'Again?'

'Why not?'

Fear. It *was* fear. This encounter with Guy was a lapse; anything else would be betrayal. This would soon be in the past, and she had long ago discovered that time was a great palliative, as soothing to the conscience as any biblical balm of Gilead. But to meet again would call for planning, and plans were in the future. Time had no power to soothe the guilt of what was yet to come.

Guy turned his head and looked at her. His smile was lopsided by the pull of gravity, giving it a wry, ironical slant. Or maybe that was there in his expression anyway. 'Let's face it,' he said. 'Meg's never going to come here, is she? Oh, for a visit, yes, perhaps – the chatelaine surveying her possessions. But she's never going to *live* here. This will be my place. And yours. Our place.'

'What would that make me. Your mistress?'

'I'm not going to get into that argument. You know the answer.'

437

'Well, what about this one? You might be able to deceive Meg, but I couldn't possibly betray Alan. Not in that manner. Not systematically, not make assignations. I couldn't do it.'

'That begins to sound very much like hypocrisy.'

'Maybe I am a hypocrite. Maybe we both are.'

He moved towards her and touched her cheek. 'Don't start an argument,' he said quietly. 'Not now.' He stroked the soft pulp of her lips, as though to soothe her momentary anger. 'What's the alternative?' he asked. 'That we walk away from each other tomorrow morning and never meet again? Is that what you want?'

'I don't know, Guy, I just don't know.'

'And one day years later we meet up. Maybe by pure chance, or maybe Meg arranges a meeting. A get-together, for old times' sake. And we look at each other and realize that the greatest thing in both our lives never happened. Is that what you want?'

'I told you,' she said. 'I don't know what I want.'

He bent to kiss her. She found that she wanted him again. There was that terrifying desire rising in her once more. 'Yes, you do, Porpoise,' he said, as he lifted his lips from hers. 'You know very well.'

30

The nursing-home was a red-brick house with a solid, Victorian air about it. It had once been a private school and the grounds that had once seethed with careless children were now haunted by forgetful adults, figures that shuffled and wandered and repeated over and over the little things they could remember.

'Mr Dewar,' said the woman at the reception desk. 'Of course.' She smiled, just to show that she knew who I was. 'We're doing very well this morning,' she said, 'very well indeed. We've been up and about all by ourself.' I hated the collective pronouns: as though somehow she was sharing in the decline. But senility is like death – it's something you experience alone.

'Is she in her room?'

'I'm sure,' she said. 'I expect we're having a rest after lunch.'

The corridor had an oilcloth floor and framed reproductions on the walls. Presumably the pictures had been chosen for their restful and positive qualities: there were bunches of flowers, bowls of gleaming fruit, that kind of thing. Children played quietly in a Delft courtyard. Cows grazed in a field near Flatford. There was a smell, of disinfectant and some kind of floral air-freshener, and beneath that, the sullen scent of urine. Gaunt faces watched me pass by. One or two smiled as though in recognition; but you could never be sure. When a nurse said, 'Good morning, Mr Dewar,' the certainty of recognition, the assurance of sanity, was almost a shock.

I paused at the door that had a card with *Mrs Dewar* printed on it. When I knocked I heard her voice, surprisingly strong and firm: 'Who is it?'

'It's me,' I called through the wood, and turned the handle.

She was sitting with her back to the door, at the desk that we had brought all the way from the hotel, the desk where she used to do the accounts and write her letters. She still sat at the desk with paper in front of her, although she no longer knew what to write, or to whom.

'Hello,' I said. She turned round to look at me, and the expression of puzzled confusion was replaced by a smile of recognition. It was like sunlight breaking through a pall of cloud. Sometimes she would frown when she saw me, and say something quite absurd like 'I don't want them today, thank you,' as though I was a tradesman who had come to the back entrance of the hotel. Or – somehow this was better – she would merely look at me with a dead expression as though I wasn't even there. Occasionally she would take me for one of the staff; often she would merely talk to me, politely, distantly, as though I were a vague acquaintance and she was happy to provide me with a few details of life in the home. But when there was real recognition in her face it brought me something like joy, a moment's connection with who I was and had been. It linked me to a past that I only dimly understood, a place in space and time that I had no wish to return to but which, being part of me, was somehow vital.

'Hello, Mum.'

That light in her face, the faint image of the young woman she had once been, illuminating from within the aged person she had become. But she wasn't looking directly at me. Her gaze was aslant, as though glancing off me into the past. 'Hello, Guy,' she said.

'It's not Guy,' I told her. 'It's Robert.'

'Hello, Guy,' she repeated.

I took the letter from my pocket and unfolded it on her lap. 'There you are,' I said. 'At least it's *from* Guy. You can't read it, but there you are just the same. I'm afraid it's about forty years too late.'

She smiled. I don't think she had even noticed the sheet lying there on the floral cotton of her dress. Her hands were laid carefully on her knees as though she were posing for a photographer, and her gaze was still directed past my face. 'In God's name, why didn't you ever tell me?' I asked her.

Diana darling,

I am writing this at camp 4, which is no more than a single tent at present, but very safe. The country we walked through to get to our mountain is a marvel – rhododendrons and magnolias almost in full bloom, more spectacular than further to the west. Do you remember the rhododendrons of Port Meirion? Multiply those by, oh, I don't know, one hundred thousand times! But now we are well up our mountain and we are going to do great things. I feel almost literally on top of the world.

Which leads me to what I really want to say, which is this: I have just had a letter from Meg, brought up with the rest of the expedition mail. We had a blazing row before I left, and now she tells me what I have always suspected: James might not be my child. Might not, is not, I don't know. Perhaps these things can be decided for sure these days. I know we two talked and talked about this and many other things the last time we were together. You said that you wanted to leave Alan and take Robert with you, and I that I could not leave Meg and the child. And now there is this news. Although, heaven knows, it is not James's fault that his mother is as she is, my loyalties must now be to you and to our son. What exactly will happen between Meg and me, I don't know – divorce, I suppose – but I will make what arrangements I can for him. That is for the future. For now all I can do is ask you this – will you accept me, Diana? In a month I will be back in England. Will you wait for me? Will you then accept all of my love, divided only between you and our son, for ever?

Guy